FLOWERS of the FOREST

The Pride of Our Land

Richard M Law

Flowers of the Forest

Tellwell Talent
www.tellwell.ca

ISBN
978-1-77370-650-4 (Hardcover)
978-1-77370-649-8 (Paperback)
978-1-77370-651-1 (eBook)

Flowers of the Forest

Chapter 1
To Paradise

A simple child,
That lightly draws a breath
And feels its life in its every limb,
What should it know of death?

~ Wordsworth

As the train began to move slowly out of Union Station, Farquhar leaned over in the seat and in a calm voice, said to me, "Jon, you know that you are going to get us all killed, don't you."

I looked back at him and said, "Why are you blaming me? You are an adult; you can make up your own mind. Do you want to back out now?"

Farquhar didn't answer; he looked away and let his head sway with the movement of the train. Elmer remained silent, gazing out the window at the passing farms and small towns. Here we were, three best friends, sharing a bench seat in a coach and wondering if we were going to die before our next birthdays. All three of us were born and grew up on the same little side street in Aberdeen, Scotland. Changing times and the approach of adulthood had separated us. Each of us had travelled at separate times across the great, grey Atlantic Ocean to Canada and settled in Toronto.

It was the beginning of summer in July, 1915, and a war in Europe had pulled us together. We were travelling in a coach, heading to St. Catharines, where we would switch to an electric tram that would take us to Niagara-on-the-Lake. The trip would only take a few hours, with a couple of stops along the way. The coach was mostly full of young men like us, few, if any, over thirty years of age, by my reckoning. We were heading for Niagara with the same purpose: to enlist in the Canadian Expeditionary Force and our goal was to teach the Kaiser a lesson. This was a short train trip, but one that would change our lives forever.

The journey down the Niagara Peninsula was eye-opening for the three of us. East end Toronto, where we lived, was a grimy, grey place. Everybody heated and cooked with coal and grey smoke spewed from every chimney and soot coated the red-brown bricks of our houses, factories and schools, turning them almost charcoal black. In winter, the air caused our eyes to water and our lungs to sting. The trees (what there were of them) were short and scrawny. By comparison, Niagara was like Eden. We could see orchards of green trees that were thick with leaves and fruit. One of our mates told us that they were mostly peach and cherry trees. There were countless rows of grape vines that seemed to go on forever. The Niagara Escarpment rose up to the south, behind the fields, like a protective wall, covered in green ivy. To the north, we could see the vast blue water of

Lake Ontario that stretched out further than the eye could see. The air was pure and sweet, cooled and cleansed by the lake. The view from our coach was so lush and green that we spoke very little as the train swayed gently on the tracks.

War had broken out in Europe in the summer, a year prior. German soldiers had marched into Belgium and parts of France. Britain was bound, by treaty, to enter the war in defence of the two beleaguered nations. My new country had a duty to come to the side of her motherland. At the beginning of the war, the Canadian Expeditionary Force had no trouble finding eager recruits. Thousands of young men enlisted and were shipped off to France and Belgium to fight the Hun. The war was not expected to last beyond Christmas of 1914, but it didn't exactly turn out that way. Instead of a quick truce, the two sides became entrenched in a deadly standoff - literally. Trenches were dug, and the long Western Front was established through Belgium and France. News came back home of horrifying injuries and deaths on both sides, and men returned with limbs missing, or babbling incoherently. We saw and spoke to friends and acquaintances who had returned home with their souls ripped out and their hearts broken forever. Young lads, just like me were no longer so eager to sign up, leave everything behind, and go overseas to fight in that mess. Farquhar McLennan was the least enthused of the three of us about heading back to Europe.

"Why would I want to go back to the old country? I just left it. I like it here. Besides, this is England's war. Let the bloody Limeys do the fighting," he argued defiantly.

Farquhar was not too fond of the "Limeys". He was a true Highlander, not a large lad, but very lean and athletic. His Highland accent was still distinct and untainted, with rolled "r"s and the vowels emitted from the back of the throat. His sister, Catherine, held the same negative opinion of the

"Limeys"- "Remember Culloden, Bloody Brits!" she would declare. She, her husband, Peter and infant son, William had emigrated to Toronto, Canada from Aberdeen, Scotland in 1913. They found a small attached house in the east end of the city in which to live. Peter was soon able to find work at a factory. Farquhar emigrated to Toronto about one year later. He was twenty years old at the time. His father died when Farq was a baby and his mother died two years before he left his siblings back in the family home in central Aberdeen. He moved into a small row house, also in the east end and had no trouble finding work. He carried a glowing letter of recommendation as a journeyman baker from his previous employer, a bakery owner back in Aberdeen. The letter described Farq as, "cheery, industrious, sober and straight; a most reliable young man"; all the attributes that a prospective employer would jump at. It wasn't easy for him to live on his own, so far from home, after growing up the only boy in a large loving family of seven. It was a good thing that Catherine lived only a short distance away. She would invite him over for dinner, or for a Sunday afternoon, to make sure that he wasn't lonely. Our friend, Elmer, was able to get Farquhar a job at the Dunlop Tire factory, which was located near Farquhar's home. Farq even joined the militia with 48th Highlanders.

The second of my mates, Elmer McLean, a tall good-looking redhead, was the first of us to leave Scotland for Canada. He was "the pioneer", as he was the first to live in the east end of Toronto and the first to find work at Dunlop. Elmer was, like me, an only child. His father was an alcoholic who could be bloody abusive to him and his mother. I know that life was very unhappy and difficult in the little house that they lived in. Elmer loved his mother above all else. We rarely spent much time there when we were young because Elmer's father frightened us. Elmer didn't pay much regard to the war. In fact, he seemed indifferent to the whole affair. I would wager that he was looking for some adventure, and fighting in a foreign land would offer more stimulation than a smelly job making all sorts and sizes of rubber tires. The stories of carnage and hell didn't seem to bother him - at least not on the outside. He even thought we might meet some pretty French or Belgian, while women on our tour of duty. For Elmer, this was a priority - always on the lookout for the ladies.

Another thing: Elmer could be a bit too forthright. He would often speak his mind when in social situations, and often left Farq and me cringing whenever he made a pointed comment to some innocent bystander. I recall him embarrassing our shift foreman one morning as he was entering the factory. Elmer called out to the foreman, saying, "You are late this morning; you are going to get fired." Normally, this wouldn't be so brutal, but Elmer had timed the comment to the arrival of the factory superintendent in our work bay. "Old Grumpy", our nickname for the manager, just glared at the foreman and went on his way. The foreman didn't know how to react to that. He just looked at Elmer and shook his head, muttering, "arsehole", while Elmer chuckled to himself. Elmer, the bugger, always got away with it!

I immigrated to Canada eight months after Elmer and about a year before Farquhar. Being a little older than the other two, I was a bit like a big brother to them, something Farquhar dearly appreciated. My relative maturity sometimes made me the voice of reason, the conscience. At first, I shared a flat with Elmer on Sumach Street, in Toronto, until I found my own flat on Gerrard Street. Because of Elmer, Dunlop Tire became my first place of employment. By the summer of 1914, we three lived within a few blocks of each other.

We worked hard at the tire plant, and we loved to play hard at football. Elmer and I had no family in Toronto, so Farq's sister would invite the three of us to her house for birthdays and special occasions. We soon became an extension of her family. Our friends called the three of us "the three Macs" because our last names had the Scot's prefix "Mc".

My family name is McLaren. Jonathan is my given name, but I prefer "Jon" or "Jonny". My father fought in the Boer War and it affected him terribly. Among his duties was removing the dead and injured, and clearing live ordinance from the battlefield. How much could an ordinary man endure of this and not break? The anguish often showed on his face, but he refused to talk about it with either my mother or me. He kept to himself most of the time, rarely left the house and was unable to find permanent work. It was my mother who went to work outside the home and my father who did the house chores and made sure that I got to school every day. I often envied my chums who had fathers who worked, or sat outside in their gardens and talked to the neighbours. I never wanted to be like him when I married and raised a family. I was frightened by the thought of turning out just like him, if I went to war.

Canada was growing rapidly with the arrival of ship after ship of young migrants just like us. Toronto was a prime destination for new Canadians, and offered jobs and housing for both the skilled and unskilled, alike. The towns and the cities were new and prospering. Farmlands stretched out as far as the eye could see. A century of innovative industry was just beginning. The future was ours, and life was promising, but only the war could destroy that dream.

Chapter 2

The Rising Star

The electric tram hummed its way up King Street in Niagara-on-the-Lake. It pulled up to the station with its nose touching up to the main intersection at Queen Street. As we got off the tram, we were greeted by several chaps in khaki uniforms. It was difficult for me to estimate, but there must have been about thirty of us who came with the sole purpose of enlisting. I was a little unsure of what lay ahead of me and my friends. I wasn't a fighter, I was more of a peace-maker; the chap who would break up the schoolyard squabbles. But I just couldn't sit back, and do nothing while our friends and neighbours were dying overseas. There was so much pressure to go. Pressure to serve my country.

"Alright, gentlemen, follow us to the camp barracks, and we will get you set up for attestation."

We picked up our bags and followed the small military contingent south down the main street of town. Within a few minutes we cleared the houses and storefronts, and entered into a very large open field. The image before my eyes was unforgettable. On the right side of the field, occupying acres of land, were hundreds of white cone-shaped tents in neat rows. It was literally, a tent city. Later, I would learn that they were called "bell tents" and the large open field was named "The Commons".

Elmer made his usual 'astute' observation, "Shite, lads, would you look at all those fuck'n tents! Thousands!"

As we walked around the perimeter of The Commons, we could see men engaged in practice drills out near the centre of the field. They were in baggy clothes, and wore what looked like large-brimmed white hats, something like a Panama hat, which made them look more like migrant farm workers than infantry. On the left side of the field, the east side, behind a curtain of lush, green trees, the Niagara River flowed out to Lake Ontario. The landscape was summer-lazy and tranquil. The camp was appropriately called "Paradise Camp". It was hardly an appropriate name for a place where young men came to learn the art of killing.

We marched into the barracks. The procedure inside the barracks started with a simple medical examination by a doctor, followed by paperwork they called "Attestation"-which we all filled out and signed, officially making us property of the Canadian infantry. Be on the ready, Fritz, here we come! We were assigned a regimental identification number and a fighting unit. I was assigned to B Company, 58th Battalion, Central Ontario Regiment. By happy chance, the other two "Macs" were also assigned to the battalion. I hoped the military knew what they were doing; having the three of us together in the same battalion could put the safety of any unit in jeopardy. You see, we were not much more than unpredictable kids. We loved to play at sports and we loved playing jokes on each other. How could we possibly be good at killing "Fritz"? We were excellent at making rubber tires, and good at football, and that was about it! We had our flats and our jobs at the factory, but no wives to worry about or children to mourn us. Above all, we had each other. There can't be many people in this angry world who can say that they travelled across an ocean and worked and lived with their childhood chums.

Predominantly, it was football that we lived for. Back in Aberdeen, the three of us played football together at various levels in school and at the club level. I must say that I was, and still am, a pretty good goalkeeper. I was born with a "club-foot" and running was not my strength. What I lacked in speed, I made up with effort and competitiveness. I don't like to talk highly of myself, but my abilities as a goalkeeper were better than average and I stole us a few wins. Elmer was a good defender, and, being much taller than average, was an effective teammate. He could cover a lot of ground with his long strides and made more than a few excellent tackles. His height gave him an advantage with headers. Farquhar, though, Farquhar was in a class by himself.

What can you see in the eyes or the walk of a person that betrays their God-given ability and that sets them apart from the ordinary? I had never seen anyone in possession of the set of football skills he had. Yet, he looked so ordinary. His eyes were piercing, blue and focused and he had thick, wavy light brown hair. He was not tall like Elmer, I think he was about 5 foot and 7 inches, but he could run like the wind. His ability to accelerate and stop was phenomenal. Farquhar could change direction quicker than you could change your mind, and he could make his opponents look absolutely silly. In one game last year, I remember watching Farq make a break with the ball, toward the opposition goal. There was one defender and the goalie between him and the net. The defender knew instinctively that he could not stop and turn toward Farq to face him because Farq would just shift and run by him. His only recourse was to run in front of Farq toward the goal. Farquhar just followed along behind and countered every shift that the defender made with the opposite shift. It was almost comical to watch. I actually felt sorry for the defender. Farquhar finished up by depositing the ball in the goal. He trotted back to centre field as if nothing spectacular had happened. It was special, very special and yet he barely noticed.

Most impressive, I think, was his skill with the ball while running at top speed. There were few players who were as fast as or faster than Farq. There were dribblers who could dribble as well or better than Farq, but none could accomplish those skills at full speed. He could, and his passes were pure genius. As an attacking midfielder, he was the heart and brains of the team. There were rumours, back in Aberdeen, that Farquhar was being scouted by teams in the Scottish Association. Farquhar never confirmed it - nor did he deny it. Of course that ended when he left Aberdeen for Toronto. I never mentioned it to Farq, but one day, our battalion coach, George Shepherd, said to me, "I have never in my life coached a talent like Farquhar McLennan."

Football was alive and thriving in Canada when we arrived. The province of Ontario was a hotbed for good football teams and leagues. Toronto had a large league in which Dunlop Tire participated. Naturally, the "three Macs" tried out for, and made the Dunlop team which played in the third division of the Toronto Football League. In 1914, we became the undisputed champions of the division, with an undefeated record. Farquhar won the scoring title by a wide margin, and he began to turn a lot of heads in the Ontario Football Association. We played our games at Ulster United Field on Queen Street East, where the stands seated over one thousand spectators and were always full whenever Farquhar played.

I felt a little guilty about prodding and goading Farquhar to enlist for this war, as he had no taste for it. He was for country but, not for King. I could feel the pull to do my part to defeat the Kaiser. I felt a commitment to the lads who had already lost their lives over in Europe. We had already lost one friend from Dunlop. Farquhar had a tremendous sporting future awaiting him, and I didn't want to be the one to take that away. What if he got hurt or worse? But when Farquhar found out that both Elmer and I were going to enlist for the war, he softened his stance.

"Hey Jon, when do you want to go and enlist?" he said, out of the blue, one day.

"What?" I said, a little surprised - actually, a lot surprised.

"When do you want to sign up for the war? I want to come too," he answered.

"Are you having me on?" I asked, not believing him for a minute. "I thought you were the guy who didn't like Englishmen. Now you want to go and share a trench with them?" Farquhar was well-read, mostly in history, and much better read than Elmer and me. None of us finished school back in Aberdeen, out of economic necessity. But Farq was very aware of the history between the English and the Scots.

"I don't want to be the only one left behind," he countered. "Me alone at Dunlop, without you and Elmer ... I couldn't. Maybe we could join a Highland regiment. Let's join the 48th."

"Farq, I am speechless."

Much of what Farq, Elmer and I had done until this moment was play. We played sports other than football, we played at attracting girls, and we explored the fields and hills near Aberdeen. Even our work at Dunlop amounted to play, whenever we could seize the opportunity. Coming to Niagara to enlist, to travel to The Front, and to kill, was not something we ever dreamt of. I hoped to have my own family one day, and have children who would enjoy the pleasures of play like I did. This war could change all of that in the flash of a muzzle.

Chapter 3
Paradise Camp

"Fall in 58th! I will take you to your beautiful accommodations," a barrel-chested, burly sergeant bellowed.

The handful of recruits fell in behind, and followed him out of the barracks and into tent city. There were tents as far as the eye could see, arranged in rows like city streets, on the west side of The Commons. We were told that there were nine other battalions and some special units sharing the camp with us, each battalion occupied a section of the camp. There were also large mess tents and as well as a section of officers' tents on the perimeter of the city. The senior officers lived in permanent quarters, located off The Commons. The sergeant led us to our section about halfway down a long street of identical tents, where we were assigned a tent of our own. Each one was occupied by four recruits.

"This one is empty so the first four in line, make yourselves to home," said Sarge, pointing to the three of us and one other recruit.

"Thank you, sir!" We all replied in unison, as we were at the front of the line. When we ducked into the white (sort of) tent to occupy our personal space, we noticed the tent was sitting on a wooden platform floor. The smell of creosote or something - probably some kind of weather-proofing - filled the air inside. The heat of the sun seemed to radiate right through the canvas above us, making it very hot. A little shade would have been nice, but wasn't going to happen because we were right out in the middle of a big, open field. The cots were arranged around the perimeter of the tent, with the pillows closest to the outside wall. At the foot of each cot was a foot locker for our personal belongings. One centre pole held up the tent, while outside, cords pegged into the hot, hard earth held the outer edges taut. The city was very dense; there were only a few feet between the tents. Soldiers got to their "homes" by walking down "streets".

The four of us unpacked with little fuss and I made sure I chose the cot furthest from Elmer, who had the reputation as the messiest fellow in the world; a one-man-slum. Farq had to deal with Elmer's clothes and supplies being spread all over top of his. I wondered if the infantry would cure Elmer of that; a victory for the army in itself.

"I am happy that we ended up in the same tent. We have to stay together," Farq stated.

A question came from the other side of the tent. "You fellas don't look very old. Are you sure you should be here?" The speaker looked a bit older than us, and I wasn't sure how he was going to fit in with this lot. He introduced himself as Leonard Long.

"Just Lenny is fine. I am from Owen Sound."

"You will get used to us, Lenny," Farquhar replied. "Sometimes we can get a little carried away with our shenanigans. I hope we don't get under your skin. Just let us know."

"Don't worry, I'll let you know. Don't get me in any trouble with the brass here. Okay?" said Lenny. He looked like he was older than, say, forty. He had a round face and short light brown hair, with a bald spot at the back. He was slightly heavy-set, but not as you would describe as badly over-weight. His voice was a bit squeaky, not quite a match for his size. I hoped he would turn out to be a pleasant mate.

"Do you have family?" I asked.

"Just my old dog, my best friend, Sailor; part Lab I think, mostly mutt. My folks passed away when I was a kid. My aunt raised me in my parents' house. Now she's gone, and it's just me an' Sailor. I didn't get any brothers or sisters. Where you lads from? Are you friends?"

We told him our stories and he seemed interested in hearing them. I think he was somewhat glad to have human companionship for a change.

"Who is looking after Sailor while you are away? I asked. "He is going to miss you."

"I have a cousin in Owen Sound, who is keeping him for me. He has three kids and they will keep Sailor happy while I am gone."

I could tell that it was very difficult for Lenny to leave his dog. His eyes seemed to tear up as he spoke about Sailor. There were a few moments of awkward silence as we contemplated Lenny's story.

The quiet was broken when we heard the Sarge's voice booming, just a few tents away from us. He bellowed that it was time to go to the QM (Quarter Master) and get our training clothes and gear. I could hardly wait to get my hands on one of those white wide-brimmed hats. At any rate, the gaggle of new recruits fell in behind the Sarge and followed him to the QM to get our clothes and supplies. Our "uniform" was a loose fitting khaki shirt, grey trousers held up by suspenders, and last, but not least, the straw hat that was aptly named the "cow's breakfast". Oh, and brown work boots. It would be a while before we actually got to wear real infantry uniforms, like the officers. We headed back to the tent to suit up in our new outfits. I laughed as Farquhar pulled up his grey trousers, fitting a little too large for him. The top of the trousers came up above his navel.

"Hi Gramps," Elmer kidded.

" *Jobby*, what are you laughing at? Do you think you look any better?" Farq retaliated, a little annoyed.

"Let's try on the hats, boys," Lenny added, "I want to see what we look like."

Naturally, the hats looked ridiculous on all of us. There was no doubt about that. Everyone fell onto their cots, convulsing in laughter, and pointing at each other. Even Lenny! The farmer outfits were so baggy; we could turn around inside them.

"Maybe if we wear these to France, Fritz will die laughing, and the war will end," I quipped, when the laughing had died down.

For the rest of day-one, the new recruits were given a tour of the entire camp. There were actually two separate campuses; one north of town, on the shore of Lake Ontario (also decorated with bell tents) and one to the south of town, where our living quarters were located. The large open commons was where all of the field training and parades occurred.

On the east side of The Commons, closer to the Niagara River, laid the remains of old Fort George. Not much of the actual fort still existed, other than some moats and parapets - remnants of another war. It was as if our war structures were sprouting from the ground of a previous war, like saplings after a forest fire. Not far away, towards Niagara Falls, at Queenston Heights, the soaring tomb of General Brock looked down on us. He was the commanding officer of the garrison at Fort George, and was killed in action at the Battle of Queenston Heights, in the War of 1812. I wondered what he would have thought at the sight that was flourishing on top of his garrison and the battleground.

When our first warm, sunny day in Paradise progressed past late afternoon, we were bugled to our meal with the battalion. There, in front of us, was the entire battalion – about one thousand men. We were all under one gigantic tent; eight to a table. The officers had their own mess tents, but the non-commissioned officers ate with us. The food was set out buffet style at one end of the tent. We found our way into line, and waited to see what was prepared for us. There was baked ham, green beans and mashed potatoes and several desserts. The offerings were pretty good, - nobody complained, and I was starving at this point anyway. After the tables had been cleared, the new recruits were introduced to the battalion and the NCOs. They weren't all strangers. Amongst the sea of tanned faces, were some friends and acquaintances from Toronto who duly hollered out our names, and waved as we stood up.

I must admit that I was excited about spending my first night under the stars, so to speak. I had never slept in a tent before. Farq was in the militia, back in Toronto, and had done this many times. Elmer had some experience as a Boy Scout. Would my tent mates snore? Would we be too wound up to sleep? Would it be cold at night?

When the hot July evening drifted toward sunset, the new recruits were given some free time to go back to the tents and prepare for nightfall. We had to be back at The Commons for the sunset ceremony and the lowering of the flag. Just before dark, a piper played a haunting tune from the far side of The Commons,.

"They are playing '*Farewell to Gibraltar*'," Farquhar explained. He knew this from his time in the militia with the 48th Highlanders. I thought that his experience would benefit him when assignments were given out in the field. I thought they might make him an NCO, and Elmer and I could benefit from having him nearby. Shite, I thought, he might save our lives "over there".

"Come on, troops, let's get moving!" Farquhar barked.

"Who made you the commanding officer around here, Farq?" Elmer replied. I took this as a good sign that they were starting to feel a little more at ease with our new surroundings. They were slipping back to our old familiar life at Dunlop, and the jabs and quips would soon return.

"*Get ye up*, soldier; or I'll send you to the brig!"

Elmer gave a hearty laugh, and waved Farquhar off with a gesture. Lenny took in this exchange with a curious expression and a slightly uncomfortable chortle. He would eventually get used to the three of us and our immature ways.

We were told that there were about ten thousand of us men at Paradise Camp at this time. We all gathered in our battalions in the centre of The Commons, facing the flagpole. We hadn't been assigned to company units yet, so we were placed right at the back of the battalion, furthest from The Front and the flag, but because we were in the back row it was almost impossible to see our commanding officers . As a matter of fact, we could barely hear their voices. This made me worry that we would get caught out, doing something wrong, like doing a left turn when everyone else does a right turn, you know, like remaining standing in church, when everyone else sits down. I always dreaded the eyes of the congregation turning and focusing on me. This would be far worse.

We made it through the last post, "God Save the King", and the flag lowering ceremony without incident, thank God, and then all the battalions were dismissed to their quarters.

We were shown where the latrine was for our section, and allowed to prepare for bed. Once the sun had disappeared, the camp was in total darkness, except for lanterns which the men used to find their way back to their tents. The sky was still grey-blue to red toward the western horizon. We could just make out the silhouettes of some tents and soldiers. The lantern in our tent cast large shadows on the white walls. We could hear all of our neighbours talking and shuffling around in and out of the tents, getting ready for bed and a well-earned rest. After a few minutes, the rustling sounds faded, and we lay in our cots and relaxed in the quiet of the twilight.

A voice shattered the quiet outside our tent.

"Reveille is at 0430 hours, tenderfeet! Get plenty of sleep!" Sarge growled, with sadistic delight, giving us the *good* news.

"Good night, Sergeant, sir," Elmer answered in a child-like voice, obviously trying to bait him.

"Uh geez, Elmer, please don't be doing that. We are not Boy Scouts; they won't let you get away with that sort of stuff. Come on," Farquhar warned. "Don't get us court-martialed on our first day." My feeling was that Elmer was totally oblivious to military decorum, not to mention authority. The next few months could be very interesting, watching Elmer transform into a deadly soldier of the 58th Battalion. We fell into our cots, as if a sniper had found us in his sights. I think we were all exhausted after a long, strenuous day. Lenny doused the lantern. Blackness. Silence. And then...

"Farq, you asleep yet?" Elmer whispered.

"Yes!" Farq answered, more than a little annoyed.

We all burst out laughing. Maybe we were "just Boy Scouts" after all.

"Shadap you assholes, go to sleep!" a voice blasted from another tent a few feet away.

Elmer answered by releasing a fart that would make any bugler proud. Sound passed easily through the walls. Again, laughter streamed through the canvas of our tent. I was getting an uncomfortable feeling about where this was going.

"Enough, you guys; let's get some sleep. Save the laughs for tomorrow," Lenny added to calm us down. Ah yes; a voice of reason and sanity and his words seemed to bring some tranquility to the tent. With everyone laying their heads down to sleep, I could hear the gentle chirps of the crickets and the odd mumbled words from nearby tents. The daytime heat had dissipated from the tent, and slowly all the talk and coughing and squeaking faded into the stillness of the dark. My cot was comfortable, and the pillow felt cool against my tired head. Paradise was shutting down for the night. An army of men would now be vulnerable and defenceless until sunrise. Tomorrow, another trainload of new recruits would enter Paradise Camp, and follow the same script that we three Macs had just followed. The war was chewing through the best young men this country had to offer. We were like those new Dunlop tires coming off the assembly line to get stacked and shipped off to a foreign land for consumption.

Chapter 4
Making Soldiers

I envisioned that the next few months would see the transformation of thousands of raw recruits into a competent fighting unit. The Hun would be shaking in their boots when they saw us marching, unstoppable, across "No Man's Land", toward their trenches and singing "Onward Christian Soldiers". I saw the fear in their eyes before they got up and ran away. Ha! At least, that was what we had all hoped for.

Our group, the newest recruits, had still not met our commanding officers. We were very curious about their appearance and their personalities. I secretly hoped that there would not be a large battery of Brits running the show. This would challenge Farquhar, to no end. He hated their accents and their arrogance. There had been chatter in Toronto about British officers commanding Canadian units, but paying little regard to the slaughter and needless casualties. We were just colonials and, therefore, expendable.

My first night in a tent was not a disappointment. After we settled down, I think I fell asleep rather quickly and slept soundly, though I had one unusual wake up, though, in the total blackness of the tent. I could feel a tickling sensation on my upper lip. My first reaction was to think that Farq or Elmer was up to some prank. I put my hand up to my lip to brush away the tickle. This was no prank. No indeed! A fuzzy-haired caterpillar with its little army of legs was doing a route march across my lips. I sat up immediately and made a disgusting (sort of) spitting noise. Of course, this woke everyone up.

"Jon, what the hell is wrong with you?" Farq asked. Now everyone was sitting up and trying desperately to see something, anything.

"Nothing, nothing is wrong. Just a bad dream. Go back to sleep." I could hear the squeaks as they lay back down on their cots and began the drift back to sleep. Within a few minutes, I could tell by their slow breathing that they had attained blissful dreamland again. I felt rather proud of myself for dislodging the offending caterpillar, and also for having the presence of mind not to let my two buddies know what had just occurred. Had I told them, every damn bug that they could find would end up in my bed, for as long as we camped here.

As promised, at the crack of dawn, we were awakened by a piper and the bugled "Reveille" on the first day of our formal military training. The honing and buffing and turning us into legitimate soldiers of the Canadian Expeditionary Force (CEF) was about to begin. The morning air was cool and damp, but had the sweet smell of new-mown hay. What a pleasure it was to breathe that air while I thought of the acrid smell of melting rubber at Dunlop. The sky was getting light in the east over the canopy of trees lining the river's edge. I felt a little apprehensive as I thought of the day ahead of me.

After flag raising and breakfast, we began our formal training. The daily routine would continue basically unchanged for our entire stay in Niagara. We had a drill sergeant, Sgt. Keachie, who put us through physical drills for about an hour. Keachie was not one of those prototypical hard-as-rock sergeants. His look was more that of an accountant than of an army lifer. These drills were your usual push-ups and sit-ups and such. After that we were put through "close order marching drills" first in small units, called "squads", then larger units, called "platoons" and finally, even larger units, called "companies". The purpose of these drills was to teach us how to march together on the parade square. "Left-right, left-right, left-right...and on and on," as Elmer became fond of saying. Later in the summer, on Fridays, they added route marches of nine or ten miles, done wearing full gear. One route was to the delightful town of Port Dalhousie, on the shore of Lake Ontario, and the other route was to Queenston Heights and the site of General Isaac Brock's tomb. These marches were supposed to build up our stamina for the long treks we would have to endure in the battle zones, overseas.

Our first route march, to Queenston, became a memorable one, unfortunately. It started out as a normal routine march early on Friday morning. After breakfast, we assembled in our assigned companies (Elmer, Farquhar and I were all in Company 'B'). Four companies made up a battalion, by the way. The weather that day, was hot and humid, not ideal for a long trek in full gear. When I say "full gear", that meant backpacks that weighed about forty pounds. The route to Queenston is uphill, which certainly added to the challenge of marching in the heat. Fortunately, we were accompanied by trucks that carried food, water and medical supplies. The battalion was led by our own brass band, so that we had a cadence to march to, and we were allowed breaks every hour to rest, drink water and consume oranges to rehydrate our bodies. Some of the merchants from the area also followed the battalion, so they could sell drinks and fresh local fruit.

Shortly after our second rest stop, my platoon was suddenly distracted by a strange, loud plea for help from within our ranks. At first, I thought it was a soldier faltering in the heat from exhaustion. That would be most understandable. I turned around to look, and, instantly recognized the soldier in distress. Our platoon was blessed with a very young set of identical twin brothers from northern Ontario; Chapleau, I think, and they came from a large family of thirteen. They were in their teens; about seventeen, I reckoned. They were short, skinny lads that weighed not much more than one hundred and twenty pounds each. All skin and bone. The twins had a thick crop of wiry brown hair that was not easy to control. They were loose-limbed and athletic. It was fun to watch them walk, the way their knees pointed outwards. The CEF wasn't as fussy about the physical qualities of the recruits as they were a year ago. Their names were Albert and George Liberty, and we could not tell who was who, and being in a sort of farmer's uniform made it even worse. We were always studying them to spot subtle differences, but we couldn't find any. To get around the problem, Elmer suggested we call them by a single name – "Wonky", because he thought they were a wee bit uneven. Everybody thought this was a great idea. From then on, they were referred to as "Wonky1" and "Wonky2" when they were together. The name caught on with the rest of the battalion, and even the officers were guilty of using it. The twins seemed to accept the name, with no complaints.

"I'm going to shit my pants!" one of the Wonkys cried. We could see that he was in agony and that this was a big emergency. I didn't think that they carried extra uniforms on the supply trucks.

"Wonky, run over there to the trees and do your business," Elmer advised. "No one will see you, and you can just catch up to the platoon when you are done." Wonky was desperate, and he peered over toward the grove of trees. There was a faint glimmer of hope in his expression. He started in the direction of the trees and then abruptly stopped. He had a quizzical look on his face.

"How will I clean myself?" he asked.

Before anyone else could come up with an idea, Elmer piped up. "There are pine trees in that grove. The army manual says that the soft shoots from the branches of pines are best for cleaning. Hurry up and get it done." Farquhar and I stared at each other in disbelief. Wonky disappeared into the bush.

Farquhar shot a glance at Elmer and said, "How could you do that to him? You *bastard*!"

"Oh, he'll figure it out, I'm sure. Don't worry. How could he be that doolally?"

The three of us turned to catch up to the platoon that had marched on, about fifty yards up the road. We fell back in with the platoon and continued to march toward Queenston. After a short period of time we were back into our marching trance, not talking or thinking of anything in particular. The trance was suddenly interrupted by a flurry of whacking and slapping sounds. The entire platoon stopped in their tracks and turned around to see what was causing the commotion. There, on the ground, in the middle of the road, was Wonky sitting astride Elmer, who was face down. Wonky was wailing away on Elmer's back and head. Elmer was just trying to cover up and protect himself. A group of us jumped in to break up the fight – if you could call it that. Naturally, the disturbance caught the eye of old Sergeant Keachie and a corporal, who ran back to the scene, to see what was going on. They arrived in time to see us pulling the two combatants apart.

"What the fuck is going on here?" Keachie hollered. He glowered at McLean and Liberty. Their farmer clothes were dusty and disheveled. "You two want to fight?"

"No sir!" They both replied in unison.

"I want to see both of you in my quarters when we arrive back in camp. Is that clear?" The sergeant yelled at the top of his lungs, his face beet red. "I want an explanation of why you two mugs can't march together in a civilized, military manner. You could be court-martialed for this kind of shit. "

"Yes sir!" They replied.

"Everybody, fall back into formation! Let's get a move on!"

We all fell back into marching formation, four abreast. We had fallen back from the rest of the battalion, so we were going to have to move a little quicker than before. The men ahead were trying to figure out what caused the altercation. Every query to Elmer and Wonky was met with silence. Farquhar and I just glanced at each other and smiled knowingly. Elmer had gotten himself into another stew, and we would have to wait to see how he would wiggle out of it. I would have loved to be a fly on the wall when they went to the sergeants' quarters for interrogation and discipline.

The plan was for the battalion to arrive at Queenston Heights in time for lunch – a sort of battalion picnic. As we approached the Heights, the sky was beginning to look a little belligerent to the west of us, and the wind was starting to gust and swirl. The day had started out clear and blue, but now was showing no indication of staying that way. We arrived at the gathering place, a large open field, as the last platoon, due to the altercation that had taken place on the road. The brass band had already put their instruments down and was resting when we pulled into the grounds. There, at the back, and high above the open field, was the looming presence of General Isaac Brock standing victoriously on the top of a column about one hundred feet high. His arm was raised in a majestic victory salute. One of the first lessons we got at Paradise Camp was the story of the Battle of Queenston Heights. The British, along with local militia, defeated a larger force of invading Americans in the War of 1812. General Isaac Brock, on horseback, led a charge up one side of the Heights in an attempt to dislodge American troops who had captured it. Unfortunately, Brock was mortally wounded by a sniper's shot to the chest. The counterattack was successful, and the Americans retreated to their own side of the Niagara River. Brock's courage and leadership was the key to the victory. He has entered British and Canadian history in glory, and his remains are buried beneath the monument. His towering image implanted a feeling of pride, as we gazed up to the top of his monumental tomb. The historic defeat of the Americans, one hundred years ago, at this spot on the Niagara Escarpment seemed to seep into our bones. We were in a hallowed place, set aside for victory and glory, and we were basking in it.

The trucks were parked off to the side of the field, and some men were assigned the task of bringing out the food and drink for the tired battalion.

"I hope they packed plenty of food, I'm starving," Farq revealed, rubbing his belly. "Hey Elmer, I think you should find Wonky and apologize to him, before we get back to camp," he added.

Elmer gave it some thought. "Why should I apologize to him? He was dumb enough to fall for it."

"Well, the way I see it, when you get back to camp with Keachie, when Wonky tells his side of the story, I don't think you are going to get much sympathy. Do you know what I mean?" Farq said, trying to reason with Elmer.

I could see Elmer thinking about it. "Perhaps you're right, Farq. I could get screwed around for this one. I'd better go find Wonk and make up to him."

"How are you going to know which Wonky to make up to?" I chirped in, snickering. Still, I could see that Elmer was thinking about it.

"I guess I will talk to the one who is walking kinda funny," Elmer responded with a silly grin on his face.

Farq and I both reacted to that line with a long drawn out "Eeeeeeeewwwwww!" Our faces scrunched up while we contemplated the Wonky's anatomical tenderness.

Elmer left to find him and try to put things right. He came back after a few minutes and informed us that Wonky said he needed time to think about granting any forgiveness.

We noticed that the sky was now growing ominously dark, as thick clouds hid the sun. The men who were emptying the trucks, and setting up tables, and preparing to distribute the food and drink stopped their work to look up at the sky, but then, continued on with their work, as if unconcerned. The wind began to gust and reveal itself and gave us some relief from the heat. When the food and drink was ready for distribution, the battalion arranged itself in several long lines in front of the food tables. After the men had received their rations, they searched out shady areas at the edge of the field where they could sit on the ground to eat and perhaps have a quick nap. The three of us loaded up our plates, grabbed our water and found a comfortable spot, under some large maple trees. None of us had the energy to speak.

While eating lunch, my ears suddenly became aware of the low rumbling of distant thunder. It must have been miles away, but my body could feel the ground tremble. As threatening as the warning was, everyone was too hungry and too tired to pay much heed. Food and rest were the priorities. The impending storm could wait while we filled our faces.

As soon as the battalion had filled its belly, and we started the cleanup, the wind changed its temperament, from refreshing to savage. Gusts began to whip paper and cups and anything without bulk into a frenzy. The thunder rolled and rumbled again, but this time it was much closer to our military picnic site, and shook the ground. The clouds over our heads were moving quickly to the east, and the colour had become a very dark grey with thin wisps of white, trailing and turning. I had never seen storm clouds like this, back in Aberdeen. There was anger in these clouds. The brewing storm had, by now, caught everyone's attention and soldiers began to hustle about, putting plates and cups back in the trucks, clearing away the food and drink, and preparing for whatever Mother Nature was about to anoint us with. Instantly, without warning, a flash of brilliant white light, accompanied by an explosion of sound that echoed in our chest cavities, threw us backward. I looked for Farquhar and Elmer behind me, and saw that they were both flat on the ground.

"Hey, are you hurt?" I yelled as loud as my voice would let me. They both looked at me, too stunned to answer. They sat up rather unsteadily, and peered around to see what was going on. "Bloody Hell, what was that? Is someone firing at us?" Farq asked me.

"Not likely. We are not in France; we are still in Niagara. I think we were struck by lightning."

Our tiny human voices were dwarfed, completely, by the painful crack of thunder. The sound made our ears ring. I couldn't see where the bolt of lightning originated or terminated but I could smell the acrid scent of electricity and burnt wood. All hell broke loose, as everyone made a mad break for the trees that surrounded the open field. Nobody wanted to be a standing target in the middle of that huge open area.

Before we could get up, a second lightning bolt followed the first. This time, I saw the spot where the lightning speared the earth. The explosion created a concussion wave and sound beyond anything I had ever experienced. The pain in my ears was unbearable and left me with no sense of hearing for a few minutes, and then became a ringing sound. As the streak of light hit a tree, it travelled along the ground to the trucks and hit them. The men who were standing beside the trucks were knocked to the ground. At first, I thought I was imagining things as their straw hats caught on fire while they lay on the ground, motionless. Immediately, ignoring the danger, the medics and engineers moved in to douse the fires and see to the needs of the fallen men. I could smell the sweet scent of the burning straw hats.

We were helped to our feet by the mates around us, and led along the edge of the field to the medical station nearby. A wall of torrential rain hit us before we could get to the station. The rain came at us sideways, with the same ferocity as the wind. I don't remember much of what happened once I got to the medical station. By this time I was in shock and I think Farq and Elmer were too. I could hear very little, other than the ringing. We and the other injured soldiers, were transported quickly through the storm, back to Paradise Camp in trucks and ambulances.

Once we had returned to camp, we were taken to the hospital tent and placed in a screened off section for observation. Several nurses, dressed immaculately in white, were busy setting up our station. Elmer saw this as an opportunity to meet some women. Despite his obvious discomfort, Elmer was trying his best to engage one nurse in nonsensical conversation. She politely ignored his attempts while she attended to his scrapes, and then moved on to another patient.

There were twenty of us all together, who had been bowled over by the lightning strikes. The three Macs were the lucky ones, as the bolt didn't directly strike us, but instead, hit one of the big maples that we sheltered under. Our ears hurt and we could hear very little because of the ringing sound. The others took a direct hit and suffered burns to their scalps, feet and hands. One poor soul received severe burns, and was sent to a hospital in Hamilton. He became the first medical casualty of the 58th Battalion. He never got overseas, and never got to see the Hun, face-to-face. The battalion was left with some very troubling thoughts. If this kind of misfortune could hit us in Paradise, what lay in store for us across the ocean?

"Do you think the General was pissed off at us for some reason?" Elmer asked no one in particular, as we sat on our cots in the medical tent.

"What general?" I asked.

"Well, Brock, General Brock," Elmer responded. I thought he might still be feeling the effects of the lightning strike.

"Why would he be pissed off at us?" Farq asked.

"Maybe he wasn't happy about us tramping around on his battleground, his graveyard," Elmer answered, his voice still a little unsteady.

"Aye, you may have a point there, Elmer, but we are soldiers; his lads, and you if think about it, he would be proud to watch over us and even command us. Don't you think? Why would he want to harm us? Not us. Fritz maybe, but not us."

Farq countered, "Look at it this way: if anything, maybe the General was giving us a taste of war. A warning. He has been in the heat of battle, heard the cannons roar, and felt the pain of hot metal inside his body."

"Mother Nature was pissed off at us, not the General," I added.

"Mother Nature ... Mother fucker, I hurt," Elmer muttered, partly to himself.

"Look, we have not even done a month of training, and already we are getting knocked about. What the hell is going to happen to us when we get over there? We are going to have to fight Fritz and Mother Nature both, most likely. Maybe we should just get back on the train and go back home," I complained, feeling a little defeated by our close call with Nature.

"Listen to you. You are ready to put up the white flag because of a thunder storm? You were the one who was all 'gung ho' about coming on this mission. You were the one who bugged me and Elmer to sign up. You are not going anywhere, Jonny! Forget it! Aren't you a bloody Scot?" Farq laid into me to try to shore me up. Shite, he seemed more anxious to get into this war than me. I felt a little ashamed of myself. I lay back on my cot and pretended to sleep. We spent one more day at medical, being poked and prodded, and then, were released when it was apparent that we were suffering no further effects. Elmer was not able to make any progress with the nurses. They were too busy to pay much attention to him. The doctors made sure that.

One good thing came out of this minor tragedy. Sergeant Keachie forgot to discipline Elmer and Wonky for their altercation on the route march.

On our first official training day, my eyes were opened to the possibility of tragedy. Until this point in time, I thought we were at summer camp; three young men, enjoying a camping experience in the loveliest part of the province.

And we were getting fed and paid $1.10 a day for doing it! What could possibly go wrong?

Life is so unpredictable. One day, we were a group of young men, doing our best to learn how to fight for King and country, our farm-worker uniforms unwrinkled and barely sweaty. Then, in a heartbeat we were scrambling for our lives, dodging bolts of fire from the sky. I rarely went to church or said my prayers at night, before bed, when I was growing up in Aberdeen. My parents never discussed God or religion in our home, and so He was absent from my life. The events that shattered our afternoon lunch on Queenston Heights gave me pause to think that someone was trying to tell us something. Someone was saying, "If you go back across the ocean, you will witness things that you will wish you had never seen."

Chapter 5

Summer Days and Nights

Lenny was happy to have us back in camp. "Too quiet here, without you three morons. I couldn't sleep at night. You got any aches and pains? Farq, what is that on your lip?"

"Uh, that is what most people would call a moustache, Lenny," Farq quickly replied.

"Ha, put some honey on it, and Sailor would lick it off." Obviously, Farq's attempt at a moustache was pitiful. It would surely take some time.

"We are as good as new, Len, thank you for the thought," I said.

"I didn't say I was worried about you. You three will survive the war. I saw you on the ground at Queenston, but I knew that you weren't directly hit. I saw the lightning hit the tree above you and then travel to the ground. I was worried that the tree or a limb might fall on you. You are very lucky to be alive," Lenny informed us.

It was apparent that he felt a little protective of us. That made me feel good and I'm sure it felt the same to Farq and Elmer.

We grew attached to Lenny, in the short time that we had known him. There was one thing that bothered us, though; we couldn't figure out why he enlisted. Farq took the step one day, and just asked him. "Why did I enlist? I am really not sure ... though ... I was married to a lovely lady... Elizabeth. She ... uh ... passed away, a few years ago ... pneumonia. She wasn't well for quite awhile. I really miss her. Sailor keeps some of the pain away. I had a stepson with Elizabeth; his name was Andrew – Andy. He was about your age. Real smart kid. Last year he enlisted and went off to The Front. Andy was ... went missing in action near Ypres, Belgium. They never found him..." Lenny let his voice fade away. We stood there looking down at our feet. "I just thought if I enlisted, too, I could try to find out what happened to him when I got over there. Maybe I could locate his battalion and find out. I don't know ... "

"Lenny, we will do anything to try to help you. Just ask us," Farq offered, in a hushed tone. We didn't raise the subject again. Instead, we left it up to Lenny; there was so much pain in his voice.

It took a few days for us to start to feel normal again after the lightning strike. The drills and parades got our minds off the misadventure in Queenston. One day we were marched to the rifle range, at the north campus, near old Fort Mississauga, another relic of the War of 1812. A number of battalions had their camp sites and tents nearby. At the range, we were introduced to our weapon of death - the Ross rifle. We were instructed, first, on how to care for and maintain the rifle. I was surprised at how heavy the weapon was. Farq had been in the militia, so none of this was new to him. When we finally got the chance to aim and fire the gun at targets, Farq proved to be as skilled as he was in football. He found the targets with little difficulty. The skinny little Wonkys were experts too; probably because of their hunting experience up north. Neither Elmer nor I could not hit a thing.

"I think Pte. McLennan is a natural sniper," one of our instructors commented, then turned to him and said, "I am going to recommend you to the O.C. for sniper training, Private." Farq looked over to me and winked. I don't think that had been in his plans.

Just a few hundred yards north of the shooting range was the beach, on the shore of Lake Ontario. This was our swimming area, and once a week, the battalion paraded to the beach for a refreshing swim. The waters of Lake Ontario are not particularly warm in the summer, but still warm enough to have an enjoyable cleansing swim. If you swam near the mouth of the out-flowing Niagara River, you could feel the current and the colder temperatures of the river's water. Swimming was a welcome break from the monotony of the military drills and the daytime heat. It seemed that the noisy cicadas were the only creatures that loved the warmth of the afternoon. We often brought footballs to the beach, and engaged in spontaneous games of footy in the sand.

During our time-off from duties, we would wander into Niagara-on-the-Lake, for recreation. Along the main street there were stores and a theatre. A series of temporary arcades and storefronts blossomed along the street, out toward the camp, as the summer progressed. Paradise Camp, itself, was "dry", so we had to head into town for a wee dram or two in the off hours. The Angel Inn was always full of soldiers on the weekends. Like the Fort, the inn existed during the War of 1812. The barkeep told us that it was haunted by the ghost of a British soldier who was killed there during the war. This was enough information to keep the Wonkys far away from the tavern, as they were extremely superstitious. We tried to get them to join us there for drinks, and Elmer even offered to buy both of them a whisky to make amends for the pine bough incident. They wanted none of it. We only got them as far as the front door.

"I am not going in dere, Elmer," Wonky1 emphatically said. "Dere's a ghost in dat place! You are crazy to go in."

"Wonky, there are women in there. Come on and get some."

"Dere ain't no women in dere, Elmer. Only guys and ghosts," said Wonky2.

"Well, your loss, Wonk. You will never get laid," Elmer added, as he opened the door and went into the inn.

Elmer was a hound, always on the lookout for the ladies. The trouble was, with more than ten thousand men camping outside a small town of a few thousand inhabitants, the ratio of men to women was extremely unfavourable. There were always a few young ladies who enjoyed the company of a platoon of soldiers, but quite often, they were escorted away, back to the safety of home by a relative, usually a father or a brother. The locals were very wary of any interactions between their daughters and the CEF. Farquhar managed to meet a lass named Nancy, at the inn one evening. She definitely took a liking to him. She was pretty, and caught the eye of many of the men in Paradise. Nancy was a not a regular around the shops of Niagara, and her pretty face and feminine figure stood out among the regular diners and shoppers of Queen Street. She was young and vivacious; about seventeen or eighteen, and lived on the outer fringe of Niagara. Her frame was compact and she walked with a quick step that put her hips and posterior in motion. One sunny Sunday afternoon, I saw the two of them walking along Queen Street together, accompanied by a little white mutt that trailed behind on a leash in Nancy's hand. They disappeared out of the town towards the camp. Later that evening, when I saw Farq back in the mess tent, I thought I would quiz him to get the details of his afternoon stroll.

"So, Fack, how was your romantic little walk with Nancy?" I said, with a hint of mischief in my voice.

"What? *Clawbaw*. How the hell did you know? Forget it...it was alright up to a point, I guess. We walked down to the Niagara Gorge to look at the river," he answered, a little hesitantly.

"And ... ?" I said, looking for more.

"Well, we sat down in a nice secluded spot with a great view of the gorge, and Nancy tied the dog up to a little tree beside us. We looked at each other and I realized that she wanted to get ... uh...romantic. We lay down on the grass and began to kiss. Things heated up real fast, Jonny. Well, just when I began to, you know, touch her, the bloody mutt, 'Ray', she calls him, gets loose from the tree, and scampers off into the woods. Off she goes, calling, 'Ray, Ray'. There I was, sitting on the ground, looking like a bloody fool! My heart was racing and I was in no mood to chase a fuckin' stupid little *scunner* dog. Shite! Shite! They disappeared into the woods. Nancy found the little mongrel, and I caught up with them, at the edge of the woods. Then that was it, just said our good-byes and went our separate ways. Shite! Don't go and tell Elmer about this."

"No, no I won't," I answered quickly. "Too bad, my lad. You will have to try again. She likes you. You will get another chance, I'm sure," I reassured him. "Unless we get sent over next week," I added with a laugh. Farq was not amused.

As the long summer days passed lazily by, our battalion was becoming more proficient with our parade drills. Some us of began to master our Ross rifles, too, and actually hit some targets. Our company, B Company, was becoming a cohesive unit. Sergeant Keachie was an effective leader, though he wasn't a screamer like some of the other company drill sergeants, and we appreciated that. He was tall but paunchy, with very pale skin and wore wire rim glasses, and probably was probably in his fifties. His wavy hair had a red tint and was well receded. To most of us in the company, he was very reasonable and well liked. Our company CO was Lieutenant George Cassels. He was not cut from the same cloth as Sergeant Keachie. Cassels didn't have the rapport with his enlisted men that Keachie had. He wasn't "one of us". He was one of those young Toronto aristocrats from a wealthy family who had had a long distinguished history as part of the establishment of the city. We were told he graduated from the Royal Military College, but his future was in law, and not in some smelly factory on Queen Street or at the bottom of a trench in France. Come to think of it, all of the commissioned officers were drawn from the upper crust; not a dirty finger nail to be found on any of them. Farquhar was not happy with this arrangement. His disdain for the "school boys", as we called them, was barely hidden, was and equal to his dislike for the English. He was smart enough, though, to realize that they held all the cards, and that pushing back was futile and would only result in his demise.

"Some things never change, Jonny. They were born to rule the world, and we were born to serve. Always has been, always will be. This is one game that you and Elmer and me can never win," was how he lamented the current state of the working class. At least Cassels was not a "Limey". Our battalion OC, on the other hand, was born in "Blighty".

Lieutenant Colonel Harry Genet, like us, immigrated to Canada when he was a young man. He lived in Brantford, worked as an accountant and served in the militia there. Genet recruited all the officers who marched at the front of the battalion. We were no different than any other battalion across this vast country. Each one was one thousand men strong; all farmers, fishermen, lumberjacks, teachers, and factory workers. All of them were commanded by the elite, the "school boys".

"We are going across the ocean to fight Fritz. Maybe Fritz is not the real enemy. I'll bet that those "Boche" troops are no different than us; poor working bastards being sacrificed for reasons they don't understand," Farq stated, with a hint of anger in his voice.

"Are you thinking of taking off and going home?" I asked Farquhar.

"Absolutely not! My loyalty is to you and Elmer and the battalion. Nobody else."

We did, on occasion, find some means of empowerment, and the Wonks turned out to be our agents. They possessed a skill that would be more than useful on the battlefields of France and Belgium. They had the ability to see well in the dark, and liked to slip out of their tent when everyone else was sleeping. They also liked to steal and sell cigarettes. We found this out when they came to our tent one day, and offered to sell us a pack of cigarettes, though not a full pack.

"Where the hell did you get those, Wonk? " Elmer asked, as he looked at them suspiciously.

Wonky1 or Wonky2, I don't know which, answered, "Promise you won't tell anybody about this?"

"Yeah, yeah, we promise, Wonk."

"We got 'em last night from a tent," Wonky said.

"Whose tent?"

"Don't know, it was too damn dark. We crawled up to a tent, stuck our hands under the flap and felt around until we found something - smokes," Wonky answered, with a straight face.

"What?" the three pals said in unison.

Then we started laughing. And laughing. We laughed till it hurt. When we had composed ourselves, we asked to see the pack of smokes. It was a pack of Sweet Caporals, about one third of them smoked.

"Who, in our battalion, smokes these?" I asked. We thought about it for a moment, and then Elmer spoke up.

"Cassels! Cassels smokes these!"

"We only pilfer from da "school-boy" tents, Jonny."

We looked at each other and then at the Wonks in disbelief. This was too good to be true.

"I love you lads!" Farq said, obviously delighted with their choice of target.

"Anybody else, anybody else smoke Sweet Caps?" Farq asked.

Elmer answered. "Listen, I don't keep track of who smokes what around here. I did see Cassels with a pack of Sweet Caps after church parade last week."

"Wonk, how much do you want for these?" Elmer asked.

"Twenty-five cents!" They both answered together.

"What, that's a bit much; don't you think?"

"Den go and get your own!" Wonky1, I think, said.

"Alright, alright, it's a deal."

Elmer managed to find the money in his lockbox. He handed it over and thanked the Wonkys. After they departed, I said to Elmer, "You don't smoke."

"Doesn't matter. I can sell these for a profit. I just need to repackage them so that I don't get caught with the pack. Those two will bring us some more of those smokes," Elmer said, with a very satisfied look on his face.

And Elmer was correct. They did come back with more, and not just cigarettes. They brought him anything, literally, anything that they could get their hands on. We saw them with stamps, razors, pencils, mirrors – you name it! The two snuck out almost every night. There were sentries in the camp at night, but the Wonkys never got caught. Their stolen goods business thrived. I hoped that we would be sharing a trench in France with these amazing guys. They could be very useful over there.

The Wonkys were impressive, but they weren't invincible. Nope! I told you earlier, that they were very superstitious. One night, after they had crawled out of their tent, they headed toward the woods at the back of the camp, towards the river gorge. As they entered the woods, something caught their eye. Within a few minutes, they came scrambling back into our tent, which startled all four of us awake.

"What the hell are you guys doing in our tent?" Lenny whispered, trying hard not to shout and wake up the whole camp. "Are you trying to steal from us, you little bastards?"

I lit our lamp to look at them. With the tent lit up, I could see the fear in their wide eyes. They could barely utter a word. Then Wonky1 tried to gather himself a bit, and stammered, "The Virgin! We seen the Virgin!"

"What do you mean? What Virgin?" I asked, exasperated at this point, and just wanting to go back to sleep.

"The Virgin Mary! We saw the Virgin Mary in the woods!"

The four of us looked back and forth at each other.

"Wait a minute! You two saw the Virgin Mary, back in the woods? Are you sure?" Farq asked. "We gotta see this. Come on, put some clothes on."

"Oh yes, for sure, come with us, and we will show you," Wonky1 answered, crossing himself as he spoke. I knew this was no trick. They were genuinely frightened; this, you could not fake.

"Do we all need to go?" Farq added again.

"Shite, I don't want to miss this," Elmer said.

"Me neither," Lenny said.

Farq didn't sound too enthusiastic. "Oooooooo, I don't know about this. We could get caught."

"I don't care. Let's go," Elmer said, his voice rising in anticipation," Before it starts getting light outside."

"OK, I'll stay behind, and the rest of you can go. I'm too old for this," Lenny said, changing his mind at the last minute.

We put pants and shoes on and crawled out the back of the tent. We let the twins get ahead of us, and followed them closely, as they crept towards Paradise Grove. It was totally dark in this area of the camp. There were some lights on, near the latrines and the officers' tents, but they were a few hundred yards away. The crickets and katydids (a local told me what they were when I asked about the racket) were still singing, which helped to cover some of the sounds that we made as we moved. It was uncanny how the twins could find their way through the camp. It is probably a skill they learned up north in Chapleau. Perhaps, it was a hunting skill. I thought Fritz should be worried.

After some time, we reached the edge of the grove. It is strange how you can lose your sense of time when you are in total darkness.

"Dis is where we go in," a Wonky told us, gesturing with his arm. We followed them down an opening into the grove, then along a trail. I was spooked by the thought of walking into a branch, and losing an eye or something. I could also hear the Wonks' footsteps in front of me, but couldn't actually see them. I could only follow the sound. Also, I could hear Farq and Elmer behind me, stumbling along .

"We are almost there. Slow down, so that we don't startle her," Wonky said. "Just ahead and around the corner."

"What corner?" Elmer asked without any exaggeration.

"Quiet!"

There was absolute silence as we edged slowly along the trail, and finally stopped still. Nobody spoke. We waited.

"Dere she is!" Wonky1 whispered; his voice shaking with emotion. Silence.

"Where?" We couldn't see where he was pointing or even if he was pointing.

Finally, with our eyes having adjusted to the dark, we were able to see the "miracle". In front of us, probably in a small clearing, we could see tiny little bright lights, floating around in the night air. It took a minute to register. They flitted about in no particular direction, mesmerizing us.

"Fireflies!" Farq spoke, in a semi-loud voice which contrasted to all our whispering. "Damn fireflies!"

"What?" a Wonky said in disbelief. "What's dat you said?"

"Hey, they probably haven't seen fireflies before, gents. They probably don't have 'em up in Chapleau," Farquhar explained. He moved gently towards the lights, careful not to trip or hit something unseen along the way. Farq managed to pick one off a branch and bring it back to show the Wonkys. He cupped it in his hands and held it out for them to see. At first, there was no glow, but as Farq slowly opened his hand, a light blinked a few times. Then the light came on and the little "miracle" flew off into the night. The Wonkys were silent and frozen. I didn't know if they were profoundly disappointed or just enlightened, pardon the pun.

We had no appetite for riding the Wonkys over the Virgin Mary adventure. I think our admiration for them actually grew. They had more cash in hand than anybody in camp, and what impressed me the most was their determination to make the best of things. They were excellent at moving around silently in the absolute darkness, and they made it pay off with whatever they could get their hands on from the officers' tents. They could operate effectively on very little sleep. I kept thinking that how much the 58th Battalion could use guys like this in the battlefields. We were told about the night-time raids that both sides took pride in executing. The purpose was to get as close to the enemy's trench as possible, in the dead of night, and to try to identify the battalions that were in the trenches, and listen to them talk. A great deal of useful intelligence was picked up this way. The Wonkys were designed for trench warfare. Now, if the brass could only teach them German...

Chapter 6
Let the Games Begin

There was only one real passion at Paradise Camp, of course. Football! Each company put together a team to play in the camp league. The Sportsmen's League contributed uniforms and equipment and the YMCA awarded prizes to the winners. Naturally, Farquhar made the team with ease, but I wasn't sure about Elmer and me. Our team uniform was impressive: the shirt was azure blue with a white "vee" accent, from shoulder to bottom to shoulder on the front, and with a white collar. Farquhar pointed out to me one day that the accent wasn't really a "vee", but was the top half of the Cross of St. Andrew. I never saw it that way until he made the observation, and then it stayed with me, like any true blue Scot. Our shorts were white and our socks were the same blue as our shirts, with a white accent at the top below the knee. Beautiful! The team loved it.

We played other sports on the large drill field, near the YMCA tent, but it was football that became the prime focus of the camp. It wasn't long before the results of our games became more important than the war reports. That competitive spirit got the best of every man, and there were tremendous rivalries between the different companies and battalions. To my surprise, Elmer and I made the starting team. Our games were played on evenings and on Saturdays, and became the highlight of the week. There were only a few people in camp who knew of Farquhar and his football prowess. After our first three games, other teams started to scout us. With the three Macs on the same team, our games were usually a little lopsided. We won a game 5-0 over C Company. The victory made us the champions of the 58th Battalion. It was now up to us to represent our battalion against the champions of the other battalions. Our coach, Sergeant Shepherd, spoke to me on the field immediately after our third victory.

"Jonny, come over here for a minute, I want to speak to you. And get Elmer over here too," he yelled from across the field. I thought we were going to get our ears boxed for some infraction or other. Shepherd was a very tough, wiry character, all bone and muscle. He looked like he could have been a boxer, because he had a flat crooked nose and a slight cleft lip. His hair was very short, maybe the shortest haircut at the camp. I gathered up Elmer and we headed reluctantly across the field to see what the Sergeant wanted.

"Listen, you guys, there is something I want you to do differently in the next few games," he said, and we were immediately relieved that we weren't going to get chewed out about something.

"I want you to speak to the rest of the team about this - except Farquhar. In future games, I want you to keep the ball away from him. Feed it to the other players; let them play more of a role. The other teams are taking notice of us, and I don't want them to see what we have got. Let's save the best for the playoffs, at the end of the schedule."

Elmer and I looked at each other, a little dumbfounded. "Are you serious?" I asked the sergeant.

"Look, I am dead serious. We can win this. You have no idea how important this football league is."

"It's just a YMCA-sponsored thing to keep us in shape and out of trouble. How is that so important?" Elmer asked, legitimately. I silently agreed.

"The truth is that it is a big deal for the brass. It is about bragging rights and discipline, and who is king-of-the-hill. These guys, and I'm talking about the COs and all their underlings, are making bets on these games. They all want that championship banner in front of their tents."

"They have a championship banner?" I asked.

"Sure do. Donated by the YMCA."

Elmer and I exchanged glances again. We couldn't believe what we were hearing. We still hadn't really met our Commanding Officer. We had seen him on our marches and church parades on Sunday, but not really close up or one-on-one. He was still a bit of a mystery to us.

"Let me tell you a little bit about Lieutenant Colonel Genet," Sarge continued. Genet was our commanding officer. All we knew was that he was a very experienced officer, and that he was well-regarded by the higher-ups in the military, and that the 58th was lucky to have him. "Genet is a football fanatic. He runs a football club, in southern Ontario; Brantford to be exact. He is on the Board of Governors for the Ontario Football Association. If he doesn't win this camp championship, it will be a huge embarrassment for him. He expects to win. Genet and McCordick of the 35th are fierce rivals. McCordick runs a football team, as well - same league. They both want to win the Ontario Championship.

Galt is the current champion and the team to beat; a real powerhouse. They have defeated teams from all over North America," Shepherd said, in his most serious voice. I could see that he was feeling some of the pressure as an NCO and football team coach in Genet's battalion.

"Aye, Sarge, we're on board," I answered him. "But it may not be so easy to do. Farquhar makes the team go, and the ball just seems to come to him. What if he catches on?"

"Don't worry about it. He won't catch on. We may have to lose a couple of games along the way," Sergeant Shepherd countered. "Just do as I instructed, and it will work out."

Elmer and I just glanced at each other and gave a shrug. This was probably the last thing we expected to hear from a sergeant in the infantry. Maybe he was asking us to throw some games so that he or someone else could win some bets. It left me with a bad taste.

"Do you think we are being used?" I asked Elmer, as we walked back across the field.

"Used for what?"

"I don't know. Betting, fixing games … whatever."

Elmer thought about it for a moment, and then answered, "I believe Shepherd. He is one of us, not a 'school boy'. I think we should just go along and play as Sarge says to play."

Our next game was against the 92nd Battalion. We knew very little of them. Some of their men were from the 48th Highlanders of Toronto and some were from Hamilton. Many were of Scots ancestry, but that is all we knew. We hadn't seen them play. It was a Saturday night game, and it seemed like everybody from Paradise Camp and from Niagara was there to watch. For the first time ever, Col. Genet was there to watch. He sat next to Col. Chisholm, CO of the 92nd, both of them in camp chairs on an elevated platform above the crowd.

Just as we thought: employing the new game strategy was not easy. Farquhar was open often and calling for the ball. His teammates, all clued in at this point, did their best to play the ball off to other players. It seemed far too obvious to me. How could Farq not figure this out? The game ended in a 1-1 draw. Farq was left off the score sheet for the first time, and had very few touches of the ball. As we left the field after the game, he gave me a curious look.

"What's going on? Nobody wants to give me the ball."

"Hang on, Farq and I will fill you in later, after we get changed," I said.

After we had showered (one big advantage of playing football was access to the officer's showers) and changed, we arrived back at the tent with Elmer. Once we were inside the tent, we were greeted by Lenny, who was waiting for us.

"Nice game lads, but not your best though. Farq, I don't think your teammates want you to score again. Nobody was passing to you."

"You struck out … just like you did with Nancy! Ha, ha," Elmer blurted out, with a wicked smile on his face.

I jumped in before Elmer could add anymore, "Uh … you're right, Lenny. That was part of our game plan. Shepherd's idea. He didn't want you to know about it, Farq; he thought you wouldn't go along with it."

"What?" Farq cut back in, with a truly mystified tone of voice. "Who told you about Nancy?" He shot a quick glance at me and Elmer.

Elmer immediately started laughing. "Here, Ray. Come on boy; nice doggy." I could see Farq getting a little annoyed. This was a good time to step in.

"Look, I told Elmer. I know I said I wouldn't, but I couldn't help myself. It was too funny. I'm sorry. Forgive me, alright?"

"I can't trust you *clawbaws* with anything. Shite, not even the football match! My friends! My friends!" he lamented. "If you didn't want me to score, you could have told me. I know how to lay low in a game."

"Sarge didn't know if you would buy in. He thought you would fight it," Elmer said, as he filled in the details. With a big grin he added, "Besides, we don't need you to win anyway. Ha!"

To break the tension, I changed the subject slightly. "Who do we play next?"

Nobody knew the answer, but it worked. It did lighten the mood. "We'll talk to Sarge, and tell him you figured it out and you are now on board. OK?" Farq shrugged, his way of agreeing.

Our next game resulted in another victory for our team, and Farq did, indeed, play a cautious, conservative game. He didn't come close to scoring a goal; in fact, he didn't even come close to the goal area, at all. He actually worked to improve his defensive play at the expense of some of his superlative offence. Sergeant Shepherd was very pleased with the outcome, and let us know it.

Midweek, before our next game, Sergeant Keachie informed the three of us after lunch in the mess tent, that we were to report to the Battalion Adjutant at battalion headquarters at 1400 hours sharp. Nice, I thought; this would get us out of bayonet practice, though. However, I couldn't think of anything that we were in trouble for.

"Are we in trouble, Sarge?" Elmer asked with some apprehension.

"Not that I know of. Just make sure that you are on time, or you will be in trouble."

Battalion headquarters was located in the old Butler's barracks buildings, just west of The Commons. The old buildings dated back to the years just after the end of the

War of 1812. The battalion commanding officers bunked in the old junior officer's quarters, a fairly humble two-storey log frame building, covered in clapboard. Farq, Elmer and I marched over promptly at 1400 hours. We made sure that we were all spiffed up and polished to a tee.

The old barracks had been pressed into service to house the battalion's headquarters. Before the war started, the barracks had been used for several years as the command headquarters for the summer officer training camps that occupied these grounds. We were greeted at the front door of the officer's quarters by the battalion Adjutant, Captain McKeand.

"Come in gentlemen, and have a seat in those chairs along the wall." He was a bland, pleasant sort with the required "British officer moustache". As we shuffled our chairs, he continued, "Colonel Genet has sent for you, and wants a few minutes of your time. Just wait here and he will be right with you."

McKeand disappeared through a door on the east wall of the room. We glanced at each other as we hadn't anticipated meeting the battalion CO. We were sitting with our backs to the wall, at the front of the office, by the front door. In front of us, was a rather small office occupied by an empty desk and several filing cabinets. There were doors to the left and right side of the office. The old barracks had that woody, smoky smell of older buildings, and reminded me of some of the old houses, back in Aberdeen or Edinburgh.

Farquhar posed a question. "What do you suppose he wants?"

"I know exactly, what he wants," I answered. "He wants to talk football."

"No! Are you kidding? *Yer arse and parsley*! "

"What else would he want to talk to us about? We are just three of a thousand men. Remember what Sergeant

Shepherd told us about Genet? What did he say … football fanatic? He wants to talk football," I said.

"He wants to trade you to the 35th for a crate of sherry, Farq," Elmer added with a chuckle.

"Shut it! He wants to trade you for a ham sandwich, McLean."

Just as Farq spit out those words, the door to the left swung open and McKeand emerged with an officer, right behind him. It was Genet. We sprang to our feet and gave him our best attempt at a salute.

"At ease, men," McKeand advised. "This is your commanding officer, Lieutenant-Colonel Genet. He wishes to have a brief meeting with you."

"Good afternoon gentlemen," the colonel said with a very smooth British 'school boy' accent. I could almost sense ol' Farq tensing up, next to me. "I don't want to take up much of your time. Would you just follow me back into the meeting room? "

We nervously followed the Colonel into the room, as he directed. I felt like I was being hauled into the principal's office for the strap. McKeand stayed outside, and closed the door behind us. In the centre of the room was a large wood table that was bare, except for a few ink bottles and pens. There were about a dozen wooden chairs distrbuted around the table. I assumed this is where the COs held their meetings and briefings. The walls were covered with maps and lists.

"Just have a seat anywhere, rest easy," he said, gesturing with his arm in the direction of the table. We three sat side by side at the table, and the Colonel took a seat opposite us. "I guess you are wondering why I called you here." We each mumbled a nervous unintelligible answer. We had not been this close to a CO before, and we were in awe. Well, Farq maybe not so much. He was giving the Colonel a once over inspection. At this distance, we could clearly see his clean crisp moustache with a fine middle part. His dark hair was neatly combed, but getting a little thin, and his face was closely shaved, showing very little stubble. His bushy eyebrows contrasted with the razor thin moustache.

"You are probably unaware of this, but I know you three gentlemen. You see, I have watched you play football in Toronto – at Ulster Stadium. I was very impressed with your skills." We nodded, a little embarrassed, and mumbled a humble thank you. "I spoke to your team manager at Dunlop Tire, I uh, forget his name, and he passed your names on to me. I run a Division One team in Brantford, and I thought that the three of you would look good in a Brantford uniform. You are much too good for Division Three. It was my intention to get you to come to Brantford and play for us, and I could have arranged for you to work for my old friend, Tommy Watson, the superintendant at the Massey plant, but as you know, the damn Huns came along and put a large shell hole in that plan. Fortunately, when your manager at Dunlop found out that you were enlisting, he contacted me and let me know. He knew that I was raising a battalion and thought I would like to have you in it. I pulled some strings at Central Ontario Regiment, and had you sent here to Niagara."

There was a stunned silence for a few moments, with just the sound of the clock ticking on the wall.

"You wanted us for our fighting skills, sir?" Farquhar asked, breaking the silence.

Genet began to chuckle. "Truthfully? I think you know the answer to that. I think you will make fine infantry once you have completed your training; there is no doubt about it. But while you are here, at Paradise Camp, I want you to continue playing the excellent football we have all seen. I want us to be the ultimate battalion football team, and we've gotten off to a fine start. Sports and recreation are an important part of training; it can't all be hard, sweaty work. Your contribution on the football pitch is good for the whole battalion – good for morale. Sergeant Shepherd coaches my Brantford team, and some of my Brantford players are on the pitch with you. You have obviously met them. This ugly war will end soon, very soon, I hope, and when it ends, I would like to keep this football team intact and continue our winning ways in the Ontario League. Anything you want to ask?" He finished.

Again, we glanced at each other, still a little stunned and intimidated by the Colonel and his revelations.

"Uh, not really, sir" I said looking to the other two for some input.

"No sir, we are clear," Elmer said, after I spoke. Farquhar said nothing. The Colonel looked at him in anticipation, but Farq remained silent.

"Well then, good, jolly good! You are dismissed. Good luck in your next game, beat the hell out of them! Oh, and one more thing. We have some new officers in the battalion and they need servants. Are any of you interested? Less exposure to frontline action."

Farq answered back, unexpectedly, "*Pog mo thoin*!"

"Well, you think about it." Genet answered, not realizing what Farq had said.

Elmer and I were stunned. Farq had just told the CO to kiss his ass, in Gaelic! I could not believe it and I nearly fell off my chair. Damn it! Thank God Genet didn't converse in Gaelic. He didn't understand or react to the comment. I gave Farquhar a look to show my displeasure and he mouthed a return, "What?"

We left the officer's quarters and headed straight back to our tent.

"Bloody Hell, what did you think of that?" Elmer said to us, as we walked back.

"I don't know what to think, right now, I need some time," I responded.

Farq still remained silent. I had an idea of what was going through his head, but I didn't want to stir things up just now. We decided to forego the remainder of bayonet drill, and just went back to the tent to contemplate.

"Let's wait for Lenny to get back, and run this past him. He may be able to give us some of his thoughts," I suggested. Nobody vetoed the idea.

When Lenny arrived at the tent, later in the afternoon, we told him the story. He just shook his head as he listened. After we finished, he let us know his thoughts.

"Well, this could be a good thing for you three. I've heard how bad Genet wants to beat the 35th in football. He just about cried real tears when they won the tug-of-war competition last week. These COs have big heads, and they want to win everything. Looks good on their war records; big promotions. Do you know what I mean? You can be sure he will look after you; you will get the best food and drinks for winning games. He might even let you guys have some hard liquor after the games; anything to keep you guys happy."

"So, while our battalion mates are getting mashed potatoes and bologna, we will be getting steak and apple pie and a shot of whisky? How is that going to work?" Farq asked Lenny.

"Geez, I don't know. They'll figure something out. Hey, maybe there will be some women."

Farq snapped back, "I haven't seen any yet."

"Probably wanted to make sure that you guys were on board first. That's why he met with you."

"You really think he would do that?" Farq erupted, his face reddening, "Shite, here we go ... the school boys are using us like play toys. Like puppets! Remember what Genet said about pulling some strings? That's just what he is doing. Having his fun. 'Would you like to be servants? Less exposure.' Fucking Limey! I'm not going to be anybody's servant! Especially not a school boy's!"

"Farq, take it easy! Think about it. We might not survive this war. Just listen to what people are saying about it over there ... at The Front. Gas attacks ... fire throwers, lice, rats - look how many boys are getting killed and shredded every day. Let's try to make the most of it! He wants to provide for us, so let him do it." I was trying to get him to look past his dislike for the English school boys.

Lenny leapt back in. "Hey, that was just my opinion; I didn't say that it must happen. I meant that is how it might happen. Give it some thought. That's all."

"Farq, it is you that Genet really wants on his team, you know that. Not so much me and Jonny. He just wants us along for the ride. Keep you happy. You know what I mean?" Elmer calmly suggested, trying to cool Farq down a little. "Just think it through, don't let your emotions decide. Rest on it for a while, be rational."

"Yeah, yeah. Give me some time. Let's just enjoy Paradise for now," Farq said, calming down considerably. He could be riled easily at times, but he was always able to keep himself contained. There was a Scottish temper that lurked there. I remember in one game back in Aberdeen, he grabbed an opponent who was a lot bigger than him, by the scruff of the neck. The player had just given him a "hair brushing" that Farq didn't ask for, or appreciate. Farq just glared at him and growled, "What the fuck was that all about, asshole?" The player just froze with a look of astonishment. But after he let him go, he didn't go anywhere near Farq for the rest of the game. Farq's tough, and he cannot be intimidated. No sir.

As the summer passed into August, we continued with our training and our football. The nights became a little cooler and the days noticeably shorter. The crickets sang feverishly at night but it was a pleasant sound to sleep to – for me, anyway. The battalion football team actually lost a couple of games, along the way, and it took some of the heat off of us as favourites. The 35th Battalion soon began to emerge as the team to beat. The three of us became more aware of the skills of our teammates, and we were able to sort out the players that Col. Genet had brought with him from Brantford. Turned out, it was the entire rest of the team.

Our Commanding Officer was obsessed with building a football dynasty, and was not going to let a global war get in the way. I thought about McKeand and I wondered if he was onboard too. Does anyone else know about this? Farquhar had good reason to feel used. I felt the same way.

"*Pog mo thoin!*"

Chapter 7
Summer's End

The summer of 1915 had been a hot one. The grass on The Commons had faded from green to brown. We hadn't had much rain, but when we did, it came down in torrents. The thunderstorm at Queenston that nearly fried us all was just a prelude. We had some wicked storms that usually brewed up in the late afternoons of hot, humid days and lashed us with gusting winds, thunder, lightning, rain, and once, even hail. The bell tents turned out to be a little leaky, and sometimes our gear inside got soaked. Fortunately, our tents were up on wooden platforms to keep us from getting flooded. Little rivers of water would just run under our tents and right on by. Fortunately, though, the storms were few and far between.

With the cooler August nights, the grass in the morning would be wet with dew. We found the footing slippery during drills until the sun got high enough to dry the ground. Some of the trees that surrounded the camp were starting to show hints of fall colour, particularly near the top extremities. The bird songs that greeted us in the morning had gone silent, and some of the birds were beginning to flock together in anticipation of the fall migration. I hated to see the summer decline. Even though we were being trained for the nasty business of war, the summer, up to this point, at least, had been like a return to childhood. There was hard work but plenty of time for games. There was regimentation but time for camaraderie. We didn't have to make big decisions; they were all made for us. If only it would last a little longer...

Farq managed to see Nancy a few more times in town. They met for breakfast once, in the Queen's Royal Hotel down by the riverfront. It was very tastefully decorated inside; very "fancy" as Nancy described it. I don't think she had ever been to an elegant dining room before. Through the summer, we had spotted her around the town, on different occasions, with other soldiers walking with her and holding her hand, or putting an arm around her. There were no illusions as to where Farq stood with her. He was just one of many and he accepted that. Besides, she was upbeat, had a sense of humour and was fine company for a young soldier away from home. Elmer and I got used to seeing them together, and stopped giving him grief. Maybe we were a little jealous.

Elmer proved to us that a leopard doesn't change its spots, as the old saying goes. He never was a neat and tidy civilian. In fact, he was just plain messy. On more than one occasion, over the summer, his goods and equipment spread over into our personal domain in the tent. Farq and I were kind of used to it, but Lenny was not amused. Elmer never used the garbage pail. His letters and wrappers just piled up around his cot, and his clothes got left on the floor. Three times we got nailed during a tent inspection, and had to serve kitchen duty to pay for it. This led to some very heated verbal confrontations between Lenny and Elmer. We had to separate them a few times when it began to get physical.

Elmer had been on his best behaviour for a while, but one day, he came up with a gem of an idea. He sweet-talked the Wonkys into stealing the 35th Battalion's 1915 PARADISE CAMP Tug-of-War CHAMPIONS banner from the section of the camp where they had it prominently displayed. They brought it back to our tent one night and Elmer went to work on it. He fastened a blank piece of cloth material over the word "War" and printed the word "Dick" in its place.

"OK, Wonks, go back and hang it where it belongs."

There were some rumours about, that we would be getting fitted for our uniforms soon. I admit that I would have felt much more like a soldier if I hadn't had to wear this floppy hat and baggy shirt. I admired the way the officers looked when they walked through the camp or in the town. It gave them an advantage with the women, which they didn't already need. The ladies would turn and look at them as they walked by. Speaking of the officers, the Wonkys had stopped stealing from them. As the officers became aware of certain things disappearing from their tents, they started putting those certain things under lock and key, and they arranged for the sentries to patrol closer to their tents at night. Of course, that meant that the Wonkys started lifting goods from the ORs (Other Ranks). The three Macs made sure that the Wonkys understood that they were not to steal from the 58th.

The rumour about the uniforms soon became fact. The new clothes arrived before the middle of August. Each company was called to the storage sheds at the Barracks for fitting. We were issued a field cap, a khaki jacket with five buttons on the front, a khaki shirt, khaki trousers, khaki puttees and shoes. This was called the Standard Dress. Most of the articles were made from wool, and were a little itchy. It took some time to get used to it. The puttees were nine-foot long strips of wool that wrapped around our legs, from the knee down to our boots. These things were a little difficult to get a handle on at first. I guess they provided some kind of protection, although I am not sure from what. What an improvement over the old farmer kit that we had been wearing! We couldn't wait to wear the uniforms to town on the weekend. We were going to have the ladies swooning! Yes sir!

Another rumour that was circulating was that there was going to be a draft of trainees leaving the camp early, probably in mid-August, to head to The Front. Some of the guys in the 58th were chomping at the bit to go. They couldn't wait to get their hands on old Fritzy. The ones most likely to go were the trainees with prior military training – like Farquhar who had done some time in the militia. Others, like me, were rather enjoying life at Paradise Camp, and didn't want to go somewhere else to get hurt or worse. I didn't feel skilled enough with the weapons or the tactics of war to last more than a day or two at The Front. Just the thought of climbing out of a trench and carrying my soft vulnerable body toward the bullets and bayonets that waited for me made my heart pound with fear, and an ache would roil through my skin and bones. As it turned out, the draft was not just a rumour. In mid-August, the 58th got hit hard. We lost more than 200 men in the draft. Luckily, our foursome in the tent went untouched. Lenny didn't think that was a coincidence.

"You fellas should find out if any other players on the football team went to The Front in the draft," he advised us. Farquhar scurried out of our tent, as fast as he could to find our teammates. He was back in a few minutes with the answer, "They are all still here."

"You know, the football schedule doesn't end till October, and Genet wants the team intact until the end. It doesn't take a genius to figure that one out," Lenny replied. "You've been spared. Especially you, Farq. You did service in the militia, didn't you?"

"Aye, in the 48th, Lenny. I thought I was gone for sure. I am shocked, but then, how could I have survived over there without my best buddies? I would have been all on my lonesome."

"You are full of shite, Farq," Elmer countered Farq's sarcasm. "You would be useless without us. You can't tie your own shoes. Fritz would eat you for lunch, *jobby.*"

With all of the battalions in uniform, the camp commander had made arrangements for professional photographers to come from Toronto to take pictures of all the assembled men: the bands, the special sections and the officers. It took up a whole day, and gave us a break from our normal duties. The final photos were panoramas of each battalion. We arranged ourselves in a semi-circle, in front of the photographer, and he panned the camera from one side to the other. I had hoped that we would get to see them before we left for The Front.

Sundays were reserved for church parades and visitors. The three of us and Lenny, too, often felt a little left out on Sunday. We had no family in Canada, except for Farq's sister. Many of our camp mates would tow around family members, showing them all of the features of Paradise Camp and Niagara-on-the-Lake. Most of the visitors would come from Port Dalhousie after taking the ferry boat across the lake from Toronto. Farquhar's sister, Catherine, and her husband, Peter, came to visit Farq one glorious, sunny August day, and saw him in full uniform for the first time. They brought their son, William, now a five- year- old, along with them. I have never seen Farq so happy. Like us, he missed his family back in Scotland, and having his sister so close by was great comfort. William was fascinated by Farq's uniform and tried on the peaked cap. Farq saluted and William returned a child-sized salute. I could tell that Farq was a little self-conscious about this scene, knowing that Lenny, Elmer and I had no family present in Canada with whom to share such good times. Catherine and Peter made a good attempt to include us in the conversation and kept all of us up on the news from Toronto and back home in Scotland. They even brought letters from home for both Elmer and me. Catherine was a delightful lady. The physical resemblance to her little brother was strong. She had the same gleam in her eye as Farq. There was a little mischief in that gleam and she loved to have her fun. She delighted in offering little William a tiny sip of her glass of dark stout. William would press his lips to the glass and take a swallow. Then, his face would pucker up as the sour taste registered, and he would shake his head back and forth, and then give a shudder. Catherine clearly enjoyed this little charade and always finished the gesture with a satisfied chuckle. We loved the way she called Farquhar, "Facker". That is the way she pronounced it, and it gave us a lot of latitude with the name, Farquhar.

At the end of the day, we all went for dinner in Niagara-on-the-Lake, and then escorted them back to the bus station to see them off. The events of the day helped to ease my home-sickness. I felt a sense of warmth inside me that I hadn't felt since leaving Aberdeen.

After watching the bus depart for Port Dalhousie, the four of us decided to walk up to Fort Mississauga, near the rifle range, and watch the ferry sail back to Toronto. We had a view clear across Lake Ontario, about twenty miles to Toronto on the other side. On a clear day, you could see some of the larger buildings jutting up on the horizon, and of course, the smoke belching from every chimney. The evening air was pure and clear, and we had no difficulty seeing the bumps of Toronto on the horizon. We didn't have to wait long to see the ferry boat sail out of Dalhousie and begin gliding across the smooth blue waters of the lake. As the sun began to go down behind the Niagara escarpment, and the sky began to darken, we could still see the ferry, but only by her lights. When darkness descended, we could not distinguish the ferry's lights from the winking city lights; they blended together into one sparkling necklace along the horizon.

"I think we should head back to The Commons, boys, it is getting late," Lenny suggested, breaking our trance, as we stared wordlessly across the water.

"Let's wait a little longer, maybe half an hour," Farq countered. "I want to see the fireworks from the CNE. We should be able to see them easily tonight." I had been to the CNE twice, and each day was ended with a fireworks display at sunset. It was a sort of giant country fair with rides, exhibits and even large permanent buildings. Toronto residents just called it "The Exhibition" or even "The Ex".

Farquhar was right. Soon we were entertained by the flashes and colours of the fireworks, projected against the black night sky. They appeared just above the horizon, tiny at this distance, casting an identical colourful reflection on the still lake water, and then floated slowly down to meet up with their reflection as one.

"Listen, you can hear them ... shhhhh ... listen."

Lenny was correct. You *could* hear them; a faint rumble, delayed from the burst by a few minutes. We listened intently, as we watched. I wondered if that is what it would be like at The Front. Distant thunder until we get dangerously close. There was a considerable time delay between flash and sound.

"We won't hear the shells coming," Farq said. We remained silent as we watched the display, and thought about shells, and maybe even the possibility of death.

Lenny's squeaky voice brought us back to reality. "I think we missed flag tonight, boys, we are in deep shit. We are AWOL."

"Shite, we'd better get the hell back to The Commons," Farq implored, rather urgently.

"Wait, wait!" Elmer countered, even more urgently. "Farq, go down to the beach and run into the water."

"What the fuck! *Away an boil yer heed*!" said Farq.

"Never mind, just do it," Elmer answered before Farq could finish his sentence. "Get into the fuck'n water and get yourself wet!"

Farq bellowed back, "You go soak yourself, McLean! What do think I am, some kinda *clawbaw*?"

"No, listen! If we can convince Keachie that you fell into the river and we had to save you, then – no court martial." Elmer cast glances around the group, looking for approval of his plan.

Lenny suggested a slight modification. "I think maybe we should all get wet. If we were saving him, then we all gotta go into the drink. Right?"

"Lenny is right. We all gotta get wet," I added. With that, we ran down the short slope to the beach and jumped in. The water was more than a wee bit chilly, and the evening was cooling off rapidly. It was a rude finish to an extraordinarily pleasant day.

Elmer made a suggestion."Let's at least get our story straight. Farq fell in the river and the three of us had to wade in and pull him out. Simple as that!"

Farquhar interrupted, "Why me? Why do I have to be the *numpty* that fell in? How about Jonny?"

"Never mind who fell in, let's just get back as quick as we can. We can't waste any more time!" Lenny shot back.

Off we scrambled, back toward The Commons, and shaking off the excess water as we ran. I could feel my teeth starting to chatter. We arrived as the ceremony was breaking up and everyone was heading back to the tents. Just at the edge of tent city, we ran into some of our battalion mates.

"Where were you guys? Keachie is steaming, and looking for you."

"Long story, mates; tell you later. Where's Keachie at?" I replied to them, out of breath and shivering.

"Heading over to the latrine. Good luck. We can't wait to hear! Hah."

We caught up to Keachie just as he was pulling open the latrine door to go inside.

"Sir, sir!" Farq hollered before Keachie could enter. Keachie turned, holding the door open with one hand. "Where the hell have you four idiots been?"

Before anyone could answer, Farq blurted out, "Elmer fell into the river and almost drowned! We had to follow him downstream and fish him out! All of us almost drowned." We turned as one to look at Farq in a kind of shock. Should have known better.

"Uh yeah, that's right. We saved his life. Isn't that right, Elmer?" I added in my most reassuring voice.

Elmer answered, "Uh … yeah, they saved me alright. I was heading out into the lake. Thank God!"

Keachie just looked down at his feet, shook his head from side to side and said. "Geez, do I have to send for your mothers to look after you? Get out of those fucking wet clothes and see me at 0800 hours. Get outta here, I need to go shit!"

I muttered to Elmer, " I think we dodged another bullet. Shite, I hope that we can dodge bullets this well at The Front."

The next morning, Keachie let us off with a day of latrine duty and driving the "honey wagon" (the truck used to transport the, ahem, human waste). We could have been sent to a court-martial. I think Keachie had taken a liking to the three of us. He could have had us back in civvies by now. Maybe the military was desperate to keep as many men as possible in uniform. The war in Europe hadn't been progressing all that well. There had been way more casualties than expected, and the outcome of the war was very much in doubt. They were in no hurry to get rid of enlisted men.

Early on the Saturday morning of the Labour Day weekend, at the end of August, all of the Paradise Camp battalions boarded one of the same ferry-boats that Farq's family had sailed on, as well as another, slightly larger, ferry. When we arrived in Toronto, we were bussed to Queen's Park, where we joined with some other battalions that were already in the city. Farq and I discussed our inner feelings as we awaited the parade to City Hall. In the company of so many other uniformed soldiers, we were beginning to feel like the idyllic days at Niagara were coming to an end, and we would soon feel the cold discomfort of long journeys, strange lands and sights that no man or animal was ever meant to see. Hearing the bands preparing, tuning their instruments, and rolling the drums made us feel like it would soon be time to go over the parapet to face the hot steel of the enemy. We could feel our bodies tense up and our hearts begin to beat rapidly. I think the emotions of war had finally caught us, and reality was sinking in. Real dread was creeping in, and our football games and pranks were not going to comfort us much longer. I started to think about being back home again; back in Aberdeen.

The huge parade started at Queen's Park and snaked along College Street, east to Yonge Street. I think most of the inhabitants of this fair city turned out to cheer us, and cheer us they did. We loved it and it made us straighten our backs, square our shoulders and stick out our chests like never before. I felt nine feet tall as we marched past the cheering crowds that were lined up along the edge of the road. The sounds of many bands, all playing different tunes, and the cheering of the crowd all mixed together to overwhelm my sense of time and place. There were many pretty young ladies that were calling to us and blowing kisses. Everybody waved Union Jacks, making the crowd pulsate with red, white and blue. I saw fathers with little children propped up on their shoulders, the little ones clutching flags and waving them incessantly. There was one group that was of school children in uniform, accompanied by their teachers, holding flags and banners. I didn't want this moment to come to an end. The adulation made all those hours of field drill worthwhile.

We marched down Yonge Street to Queen Street, where we made a right turn. Then, we did a march-past at City Hall, in front of the viewing stand, where we were perused by the Mayor of Toronto, some other politicians and Col. Sam Hughes, the Minister of Defence.

"Eyes right!"

The parade ended at the armouries on University Avenue. At this point, we were told that we would be bussed back to the CNE, and given free time there until after the fireworks. The three Macs and Lenny, of course, were overjoyed. In the time that we had lived together in Toronto, we had never been fortunate enough to attend the CNE together. What a great opportunity to relive a little of our childhood, and watch the fireworks from close up.

As the troops walked about in small groups along the streets of the CNE and the midway, civilians cheered us and patted us on the back.

"Go get 'em, go get those Krauts!" "Kill Kaiser Bill!" they yelled.

The cheers were meant to do us good, but again, they seemed to bring back some of the apprehension we had felt at the start of the big parade. The rumble of those drums caused a fear to surge through my veins and a knot to form in my stomach, as if I was being stalked by danger. I didn't know what it is like to kill someone, and I wasn't sure I wanted to know; Hun or not.

We engaged in some fun on the midway, playing games of chance and trying some of the rides. The best of the midway was a little game of flirt, which we played with the young ladies. Not just any young ladies, but the ones who were accompanied by mother and father, and dared not to get caught making eye contact with the rowdy soldiers. It was a game that had to be played with skill and some stealth to avoid any parental nastiness.

Once darkness overtook the Exhibition, we headed down to the lakeshore to watch the fireworks. A crowd began to gather along the grassy raised edges of Lakeshore Road to see the grand event: the termination of the day. The display would start at ten o'clock to signal the daily closing of the Exhibition, and the day itself. You had to brace yourself because the first explosion was guaranteed to startle you. The spectators couldn't see the charge being launched from the ground. It rose in silence, only to spark and cover the black night sky in diamonds. Everybody, braced or not, gasped and jumped. The ground lit up as if a giant lamp had been turned on. Night turned to day. Some fireworks exploded with a small flash and a puff of smoke, but then were followed, a few seconds later, by a shattering bang that resonated inside my chest cavity. It made our ears ring and actually hurt. I wondered, does it feel like this in Ypres? Do the troops watch for the flash with the same anticipation as we did along the shore of Lake Ontario? Would I be able to see and hear the horror, and stand up to it without crumbling to the ground?

The ferries took us back to Niagara at midnight. We were exhausted from the activities of the day, and it felt good to be back in our tent-city and in our cots. Tomorrow would come too quickly, and we would be back to the process of our preparation for the war.

That night I had a disturbing dream that may have been triggered by the dread I was beginning to feel about going to The Front. The late-night ferry boat ride became a nightmare as the vessel began to list and take on water. I don't remember why. I don't recall the ferry hitting anything. The ship was jammed with troops, and there was complete chaos as the ship leaned. Men were pushing and fighting with each other to get to the life boats, but there was no room to move. I could only move to where the crowd carried me. I saw an unoccupied life boat but I couldn't get to it; the surge of the human mass carried me right past it. Then, another empty life boat appeared, but was followed by the same futile result. The cold Lake Ontario water began to rush over the deck, and soon soaked us up to our waists. I was beginning to panic with the thought of dark water rushing in through my mouth and nostrils; unable to gasp any air into my lungs.

Suddenly, the dream smacked me awake, and I sat up at the side of my cot. It was so dark that I didn't know if I was dead or alive. After I got my bearings, and my eyes adjusted to the dark, I could sense that my tent mates were all sleeping and unaware of my sweaty, panicky presence.

I sat on the edge of the bed until my pulse slowed and I could relax again, enough to find shelter in sleep.

September continued with the beautiful sunny weather that had accompanied us since June. It seemed like every day dawned clear and blue. The nights were getting cooler, but it just made it easier to sleep and, conversely, harder to get up in the morning. We had heard rumours that we would be shipping out at the end of October. The rumours didn't specify if it would be all of us or just some of the battalions. The news that was coming back home from The Front wasn't encouraging. The number of casualties was growing at an alarming rate ,and the use of gas by both sides had increased. We were now being trained in the use of gas masks during our trench training sessions.

I never thought I would say this, but our infantry skills became very formidable, and I don't mean just the three Macs, but the entire battalion. Our parade drills were near faultless and we had achieved cohesiveness as a battalion. We became more comfortable with our weapons, particularly our Ross rifles. There had been a lot of controversy at The Front over these rifles. Our troops had been complaining that they jammed easily in the filthy battlefield conditions when they got too hot or dirty. On the range here in Niagara, we had no problems with them. I grew to enjoy my practice time on the range. There was a sense of satisfaction that registered in some part of my brain when I saw that little puff of dust on the surface of the target. It reinforced my confidence and made me want to fire at that target all day long. The more I hit it, the more I wanted to shoot at it. The recoil that I felt at the butt of the rifle became a reward for my excellence. It was addictive.

Farq has been deadly accurate on the range (why was it always him?) and he looked like a sure thing to be a sniper when we got over there. He would be amazing, especially if he had the Wonkys as spotters; I'll have to remember to suggest that to Sgt. Keachie. We have also been practicing bomb-throwing, using dummy wooden bombs made to look like real Mills Bombs, and all three of us have done well in this sport. I can't wait to try out the real ones so that we can make our own "end of the day fireworks display".

The football season was coming to an end near the beginning of October. The 58th team (we called ourselves the "Victors" because of the white vee on the front of our sweaters) was in second place in the standings with eight wins. Our dreaded rival, the 35th, were out in front, in first place, and undefeated. They had managed to repair their vandalized Championship Banner and promised to avenge the dirty deed. I think Col. Genet was pleased with these standings; he didn't want to go into the playoffs as the favourite.

He said to us one day after a game, "Let's just lie low in the grass and surprise them in the playoffs." I knew that the 35th would be no easy victory. They were stacked with first and second division football players, just like the 58th.

The Wonkys' business continued to prosper as the summer faded. They had branched out from fags to mickeys of rum, watches, pens or whatever came their way. Our tent was always their first stop on their sales route, so, despite Elmer's route march, pine-needles-for-toilet-paper run-in with them, our friendship blossomed. They were, after all, very likeable, and we became like big brothers to them. Lenny couldn't have been more pleased with this arrangement. He was never without a wee flask of whisky to help him with his aches and pains at the end of a long day of training. For an old guy, he was keeping up with the younger recruits very well. It would have been nice if he could have gotten a visit from his old friend, Sailor, before we shipped off to England. He told us stories about him and Sailor just about every night, and I think we had heard a few of them more than once or twice. One night, a few weeks prior, he fell asleep right in the middle of one his stories. Right after the word "and", he was gone; snoring away to beat the band. It felt like we were growing as a family. The loneliness of being away from our homes was eased by the comfort we gave each other. I wanted to make sure that we took this feeling with us when we crossed the ocean to fight a war. No one wants to die alone.

Chapter 8

The Showdown

It was becoming clear to everyone at Paradise Camp that the football championship playoffs were going to be the great event of the year. Forget parades. Forget route marches. Forget musketry competitions. Football reigned supreme. I don't want to sound unpatriotic, but it was like we were saying, "Forget the War!" Maybe this was all about forgetting the war. The men just wanted to talk about the teams and the championship. Col. Genet was correct when he told us how good the competition was for the morale of the troops. The rivalry between the 35th and the 58th was becoming very intense. When we were doing battalion drills out on The Commons, we always kept an eye on the 35th to make sure our lines were straighter or our steps were tighter in unison, and I am sure that they were doing the same. Even the route marches became a competition. Who could do it faster? Who could do it with fewer rest stops? The irony was that we might not even get to play against the 35th for the championship. We had to play a semi-final game against the 75th Battalion first, and if we lost that game, then the big showdown with the 35th would never happen.

When I think of Genet's words about morale, it gets me to thinking a little deeper. Keeping our minds on football was keeping our minds off other things. What other things? The answer to that was very obvious. Life in camp was very pleasant in many ways, but we were not isolated from the outside world. We heard the stories that were coming back from The Front. The newspapers carried stories of battles and terrible losses, and listed the local lads who had been wounded or killed. One evening in the tent, Farq was reading a letter from his sister, Johann, back in Aberdeen.

"Hey you guys, listen to this. Frank McGoey was killed in action at St. Julien, in Belgium a couple of weeks ago. Sniper got him."

Frank was one of our old gang back in Aberdeen. He lived on the same street, just two doors west of my family. He wasn't interested in sports like the rest of us, because of some physical disabilities, but other than that, he was always in the thick of things with the rest of us chaps. Frank had a pigeon coop, out behind his house where he kept his collection of racing pigeons and this made him a valuable commodity for the British Expeditionary Force (BEF) soon after the war started. Communication at The Front during a battle was very difficult by normal means, so somebody came up with the idea of using messenger pigeons. Frank, more or less, got drafted. I can still remember hearing him scraping his coop out every evening, summer and winter, before he turned in for the night. He loved his birds, and was dedicated to them.

The bad news cut us deeply. It brought the war closer than we wanted. It was always somebody's cousin, uncle or friend that we heard about, as we lived our lives in safety at home. We saw Frank every day, and attended school with him. We knew his mother and father, and I could see them in my mind, sitting in their parlour with a death notice in their hands and tears streaming down their cheeks. Frank was an only child, like Elmer and me. What would they have left to live for?

Elmer's grief and anger burst through.

"A fucking sniper! Farq, if you become a sniper, I want you to take all them Boche snipers out. Bastards! All they do is skulk around all day and all night, waiting for some poor bugger to lift his head above the parapet. You can't even look up at the stars or the moon without taking one between the eyes. Frank was probably just tending to his birds, just like he always did. Killed in action … .yeah like shite he was!"

Farquhar answered, "I don't know if I want to be a sniper, Elmer. I really haven't thought too much about it. I guess killing from a long distance is easier than killing face to face. Could you kill somebody right in front of you, face to face, with your bayonet? Could you kill somebody with a Mills Bomb, and watch the pieces fly through the air? I never liked to think about it. I wasn't interested in killing anyone until now."

"Better to think about football, eh?" I added.

Lenny then joined the conversation from his cot.

"You know, this is the first time that I've heard you guys talking seriously about that big mess in the trenches without making a stupid joke about it. Maybe you are finally starting to realize what lies ahead of us. This is not some game of football, and when your friends start dying and getting blown to bits, it feels different."

There was silence in the tent as the younger guys digesting what the older guy had just said.

"Look at each other. You've grown up together, but one day you may see one of you, or even two, die right in front of you. Or maybe all three of you will die together, at the wrong end of a mortar shell, and not even know it was coming."

I could feel my heart beginning to race, like that day in Toronto, at the parade when I heard the drums, the drums of war start to beat and the band instruments warming up. The thought of going across the ocean and living in cold wet trenches, for who knows how long, gripped every part of me, not just my mind. Occasionally, snippets of thoughts, like going back to Toronto and back to Dunlop, invaded my mind, but then were erased. I was in turmoil, trying to battle my fear.

"Do you lads ever think about taking off – you know – just going back home or somewhere else?"

Again, there was a moment of silence.

Then Lenny answered, "There is nothing wrong with having those kinds of thoughts. You are no different than anyone else here at camp. We've all had thoughts like that. There are men here who have lost several friends, or brothers in this war. At Paradise Camp, we have to live day-to-day, drill to drill, semaphore, fatigues, spit and polish, and we don't think too much about what can happen down the road. It will sap you of your strength and your will. Just do your best to whup the 35th."

Sleep didn't come easy for any of us that night. We all tossed and turned in our cots, wrestling with the loss of our friend, Frank, and thoughts of what was waiting for us across the ocean. If Frank could die over there, so could we. Is there a sniper waiting for me to arrive so he can put a German bullet in my head? What will it feel like if I get shot? Will I scream for my mother? They say men scream for their mother when they lay dying in the mud.

The football team had a week to practice and prepare for the game against the 75th. We had seen a few of their games, and we knew what to expect from them. Their attacking forwards were very fast, and they liked to play for the long passes up the field. Their inexperience, though, often put them offside, when they tried to play this kind of game. Our team was not as quick as they were, but we had the experience and teamwork to offset their speed. However, we did not anticipate an easy victory.

On the Saturday of the game, the sky was clear and the temperature was typical of a warm autumn day. Every soldier from Paradise Camp was gathered around the outside of the playing field, which was located in the middle of The Commons. The field looked like it was framed in khaki. They were joined by what looked to be, about half of the inhabitants of Niagara-on-the-Lake. Front and centre, at midfield, was the 35th, wearing their red shirts and white shorts, and accompanied by Col. McCordick, sitting in his seat, up on a riser. This was the biggest crowd we had ever seen at one of our games. Even our championship games, back at Ulster United Field, only drew a fraction of this.

The game began in a cautious manner, with both teams playing a tight defence, and not allowing any attacks deep into either end. We waited patiently for them to start trying the long passing game. I wasn't getting tested at all in our goal, with most of the play concentrated at midfield. Neither team looked very sharp, as if they hadn't had much practice or preparation. I think nerves were getting the better of both teams. The first half ended with the score tied nil – nil. I did not have to stop a single shot on goal. We had only two shots on the opponent. During the break, Sgt. Shepherd let us know that he wasn't happy with our sloppy play. Then, he revealed our second-half strategy. “Listen, I don't think we can wait any longer with keeping Farquhar back. We have to let him play his game. It is too easy to lose a game one to nil to an inferior team, and I don't want to face Col. Genet if that happens. Are you ready to play some offence now, Farq?"

"I thought you would never ask, Sarge," Farquhar said, beaming like a small child on Christmas Day.

It didn't take Farquhar long to show his magic. At about the fifty-three minute mark, he manoeuvred the ball through the midfield, leaving two defensive backs on the ground behind him. Suddenly, space opened up in the middle for our left striker, Norman "Tout" Leckie. "Tout" was the only officer on the team, but he was a superb athlete who played both association football for Genet and rugby football for the Toronto Argonauts. Farquhar looped a beautiful pass, up high over the defenders, and let "Tout" catch up to the ball, and he headed it high in the air to the back of the net. It happened so fast that the 75th seemed to lose their concentration , along with their speed and energy.

In desperation, the 75th began to try the long pass game, but it backfired. Pass after pass was either intercepted or went offside. Their defence began to wilt, and the 58th was able to generate many excellent scoring opportunities. Even Elmer was able to move up the field into their defensive territory, and make some passes up to the attacking forwards. Farquhar scored the next goal at the 70th minute, and ended any chance that the 75th could get back into the game. The game was easy for me in goal. There were never any serious scoring opportunities that I had to deal with. Most of the time, I was just a spectator. We scored twice more, and when the game ended, the crowd let out a boisterous cheer and rushed onto the field to congratulate the winners. Col. Genet ventured out of the crowd and headed straight to us, looking like a proud new Papa. He slapped us on the back and hugged us while chuckling heartily. It was strange to be hugged and slapped by a Commanding Officer, as if he was one of my best friends. It always seemed like OCs were untouchable. After Genet did his rounds with the team, I saw him search the sidelines for McCordick. At least, that is what I figured he was doing; scanning the sideline where the 35th had stationed itself. There were no signs of the 35th and no McCordick. They had vanished.

We had one week to prepare for the championship game. Both teams did their best to avoid each other. No eye contact. No conversation. Sgt. Shepherd informed us that our team practices were being shifted to the north fields, where the rifle range was located. He didn't want anyone watching or spying on us. We made use of the other men in the battalion to keep prying eyes away from our field. Back in August, we had spent weeks learning how to lay barbed wire in the battlefield. During one football practice, Elmer reminded Sgt. Shepherd about it. "Hey Sarge, can we get some of the sappers to dig a trench around our field and lay some wire?"

"Sure, why not, MLean. Maybe we can place some snipers in the trees, too!" This got everyone laughing, and brought the practice to a halt. We all laughed and gave each other a knowing look. I think that, all at once, we realized that we were preparing for war. Not just one war, but two.

The week of waiting and practising went by quickly. I don't remember anything other than our practices. I couldn't remember eating, sleeping, drilling, anything. We just wanted to get the game over with. We all had trouble sleeping on Friday night, before the game. Lenny volunteered to sing lullabies to us, but his squeaky voice was no comfort. We tried playing *would you rathers*; a silly game we made up back at home.

Elmer started off with, "Farq, would you rather kiss Sgt. Shepherd's ass or go over "the Falls" in a dinghy?"

Farq answered instantly, "The Falls, the Falls; no contest!"

He went next: "Jonny, would you rather have Lenny fart in your face or get pushed into the latrine hole, head first?"

Jonny came back with, "The latrine, give me the *cludgie* any day!"

Lenny added his voice to the insanity. "You guys are *numpties*!"

Then a voice came from another tent beside us: "Quiet, assholes! We are trying to sleep here. Go to fucking sleep!" The game went on for awhile until either we got tired of it or we ran out of "*would you rathers*". Sleep eventually came, soon after.

With the arrival of the big Saturday afternoon game, the khaki frame started to form around the outer edge of the playing field. The gentle people from town began to fill in the empty spots in the crowd. The brass bands from the rival battalions tried their best to outdo each other, playing louder and faster. People had to shout to be heard. Col. McCordick was in his usual spot at midfield; in his chair above the crowd. This time Col. Genet was right beside him on the riser. There was a small table between their chairs that held a carafe of some liqueur that they were sharing. For two intense rivals, they seemed very collegial.

When the two teams ran onto the field of play, the crowd erupted in a mighty cheer. The 35th Battalion were the team favoured to win, but it was impossible to decide if there was a crowd favourite. Bets were being made on both teams, and my guess is that people were cheering for whoever they had placed their bets on. There was a rumour that the Wonkys had bet on the 35th Battalion. Over on the sidelines, Sgt. Shepherd gave us our last words of encouragement, and then he grabbed Farquhar by the arm and whispered into his ear. "Give it your best, Farq." The game was on and I felt like I needed to puke.

In terms of pure skill, the 35th were, by far, the best opponents we had ever faced. They weren't as fast as the 75th but they didn't need to be. Like our team,, they were stacked with Division One players. As Sgt. Shepherd had predicted, they brought the game right to us, and forced the play in our end. In the first minute, I was called on to make a diving stop on a long hard shot that stung my hands like a hundred bees. I had not felt a shot that hard all summer. A few minutes later, I had to make another challenging stop on a corner kick. The pressure was tremendous; shots were coming from every angle. Elmer blocked two shots that probably would have gone in if he hadn't been there. It seemed like it took forever to get the ball out of our zone and past the centre line. Once this was achieved, however, our team seemed to catch its breath and moved the ball with some quick short passes into their end. At this point I noticed that the 35th were keeping two midfielders close to Farquhar's shoulders. Wherever he went, they went. This wasn't the first time he had been "double-teamed" and he knew how to deal with it. A "double-team" would open up the field for other players and give them scoring opportunities they otherwise might not get. Farq would just make sure he fed the ball to the open areas.

The first half ended in a scoreless tie. We left the field and headed into the mess tent for some oranges, water and a chance to discuss strategy, and nurse our scrapes and bruises. The 35th were playing a physical game, and tackled without mercy. The referee, an officer from the 37th, was not making many calls. Our uniforms were as dirty and grass-stained as I had ever seen them. We decided that if the 35th continued to double up on Farq, we would play the long pass game to try to open up space on the field; much like the 75th had tried with us. Farq would move the ball less and try to draw his checkers away from the play. It sure sounded good, but could we deliver?

When the game resumed, the 35th immediately took the play into our end, and controlled the ball. They passed quickly, and deftly around our defenders, keeping us off balance. Then they struck with three quick hard shots from within fifty feet, but I was able to stop only the first two. Before we had a chance to react, we were down, one to nil. McCordick jumped to his feet on the stand. The supporters of the 35th cheered and danced on the sidelines. Somebody in the crowd played a charge on a trumpet. It was important for us to remember not to panic, and to play the game we had decided to play during half time.

Each time the ball came to our fullbacks, they would play it quickly up the sidelines, to the attacking midfielders. Farquhar was still double covered, and kept the extra defender occupied. At around the sixty minute mark, we were starting to show more speed and began backing them up into their own end. "Tout" Leckie had two great scoring chances in close, and his opposite side striker, Bill Prosser (the elder of the two Prosser brothers on the team) had one opportunity on a header. Finally, we were playing up to our abilities and experience as well as Genet's expectations. We began to return the vicious tackles that our opponents had showed to us. The uniforms of both teams became almost indistinguishable in brown and green, and showing spatters of blood. Their goalkeeper was being severely challenged by our shots for a change.

Suddenly, Farquhar made one of those amazing efforts that people talk about for years. As we pressed them in their end, and controlled the ball around the perimeter of their defence using quick accurate passes, Farquhar suddenly slipped from his midfield position, and caused his two tormentors to collide with each other when they reacted. Free now, to move anywhere, he glided into the scoring area to take a beautiful pass from the other Prosser brother, Art. Farq, with his back to the goal, leapt into the air, inverted himself, and kicked the ball past the goalkeeper and into the net with a seemingly impossible upside-down kick. It happened in a flash, and all the players, both teams, stared at him as he picked himself up off the ground. The huge crowd let out a deafening cheer that must have been heard as far as Hamilton. Tied game; onc to one, and that was how it remained until full time. We had to play a ten minute extra period and a possible shoot-out.

In extra time, the 35th came at us again, with tremendous determination. They pushed us close to the net, and put us in an entirely defensive position. Their middle striker was gifted with a gorgeous pass, and was ready to put the ball past me from about twenty feet out. Elmer made a mighty diving tackle to knock the ball away before the striker could pull the trigger. Unfortunately, Elmer knocked the striker's feet out from under him, sending him hurling to the turf with a thud. Penalty shot!

As my opponent placed the ball on the turf, exactly as he wanted it, and then backed away from it to view his target, I studied his moves, gestures and face to see if he would give anything away. Would he go high or low? Would he shoot left or right? I think my heart was about to explode. I set my feet apart, so I could dive either way. I saw no clues in his actions that could give me an advantage. I felt helpless; I might as well have been blindfolded in front of a firing squad.

My opponent began his stride toward the ball. All I could remember was the sound of his foot connecting with the ball, and, followed by a fraction of a second, the sound of the ball hitting me square in the face. I went down like I was hit with a Howitzer. Then, silence. I was out cold. For how long I don't know. When I regained consciousness, I could barely make out my teammates hovering around me. Everything was blurry. The battalion doctor, Capt. Cosbie, was holding a cool cloth on my swollen forehead.

"What is your name, son?" He asked me.

"J … J … Jonny, I think. Jonny McLaren."

"What day is it?"

I answered, "Saturday?" Apparently I passed the test.

"OK, we are going to put you on a stretcher and take you to the medical tent. You need to stay there for awhile."

The stretcher bearers hauled me to the tent, and placed me on a cot. Then, a thought entered my mind. Did we win the game? There were two nurses standing a few feet from my cot.

"Excuse me, nurse … excuse me. Can you tell me if the game is over?"

"Oh yes, it ended a few minutes ago."

"Who … who won?"

"Oh dear, bad news, I'm afraid. The 35th won the championship." I think I passed out.

Chapter 9
The Great Trek

I never even saw it coming. The ball hit me right in the kisser, then rolled into the net. My teammates were gracious, and placed no blame on me for the loss. The hated 35th were the champions and they certainly deserved it. I hoped Col. Genet did not take the loss too hard. My face was still throbbing with pain and both my eyes were shades of purple. Fortunately, my nose wasn't broken, but it sure was crooked. Capt. Cosbie, our battalion doctor, said it would eventually straighten out. He said he might have to adjust it once.

With football now concluded, the next few weeks were taken up by two "Bigwig" visits to Paradise Camp. The news of the visits started rumours among the soldiers that "our time" was drawing near. We were aware of the stories from the Western Front, where the casualties were enormous and the losses were quickly mounting. Canada was a small nation in terms of population, and our losses were very large compared to other countries. We knew that our boys were right in the thick of the battles, particularly in the Ypres Salient in Belgium.

Two days passed before the three of us had an opportunity to rehash our loss to the 35th. We were ending the day, as usual, in our tent, and getting our cots prepared for the cool night. "How is your nose, Jonny?" Elmer asked, as he unfolded his wool blanket.

"I still have trouble breathing properly, but the pain has lessened. My eyes still water, I'll live. The loss hurts more."

"Why should the loss hurt, Jonny? It wasn't your game to lose," Farquhar added.

"What do you mean 'not my game to lose'?" I don't get it."

"Listen, it is like I explained to you before. That game belonged to Genet and McCordick - the school boys; not us. It is no different at The Front. We are nothing but pawns, we don't win anything. It is the same for Fritz in the trenches, too. They have their school boys, the same as us. No matter what happens on the battlefield, we can't win. Don't you get it?"

"I don't know if that's true, Farq," Lenny cut in. "The school boys are dying too; not just the ORs."

"That's just what I am talking about, Lenny; the ORs. Have you noticed how the papers report our losses? They will print that Col. So-and-So was killed in action, and then they will finish up with, you know, almost as an afterthought that forty-two ORs perished, as well. Those forty-two ORs are us; fathers, brothers, sons, friends ... no different than anyone else. Why should we just be an afterthought? Did you see Genet and McCordick sitting there in their chairs, sipping their 'whatever' like they commanded the play of the whole game? Like puppeteers. Doesn't that bother you?"

There was complete silence, and then Elmer spoke. "Fack, did you let up? Did you spike the game?"

"Shite, Elmer, I could never do that. I could never let my mates down. I knew how much you wanted to win, everyone on the team wanted to win; even Shepherd. I played my heart out. It will be no different when we go to The Front. I would die for you. I would die for anyone in this battalion or any other battalion. I hope everyone else feels the same way."

The next morning, the announcement was made at breakfast mess. Some of the battalions were to leave Paradise Camp at the end of October. They were to march from Niagara to Toronto, over a period of six days. One battalion would leave the camp each day, and treat the march as a battle exercise simulating an advance through enemy lines. Scouts and pioneers would be sent in advance of the battalion to keep a lookout for the enemy. This would be the test of whether all those long, hot route marches had adequately prepared us for the great trek. We would be issued our new Ross rifles and Oliver harnesses, to complete our uniforms and accompany us to Toronto. The 58th was one of the lucky battalions.

The weather in October had cooled considerably, in comparison with September. There was heavy dew on the grass in the mornings, and even on the inside of our tent walls. We could see our breath in the morning, up until the sun warmed the chilled air. We couldn't get to the hot tea or coffee fast enough at breakfast mess to warm up our shivering bodies. Marching around in the parade drills actually felt invigorating; it got our circulation going, our muscles moving. As much as those sunny, sultry, summer days challenged our strength and stamina, we were sad to see them go. The crisp coolness of autumn was definitely easier on our bodies during the drills, but it was so much more difficult to get out of that warm cot in the morning, and step on an icy cold floor, and put on our cold damp uniforms. There were some delightful qualities to the Niagara

Autumn, though. The abundant trees had changed from a lush green to a rainbow of colours. Red, orange and yellow were splashed everywhere, with the odd dab of green defiantly holding its own. Some mornings broke, shrouded in fog that slowly lounged across The Commons, and down into the Niagara Gorge. By noon, the sun was strong enough to burn away the mist and reveal the intoxicating colours of Ontario. The Garden of Eden: Paradise Camp.

The first politician to visit our beloved camp in mid-October was Sam Hughes, the Minister of Defence and the Militia. My feeling is that he wanted to see if the infantry that had been training here all summer was up to his expectations. He knew we would be leaving in a few weeks, and he wanted to look us up and down. All of the Paradise Camp units and bands took part in a march past, as Hughes stood on the same riser that Col. Genet and Col. McCordick had used to watch the football championship. Many of the residents of Niagara came out to watch as well as well as the newspapers of southern Ontario and New York State sent reporters to cover the event. At the end of the day, when the formal activities concluded, Hughes presented the Paradise Camp Football Championship banner to the 35th and Col. McCordick. It made me feel somewhat uncomfortable because I still blamed myself for letting in the winning goal. I had not slept well since that moment; it felt like a permanent stain on my body that I would carry with me forever. I had let my mates down. I should have stopped that ball, even though it knocked me silly. I gagged and wanted to throw up. I knew Genet felt even worse.

One week later, Prime Minister Borden made an appearance at Paradise Camp. The spectacle was much the same as the previous week, except that this time, there were more people from the press. After the ceremonies were over, it was announced that ten of the battalions would be going on the trek, starting on the 25th of October.

The hated 35th were to leave in a few days. They would not be missed because we were pissed off with their championship banner-waving parades, up and down the "streets" between the tents. A man, no, a battalion can only take so much of that. They were rubbing it in a bit too much.

The departures would be staggered over twelve days. The first night would be spent in St. Catharines, the second in Grimsby, and the third night in the city of Hamilton. The last two nights would be spent at Camp Merton, in Bronte, and then Port Credit. Most of the men in our battalion were excited about the idea of a grand exit from Paradise, though nobody was happy about leaving our memories of the camp behind. The conditions were changing in favour of warmer facilities. Our new billets, we were told, would be in one of the large pavilions at the Exhibition grounds. Training in the city would not be very different than it had been in Niagara, but it would allow the men who had families in town frequent visits. Farquhar would be happy to be near his sister again. Maybe we could pay a visit to Dunlop, too. We would remain there, and continue our training until we shipped out for England. The date of our departure across the ocean had still not been determined.

"Hey Fack, are you going to have a tearful good-bye with Nancy before we go?" Elmer was trying to get Farquhar riled up. "I hope she likes your moustache."

"Don't worry, Elmer, she loves my moustache. It tickles her in all the right places."

The departures started on the 25th of October, as planned ,with 37th Battalion leading the way. There was a hearty celebration the night before they left. Alcohol made its way into the drinks of the celebrants, and we noticed that the Wonkys were in the middle of the party. Afterwards, they dropped by our tent to show us how much money they had made at the event. Their skinny faces clearly showed the delight that they felt with the weight of the coins in their pockets. Wonky1 pulled out a flask and passed it around the tent, until we were feeling no pain. I loved those guys.

Our battalion was the next to leave. We were being paired up with the 74th. We decided to have a bigger and better departure celebration than the 37th. The party started in the mess tent, with a banquet that was catered by the local inns and taverns. They served beef and chicken with beautiful fresh vegetables from the local farms. One huge advantage in having our training camp located in the Niagara Peninsula was the abundance of fresh fruits and vegetables. The flow of crops started in August, with Concord grapes, cherries and peaches. They were followed in September by apples and pears that were sweet and crisp. October brought the pumpkins, squash and corn. Our meals here were never a disappointment. After the banquet, we left the mess tent to head out into The Commons. In the darkening evening light we gathered around a stacked pile of firewood with an effigy of the Kaiser, dead square in the middle. Everybody wanted to be the "fire starter", but Col. Genet was the one who got the honours. We would rather have seen an effigy of McCordick in the middle of the flames. When the fire was well-established and the sparks were twisting like fireflies up above the flame, our boys sang along to popular war tunes and stage songs. Somehow, again, liquor was mixed into our cups of juice and soda. The singing got louder and some of the other battalions wandered over to enjoy the spectacle with us. Much to our delight someone dragged the wooden riser that Genet and McCordick had used as a viewing stand, over to the bonfire, and in it went. The impact of the stand on top of the embers caused a cascade of sparks to swirl high into the black night sky. I imagined the people in Toronto seeing those embers in the sky over the lake.

As the clock passed midnight, most of the battalion celebrants were at least a little drunk, and many had wandered back to the tents. We would be leaving at 1400 hours the next day, and a good night's sleep would help immensely. I did not sleep well. I couldn't stop thinking about the road that lay ahead, and not only just the road we were marching on, tomorrow. My mind was trying to deal with the road into the trenches, into the flames of the guns, our khaki stained bright red with blood. Leaving Aberdeen and my family never felt like this. I didn't fear my death; I feared the death that would linger all around me.

When the dark cold morning arrived, we were faced with the chore of getting out of our cots one last time, dressing, having a hearty last breakfast in Paradise, and packing our gear for the trip. Our departure would take place right after lunch, but first, we had to dismantle our tents, and fold up the floor platforms. I admit to feeling a little sad in seeing "our home" sag to the ground. The leaky bell tent had been our base and shelter for four months. Many laughs and snores were shared under that canvas. I would never forget the particular smell of the "water-proofed" canvas as long as I lived.

Each of us had to carry a kit that weighed more than fifty pounds. I paid particular attention to the Wonkys as they suited up. The kits weighed almost as much as they did. How on earth could they march to Toronto with these immense burdens? As we formed up in The Commons, the remaining battalions gathered around to cheer for us and wave us off.

During this long trek, the battalions that were taking part, engaged in a fictional war scenario. Two nations, "Northland" and "Southland", were in a state of war.

The enemy for us were the "Northlanders", and they had managed to invade our territory from Toronto to Niagara, and occupy all of it except our fortified garrisons in Niagara, St. Catharines, Hamilton and Toronto. We played the part of Southland reinforcements, and we were needed to strengthen the line at Newmarket, just north of Toronto. We would encounter enemy forces along the route. The idea of playing a "war game" made the three of us eager for some military action against the "enemy". When we were young lads, back in Aberdeen, we indulged in this type of battle play all the time. Now we had the opportunity to play with two whole battalions for mates.

The first sections of the 58th to leave Paradise were the scouts who were to act as a screen for the main group. There were twenty scouts who were ordered to find the enemy, in advance of the rest of the battalion, and warn us of the danger. The next departure was A Company (58th) who was an advance guard, placed well in front of the remainder of the infantry group. They were followed by the band that led B and C Companies of both battalions. Behind them, was the transport train with five "steaming kitchens", stretcher- bearers and an ambulance. D Companies (from both battalions) brought up the tail end, as a rear guard. Grand marching music carried us up Queen Street, along the dusty road to St. Catharines, the first overnight stop of the Great Trek. We were blessed with fine weather; cool, clear blue skies with a warming sun.

We made it to St. Catharines by early evening with no casualties. Many of the cheering citizens lined the route as we marched into the city. The battalions had supper and were billeted outside the Lake Street Armoury, in hundreds of the old bell tents (there is no place like home). To the last man, we were starving and exhausted. The parade floor of the armoury was used as a mess hall where we ate our meals. Breakfast was served at 0700 hours the next morning. The citizens of St. Catharines were more than generous to the weary arrivals. The YMCA provided us with an evening concert, as well as laundry services, too. The "Y" also coordinated a service to match soldiers with residents who were offering meals and baths in their own homes. Never had any of these men witnessed such generosity and concern from complete strangers. We were dumbfounded. It made us so proud to be wearing that itchy khaki uniform with the red Maple Leaf on the shoulder. I could feel the strong urge inside my heart and my body to get to The Front and make these people proud.

Elmer found the Wonkys at one of the mess tables, and asked them how they made out with their heavy kits.

"Hey, Elmer!" Wonky2 (I think) answered, with a big smile on his face. "We had no trouble with them kits at all. We paid some of the udder guys to put some of our gear into dere kits for us. You want to make some cash?" Elmer rolled his eyes back and gave them a dismissive wave of the arm.

I looked at Elmer and said, "Those two bumpkins might be the smartest guys in the battalion. They got more money than anybody, including the school boys. They should be up at the front of this parade!"

At 0900 hours, the battalion was ready to begin the second leg of the trek to Grimsby, a small farming town at the base of the Niagara Escarpment. It was nestled right in between the escarpment and Lake Ontario. Col. Genet joined us for this segment and rode on a beautiful chestnut horse at the front of B Company (58th) with the other officers.

"Farquhar, you should ask Genet if he will let you ride the horse for awhile," Lenny kidded.

"Not after our disgraceful loss to the 35th," Farq answered. "He might prefer to drag me along behind the horse."

Elmer saw his chance. "Not you, he would throw Jonny behind the horse; he was the one who headed the ball into his own net."

"Get it up ye, McLean; I didn't head it into the net!"

"OK, sorry; faced it into the net!"

"Very funny. Very fucking funny, Elmer," I shot back.

The band struck up a marching tune, and the column of two thousand (give or take a few) headed north, up the Lakeshore Road toward Grimsby. The good weather continued, and we were often met along the road by farmers who would offer us food and drink as we passed by. Some farmers placed crates of apples along the side of the road for us to eat. It was odd, watching the men break ranks to head over to the side of the road for apples. Where was our discipline?

At Vineland, we came across a very welcome sight. It was a "Pie Wagon" loaded with pies (naturally) and drinks. The generous people of Vineland served enough pie slices for everyone. We ate and drank until our bellies bulged. The incredible Wonkys, sneaking in for seconds, ate more than anybody. Too soon, we were back on the dusty road again, full of pie and happy.

Once everyone was marching in rhythm, we became sort of hypnotized; you didn't really notice the passage of time, or anything else for that matter. We were in such a trance when, suddenly, there was a "crack, crack, crack". Somebody was firing at us! We quickly dispersed into the weeds along the side of the road. No one seemed aware of what was happening to us. There was momentary chaos until we realized that the unit had been engaged in a sham "battle" by the "enemy", just west of Jordan. This didn't go too well. The Northlanders had eluded our scouts and advance unit, and concealed themselves in the bushes along the side of the road. They waited until the main body of the 58th and 74th

arrived right in front of them. All Hell broke loose as they emerged from hiding, firing their weapons (blanks), and forcing us to hit the ground and defend ourselves. While the infantry was occupied in trying to confront the enemy on our flanks, the Northlanders brought in a second unit of infantry that had plans only for our startled officers. The nasty scoundrels surrounded the mounted officers and forced them to surrender. Our full contingent of officers was captured and constrained.

After the dust had settled, and the Northlanders had been declared victorious by the judges, the two defeated battalions took some time to assess the battle along the side of the road. Our officers conferred and then took some time to suggest changes. Then the CO got up to address the battalion. Genet was furious and he let us know it. "The Boy Scouts would have been more effective combatants than you clowns! God help us at The Front! Were you all asleep? Did you eat too much fucking pie? Damn you, what took you so long to react?"

His face had turned bright red. "And just one more item you should be aware of, you louts. The battalion that man-handled us today was the 35th. That's right, the 35th! Another loss to the 35th! I'm still pissed that they beat our asses in football. A game we should have won!"

"God, Farq, did you hear that? How is he going to face McCordick after this loss? It was bad enough losing the Football Championship. Now this."

Farq thought for a second, and then answered me. "I hate those guys almost as much as I hate the Heinies. I don't know if we will get another chance at those dolts before we get to The Front. They are always one up on us. I actually feel bad for Col. Genet. I never thought I would say that."

Neither did I.

We made our way into Grimsby by late afternoon, to the cheers of citizens and wailing factory whistles. Old Lenny was worn out at the end of the hike. We knew this trek would be tough on him because he wasn't a young man, and he wasn't in great shape. We did our best to encourage him, while the Wonkys kept him fortified with rum.

The battalion encamped on the beach beside Lake Ontario in Chautauqua Park. We were able to bathe in the lake, which at this time of year was numbingly cold, and no one stayed in the water more than a few seconds. There were no tents for us tonight. We slept under the stars, right on the beach and woke up in the morning with frost on our moustaches (those who had them) and on our blankets. The shivering battalions crawled reluctantly out from under the sheets like bears emerging from their dens after a winter's sleep. Nobody wanted to move. If our enemy wanted to take us, now would be the time. It wasn't long, though, before the air was tinted with the aroma of bacon. The steam kitchens were fired up and we were served a generous portion of bacon, eggs and fried potatoes. The meal was topped off with excellent (for the army) coffee.

"Are you going to be OK to march today, Lenny?" I asked, after taking a sip of hot black coffee.

"I'll be fine; don't worry about me. One good meal and I am as good as new." He sounded confident but, I had my reservations. He had struggled a bit near the end of the last sector. So far, there had been no casualties in either of the battalions, but we weren't halfway there yet. The total distance of the Trek was about one hundred miles. There were probably close to seventy miles in front of us. My left knee was starting to get a little sore and stiff but I wasn't going to let anybody know about it.

Lt. Cassels walked back to our company, to make sure everybody was in good shape. As an officer, he was on horseback for the journey. Where our uniforms were rather dusty and dirty from the roads, he looked like he had just come out of the country club after a glass of port and a game of cards. "Let's show everyone that B Company is the best of the lot!" he said as he gave Farquhar a paternal pat on the shoulder. Farquhar gave him a look that would set a box of matches on fire. I thought to myself, "Keep a lid on it, Farq. Stay calm." Lucky for us, Farq let it pass. I exhaled.

Hamilton was our next objective. This was one of our fortified encampments. We got on the road early and began our march at 0900 hours. By 1100 hours, we ran into some rain, but not of the heavy variety – just a lazy drizzle. There was a blustery north wind, bringing the change of the season. Normally, this would be a bad thing, but the rain was washing the dust out of our filthy uniforms. On the negative side, the uniforms were becoming itchier as they got wetter. Lenny was slowing down a little more each hour. The three of us stayed with him, but then, we began to fall back into the rear guard.

The battalions stopped in a tiny village called Fruitland, where we rested at the side of the road and had lunch. As we lay down on the grass beside the road, we were approached by a large number of women and children. Suddenly, Farquhar stood up and shouted, "Look lads, the enemy have cleverly disguised themselves to try and capture the whole damn battalion. Quick, stand to."

B Company exploded into laughter. As the "enemy" got closer to us, we could clearly see that each and every one of them was armed with a slice of pie. There was plenty to choose from; apple, blueberry, pumpkin and cherry were only a few that I could distinguish. There was enough pie for all; it was truly a miracle that could rival Christ with his fishes and loaves of bread. Did God, himself, send these angels to us? And a miracle it was.

"Genet will love this." I thought.

Every man in every company was re-energized by the kindness and goodwill shown us by these thoughtful people. The remainder of the journey to Hamilton became less of a burden.

The arrival in the City of Hamilton was a jubilant one. Like St. Catharines, the streets were lined with citizens cheering and waving flags. The noise was deafening. We marched to the James Street Armoury, and there we were fed and billeted for the night. The Armoury was large and spacious inside, and echoed the sounds of the men preparing their cots and kits. There were shower and laundry facilities for us to use to clean off all of the road dirt and dust we had picked up.

The next morning was windy and rainy, so it was decided that we would have the day off and stay in Hamilton for an extra day. Most of us spent our time resting and playing cards in the armoury. The Wonkys disappeared into the streets of Hamilton and weren't seen again, until curfew.

When the pair of them wandered past my cot in the armoury, that night, I stopped them to find out what they had been up to. "Hey mates, where have you been all day? We didn't see you around here with the rest of us."

The twin's faces were lit up with mischief, but they were hesitant to answer which of course, caught the attention of everybody within earshot. Their silence was deafening and everyone turned to see what possible explanation would follow. "We found the ladies," Wonky1 (I think) answered in a kind of whisper.

"Pardon?" I asked.

In a slightly louder voice, he said, "We found the ladies."

"What ladies?" Elmer blasted back at them. Elmer sat straight up on his cot almost at attention.

"Fuck, Elmer, we found the ladies of the evening," Wonky answered, with some pride.

"Did you say ladies of the evening as in, you know ... prostitutes?" I asked, in astonishment.

"Uh yeah, doze," Wonky answered.

Farq cut in, "What the ... Why didn't you tell us?"

"You don't have enough money; any of you," Wonky explained, leaving the rest of us glancing back and forth between us like we were lost in a strange land. There was total silence and disbelief after that exchange. But the Wonkys were correct. We didn't have enough money with us at the time. It was not a pay day and none of us had any money in our kits. The Wonkys always had money, and plenty of it. We just didn't think they would spend it in a normal way, like the rest of us. Shows you how wrong you can be about people.

It was a treat to sleep inside again. I had almost forgotten what it felt like. We had the best sleep since those warm nights in Paradise. With our departure from Hamilton, we were now heading east, along the north shore of Lake Ontario, toward Toronto. The extra day of rest in Hamilton soothed our tired feet and legs. We could still boast of not having lost a man along the route. The rain had ceased, and the day was clear and crisp.

It was important to keep an eye out for the "enemy" that lurked in the weeds along the route. We wanted to avoid another embarrassing "defeat" like the one back in Jordan. Bronte was our next stop, about sixteen miles east of Hamilton. There was a large camp at Bronte, near the Grand Trunk Railway station, called Camp Merton. It, too, was set up with bell tents, just like the ones we used in Niagara. The battalion arrived late in the afternoon, just as it was getting dark. The sun sets quite early at this time of the year, and the temperatures in the daytime were cool but pleasant; perfect for the long march. My left knee by now had become swollen, and because I was favouring that one quite a bit, my right side was becoming tender and sore. Farquhar had noticed the limp and asked me if I was in pain.

"I am used to it Farq, I have dealt with this all my life. Don't worry about me."

After an uneventful night at Camp Merton, we set off in the morning, for the town of Port Credit. The weather stayed cooperative and let us march in the warming sunlight. Lenny began to slow again, and was struggling to keep pace with the rest of us. Lt. Cassels noticed Lenny's plight, and rode back to see what the problem was. The Three Macs were stunned at the sight that followed. We collectively thought that Cassels would give him a speech to urge him on or suggest that Lenny take a ride in one of the trucks. Instead, Cassels offered Lenny the use of his horse. Lenny was not a rookie rider, and accepted the offer. Lt. Cassels walked toward us, joined our company and continued the march with us. "Maybe I have misjudged him," Farquhar suggested in a whisper.

"Maybe we all have," I offered back.

The Lieutenant marched all the way to Port Credit with our company. He engaged us in conversation; asking us where we were from, how we were holding up, and basic questions to get to know us. It seemed to give us an extra push to move along the road; an inspiration. And we got to know a little more about him. He was very articulate, but not smug or arrogant, even though he was from a prestigious family. His voice was a deep baritone, yet it was smooth and soothing. It felt to me that he would be able to keep calm and cool in the face of enemy fire and hot metal. He would make good decisions, and not needlessly sacrifice his men. Maybe that was just wishful thinking on my part.

The village of Port Credit, along the north shore of Lake Ontario, was our last stop before we marched into Toronto. The unfortified camp at Port Credit was quite large, and surrounded by a concrete walkway. The town supplied us with electricity and water, and a local starch company supplied us with laundry and washing facilities. As at Camp Merton, we slept in tents. This encampment was very comfortable and pleasant, and we all enjoyed our short stay here. Lenny felt much better about finishing the trek on foot. My pain was still present, but I knew I could make it to Toronto without aid. If it gets any worse, I thought, I will ask Lt. Cassels for a ride. How could he refuse me now?

Our destination in Toronto was a place called High Park, in the western end of the city. The battalion arrived at this beautiful, hilly landscape just before sunset, and we were able to get our tents set up before total darkness came. Finally, the Trek was done. Not one man of the battalion had faltered during the entire journey. We were told that the 58th and the 35th were the only battalions with that distinction; that would give Col. Genet some satisfaction. We were tired and worn, but proud of our accomplishment. At supper, the battalion stood to toast and cheer ourselves and our officers. We gave three cheers to Col. Genet and sang "For He's a Jolly-Good Fellow" and then a rousing rendition of "God Save the King". There was a sense that we had finally come together as a fighting unit.

The park was spacious, and could easily accommodate both our battalions from Niagara together for a few days of training. The senior staff of Military District Two decided to make the arrival of the huge number of men in uniform a stimulus to recruiting. A huge parade was planned to march into the city: a parade that would be twelve miles long, and like no other parade in the history of Toronto.

We waited a few more days for the arrival of the remaining battalions from Niagara. When all of the units had finally gathered in High Park, there were close to ten thousand men. The next day we mustered for the parade, the 58th, 37th, 74th, 75th, 81st, 83rd, 92nd, and 95th Battalions, all accompanied by sixteen military bands, field kitchens, ambulances, transport vehicles and guns. We marched along Bloor St. to Yonge St., and then south down Yonge to Queen St. Motor vehicles in the parade carried signs, "Your King and Country Need You, Step on Board." All along the route, homes and businesses were decorated with Union Jacks and signs. Each time the parade stopped, the populace cheered, and showered the soldiers with gifts of tobacco and cigarettes. It looked like the whole city was in attendance, lining the streets six or seven deep and even climbing to rooftops or up trees to get better vantage points. I felt my pulse race with excitement, or was it fear?

At one point between Bay and Yonge streets, the parade halted and the men sang one of their favourite camp ditties to the tune of My Bonnie;

"They say we get milk in our coffee;
They say we get cream in our tea.
They say we get milk in our cocoa;
But it looks more like whitewash to me."

After we reached the City Hall, the units dispersed to the Exhibition Grounds where we once again mustered for an inspection by Sam Hughes.

Afterwards, we were assigned to our billets in the Exhibition buildings and managed to relax and get some badly needed rest. Even though we had been humiliated in the recent ambush by the 35th, we had good reason to feel proud of ourselves. The receptions that we had gotten along the way made us feel like a conquering army. The march was gruelling; a fitting test for a battalion that was heading to Europe to fight for King and country. Only a few months ago, I was a rubber worker in a tire plant. Now I felt like a knight on a quest, having marched into the city in triumph, and waving to the adoring crowd.

It seems like very little time has passed since we three boarded the train for Niagara. When we left this city, we didn't have any idea (except for Farquhar's militia experience) of military life. I felt that I had grown to be more focused and disciplined, owing to the training that I had been subjected to. I couldn't speak for Farquhar and Elmer, but I could comment on what I saw in them. They were a bit younger than I, so the changes may have been more evident. They had cut back on some of the shenanigans they had exhibited before we left Toronto. They still engaged, but not as frequently. Humour bonded the three of us together, and this would, hopefully, never fade away. They had tempered it with an increased level of intensity toward their combat skills. They are very good soldiers. The Front was closer to us than it had been a few weeks ago, and when we had seen, with our own eyes, what we meant to those strangers who cheered us on, at the side of the road, we were sobered and shaken in the realization that we had become full grown men: strong, competent soldiers in the Canadian Expeditionary Force.

Chapter 10

Back in the City

Our home, for the next few weeks, was in the Horticulture Pavilion at the Exhibition grounds. The building was very large, and warm and filled with wooden bunk beds. There was enough outdoor space on the grounds of the Exhibition to continue working on our drills, just as we had at the Niagara location. It was a reunion of the battalions from Niagara, minus the bell tents and outdoor latrines. This was a fortunate change for which we were grateful, as the winds of November were bitterly cold. The blue skies of summer in Niagara were a vanishing memory, having been replaced by steel grey skies and stinging winds from the north. Gone was the sweet smell of new-mown grass, the singing birds and buzzing insects. Our senses now had to deal with our less than cherished reality of urban life. The mornings were now greeted by the city soot, the rumbling, huffing trains, the sputtering autos and occasionally, wet snow flurries. I no longer heard chickadees singing to me in the morning; instead it was the mournful hoot of the slate coloured pigeon that mocked me. If I could have turned back the clock by a few months, I surely would have. Those summer days were just a dream now.

The "brass hats" encouraged us to visit our friends and relatives who lived in the area. I was looking forward to returning to Farquhar's sister's house on Epsom Avenue in the east end. We hadn't seen the family since their visit to Niagara in August. Farquhar was eager to pack up his belongings at his flat on Boulton Avenue and store them at Catherine's place. He suggested that we could help him do that, and then, we could also visit our mates at Dunlop. I thought that was a great idea. Elmer did too. We even invited Lenny to join us but he told us he had plans to travel to Owen Sound for a couple of days and visit with Sailor. The Wonkys had relatives in the "Cabbagetown" area of the city and planned to visit them. I hoped their cousins or whomever, had the sense to hide the silverware and tie everything down that could be lifted.

Our first excursion into the city was a visit with Farquhar's sister, Catherine. The "three rascals" were invited to spend a Sunday with the Law family. Catherine had given us that nickname when we were about eight years old, back in Aberdeen. She seemed almost as fond of Elmer and me as she was of Farq. We always told Farq that she liked us better. We boarded an electric tram at the Exhibition and travelled east on King St. It had been a few months since we had travelled through the city, and this Sunday was no exception. Sunday in Toronto was like no other day. Everybody was either in church or at home with the family. You could fire a Howitzer down Yonge St. and never hit a soul. No autos and few pedestrians. It was like a ghost town. If this was a Monday or a Tuesday, the tram would be full of citizens, standing shoulder to shoulder.

We were greeted at the front door like long-lost travellers. Little William jumped into his uncle's arms and hugged him while pulling off his cap. The cap went immediately onto his little head, covering over his eyes and ears. The little fellow was fascinated with our uniforms and always wanted to wear the cap or try the fit of the tunic or the Oliver harness.

His father, Peter, said, "William will be in uniform himself, one day. You can bet on it!"

I laughed and added, "Tell him to go into the Navy. Believe me, it has got to be better."

We spent the entire day at the house on Epsom Ave. The neighbours dropped over to visit us and wish us well at The Front. They treated us like kings, fed us and filled our glasses with stout, slapped us on the back and made sure that we wrote to them so they could send us "goodies" during our time in the trenches. We even went outside of the house and stood in front of it to pose for photographs with family and friends. Everybody wanted to have their picture taken with a hero or two. The whole time, I watched Catherine's face to see how she was dealing with the imminent departure of her younger brother. She tried to laugh and smile, but to my eyes, it was rather forced. Her eyes never sparkled or smiled with the rest of her features. The eyes are the well of truth. I saw an occasional tear trickle onto her cheek, only to be quickly wiped with minimum gesture to avoid detection. It made my heart begin to hurt, too. I was beginning to feel an aching loneliness that was added to the fear of going to The Front.

Appropriately stuffed with delicious food, it was time for us to get back to barracks.

"When do you leave for Europe?" Catherine asked us before we were out the front door.

Farquhar answered quickly, "We have not been told the date yet, but everyone believes it will be before the end of November."

"Please let us know when you find out so that we can come down to wave you off."

"I promise to let you know, and there is a good chance that I will be back to visit you before we leave. We have other missions to accomplish in the city before we ship out. The three of us want to visit Dunlop and then we can drop by here afterwards. I would like to bring some of my belongings up from Boulton and store them here. Don't worry; we will see you again soon." We headed back to the tram line and made it back to barracks before curfew.

The battalions continued to do open and close order drills, rifle practice, trench and sap construction, and bombing drills at the Exhibition grounds. We also travelled to High Park and Riverdale Park to engage in some battle simulations. In the second week of November, the 58th was told that we were going to ship out by train to Halifax on the twentieth of the month. In Halifax, we would board a troop ship and sail across the Atlantic to England. No other information was given because it might have fallen into the hands of the wrong people. We were informed of the presence of spies in the city. Time was running short to finish up any personal business in Toronto.

Lt. Col. Genet addressed his battalion soon after we heard about the departure. One thing he advised us to do was to get a formal portrait photo taken of us in uniform. He suggested that we gift the photos to our next of kin before we left for Halifax. When I heard, this it gave me a terrible shiver. There was a feeling of finality or doom in giving the photo to "our next of kin". It was like, "Here is something to remember me by, Ma and Pa", or "Here is a last memento of our late son, killed in action".

"Elmer, we should have our photos sent back home to Aberdeen. Maybe your sister could look after that for us, Fack," I suggested, when I thought about sending pictures to my next of kin, my parents back in Scotland.

"She would happily do it for you, my fine friends."

Farquhar knew of a photographer on Queen Street that could take the pictures and develop them for us. We had only one day to try to get them our pictures taken, visit Dunlop and get back to Epsom Ave to see Farq's family. When we set out that morning to get our tasks done, Elmer happened to notice a change in Farquhar.

"Jesus, Farq, what happened to your moustache? Did it fall off? Did the glue give out?"

"Oh, you are really funny, McLean!" Farq replied, without a hesitation.

He rubbed his upper lip, just to emphasize what he had done and that it was gone.

I couldn't resist. "I don't blame you, Farq. I wouldn't want to be remembered by everyone with a piece of cotton candy stuck on my upper lip. You did the right thing, taking it off."

"Maybe I'll grow it back once we get to The Front just to scare the Heinies."

Our first stop was at the Walter Dickson Studio on Queen Street. The three of us, had individual portraits taken of ourselves in our uniforms, and a couple of posed portraits of the three of us together (inseparable). If we had swords, we could have been the Three Musketeers. We had some fun with the group photos; not the kind of pictures that we would want our CO to see. There is a pattern to our behaviour when the three of us are together. Things may start out straight and serious, but, they rarely end that way.

It didn't take us long to get from the studio to our old place of employment – Dunlop Tire. As soon as we walked in the front doors, the odour of cooking rubber assaulted our senses and brought back the memories of long days on the shop floor. We were greeted in the front lobby by Mr. Beynon, the factory superintendent. He greeted us with great kindness and enthusiasm, which was quite different from the way he used to greet us when we were mere employees. He actually made eye contact with us; something I don't remember him ever doing before. We were soldiers of the King now, and everyone treated us like celebrities; even Mr. Beynon. He led us into the bay where we used to toil, and, as soon as our mates saw us walk in, they put their work down, shut off their machines and came up to us to shake our hands and slap our backs. There were a few others from our shift that too, were also missing; they had departed to enlist. We enjoyed the reunion while it lasted; we didn't want to stay too long. As we were leaving though there was something that struck me. Every man shook our hands heartily and wished us safety, but the smiles were absent from their faces. To a man, their expressions had changed from delight to sadness, or maybe even fear. I knew what they were thinking, and it was probably very close to what Farq, Elmer and me were thinking. My gut instantly tightened up, and the joy that I was feeling from seeing my mates died inside me.

"Kill the Kaiser!"

"Kick Fritz's ass!"

"Bring me a Luger!"

We just waved and made our exit back out through the front door. I couldn't look back, even though I wanted to.

We departed the factory and headed over to Farq's old flat on Boulton Avenue, a few blocks away. Farq had left some belongings there, with another tenant, and each of us picked up the items that we could carry and then sped, on foot, to Epsom Avenue. The day was running out on us, and we wanted to spend some quality time with Catherine, William and Peter.

"My God, look at you three! You are far too good-looking to be sent to the front. Come in, come in."

Catherine welcomed us at the modest door on Epsom Avenue. Peter and William joined in the greetings as we were ushered into the house for our last visit. Catherine had prepared a delicious roast pork dinner for us, and during dinner we told them of the Great Trek and everything that happened to us during the march.

We were roundly (and deservedly) teased about our defeat at the hands of the 35th. Peter took special delight in giving it to us.

"I hope you are better at handling those German guys than you are with the 35th. Are you that bad or are they just that good?"

"Sometimes, you just get lucky," Farq answered. "They got lucky with their tactical win – we had just filled our bellies, and were in no mood to fight. Oh yeah, and they are lucky enough to have a better goalie than us – that's all."

I shot a nasty glance at Farq to show my displeasure.

"I didn't see you doing anything to stop that shot from going in."

We traded insults for a few minutes and everyone was laughing and in good humour. Then Catherine changed the subject.

"When do you ship out?"

With the rest of us suddenly silenced, Farquhar picked up the conversation. "We leave for Halifax, by train, on the twentieth, and then we board a troop ship bound for England on the twenty-second." There was complete silence and everyone stared at their food for a short interval.

The silence was broken by Elmer.

"Will you come to the Ex to see us off?" Peter assured him that they would come. The remainder of the supper was finished with very little being said, but a whole lot was being thought.

When it was time for us to leave and head back to barracks, we put on our greatcoats and stood by the front door. At this point, powerful emotions emerged after being suppressed through dinner and dessert. Catherine had tears streaming down her cheeks, even though she was not audibly sobbing. They were silent tears of pain, of loss. The expression on her face showed that she was aware that she might never see Farquhar again. Catherine pulled Farquhar to one side and wrapped her arms around him. She kissed him gently on both cheeks as her eyes welled with tears.

"Take good care of yourself. Stay safe, if that is possible. I shall be thinking about you every day. I will write to you and send gifts. We love you."

Peter embraced Farquhar and Catherine.

"We will miss you, little brother. Keep your head down over there. Look after those other two guys," he said, with a gesture toward Elmer and me.

Farquhar spotted William standing behind his father. "Come here, little fella," he said, as he stooped down and lifted William into his arms. Farq kissed him and hugged him.

"I love you."

William leaned back in Farq's arms and said, "Good bye, Uncle Facker. Please don't get hurt."

Farquhar squeezed his little nephew and kissed him gently on the top of the head. He held the kiss and savoured it for a few seconds, tears visible on his face.

Peter reminded Farq to look after his two chums.

"We love these guys, too, Facker. Make sure they come home with you."

"I will if they don't shoot each other first." Farq answered, brushing away the moisture.

The news from the Western Front had made it clear that the future of any young man who went there was, at best, uncertain. The odds were against Farquhar, and Catherine knew it. This scene was not limited to the doorstep of Epsom Avenue; it was being enacted at thousands of doorsteps in Canada, Great Britain and the rest of the Empire. Nor should I forget the other participants in this inglorious fight to the death. Germany too, was quickly sacrificing a whole generation of its best for a few yards of muddy, bloody soil. We had forgotten why.

Our time in Toronto was coming to an end. Hundreds of people showed up at the makeshift station, on the north side of the CNE, to see us off. The Law family was there to hug us and wish us a safe return and wave with the rest of the crowd when the train departed. The Grand Trunk train would take us to Montreal where we would switch to an Inter-Colonial train to Halifax; a journey of just over one thousand miles. It would take us two days to get there, just in time to board a troop ship on November 22. We enjoyed a comfortable ride with good beds and good food, and most of our waking time was taken up with playing cards or reading books. The Wonkys had somehow slipped some alcoholic beverages into their gear and were peddling it aboard the train.

"Wonky, what are you selling in those little bottles?" I enquired, as one of the Wonkys wobbled past me in the aisle.

"Rum! Do you want to buy some?"

"No, not right now, maybe later. Where did you get it from?"

Wonky laughed and wiggled his scruffy eyebrows at me. That told me everything. They got it from the

Quartermaster's Stores. It was our own rum and they were selling it back to us.

"Where did you get the little bottles?" I asked.

"Same place. They're medicine bottles. Much easier to carry around than a cask."

An image passed through my mind of the two of them hustling a rum keg out of the QMS, under the cover of darkness.

We found Lenny in one of the cars further back in the train. "How did your visit with Sailor go, Lenny?" I asked as I was passing by his seat.

"Hey Jonny, the visit was great. He was so happy to see me. I think he has gained some weight though. My cousin doesn't walk him as often as I did, but I will work that flab off of him when I get back home. It sure was tough to leave him and come back to camp."

We talked about my visit to Dunlop and to Catherine's house. It was great to connect with him again. He seemed in great spirits.

The train arrived at the Halifax rail station on the morning of the twenty-second.

No time was wasted in getting the battalion down to the dock to rendezvous with our next ride. There she was, tied up at the dock – the HMT Saxonia. Several gang planks stretched from the dock to the side of the ship. Supplies and horses were being loaded onboard when we arrived. I never thought I would be sharing a ship with horses.

"Jonny," Elmer said, "You are going to be sharing a room with a horse!"

"Rather a horse than you, Elmer. Smells better."

The Saxonia was a large ship. It was a converted Cunard liner; converted to carry supplies and soldiers to The Front in Europe. The luxurious amenities had been removed and she was stripped to the bare bones. It had been loaded with ammunition while it was in New York, a few days earlier. Now we had to wait awhile for the ship to be loaded before we boarded.

Later in the day, the citizens of Halifax began to gather at dockside. They were there to "see us off," and similar to the Great Trek, they brought along food and gifts for us: fruit, tobacco, bread, cake, books … too much for me to list. They were so generous and loving. We were hugged and kissed as if we were their sons. When we began to board the ship, the crowd waved and sang to us. Some tossed fruit up to the soldiers who lined the railing on deck. We felt as proud as the day we paraded through the streets of Toronto. This was quite a step up for three chaps who made rubber tires for a living. I knew how King George felt when waving from the balcony at Buckingham Palace. What an emotional moment; a sight I will never forget.

Chapter 11

The Atlantic Beckons

The HMT Saxonia pulled away from dockside at about 1730 hours on November 22. The sky was dark, but the dock area and the ship were both alight. As the gap between the hull of the ship and the wooden wharf opened up, the throng of spectators continued to sing their farewell. The 58th was sharing the vessel with the 54th Kootenay Battalion and the No.1 Siege Battery of Halifax. Along with numerous horses, there were about 2400 men, not counting the ship's crew. The Saxonia, normally, was meant to carry 1100 passengers. Without a doubt, this was going to be a cruise in close quarters.

The late November weather was turning cold, and the North Atlantic could be a nasty place at this time of the year. Storms could appear from out of nowhere, and toss a ship around like a cork in a river. The Captain and his crew filled us in on what to do in case we encountered any storms of large magnitude. They also warned us of the possibility of encounterting German submarines as we got closer to Ireland. In either of these eventualities, we were informed that we had to sleep in our clothes, in case we had to abandon ship. This was not going to be as comfortable as the train ride to the East Coast. In fact, it brought back the memory of the dream I had after the gentle ferry ride across Lake Ontario. I became angry at myself for recalling that dream. Now, I was in a place where that dream could very easily manifest itself, leaving me frothing and fighting for my life in the frigid November waters of the Atlantic. If I was prone to having nightmares of Lake Ontario ferry rides, what effect would this epic run across the angry Atlantic have on my imagination, my inner fears? I would know shortly.

"No turning back now, eh?" I offered to my two friends as the lights of Halifax disappeared into the cold night. "Let's get below deck and find our quarters. It is too cold to stay out here."

We headed down into steerage, and found our cots in a large room we would be sharing with well over two hundred other soldiers.

"Let's grab three cots and put our equipment on them to mark our territory, while we can," I suggested. "It is going to fill up quickly down here."

"There's going to be a hell of a lineup for the toilets in the morning," Farquhar observed as he took in the huge number of cots, neatly arranged on the large floor space. "How are we going to keep these cots all lined up when the sea starts tossing us around? We could all be crashing into each other!"

"Let's tie our cots together so that we will have more weight than anyone else. We can knock the other cots out of the room!"

"Great idea, Elmer," I answered. "Then we get the room to ourselves – noline up for the toilets in the morning."

I think the humour was an attempt to cover up the fear inside of us. Everything that we had encountered up to this point, was like a game played by three young boys. The stakes were never high. Our lives were never in jeopardy, except for an encounter with a lightning bolt. This was different. Our senses were assaulted by strange sights and sounds. The sound of the huge steam engines vibrated the hull of the ship all day and all night, never ceasing to take a breath. We were headed out into a black vastness, not knowing if we would ever see light or land again. Even the oily odour below deck seemed to have a threatening edge to it. This was the interior of a massive machine, a whale that could swallow us up, and spit out our battered bodies into the cold Atlantic; like the Titanic did, three years ago. We were on the same route as the Titanic, only in reverse. Every wall, every step, every edge was cold, grey-painted metal. There was no welcoming softness anywhere. No lounge chairs or chesterfields to sit in to read the newspaper. There were no crickets, no katydids to sing us to sleep at night.

We had, of course, been on passenger vessels before, when we immigrated to Canada. Those ships were of similar size to the Saxonia, but they weren't stuffed to overflowing with human cargo, horses and ammunition. There was very little space onboard during this trip, that wasn't occupied by somebody or something. How were the officers ever going to contain the pent-up energy of 2400 young men, confined to such tight quarters for the duration of this trip – seven, eight days, whatever?

The sergeants were given second class passage, with very good accommodations. Of course, all of the officers were in first class. They, at least, had some privacy, and some room to manoeuvre, compared to what the other ranks had.

Our meals were taken in the saloon. It didn't take long for opinions to surface regarding the meals. Breakfast may well have been the pinnacle of the day. We were served porridge that was sometimes hot and sometimes not, but we knew it was porridge. Tea served at breakfast that was more than acceptable, and always hot. A fruit always accompanied the porridge; sometimes an apple, an orange or a banana. The condition of the fruit could be described as varied, and was always a surprise. One day, I received an apple that was actually crisp and tart, and the next day I received a banana that was almost black on the outside, and mush on the inside. This kept life interesting and unpredictable.

Lunch, on the other hand, was a step down from breakfast. The sandwich was the entrée of the middle meal. There was a sandwich that might or might not have been a pate; we were never really sure. Another attempt at a sandwich was labelled "jam", but we could never really find the jam in there. Maybe it should have been called a "bread" sandwich. The sandwich was always accompanied by some veggie sticks like carrots or celery; rubbery carrots and celery. There were days when a soup appeared, and then we would spend some time trying to guess what kind of soup it was, and what was in it. Then, after we consumed the soup, we would vote to determine what kind of soup it really was.

Supper was the biggest disappointment. The main ticket was always some kind of bully-beef affair that we could garnish with HP sauce, to give it some flavour and colour. On the side, there was usually a glob of mashed potato, but occasionally, for some variation, it was a glob of squash. The vegetable might or might not have been warm, upon arriving on our plate. It depended on whether you were at the front of the line or at the back. Tea was served with supper. The dessert was a slice of fruit cake most times, or other times it might be pudding.

I did not mention the portion size. The portion size became an issue as we got further away from Halifax. The breakfast portion was adequate, but the other two meals were puny in comparison. The sandwiches that I described were not much bigger than a playing card. We left the table with our stomachs still growling with hunger. The supper portions were no better, and the men were not happy. Some men complained to the officers, who said they would talk to the Captain and the cook on our behalf.

One day, as we were sitting down for supper, Farq made a comment. "I think there is going to be a mutiny, Jon. The men are getting a little fed up with the food. I hear them grumbling about it all the time. It never stops."

Elmer answered, "Lt. Cassels says we got spoiled at Niagara, and we should be thankful for what we got."

Farq chuckled a bit, and said, in an attempt at an English accent, "You boys are ungrateful, and should think of those less fortunate than you. That's probably what his mother told him when he was a kid and complained about his food. Thank you, Mrs. Cassels."

While we were complaining, the Wonkys never missed a trick. Ever. "Hey Wonk, how do you like the food today?" I asked one of the Wonkys (not sure which), just trying to make idle conversation.

"Loved it!" He replied, with a silly grin plastered on his face. "Roast beef sangwhich with HP sauce, and rice puddin'."

I stared at him, wondering if he was making this up to get me going.

"Yeah, right, and I had rack of lamb!"

"In your dreams, Jonny, in your dreams. I know what you had. Jam sangwhich! Farquhar told me. Disgusting!"

I was becoming a little annoyed at being bested by a Wonky.

"Where the fuck did you get a roast beef sandwich, ya numpty?" I spat back at him.

"From the ship's crew. They got their own kitchen and a real chef. I give dem a nickel and dey give me a roast beef sangwhich; a real sangwhich, not a pretend one. We sell dem to the men, three for a quarter."

Shite! Shite! Shite! I should have known. Little bawbags!

On the 25th of November, one of the three Macs celebrated a birthday. Sort of.

"Hey Farquhar, isn't today your birthday?" I queried when the memory tickled my mind.

"Yeah, Jonny, it sure is."

"Then happy birthday, old chum. Twenty-three, right?"

"You got it; twenty-three and never been kissed."

At this point, Elmer couldn't resist a dig. "Shite, Farq, I'm not going to kiss you for your birthday or any other day. You'll have to get Nancy to do that. Too bad she's a million miles away. We'll find you a girl to kiss when we arrive in Blighty. That can be our birthday present from both of us."

Farquhar laughed. "Thanks lads, but I won't hold my breath 'till you do it."

On the fourth day of the voyage to England, the soldiers finally snapped. There was no improvement in the quality or quantity of food, even after the officers had supposedly spoken to the captain of the ship. After curfew and lights out, a platoon of soldiers, led by the Wonkys naturally, raided the food stores aboard the ship. Tins of meat, bags of fruit, loaves of bread, and more, were hustled back to the sleeping areas, and hoarded away in secret hiding places. The rats aboard the ship would have been proud of us. Most of the men were generous with sharing this bounty with the ORs onboard.

I don't think it took the ship's Quarter Master very long to figure out that some items were missing from the food stores. As a consequence, each Company was summoned by their CO, and grilled about the missing food. Of course, no one knew anything. What did they expect? To make a short story of it, the matter was dropped, and the quality and quantity of the food that was served to us improved substantially from that night on. You can't expect us to exterminate the Hun if we are operating on empty stomachs.

The weather remained calm for most of the voyage. There was one night, I think it was the fifth night aboard ship, that we got tossed around a bit. The cots did as we expected, and slid slowly around the floor. I had pictures in my mind of all the cots, and there were hundreds of them, sliding in unison, from one wall and piling up into the other wall; and then back again, all night long. But it wasn't nearly that bad. We did slide into each other, but that is as far as the cot would go. At first, we thought it was fun. The men were laughing at the commotion as the cots banged around a bit. There were a few loose items that rolled around the floor, adding to the racket. It sounded like some bottles rolling around, and a few metal objects. Pretty soon, we realized that we were not going to get much sleep. We did the best we could in securing any loose objects, and under the circumstances, may have achieved a couple of hours of sleep. I don't know how they kept all the horses upright, or all the ammunition from exploding. Through all of this, I was kept awake by the recurring memory of the dream that shattered my sleep back in Niagara. The ferryboat dream.

By this point in the voyage, about four days in, the Saxonia was starting to take on a lingering, pungent odour. The facilities for bathing and showering were not designed for this many people, never mind that they were almost all active young men. The further you penetrated the bowels of the ship, the worse the aroma got. Because of the cold Atlantic climate, the interior was sealed to keep in the warmth. In the daytime, there was often an excess of heat. The cold outer walls of the hull became covered in the moisture exuded from our bodies, as the grey Atlantic transferred it icy chill to the steel. I have one vivid childhood memory that duplicated the smell of our ship. When I was about ten years old, I volunteered to help distribute Christmas gifts to needy families in our church parish in Aberdeen. One cold December evening, I entered the front door of an old row house to make a delivery. I was confronted by the acrid smell of urine, stale sweat and stale food. I handed over the gifts to a toothless woman and tried to make a quick exit without looking like I was going to puke.

Our daytime activities were very limited. There just wasn't enough room onboard to engage in any physical action. We made a few attempts to play indoor football in the steerage area, with all the cots pushed to the sides. However, it didn't work out too well. We were told that it was too dangerous to try any activities on deck. It didn't stop us, though, from trying. On one sunny semi-warm day, we tried to kick a football around a bit. We formed a tight circle on the forecastle deck, and gently passed the ball between us. Unfortunately, one participant (not one of our teammates) got carried away, and hoofed the ball into the Atlantic. He disappeared instantly, below deck when we threatened to throw him overboard to retrieve the ball. Most of the men passed the time playing cards, writing letters or reading. The Navy retained a small library aboard the ship that had a good supply of books, courtesy of Cunard.

As the Saxonia approached the coast of Ireland, submarines became a real threat. We were ordered to wear our life vests and clothes, all day and all night. The ship's speed was reduced during the daylight hours, and many of the soldiers remained on deck to keep watch for the lethal foe. The German vessels had sunk a large number of our freighters and warships. The level of tension onboard rose dramatically in the frigid waters off the coast. Our nerves became frayed.

For some reason, Elmer seemed the most affected by the silent, invisible threat. "Jonny, did you get any sleep last night? I couldn't get any fuck'n sleep, thinking about those German subs. I can't swim!"

"Listen," I said to him. "It doesn't matter if you can swim. That water is so bloody cold; it will kill you before you can get your arms and legs moving. We should be in Portsmouth in a couple of days, and we are supposed to pick up an escort any time now. Stop your worry."

We were just resting on our cots, reading some books and passing time. Without a whole lot of things to do, there certainly was plenty of time to worry. Fear didn't seem to loosen its' grip on Elmer, despite my attempt to soothe his anxiety. It is a good thing that he didn't know that I was more frightened than he was.

"Do you really think we will die before we can start to swim?" he asked with a very nervous quiver in his voice.

His question was taken up by another soldier, two cots to the left of us. "I lost two mates last year ,when their transport was sunk near here by subs. No survivors; all dead within a few minutes of hitting the water! I guess that's better than suffering for hours in the water and getting eaten by fish."

Bloody Hell, why couldn't he keep his comments to himself, I thought.

Elmer inquired quickly, "Oh, do you know the ship?"

"Well," my neighbour answered. "I think it was the Concordia or something like that. Not sure now. The Navy has beefed up around here since then, and it is safer than last year. We'll make it." I'm glad he threw in those last remarks; it calmed my fears somewhat and maybe Elmer's, too.

We did get our escort shortly after the conversation. Two British destroyers showed up on our port side. One destroyer moved in to the lead, and one shadowed us from behind. Elmer seemed to feel more at ease when he saw the two ships. One other troop ship was sunk by a sub on this route last year. All souls were lost in the darkness of the ocean.

The next day, there was one sighting of a periscope, a few hundred yards to our port side. The cargo of infantry men became very anxious and poured out on deck, to try to get a glimpse of the enemy. This would be the first time that anyone in the 58th, or the other battalions onboard, would have a chance to see the object of our loathing: The Hun! The order was given to "stand to". We made note of the location of the lifeboats that we had been assigned to. Thousands of eyes scanned the grey-green water for the offending protrusion. The Captain put us into a zigzag course to avoid being hit by a torpedo. The two escorts manoeuvred around us in search of the sub. Maybe there was more than one. Who knows? The search lasted for several hours. It was too cold to remain on deck, so we all went below and sat around, waiting for something to happen. No one spoke; we just sat and listened and looked around at each other. Would we see the cold Atlantic spill in onto us from a gaping hole in the hull of the ship? Would we fight with each other to make it up to the deck and into a lifeboat?

Farquhar broke the silence.

"I have never been so frightened in my life. I can't swim, and even if I could, it wouldn't make any difference."

That made three of us.

We could feel the vibrations of the engines, straining to make speed, and the hull of the old ship groaning with every course change. If we were at The Front, at least we could fight back. Here, we could only sit and wait. Helpless, we had trained so hard to be helpless.

When the periscope failed to make another appearance, the Captain put us back on a straight course while the destroyers moved to our sides, one port and one starboard, to act as pickets as we sailed toward the safety of port. Good fortune smiled down on us, and we saw no more of the enemy as we moved around to the south shores of England. On December 1st ,we arrived in Plymouth, safe, tired and relieved. Tomorrow would be another day, and we would bc back on a train to our new destination: Camp Bramshott.

It seemed very strange to be back on the island in the Atlantic from which we had emigrated just a few short years ago. It took a great deal of effort and money to get to Canada, and now we were back to where we started. It felt like an exercise in futility. We left for a better life in a new country, and now we were leaving its safety and comfort to go live in mud holes in France or Belgium. It didn't seem like something a rational person would do.

Chapter 12
Blighty

After spending a day in Plymouth, the mighty 58th was loaded aboard a train that would take us to a place named Liphook, in Hampshire. The weather was what we expected in England: cold and damp. The train ride, though, proved to be inspirational. People came to trackside to wave at us and cheer us on like we were true heroes. We hadn't even fired a shot in anger yet, and already we were celebrities.

"I don't believe it," Elmer said, as he pressed his face as near to the window as he could. "Look at all those pretty young things just dying to meet us! This could be very interesting when we are on leave. Come over here and have a look, Facker."

Farquhar leaned toward the window so that he could see what Elmer was referring to.

"You're right, Elmer, they love a man in uniform."

I looked out the window too, and was delighted to see that they weren't exaggerating. A good portion of the cheering

English citizens were pretty, young ladies who were waving hankies or whatever they had in hand.

"Fack," I teased, "no English crumpet for you. Remember Culloden."

Farq gave me a glance and shot back, "I just forgave them."

When the train pulled into Liphook, we were informed that we had to march to Bramshott Camp, a distance of about nine miles. Our bellies were empty, and we had to carry our full packs with us. There was a bit of a cold drizzle going on at the time, so this was not going to be a pleasant march. The route that we travelled became very muddy as we marched, which caused our boots to get heavy with clinging mud. This made the march seem like fifteen miles rather than nine.

When we finally arrived at Bramshott, we were shivering right through to the skin with cold and damp. We were shown to our barracks, but all we wanted to do was get dry and then eat. Luckily, the three of us were able to get into the same cabin. We managed to get a hold of Lenny, and get him in with us as well. It was nice that the four original campers from Niagara were able to be reunited. The entire campsite was a muddy flat plain, up to fifteen inches deep in some places. This was going to be our home until we were sent across the channel to fight.

Elmer summed up everyone's thoughts accurately.

"Damn! When do we eat? I am starving!"

There were about forty of us in our cottage. We would be sleeping in wooden bunk beds, similar to the ones we slept on, at the Ex in Toronto. Sergeant Keachie popped in, and informed us that we would be called to mess in thirty minutes. Every man gave a hearty cheer on receiving the news. It is bad enough being cold and soggy, but totally unacceptable being cold, soggy, AND hungry!

I was impressed with our first meal at Bramshott. They served us bacon and beans with green peas and hot tea. The meal was a huge improvement over the ones on the Saxonia, but not quite up to the excellence of those in Niagara. As the time passed here, nobody ever complained about the quality of the meals. We were used to larger Niagara portions, and the Canadians tended to be a little bigger and a little brawnier than the Brits.

The terrain around Bramshott was rather flat and always muddy. Of course, it was December, and it rained almost every day. The sky was always grey and the wind swept past the camp, making it impossible to get warm. We did the same field drills that we had practiced back at Paradise Camp. The biggest difference here, other than the soggy weather, was the fact that we had to do our drills while wearing boots coated in what seemed to be ten pounds of mud. By late morning, our legs were burning with fatigue and we could barely lift them up. I was sure that by the time we got to France, we would be able to leap over the German lines with little difficulty.

In the afternoon, we practiced musketry, signalling, bombing (we were introduced to the new Mills bombs, which were very easy to throw properly) and trench work. The trench work was the worst. It was physically exhausting, digging mound after mound of sodden mud. Each shovelful felt like it weighed fifty pounds. Our shoulders and arms ached at the end of the day. In the first few weeks at Bramshott, we could barely crawl into our bunks at night. The poor bastards that were in the upper bunks needed help to get up there. I was one of them, and needed a boost from Elmer and Farq. Oh, I almost forgot; one night those two slimy devils removed the wooden pegs that secured my mattress above the lower bunk. After they boosted me up, they buckled over in laughter as they watched me descend rapidly to the lower bunk. Naturally, the loud bang attracted the attention of all the other recruits and, within seconds, they were all doubled up in laughter.

I looked over at them, rolling on the floor.

"Scunners, you will pay for this!" were the only words I could express at the time.

They were laughing so hard that they could not breathe, let alone speak. After the ruckus calmed down, my two fine friends put my bed back together.

"Next time you do that, Farq, wait till Elmer is all nice and comfy in the bottom bunk."

The lack of daylight at this time of the year meant that some of our drills and exercises were done in the dark. We were told by the officers that this was good, because once we were on or even near the frontlines, many of the duties had to be performed in the dark. Work platoons would be sent out at night to rebuild the trenches that were blown up in the day. Night time provided the cover needed to do this work. In the daylight, a work team would be an easy target for the Hun.

The prolonged darkness also meant that Christmas was just around the corner. We were given generous amounts of leave time around the holiday. Many of the lads in the battalion had family in England that they could visit for the festive time. The three of us discussed going back to Aberdeen, but we concluded that it was too far to travel after all the travelling we had just done. We sent letters to our families, to let them know that we were here. Hopefully, some of them might travel down to visit, but at the least, they would send us some generous Christmas packages. About half of the men in the 58th were able to get leave for Christmas, and left the camp to visit their families.

As Christmas Day approached, the people from nearby Liphook brought us a Christmas tree and beautiful decorations to place around the camp and the barracks. For the men who were staying through the holiday, the addition of the décor and lights brought a joyful spirit. Some of the churches in the area conducted Christmas pageants for us and sang carols to us. They were so thoughtful and generous to these young men who were so far from the comforts of home.

The Christmas packages began to arrive about a week before Christmas Day. They brought treasures of cookies, cake, jam, tarts and other delights to keep us stuffed and happy. Every man shared equally with his mates. The "dry rule" was relaxed, and we were able to share some of the alcoholic beverages that were in the packages. During this time the number of soldiers left at camp was down to only a few. There was, perhaps, half of the battalion still in camp. As happy as we were, we still envied the men who were at home with their families and their lovers.

Christmas Day arrived with no snow, but lots of rain. I think it rained almost every day in December. In Toronto, a little snow, on or before Christmas, was normal. It always looked so clean and beautiful, adding to the spirit and beauty of the season. The day started off with church parades, carols and speeches by the "brass hats". The officers had arranged for a band concert later in the day. We concluded the day in the Yule-decorated mess hall, with a Christmas feast of roast goose, cranberries, mashed potatoes and carrots. Dessert was the best rum cake we have ever savoured and the baker did not spare on the rum.

"Farq, can you bake a cake as good as this?" Elmer asked, remembering that Farquhar was a journeyman baker before he came to Canada.

"Hell yes! With enough rum, anyone could bake a cake as fine as this."

We managed to get some second helpings of the rum cake and before we headed back to the barracks for some rest. When we arrived, the Wonkys were already there, they had in their possession, two whole rum cakes and a cask of rum. As the rest of the battalion filed back in to the barracks, they made a track straight to the cake and the rum. In less than half an hour, the cakes were devoured and the cask was empty.

In astonishment, I asked the Wonkys how they managed to make two cakes and a cask disappear, and then reappear in the barracks. "It was easy, Jonny. We bribed the QM. We gave him a little Christmas bonus, and suddenly goodies appeared – right here!"

"How much do we owe you?" I asked, as humbly as I could.

"Nothing, you owe us nothing. It is our gift to all of you. The 58th."

I thought about the Wonkys and their generosity when we went back to the barracks that night. "You know something, Farq? Do you think that the Wonkys ever go to confession?" Farq and Elmer remained silent for a few minutes, obviously pondering the question.

Finally, Elmer spoke up. "I can see them going to confession, being devout Catholics and all, I think, but I can't see them telling the priest everything that they'd have been up to. Too risky! They could get court-martialled for their shenanigans. I don't know, maybe they describe it a little differently."

We pondered those thoughts for a minute and then Farq added his opinion. "Those two are way smarter than they seem. That little Christmas favour that they gave to the boys tonight wasn't just done for the Christmas spirit. Don't get me wrong; I think they were being genuine with their generosity, but there was another purpose. Now, everybody owes them a little favour now and again, and especially when we are at The Front with Fritz. I expect to be asked for a favour in return. And yes, everybody likes them. They have never stiffed anybody while doing business."

"At least not in the 58th," I added.

Farquhar leaned over towards Elmer and kind of mock whispered in his ear, "Elmer, do you remember the fun you had with Wonky1 or 2 on the route march to Queenston Heights? Who's having the last laugh now?"

Elmer looked at Farquhar and thought about what he had just heard.

"What do they say?" Elmer replied to Farq. "Never judge a book by its cover, or in this case, covers. They may be from God's country, but they are very savvy. Who figured? I sure didn't."

Then another thought occurred to me. "If anybody makes it through this war unscathed, it will be them."

The next few days following Christmas were uneventful. Oh, I almost forgot. Two of Farquhar's sisters came to Bramshott to visit him. They took the train from Aberdeen to London and then a train from London to Liphook. They were Jesse and Johann, both older siblings and they were half-sisters. (from different mothers). The younger sister, Johann, looked very much like Farquhar. In their baggage were some delicious treats and goodies that Farq was happy to share. There were cookies, tarts, bread and some amazing cake from the bakery where Farq worked before he came to Canada. Bramshott was not a nice place for two ladies, so they didn't stay more than a few hours. They were eager to go back to London to shop and see the sights. I could tell that Farq was sad to see them leave, and some tears were spilled when we saw them off at the train station.

The visit did give Elmer a very brilliant idea. "Why don't we do the same as Jesse and Johann, and go to London for a few days of furlough. Let's go for New Years."

"Perfect! We should go to Lt. Cassels and get permission to go. We could stay there for two or three days," I suggested.

Elmer then added another idea, "We can treat Farq to dinner at a pub to celebrate his birthday."

Farq liked that idea a lot. "That would be rather nice of you laddies. I am so good to you all year, so I deserve it, don't you think?"

The persistent rain had let up a day or two after Christmas. We actually got to see the sun a few times, but the temperature had dipped to the freezing point. We went to see Lt. Cassels, and he granted us three days leave to go to London. "While you are in uniform, you can travel on trains, buses, carts and the tube in London for free. That will save you some money. There is a hostel near Soho called Earl Roberts Rest House for Sailors and Soldiers. You can stay there for a small fee. Enjoy your holiday, men, and we will see you when you get back."

We thanked him and told him that we would be "good boys" and would stay out of trouble. Cassels gave us one last word of advice before we left. "Oh, and one more thing: stay away from the ladies unless you want to get V.D."

"Shite, did you hear that? We are going to see women in London and do what men do. We just have to be careful, that's all. What does he think we are going to London for? The museums?"

Elmer was a little agitated over the suggestion that we stay away from the women.

"You know, Elmer, I wouldn't mind seeing a few things while we are there. We could visit the Tower of London and such. We'll have lots of time," Farq said. "Oh, and Westminster; damn, I'd love to see Westminster."

The excitement about going to London grew on us over the next few days. We would leave one day before New Year's Day and return to Bramshott the day after.

When the day arrived, we caught the first train from Liphook to London; it departed at 0600 hours, and was scheduled to arrive at the station in London in the afternoon, around 1400 hours. During the trip, we discussed our itinerary. I took Elmer aside to where Farq couldn't hear us, to discuss an idea. "Elmer, we didn't do anything for Farquhar's birthday; let's treat him to a great dinner. We can find a steak house. I know he loves steak or roast beef."

Elmer liked the idea. "Let's make sure we get him good and drunk."

The train arrived at Waterloo Station, right on time. The weather was still in our favour, being somewhat sunny and cool. When we emerged onto the street, we could see that the city was still in full festive flavour. The street was full of bundled up citizens, moving around from store to store, window to window. There were spruce wreaths adorning the street lamps (darkened on the tops and sides) and above the shop doorways. The stores still had their Christmas decorations in the windows, while all the buses, cabs and carriages were decorated on the inside for the passengers. To see this lifted our spirits, and immediately pushed the thoughts of war and death out of our minds. This was our first time in London, and we were in awe. The first thing to do was to find our hostel.

We rented a carriage at the station entrance and headed toward our hostel. The streets were crowded with buses and cars, much more than Toronto. Few words were spoken as we clopped through the streets of London. Our eyes were fixed out the windows as we breathed in the sight of the Thames River, Westminster to the west, and finally, Trafalgar Square. Within a few minutes, we arrived at Earl Robert's Sailors' and Soldiers' Rest House. It was an old refurbished hotel that had seen better days. The brick face had been painted white and was beginning to chip off in places, revealing the original reddish brick colour. The front entrance was rimmed in polished black stone and may have been elegant at one time. We entered and were taken to our room on the second floor. Walls had been removed between the small guest rooms to create a large common room. We were used to this kind of accommodation – a large room full of bunk beds.

We were eager to get our first taste of this great city.

Elmer was bursting. "Let's check in and go find a pub. I am starving and thirsty as hell. We've got some sights to see, boys."

Nobody could argue with that. We were in and out of the hostel in a flash. Trafalgar Square was our first destination. When we passed by, on the way to the hostel, we noticed the large number of khaki uniforms decorating the Square. We wanted to be among our own. It is true what they say about "birds of a feather".

With all of our training and route marches, walking the streets of London was less than a challenge. It didn't take us long to arrive in Trafalgar Square and my pulse jumped as we arrived in the vast open space. There were thousands of servicemen milling about, taking in the awesome sight of the statue of Nelson that dominated the square. We looked for the shoulder patches that identified the Canadian battalions. I was struck by the number of men from around the Empire all gathered here, with one objective: to send the Hun packing and end this war. There were troops from Australia, New Zealand, South Africa and even India. I thought, how could the Kaiser ever think that victory would be his? Being amongst all these men from different lands made us feel a sense of invincibility. We can't lose. Hundreds of civilians were in the square to greet us and wish us success and long lives. As I was taking in all of these sights and sounds, something in the centre of the square caught my attention. It was the monument. My gaze travelled up from the base to the pinnacle.

"Look Farq, look at the monument."

Farquhar, who had his back to me, and was obviously entranced by something else, turned to look.

"What? What am I looking at? … Oh I see what you mean. It's the General. General Brock. He is here in London."

"That's not Brock, you idiot; It's Nelson! It's a monument to Nelson."

A British soldier, a Tommy, who was obviously standing within earshot of us, corrected the mistake.

"That's why they call this Trafalgar Square, to celebrate the battle of Trafalgar. You fellas don't sound like Canucks. You are Scots!"

Farquhar didn't hesitate to inform our friend, "Bloody right we are Scots. Don't let the uniform fool you."

I sensed that Farq might be getting a little hostile, so I suggested to him that we find Elmer and move on. I gave him a nudge and got him moving away from the Tommy before an altercation got started.

"I knew that wasn't Brock, Jonny, I was just reminded of his monument in Niagara; they look the same. He called me an idiot, the scrawny bawbag!"

"OK, OK," I answered. "Let's find Elmer and go have some fun."

Elmer had wandered off by himself, and, with so many soldiers in khaki, he was difficult to find in the crowd.

"I see him on the other side of Brock – I mean Nelson. What a surprise! He's talking to some ladies."

I think we'd better go and help him out," Farq observed, as he started weaving his way across the square. After some skillful manoeuvring through the throng, we made it to Elmer's side.

"Good afternoon, ladies, is this man bothering you?" Farq said, as he inserted himself between Elmer and the two pretty young women.

Elmer tried to push Farq off to the side, but he was not very successful, and I could see this getting awkward very quickly, so I decided to try and salvage the situation.

"Uh, Elmer, could you introduce us to your two friends?"

Elmer instantly calmed down, straightened his tie, and tunic and said, "I just met them; I don't know their names yet. Give me a chance, will ya?"

Elmer was strutting like "cock of the walk", having been the Casanova who made the catch.

The two girls took the cue and introduced themselves to us as Karen and Emma. They were as pretty as any girls we had met in Toronto. I think they were a little shy, because they spoke very softly. Karen, who seemed the less shy of the two, told us that they were sisters and that she was the elder by two years. The sisters looked to be around twenty years old. They both had green eyes and long brown hair, with just a touch of red. We introduced ourselves and began a friendly conversation with them. The two worked nearby, in a clothing shop, and were just on their way home to East London. Elmer made them an offer.

"Can you join us for one New Year's Eve drink?"

There was a hesitant silence for a second or two while the ladies looked us over, and then at each other.

The girl named Karen answered. "We can join you for one drink, and then we have to catch our train home."

With that, we went in search of a pub, and found one, just off Strand. When we entered the front door, there was very little room inside.

"Let's go in; let's give it a try," Karen suggested.

One glance around and it became evident that we would never get a table, so we just found a corner to stand and huddle in. The volume of noise inside was incredible, almost painful. It was so loud that everyone needed to holler to be heard. Indulging in a decent conversation with the sisters was very difficult. A waiter brought us our ale and we drank it without much conversation. We would take a drink, look at them and smile and repeat. The girls would do the same. Over the noise, we finally arranged to meet with the sisters the next day, New Year's Day, at the same spot and the same time that we met today. Hopefully they would bring a friend with them.

When we finally emerged from the pub, it was dark except for the yellowish street lamps and warm glow from the shop windows. The streets were coming alive with New Year's celebrants heading off to dinners and parties or whatever events that they had been invited to. We walked the ladies to their tube station and then set out to find a restaurant where we could celebrate Farq's birthday. Our treat!

"I am starving and could eat a whole roast beef – prime rib!" Farq said, rubbing his belly. And with a little luck, we found a small tavern on the same street, just off Strand, that offered just that.

Gesturing to Farq and poking him in the ribs, I suggested. "Let's go in and see if we can fatten this guy up."

The room was very narrow, but ran quite far to the back. There weren't many tables left unoccupied, but we got one near the back of the tavern. It was hopping with sound and aromas and people, all ready to celebrate the incoming year. Like the pub that we visited with the sisters, it was difficult to have a conversation above the general din of the place, but we didn't care one bit. We were bloody hungry and we were bloody thirsty.

When our waiter arrived, we demanded "The best roast beef dinner in London for our friend here. And the same for us. It's his birthday. Bring us some ale to wash it all down!"

The waiter chuckled and said, "We'll give him our best."

The roast beef was juicy and rare, the way we like it. Beside it, on the large plate, were mashed potatoes, green peas, carrots and Yorkshire pudding. The food disappeared off our plates with not a morsel left. What a contrast to our army fare!

"Best meal since Niagara!" I declared, as I pushed my plate away to make room for my beer mug. The room was full of khaki, and I bet they were all making the same declaration about their meals.

"Best meal, including Niagara!" Farquhar added. "I thank you two gentlemen for filling my belly like my mother used to."

"Happy birthday, Facker. The drinks are on us, too, so drink up!" We picked up our mugs and clicked them together. "*Co latha breith sona dhuibh*!" We all said together. "Happy birthday!"

Farquhar then shouted "*Bliadhna Mhath Ur*! Happy New Year!"

The evening passed quickly, as we were enjoying the ale and the noisy celebration. I was beginning to feel the effects of all that drink just as we were getting ready to leave the tavern. Elmer pulled me over to one side as we stood at the side of our table.

"Let's buy Farq a lady. What do you think? How much money do you have?"

A little unsteady on my feet, I looked at the change in my pocket. "I think I have about one quid and a bit." We both looked over at Farquhar to see if he was listening in. He wasn't. He was feeling a little unsteady, himself.

"I have two quid, I think. Let's head over to Soho."

Once out the door of the tavern, we were greeted on the street by hundreds of people, dressed in their best evening outfits, and filling the sidewalks to overflowing. To get past anybody, you had to step off the curb and onto the road. There seemed to be almost as many soldiers and sailors as civilians. Everyone was in a festive mood as they made their way to their New Year destinations. Our first objective was Trafalgar Square, where we could get our bearings and try to find Soho.

When we reached Whitehall, Farquhar stopped in his tracks on the edge of the sidewalk.

"Look down there." He gestured to his left.

We turned our heads almost simultaneously. At the end of Whitehall, we could see the tower and the clock.

"It's Big Ben!" Farquhar stated, as if we didn't know. "Shite! I never thought I would see Big Ben! When I left for Canada, I thought I would never see London."

Elmer and I looked at each other. I think we were surprised at Farquhar's excitement at seeing the sights of London, the centre point of all things English. Farquhar was full of surprises; that was for certain. We stood and admired the sight for a few minutes. Not a word was spoken or needed to be.

When we arrived to a packed Trafalgar Square, Elmer whispered in my ear, "I'm going to ask somebody for directions to a place, you know, where there might be some lovely ladies for us."

"OK," I said. "I'll stay with Farq."

Elmer made a straight line for a group of Royal Navy lads. If anybody would know about the ladies, they surely would.

After a few minutes, Elmer returned. "A street named Berwick, in the middle of Soho. There is a hotel called the Warwick. They told me how to get to it."

Elmer and I gathered up Farquhar, who, by now, was really beginning to show the effects of all the ale he had drunk at the tavern, and led him in the direction of Soho. When we left the bright lamps and loud noise of the Square, the narrow side streets felt like dark little canyons. We could hear the hoof beats of carriage horses or a door closing nearby, but otherwise, it was silent. The low small street lamps cast long shadows that stretched to almost the length of the roads. Elmer and I were not as tipsy as Farq, but we still could not walk a straight line down the streets together. We made a few wrong turns, bumped into a few other drunks, and fumbled around Soho until we found Berwick. A little further up the street, we could see a marquis sign that spelled "Hotel". That must be it – the Warwick.

There was a big yellow sign attached to the face of the building and lit by bright lamps. It was an old building that looked a little beat up and rough. It had two large glass front doors that gave it the feeling of a theatre entrance. We stopped on the sidewalk. across the street and pondered for a few minutes.

Farq blurted out. "Where we going? Waz this?"

"Come on in, Farq; we have a surprise for you," Elmer said, taking Farq's arm and leading him into the lobby.

The lobby was quite large and open. It was somewhat dimly lit, making it difficult to see a lot of the details. The air was filled with the aroma of stale cigarette smoke. To the right of the door was a check-in desk, and at the back of the lobby there were several easy chairs and a chesterfield. More important, there was the presence of pretty young women sitting on the chairs and the chesterfield. They were gesturing, smoking and keeping occupied until they noticed us walk in to the lobby. Immediately, several ladies got up off their chairs, and headed straight for us, then stopped us before we got very far into the lobby, or could turn to leave. They were dressed in flimsy slips with frilly lingerie which was visible underneath. Their scent preceded them, and smelled of lilacs or some other type of fragrant flower. Their slips swished as they walked.

"Are you soldier-boys lost? Do you need directions?" one pretty lady asked us, as we stood there with our mouths agape.

"No ma'am, uh Miss. We are not lost," I muttered, a little embarrassed.

"What would you handsome Canadian lads like, then? We love Canadians!" Another of the pretty ladies chimed in.

Elmer took charge. "It's our friend's birthday," he said, gesturing at Farq, who was smiling like the Cheshire cat by now. "We would like to buy him a birthday gift of sorts."

"Happy birthday, soldier-boy. What about you other two privates? Are you just going to sit around and play with yourselves while he is having all the fun?" she said, throwing out a challenge we weren't prepared for.

Elmer took up the challenge immediately. "Well, we took him out for dinner, and we don't have a lot of money left between us."

"Take a minute to count your money, and we will see what we can do. OK?"

Elmer and I turned around and fished into our pockets to see how much was there. We pulled our hands free and held them out in front of us to see what our total would be.

"Shite. We only have two quid and some shillings. We are out of luck. Just enough for Farq," Elmer whispered.

We turned back around and showed our meagre fortune to the lady in front of us, our hands extended like kids in a five-and-dime store. She looked at our sweaty palms and then turned to look at the girls behind her. They all started laughing. Our faces and shoulders drooped.

"I tell you what. Business is slow here tonight. Everybody is out celebrating New Year's Eve. Besides, we like Canadians. You are the sweetest! Farm boys! Mamma's boys! We'll give you something to remember your time in London. Pick three girls."

She relieved us of our money, and then let us peruse the harem, to select our bed mates. We were speechless, and wandered into the midst of the ladies. They batted their eyes at us and gave us seductive smiles. Elmer selected a very petite girl with bright red hair and pale white skin. I was attracted to a shorter lady, who could have been Japanese or Chinese. Her long straight hair was shiny black. I looked over at Farquhar who was holding hands with a girl with long brown hair and olive skin, and she was by far the most buxom and voluptuous of the three. When we had made our selection, the remaining girls strolled slowly back to their lobby seats, seeming resigned to their rejection by the three most handsome men in London. There they resumed their conversations, nail filing and what-not.

The woman who had negotiated with us made one more comment. "You will have to pay for the room. Go over to the desk and give the remainder of your money to the hotel keep."

I turned to walk over to the front desk, but Elmer grabbed me by the arm. "Did she say room? As in one room?"

I looked back at Elmer, and answered, "That's what it sounded like to me."

Elmer and I then dumped all the change that was in our pockets on the front desk. A whiskery old fellow with overgrown white eyebrows shuffled to the desk and scooped the money without muttering a word. He eye-balled the change in his dirty hand once, then twice, and then muttered before he disappeared into a back room. "Three O Eight!"

The three of us, escorted by the three young ladies, proceeded up two flights of rickety stairs to room 308. The door wasn't locked, and the red-haired girl just pushed it open to reveal its complete darkness. She reached into the room, just inside the door, and pulled a chain on the wall, instantly casting a yellowish glow into the space. With boyish apprehension, the three Macs peered into the semi-lit room to do a bed inventory. One, two ... two, uh, beds! One, two, three ... three couples! Bewildered glances were exchanged, while the three young ladies disappeared into the room ahead of us.

We followed in behind them cautiously, and then Farquhar blurted out, "I get the far bed and you two can share this bed. After all, it's my birthday!"

Who can argue with that logic?

The room was not very warm, and smelled a bit odd - dusty and stale - like it hadn't any fresh air flow through it for a while. It was a dark Oriental carpet that may have been the origin of the smell. We introduced ourselves to our hosts, and told them a few things about ourselves. We were just trying to relax and make easy conversation. They listened patiently, and then, introduced themselves to us. I think they said their names, probably not their real names, were Mandy, Orchid and I can't remember the third name; some kind of exotic bird or something.

Now that the introductions were over, and the bed situation had been straightened out, it was time to get down to business, excuse the pun. "Are we doing this in uniform, or are we at ease, soldiers?"

We immediately began taking our uniforms off. The ladies took us by the hand, and guided us into the small loo that was attached to the room. One at a time, we were baptized at the font, so to speak. Each girl gently washed our stiffening penises under the warm tap water in the sink. We weren't expecting that, and it had the embarrassing effect of making us feel like young lads getting a hand wash before supper. There was an awkward silence in the loo during the procedure. With effect of the ale still coursing through our veins, we became a little giddy. Speechless, giddy and a little red-faced! Maybe we shouldn't have drunk so much.

The birthday boy headed to the single bed with his mate, while Elmer and I staked out our territory on the double bed. We each wanted to make sure that nobody ventured past no man's land, down the centre of the mattress.

"Keep your dangly parts on your side of the bed, McLean," I warned.

"Yeah, well keep your hairy ass on your side."

"Do you soldier boys want the lights out?"

The answer was a simultaneous "Yes!" The lamp was shut off. Both Elmer and I indicated to our ladies that we wanted to be pleasured orally. We had no idea what Farq was doing on the other bed, but we could hear a conversation, which indicated to me that those two were engaging in something different. The complete darkness seemed to heighten the sensual pleasure as my partner began to gently stroke me. The bed squeaked as I lay back on the mattress. I was barely aware of what was taking place on the other half of the mattress or in the other bed.

For me, anyway, things were progressing very satisfactorily, as the double bed began to shake and squeak, somewhat. In the darkness of that little bedroom, three soldiers of the Canadian Expeditionary Force were relieved, temporarily, from the thoughts of war and oblivion. Our mission was accomplished, and the objective had been taken. The room returned to stillness and silence, but only for a brief moment. I could hear some light laughter from Farq's bed.

"What's so damn funny, you two?" I asked, as I sat up on the mattress.

"Oh, you don't want to know," Farquhar answered, in a smug tone, and then added, "Are you finished over there? I am not quite finished here yet, give us a few more minutes."

Elmer and I and our ladies engaged in a light conversation to try and give Farq and his olive-skinned beauty some private time. The room was small and we couldn't go very far. After some time passed, we heard what sounded like a conclusion to the activity in the next bed.

"Light, let's have some light!" my lady said, as she moved cautiously off the bed in darkness, in the direction of the lamp.

I could hear her feeling around for the switch on the wall, and then, with a click the lamp lit up the room. We looked around the room at each other as our eyes adjusted to the light. Farquhar's hair was all messed up. His face was aglow and red, but he was grinning. Mission accomplished.

Elmer decided to have some fun with him. "Fack, you look like you just got mugged. Are you going to live?"

Farquhar tried to straighten his hair a bit with his fingers and shot back, "Just building up my stamina for The Front. I intend to go home in one piece after the war."

Elmer couldn't let it go. "Looking at you right now; I think you better stay away from The Front. They'll put you on kitchen duty. Jonny and I will do the fight'n."

The olive-skinned girl jumped in, "It's OK. Farquhar's a lover, not a fighter."

Elmer still couldn't stop, "It seems that Farq's dislike for the Limey doesn't extend to the ladies. Eh Farq?"

The ladies soon grew tired of the schoolyard insults, got up off the beds and began putting their clothes on. This seemed to cool us down, and we were finally able to shake off the laughter.

"Are we done for the evening?" Elmer enquired.

"I don't think you gentlemen are in any shape to go any further. We are happy that you enjoyed yourselves so much," the redhead answered good naturedly.

"Fack, what was so fucking funny? " I asked.

"Never mind," he said. "I'll tell you later."

With that, the three young women said their goodbyes, closed the door behind them, and headed down to the lobby. We just laid there on the beds and looked at each other until the laughter started up again.

"Can you tell us now, what was so funny?" Elmer asked, a little impatiently, trying hard to stifle his laugh.

"Alright, alright, I will. Give me second to get my breath." Farquhar inhaled and exhaled slowly a few times in order to calm himself down. "Well, you know it was pitch dark in here, right. I couldn't see a thing." At this point, Farq started to laugh again. Elmer and I patiently waited for him to compose himself. "So, I couldn't see anything, but I could hear everything."

The laughter started again. Now I could see where he was going with this. I paused to imagine what Farquhar could hear. Then it hit me. I let my mind's ear imagine the sound coming from our bed with two couples fully engaged in sexual activity. My face contorted into a smile, followed immediately by a belly laugh. It was infectious, because Elmer started as well, and the room was full of uncontrollable laughter once again.

When the laughing and snorting had run its course, the three of us managed to get our breath, and put our uniforms back on. We sat down on the edge of the beds and looked at each other. I know that my mind was racing with the thoughts of what had just transpired. I just needed to take a few minutes to digest it all. I think that my two friends were feeling the same. There were a few minutes during which no words spoken.

Elmer broke the silence. "Don't tell my mother that we did this. Ever!"

Farq added a thought, "Only if you don't tell my sister." Again the room fell silent.

Then, a new thought entered my mind. I wish it hadn't.

"You know, in a very short time, there could be something else we might have to tell your mother that is a lot fuck'n worse." The air left the room. The expressions changed.

"I'm not sure I want to talk about that tonight," Elmer said, as he let his head droop down toward his knees. He rested his elbows on his knees and propped his folded hands under his chin. Then he turned toward Farquhar. "Do you think it is as bad as the rumours that we hear? Not rumours really, but actual stories – mud up to your knees, lice and rats in the trenches, bodies rotting in the sun."

Farquhar thought it over for a few seconds before he answered.

"I was in the militia, but never saw any action. I can't answer from my own experience. I don't think it is exaggerated. Look at the mud we slopped through at Bramshott. Can you imagine fighting for your life in that? Can you imagine sleeping in a trench or a shell hole? I think I want to visit my mother back home. I want to see her before we go over there."

Now, I was feeling guilty for changing the mood of the evening. This was, though, the first time that I could recall, where the three of us actually began to think and talk about the consequences of signing up for this war. We had been "whistling past the graveyard", up until now. I recalled the feeling of fear and apprehension when I heard the drum beats at parade, and thinking of the drums of war – and marching into the bloodied hands of death.

It was difficult to make eye contact with the other two now. We sat on the edge of the beds, looking down at our feet, at the floor. Time to change the subject. The three of us made efforts to talk of other things, in an effort to bring back the spontaneous joy of only a few minutes earlier.

I thought of something. "Do you miss the football, Fack?"

"What kind of question is that? Yeah, I miss it. It was good to focus on other things, you know, not the killing stuff. I miss playing at Dunlop with you two. I am not so nostalgic about playing for Genet at Paradise Camp. I am not so sure I want to play for him after the war."

"It's Division One, Farq. How can you not want to play Division One?" I asked.

"I didn't say that, Jon. I do want to play Division One; just not for Genet."

I tried to reason with him. "Do you want to stay at Dunlop? You are wasted in Division Three."

"I'm not sober right now, Jon. I want to go back to school. Let's talk about it another time, when I am sober, OK?"

"Alright, another time. Enjoy your birthday."

Time passed. It was a while before we realized we had been sitting and talking for some time. "I think we should get moving. Let's head back to Trafalgar and celebrate the New Year."

When we arrived downstairs in the lobby, the girls had all returned to their places, replicating the scene when we arrived at the front door.

One of the girls shouted out from the group, sitting at the back of the lobby, "What took you boys so long up there? Were you playing with each other?"

Elmer shouted back. "I wasn't. Those two were." and he was pointing at me and Farq.

The laughter erupted again and the sullen mood seemed to be broken – at least for the time being.

We exited the Warwick, stopping briefly to look back at the front doors' in reflection, and headed back toward Trafalgar Square. Midnight was approaching, and we wanted to be there to ring in the New Year. Farq suggested that we go to the part of the square where we could see Big Ben and the Clock Tower, at the end of Whitehall. We waited with all of the other soldiers, sailors and civilians as the hands on the clock face approached midnight. The crowd became silent as the gap between the hand on the clock and the midnight numeral shrunk to nothing. Then, we could hear Big Ben toll midnight and the announcement of the New Year. We all shouted "Happy New Year! Happy Hogmanay!" over and over, as everybody shook hands, kissed and slapped strangers on the back. Somewhere, a chorus of Auld Lang Syne began to float above the noisy crowd. Flasks and bottles appeared from under coats or out of pockets, and people began to clank them together and toast to the occasion.

"Happy Hogmanay! Happy Hogmanay!" we yelled as loud as our voices could.

You would never know that somewhere across the Channel, some young man, a Canadian, a Brit, a German, was laying on the muddy ground in mute bloody agony, unable to witness the passing of one year into the next.

I suggested to my chums that we make our way back to the hostel. Tomorrow would be a chance to see more of London, and it would be good to sleep off the effects of our drinking and our fornication in Soho. It had been an eventful day that had exceeded our expectations. Before long, we were back in our bunk beds in the hostel, sleeping off the remains of the day.

"January 1, 1916." I kept saying that to myself, as I lay in my bed and stared at the dusty ceiling panels. Every New Years challenges my ability to get used to saying it. "January 1, 1916".

Eventually, morning arrived and the three groggy Romeos rolled out of bed and prepared for the day of sight-seeing. I think Elmer must have showered in cologne; we could barely keep our eyes from watering when he came near us.

"Elmer, do you think your lady friends will show up?" Farq asked, while he combed his thick brown hair.

"Your guess is as good as mine. I hope they show up because none of us has a clue where to go except Trafalgar Square."

I suggested that we have breakfast at the hostel, and then head back to Trafalgar to look for the girls. "Do you remember their names?" Farq asked Elmer, as we headed down the steps to the canteen.

"One was named Karen and they were sisters. I can't remember the other name ... ."

I knew the answer. "The other was Emma. She was taller than Karen. They both looked good, though, and very similar. It would be just our luck if the Wonkys stole them from us before we get back to Trafalgar." There was silence as we contemplated that scenario.

We had some spare time before we were to meet the ladies, so we wandered past Trafalgar Square and down Whitehall. The large white buildings were most imposing, on a bigger scale than we were used to in Toronto or Aberdeen. We cut between a couple of buildings and ended up on a street that ran next to the Thames. On the bank of the river, we could see Westminster and the Westminster Bridge. It was interesting to stand there and watch the boats and barges travelling up and down the Thames, carrying people and goods, like there was no war. The weather was still very cooperative, providing us with sunny but brisk temperatures. It was a hell of a lot nicer than Bramshott. I didn't want to think of bloody Bramshott. I thought it would be nice to just stay here in London and become a Bobby or something. Carelessly, I let my thoughts speak out.

"Would you like to stay here, and forget the war, and just go on with our lives?"

My two chums looked at me for a few seconds, with their mouths open.

"Are you suggesting we go AWOL, Jon? Are you serious?" Elmer asked.

Farquhar spoke up next. "I could never leave the 58th. I cannot let my mates go over to fight without me. Too many Scots have spilled their blood … and Canadians too, for me to walk away."

I tried to explain where I was coming from. "I wasn't suggesting that we go AWOL or abandon our mates. I was just musing about London, and everything that has happened here. That's all. Nothing more."

Farq then asked me a question I hadn't anticipated. "Does your father know that you enlisted?"

I hesitated a second before I answered, "No, he doesn't know. It would be too hard on him."

Then he asked me another pointed question. "Do you ever think that you might end up like your father when we go home?"

I hesitated again. "Yes, I have considered that. He is a difficult man to live with. My mother has sacrificed so much for him. She is a saint. I know that he can't help being who he is; it is the horror of war that makes him like that. As a child, I missed out on having him as a companion or a father. It keeps me awake some nights, but not as much as the thought that I may never come home."

Elmer sensed the mood change. "We should get back to Trafalgar and look for the girls."

Once we arrived back at the square, we scanned the area for our friends, our girl friends. Elmer's sharp eyes spotted them near the same spot that we first met them. "There are just two of them; I guess you are out of luck, Jonny." Elmer said.

"Me? Why am I out of luck?"

With his usual rude humour, Elmer shot back, "'Cause you are the ugliest, ha!" He loved to get under my skin; get me going. Then Farq would join in and I would have to joust with both of them. Some things never change. Some people never grow up.

The two girls looked even prettier than I remembered from yesterday.

Karen and uh … Emma were very happy to see us again. They were dressed differently than yesterday; not in their work clothes but colourful dresses down to their ankles, white blouses and hats. They wore long coats to bundle them up from the cold. What a contrast they made to our drab khaki greatcoats. I wasn't too sure that they would show up, but they fooled me. We greeted them with hugs and kisses and exchanged stories of New Year's Eve. I loved the way they smelled. The scent of these two young ladies was the complete opposite of the scent of two hundred men sharing a steerage dormitory aboard the Saxonia. Their feminine aura was of fresh air and flowers, but not overpowering, and it made my insides quiver in delight.

Of course, we didn't tell them about our adventure at the Warwick, in Soho. Elmer suggested that we would like to see some of the sights around London, and the girls could be the guides. "We have only one more day here before we go back to Bramshott tomorrow. All of us can travel without cost and you know your way around."

And show us around they did. We saw Westminster, Buckingham Palace, the Tower of London, and travelled on the Thames on a ferry. The only thing that reminded us of the war was the soldiers and sailors that were sightseeing, too, and the people of London who greeted us with slaps on the back and good wishes. We stopped at a restaurant in Covent Garden for supper. Our bill was paid for by another patron, who was a diplomat from Canada, and who had spotted us in the restaurant. The day passed quickly, and the dark of night time came early. It was time to see them back to their station. London, at least what I saw of it, took a piece of my heart. I loved the grand buildings and architecture, the busy streets and the lively people. One day, I will return.

As we were about to take leave of them at the station, Elmer made another good suggestion. “Would you two ladies consider writing to us at The Front if we give you our military unit information? Jon, do you have your pencil?”

I handed him a pencil, and addresses were exchanged before we said goodbye to them. It made me feel good to know that someone other than my mother and Farq’s sister, Catherine, would be writing to me at The Front. It was icing on the cake that it was a pretty girl who would be doing the writing.

The time went by too fast in London. The train trip back to Bramshott gave us an opportunity to reminisce and clear our heads. We had had too much to eat and too much to drink.

I asked Farquhar a simple question, as we rode the train. “So Farq, did you enjoy your birthday?”

“Aye, that I did. Thank you, my friends, for treating me. I will return the favour when your birthdays roll around. But … ”

“But what?”

“No women. No women for you!”

Elmer took the bait. “What are you blathering about, no women? You got one. Why not us?”

Farquhar just laughed it off, and then Elmer realized then that he had been baited and caught.

I asked Farq another question. “When are you going back to Aberdeen to see your family?”

"As soon as we get back to Bramshott, I am going to ask for leave to go. Do you want to come too?"

"Farq, I can't go. My father doesn't know that I have enlisted. It would destroy him if he found out. Why don't you take Elmer?"

Elmer answered quickly, "I'll go."

Farquhar and Elmer were both granted four days leave to go to Aberdeen. Some of the men in our battalion were surprised that permission was granted. A few men even made mention of the benefits of being on the football team. That thought had never occurred to me, and then I thought back to some of Lenny's comments about the football players getting special privileges. I became convinced that this really was the case.

When my two chums departed for Scotland, they took the decent weather with them. The same cold, fog and drizzle that had made our lives miserable before Christmas had returned. Before they left, I gave Farq a letter to give to my mother. She knew that I was enlisted, and I wanted to tell her of the events that had unfolded in the last six months. It was hard for me to forgo seeing her. I missed my mother dearly, and my father, too, but it would be very difficult to visit them without my father knowing of my enlistment. I couldn't face him in uniform. I couldn't lie to him; it was best to stay away.

Of course, the field drills returned with a vengeance. Every morning, before daylight, we were up and out on a six mile hike to the rifle ranges. Our boots became clogged with mud, as we marched, and the added weight made marching a tiring challenge. The NCOs were kind enough to add some rest breaks, but as we rested, we just got wetter and wetter in the drizzle. Give me the sun and heat of Niagara. When we got to the range, we added to our misery by kneeling and lying in the mud to shoot. I had heard stories about the miserable, muddy trenches of Belgium, from soldiers who were on leave in London. I thought that they might be exaggerating. I don't think that now that I'm lying in one.

My company, B Company, received some bad news while Farq and Elmer were away. Our CO, Lt. Cassels was transferred to A Company. Our men had learned to respect, even like him. The Great Trek was the event that bonded us (indeed, Farquhar as well) to him. He treated us like equals, and that was important for the men who, in their daily lives, were often held in low regard by the "upper class". Few officers made the effort to transcend the class divide. Fewer still, understood how it would make them more effective as officers, and make their units more effective and cohesive as fighters.

When Farq and Elmer returned to Bramshott, they were greeted by more bad news. The camp was rife with sickness. Several of the barracks were quarantined for Spinal Meningitis. The cold damp weather and the cramped quarters were being blamed for the outbreak. One of our men from B Company had been sent to Aldershot Hospital for treatment. His name was Gallagher, and he was from Haileybury. Lenny knew him well, and he was liked by all of us in the company. Lenny told us that he was only twenty-two, and he had just got married before he enlisted. They didn't expect him to survive. He would be our first fatality of the war if he succumbed. To counter the disease, we had been instructed to gargle every morning and night with a salt-water solution. A medical team came by yesterday to disinfect our hut. The meningitis snuffed out the young life of Private Gallagher one day after he was hospitalized. A day later, we lost a second man to the disease; Private Rance. Fortunately, those two were the only fatalities, and the others who were infected managed to survive.

My mates handed me a letter from my mother. She had read the letter I had sent and thanked me for the pictures that were taken in Toronto of me in uniform. Farquhar and Elmer had spent some time with her, and told her some of our adventure stories from Niagara and Toronto. She wrote that she prayed for my safety every night, and that she was happy that my two best friends were with me, "along with Jesus." I wept as I read.

Rumours began to circulate that we, the 58th, were being considered for movement to France in early February. As January came to an end, the rumours became solid truth. We were told by Lt. Col. Genet that we were being placed in the 9th Brigade of the 3rd Division. We would be joined in the 9th Brigade by the 43rd from Winnipeg, the 52nd from Port Arthur, and the 60th from Montreal. The rest of the 3rd Division would be made up of the 7th and 8th Brigades. There were some well-regarded units in our Division with us. The Princess Pats were part of the 7th Brigade, and the Canadian Mounted Rifles made up the 8th Brigade. In total, the 3rd Division was comprised of 12,000 men smacking their lips and drooling over the thought of taking on the best of Germany. In an elaborate ceremony at Bramshott, which was attended by Sam Hughes, the Minister of the Militia and Defence, we were presented with our Division Colours.

Near the end of February, on the 20th, to be exact, we boarded the train in Liphook, and were shipped to Southampton. The next day would be our last in Blighty.

Chapter 13

One Step Closer

I was uneasy about traveling across the water again. The distance across the English Channel, from Southampton to Le Havre, France, was almost the same as the distance from Toronto to Port Dalhousie. We were warned that German subs could be present when we crossed the Channel. One encounter with a German sub was enough for me. One nightmare about drowning in cold water was more than enough. The troop ship would travel at night, so it would be more difficult for any subs to detect. I hated the specter of cold black bottomless water beneath my living, breathing body. I could imagine all sorts of creatures peering back at me through the darkness. I could hear German voices directing torpedoes into the paper thin hull of our ship.

Fortunately, our cruise to Le Havre passed quickly, with no death or drama. We arrived dry and safe on the continent where all the death and drama was taking place. How ironic that I feared my departure more than my arrival. Upon arrival, we were informed that we would spend the night in Le Havre, and then be shipped by rail, to Belgium, in the morning.

There were some good pubs in Le Havre, and we managed to have a decent warm dinner and some excellent Belgian beer. We were very tired, and decided to take a short walk around the town before we went to bed. One thing caught our attention on that walk: there were some houses that were adorned with a red light outside the front entrance. We knew what that meant. It was the houses with the blue lights that piqued our curiosity. Seeing a military policeman, we decided to find out the answer to the puzzle.

"The blue light is for officers and the red 'un is for ORs," was the gruff answer that we received.

Farq looked at me and said, "I guess the banquet is behind the blue light, and the cold leftovers behind the red. What do we get; their grandmothers? Didn't I tell you that we can never win? This game is rigged, no matter where we are or what we do."

"I can't argue with that, Fack. I would never have believed it if I hadn't seen it."

We spent a comfortable night, billeted in LeHavre, and were up before dawn to head to the train station. My fond memory of pleasant trips back in Canada, particularly the ride through the Niagara fruit belt, did not prepare me for my first train ride in Continental Europe. It didn't help that the outside temperature, that morning, was well below freezing, but at least the rain had stopped.

"Box cars? We are riding in bloody boxcars?" Elmer didn't seem impressed. "I guess we should have bought first class."

About three dozen of us were shown a boxcar, roughly halfway down the length of the train, by an anonymous British sergeant. "There's your cabin, boys. Enjoy!"

We marched halfheartedly, to our "cabin" and climbed in to be greeted by four large smelly horses. "Crikey! What the ... ," Elmer bellowed. "They never told us that we would have roommates!"

We discovered, after the train got moving, that having these roommates was a wonderful benefit. Their large horse bodies were like big furnaces, radiating heat throughout the box car. They kept us warm in the freezing car, and the straw made a comfortable, soft place for us to lie, as the car wobbled along the tracks.

"Hey, I recognize one of these horses," Farq decreed. "The chestnut: he was on the Saxonia with us." I gave him a questioning stare.

"You can recognize horses?" Elmer added. "Fack, you can't tell one Wonky from the other."

Farq started to laugh heartily, and we realized that we had been bitten. We passed the rest of the trip in relative comfort, and even slept a little.

Within a few hours, we arrived at our destination – Godersvelde, Belgium. We were moved from there to some farms at Sylvestre-Cappel, just southwest of Godersvelde, where we were greeted by cold, clear weather. We shared our sleeping quarters in a barn with domestic livestock, yet, a second time. There wasn't much room to spare, with close to a thousand men and dozens of animals, all packed into a few barns. The fucking officers were billeted in the farmhouse.

There was a lot of talk about the fact that we were now only a few miles from The Front. One corporal, who was stationed at the farm, told us of hearing the big guns – both German and British. "It is worse at night, when you're trying to sleep. The rumble shakes the ground beneath you. You can feel the concussion of the explosions, `specially the big naval guns; the big fifteen inchers. It will go quiet, sometimes, for days. Then it will start up, all over again. Oh, and the worst is when somebody, it could be either side, detonates mines – thousands of pounds of explosives. It is like an earthquake."

We had no words for each other after hearing the corporal's descriptions. I think we were in severe shock. I had heard of the term, "shell-shock", used to describe the after-effects of heavy artillery bombardment. It seemed that we had shell-shock before anybody had thrown even a stick at us. My gut tightened into a terrifying knot. I felt sick to my stomach. I just wanted to go home.

"None of us are going home!" Elmer stated, as if he was reading my mind. I couldn't properly answer that statement, and neither could Farq. I could feel a change coming over us, and the bravado was bleeding quickly out of our souls. The tone of our interactions was changing from brotherly and playful to cautious and almost timid, like the newest kid in the class. Everything changed with that short trip across the English Channel. I felt like we had just been locked in a cage with a wild animal that was coming to consume us.

Our first night in the barn was uneventful and quiet; no big guns, just the intermittent mooing, bleating and flapping, which posed us no threat. It made us realize how good we had had it in those leaky bell tents at Paradise Camp. We learned from our new company CO, Lt. Thomson, that we would soon get some exposure to the Belgian trenches, and learn how to navigate through them and to them, in the battlefields. He gave us a description and a history of the fighting that had been going on in this part of Belgium. The area was called the Ypres Salient. A salient, I had been told, was a bulge in the frontlines. In this case, the British frontline bulged into the German frontline, forming a sort of triangle. The battle lines were stationary and supported by trench networks. Because the water table was only a few feet below the ground level, the trenches tended to fill up with water. The constant rain and drizzle only made it worse. Some trenches were filled to the knees, making it impossible to keep your feet dry. Everywhere was thick, slimy, gooey, brown-grey mud. It covered everything.

There were only a few hills or rises in the flat farmland, and these became desirable locations, both tactically and from a comfort standpoint. Certain areas contained small forests or copses, that provided some shelter and cover from enemy eyes. Small villages dotted the salient, and most of them had been flattened by artillery, leaving them ghost towns.

Ypres was an ancient medieval city, now located in the locus of the salient, and it was a target objective of the German forces. It was the largest city in the area of Belgium called Flanders. The Allies were determined never to give it up. It had been smashed by large caliber shells and reduced to stubborn walls and chimneys, where once stood ancient homes and cathedrals. The citizens had fled to other safer places, and what was left of the city was used by the Allies for dressing stations and rest sanctuaries.

Already, less than two years into this war, too much blood had been spilled over this muddy, cratered piece of land, which had at one time been peaceful farmland like Niagara. The trees were winter-clear of leaves, and everything had a brown-grey tint to it, the buildings, the farmland, the villages and even the soldiers. Any slight elevations allowed the occupant the advantage of being able to see into the enemy's lines. Many a bloody battle had been fought over the innocuous bumps in the once-generous farmland of Flanders.

Thousands of young men now lay motionless and cold beneath the soil. They would never again see their mothers, sisters, fathers and brothers. With the steady barrage of heavy artillery, they would never find peace, as they were constantly churned up from the soil as reminders to the new cohort of young men who followed them of what may lie ahead.

The field kitchen was set up in the farmyard, and breakfast was served to us there. This would be our home for a little while, before we got our first glimpse of the frontlines. We spent the next five days engaging in the same field exercises and route marches as we did at Paradise Camp. This gave us an opportunity to reconnect with Lenny, who had become separated from us at Bramshott. Elmer spotted him sitting at a table, eating breakfast. He had been transferred out of our platoon because he was having some difficulty with the physical drills. His age showed at times, and he tired quickly when shoveling or climbing. He was back in our platoon again, but I felt he wouldn't be staying with us for long. The brass wouldn't post him to the frontlines or reserve trenches. They would keep him back in the support trenches, where he could be useful at supplying the frontlines.

"Lenny, my pal, welcome back to the Pecker Platoon." – our nickname, given to us by Sgt. Shepherd. "We thought we had lost you for good," I told him, on seeing him at the breakfast table.

"Did you miss me?" he asked.

"Yes, we missed you like a case of the crabs!" Elmer said, in typical Elmer fashion.

Lenny passed on some information to us: we were to remain in Sylvestre-Cappel until the first of March. Then, we would march to a place called the Aldershot Huts, and we would remain there for ten days to partake in trench training and bombing. It was obvious that the brass hats were slowly moving us closer to the frontlines. We were still green, raw recruits, and not ready for the stage and showtime. Lenny added one more thing, "At Aldershot, we will be in range of the biggest German guns. We may get our first taste of cordite and hot metal."

That was one message that I didn't need to hear. I could feel my inner strength slipping away, and I began to wonder if I might not be able to handle any shelling. The last thing that I ever wanted to happen was to let Farquhar and Elmer down. I didn't want them to see my fear. The feeling that I was responsible for getting them into this mess wouldn't abandon me. How could I look them in the eye? There was a memory that kept me from succumbing to my deep fear. I would think back to the day at Queenston Heights, when the Good Lord Himself sent His Heavenly artillery to give us a taste of death. We survived that white-hot burst with nothing more than a slight concussion. Even the soldiers who took the direct hit survived to tell about it. I was half-a-year younger then, and not as well-trained as I am now.

On the first day of March, we were assembled at dawn for a route march to Aldershot. It was the last time that we would be able to make any tactical movements in the daylight. Once we were within range of the German artillery, we would be under constant observation. We would have to travel below the surface, in communication and support trenches, and under the cover of darkness. We'd have to keep our heads down at all times. The enemy used large observation balloons to keep an eye on activity behind the lines. If we were spotted moving into a work location, the Boche would send some shells our way to make life difficult, if not impossible.

The new camp, at Aldershot, consisted of a collection of wood huts that were our sleeping quarters. They were not heated, but each hut contained cots, much like the ones we slept on in Niagara. Anyway, it was better than sleeping in a barn. Here, we began intensive training in trench warfare.

Sgt. Major McKnight was our platoon OC and teacher. He was a big gruff Irishman, who looked almost as wide at the shoulder as he was tall. Trench warfare was his specialty because of the experience he had in France before he was attached to the 58th. His large head was shaved clean and he had a thin grey-brown moustache. Beneath the gruff exterior was a very wicked sense of humour, accompanied by his ability to tell stories in a variety of accents and voices. His confidence was infectious, allowing me to keep a handle on some of the fears that kept creeping through my mind. One thing that was abundantly obvious was the respect that the platoon carried for him.

Under McKnight's watchful eye, we learned the skills necessary for survival in the Salient. Our first days were spent learning how to lay cables beneath the ground and through the trenches. These would carry phone messages and commands from The Front to the Headquarters and various redoubts (strong points or machine gun nests). Cables would often get chewed up by artillery, so we also learned how to repair the ones that were broken. All of these tasks had to be performed in the dark.

Bombing was another skill that we spent considerable time practicing at Aldershot. It was here that we learned that Farquhar had been designated as a platoon bomber. Elmer and I remained in the normal infantry. In an attack on enemy trenches, platoon bombers advanced up through the communication trenches and saps (trenches running toward the enemy frontline trench). The bombers carried sacks of Mills Bombs, and they lobbed them into the enemy frontline trenches in an effort to clear them out. It was an extremely dangerous assignment, and I was shocked that Farq was being used in this way. It put Farq out in front of the advance, in a most vulnerable spot. I wanted to be with him when he did it. It was the first time we had been separated in the field since Niagara.

The level of danger ramped up considerably when the companies were assigned to "working parties". B Company was attached to the 2nd Brigade, and went out at night to do repair work on trenches and cables that had been damaged during the artillery exchanges closer to The Front. The first exchange of artillery occurred a few days after we had arrived at Aldershot. The battle was only a few dozen miles away from us, but we could feel the ground shake from the concussion waves of the big guns. It was a terrifying experience for us, but it must have been unbearable, for those who were closer to the action. I could picture two gigantic iron beasts battling each other over a mate or hunting territory; battling to the death, with sparks and metal chunks flying. We couldn't see them, but we could hear and feel their fury. As night fell on the battleground, the beasts tired and retreated to their lairs, leaving the land smashed and pockmarked with shell holes. All our months of preparation had brought us right to the edge of Hell. We were now getting our first taste of the real war. The time had come.

That night we gathered our company and hopped aboard a small narrow gauge tram and rode it toward The Front. When we were within a mile or two, we got off the tram at an old farmhouse which was being used as general headquarters. Here, we were met by a guide who knew the trench system intimately. We followed him, in single file, into a darkened trench that would lead us toward the battlefield. Sgt. McKnight gave us our final orders as we set out. There were trenches that had to be repaired and severed cables to mend. Also, we were told that there were some wounded men that had to bc moved back to the dressing stations.

The trenches that we moved through were narrow, V-shaped slits in the muddy ground. We carried shovels, empty sandbags, and other pieces of equipment for repair work. Some men carried stretchers to bring back the wounded. I carried a shovel. The nighttime air was frigid, and my mouth was so dry, I couldn't speak. Just moving through the trenches, with no light and only the sound of the stumbling footsteps, in front of me, was far tougher than any challenge that I had faced at Paradise Camp. Sometimes there were duck boards under our feet, and sometimes there weren't. I kept one hand in front of me to feel my way. These communication trenches ran fairly straight, only deviating around large natural objects that were too difficult to move. There were a few large trees to get past, and we had to be careful in the places where their roots had invaded the trench.

I was led to a section of a communication trench that needed reconstruction. It had been filled in, to a great extent, by shellfire. I shoveled as best I could in the dark, but I couldn't see the result of my effort very well. It was cold tiring work, and as I dug deeper into the mud, I found water. The water table was only a few feet below the surface here, and it caused loads of grief for the men in the trenches. Their feet were constantly wet, and some eventually developed a condition called "trench foot". Duckboards were placed across the bottom of the frontline trenches to keep the soldiers feet out of the water. The constant rain in this part of the world didn't help matters.

Before the sun rose in the morning, our unit was led back to the huts where we could get breakfast and some badly needed sleep. The trip back was no easier than the trip to.

Back at camp, we had some time to reflect on our first taste of the Western Front: the Ypres Salient. In our hut, Elmer was the first to speak up. "Fuck, ladies! I wasn't prepared for that! I couldn't see a thing out there. There were rats running over my feet. I tried to whack one with a shovel but I hit my toes."

There was silence for a minute or two, then Farq answered, "And that was just a warm-up. We got wet and muddy, but nobody got hurt. Fuck, did it stink out there, and I couldn't see anything either. I was repairing a wall in one of the communication trenches, and my shovel hit some metal in the ground. I brought a torch close to have a look, and I could see that it was a live shell. I just about shite myself! I called some sappers over and they removed it. It was a 5.9 inch shell; they call them 'Whizz-Bangs'."

After digesting that, Elmer spoke up again. "It is so dark out there. I don't know how those guides find their way. Fucking lads are amazing; they know every turn. It's like following the Wonkys in the dark, looking for the Virgin. I swear, if I see the Virgin here it, means my number has come up. Where *are* the Wonkys? I haven't seen them all week!"

"I heard that they are getting special training for night raids," I replied.

"No! They are doing night raids? *Those* little buggers?" Elmer seemed intrigued. "Well, think about it: this is where they excel. Those gits have unbelievable night vision. They can move around in absolute silence ... and if they can fucking kill like they pilfer cigarettes, they'll be deadly. Makes me happy just thinking about it."

Farquhar had been sitting on his cot, listening to the conversation. After a brief silence, he spoke to us again. "I keep thinking about Frank ... 'Magoo'. I can't get him off my mind. He died out here; not far from this place. Maybe we can get some time so we can find his grave. I don't know. I want to take Genet by the hand, and I want to show him Frank's grave. He thinks this is another grand football game. Not on a grassy pitch ... on a muddy, pockmarked, blood-stained swamp. Does he feel the pain? How does he expect us to survive this war and play for his team? His championship team. *Pog mo thoin*! Kiss my ass! He won't even get his boots dirty in this war."

"Farq," I answered, "you don't know how Genet feels. Shite, maybe he does feel the pain. Give him a chance; we haven't even fired a shot yet. He might turn out be a good CO, after all, you know, he is a human, like us."

Farquhar didn't answer. I thought he needed a little time to think matters through. He could be a little quick to judge people.

We were exhausted, and it didn't take long for us to begin to fall asleep. It seemed odd, trying to adjust to being awake all night and going to bed in the morning. I did some night shifts at Dunlop, so, at least I had some experience with a shifted schedule. At Ypres, there were some other factors to deal with. My uniform was wet from the knees down to my feet, so I took my pants off. My socks were wet, and I took them off, too. The wool blankets that were supplied to us were a very good quality, but no match for the cold temperatures that we were enduring in early March. We shivered as we slept.

Our too-short sleep was ended by a duty call, late in the afternoon, pulling us out of our beds and back into our damp uniforms. I would have killed for some warmth; anything to stop the constant shiver and to dry my cold wet pants and socks. All of the discomfort was magnified when I had to wrap the wet puttees around my legs and ankles. Stuff my foot into a cold, damp boot? Where is that sniper's bullet to end my agony? We had just started our time here, and already, I wanted to go home. Where was my strength?

"Shite! Everything is still wet! We gotta put this stuff back on again?" Elmer complained, from his corner of the hut, as he began to get dressed.

I felt some perverse satisfaction from knowing I wasn't alone in my pain. I looked down at my boots so that I could fit my miserable feet into them. They were caked with wet grey mud, and I couldn't find the laces. The memories of Paradise Camp crept back into my mind, and I thought about the complaints that I made to myself about having to walk on the grass, wet with morning dew. Heaven forbid! My boots got wet. Not soaked all the way through to my waxy white feet, just a little moisture on the shiny leather. Was I so weak?

We did a few more nights of working parties without any incident or injury, and then, we were rewarded with a welcome day off to recuperate, adjust our body clocks and dry our uniforms out. The following day, it was time for us to go back to school again, with Sgt. McKnight as our professor. We were anxious to see what was in store for us next. He led us out to the training trenches to learn more about the ins and outs of trench life. The trench system works much like a city, with infrastructure and a network of connected trenches. The frontline trench paralleled the enemy's frontline. In the Ypres Salient, these frontline trenches were as close as forty yards, and as distant as one hundred and fifty yards. When they are close together, you can hear your enemy talking, laughing or farting, whatever. I found that situation very hard to digest, as it didn't fit with my image of trench warfare, what we had learned back home in Toronto and Niagara. How can you be so close to someone, like a next-door neighbor, you are supposed to loathe and kill? Elmer suggested that we heave our latrine buckets at their trenches every night.

Running behind and parallel to the frontline trench were the support trenches. This is where supplies, weapons, ammo and water were kept. Sometimes the latrines were located in short saps that ran off from the support trench. No matter what war you fight, or what side you are on, when you have to go, you have to go. Elmer, as usual, had a comment when Sgt. McKnight pointed this information out to us.

"With my luck, I'll take a "crump" (large bore shell) in the head, just when I am having a crap."

The sergeant shot back, "We'll put that on your headstone, McLean."

The communication trenches, like the ones that we were repaired a few days previous, ran perpendicular to the frontline and support trenches. They were used, mainly, for travelling to and back from the frontline. When there was a shift change, the fresh troops would travel up the communication trenches to get to the frontline. All troop movements were done at night, to thwart detection.

Sergeant McKnight explained to us that on each day, at daybreak, the troops on duty would conduct "stand to". This meant that everyone got into position on the firing step behind the parapet, or in their battle positions, in anticipation of an attack. Sometimes the troops engaged in a "mad minute" during stand to. Everyone fired their weapons toward the enemy trench, in hope that some nasty Heinie might get hit. It was a brutal and crude game. This war was like two men hammering each other over the head with sledgehammers until somebody dropped. Such nastiness!

As we became immersed in the theatre of war, I became more reflective on the safety of my two mates. Farquhar was so bloody competent in musketry, bombing and just about anything else he chose to do, that he would survive the worst of this inferno. That was how I thought and that is what I wished for. I could not imagine a Fritz who could get the best of our Farq. Nobody could do it, either on the pitch, or on the battlefield. It was no coincidence that Farquhar was chosen to be a bomber: the flower of the battalion. But they were also called "the suicide squad". The first into the enemy trenches, the "stormtroopers".

Elmer was a different equation. He was a risk taker, but not a planner. He was impulsive, and often got into situations that were not easy to get out of. I am not saying that he was careless or incompetent; far from it. He just tended to go his own way, and did things differently than most people. Back at Dunlop, the worst that could happen was sudden unemployment, but I must say that he got through some scrapes there, without a scratch. I was not so sure that he carried his lucky charm with him to The Front, though. He wasn't dealing with Mr. Beynon here; he was up against a foe much more determined to do him in.

What about me? Was I going to walk away from this conflict? Was I going to play football again? My biggest fear was not the bullets or the bombs. It was becoming like my father, a broken man. I felt the trembling hands and the tightness in my gut, back in Toronto whenever I heard the drums of the battalion band. The bolt of lightning at Queenston didn't make me aware of the possibility of death coming our way in Ypres. I saw something else. When I looked up at Brock's Monument, I saw my father, and not Brock, atop the column. He was not gesturing in triumph, he was pointing at me. If my father could be broken by war then I can as well. My father lived in a prison cell of memories, for the rest of his post-war life. That is what he was telling me from the top of the monument. My fear was what I might see and hear and feel while living in those hell-hole trenches. I already had a whiff of it and it made me shudder.

The three of us had been very fortunate, up to this point, that we had been able to do everything together. I never dreamt that we would be together this long. I knew that it was all going to come to an end, and soon. It was impossible to keep friends together, once the combat began. They always broke the larger units, like platoons, into smaller sections, for combat missions. What we had together was not reality. It was a dream, just like Camp Paradise was a dream.

As we got closer to the middle of March, the weather began to warm a bit, not so bone-chillingly cold. The windy conditions helped to dry up some of the muddiest areas of our training camp. Sgt. McKnight thought it was time to introduce us to trench mortars. He had our company stand on a slight hill rise so that we could all see his demonstration. The sergeant had placed trench mortars of different caliber out for us to see and hear.

"Listen up, company! Trench mortars are, perhaps, the most dangerous artillery pieces of the modern trench battle era. What makes them so dangerous is their high trajectory, allowing them to drop right beside you into the trench. You do not hear them coming, and so, most times, there is no chance to duck for cover. They are also very effective at breaking up the enemy's barbed wire. As you can see, there are different calibre mortar bombs. My assistant, Sgt. Carley, and I will demonstrate the different mortar bombs for you, so that you can see the procedure for arming and firing. Then, you will be separated into small sections to practice by yourselves. Pay special attention to the sound of each mortar being fired. You need to learn that sound, so that you can identify the artillery equipment being used against you."

Sgt. Carley was even bigger than Sgt. McKnight. He was over six feet tall and sported a large bushy black moustache and thick black hair. He had a presence that could intimidate an entire Heinie company. His expertise was ordinance, and he set up the weapons like a waiter setting the table. We watched the demonstration, at first, flinching a bit, in reaction to the volume of the sound, as he fired the weapons. As the wise sergeant advised, we noted the different sound qualities of each calibre.

"The Heinies call them minenwerfers; mine throwers. They use them very effectively. You need to stay very mindful of them, and pay attention to the sound when they are fired. You need to know what is coming at you," Sgt. Carley noted when the demonstration ended. "Now you will have a chance to play with these babies." The sergeant's voice was deep and authoritative. We moved quickly, to our positions.

Play with them we did. We spent the rest of the day practicing the art of mortar bombing. The trick was to learn the range of each piece, and adjust accordingly. The mortars were not sophisticated weapons, but deadly, nonetheless. We enjoyed watching the flame belch out of the cannon's mouth and the mounds of earth thrown into the air as the shell struck the target.

Sgt. McKnight finished the afternoon session with an announcement. "Tomorrow will be your last day here at Aldershot Huts. We will spend the day learning how to defend ourselves against poison gas attacks. The day after, we will be marching to Fletre. You are dismissed."

I didn't think too much about the poison gas demonstration that night. My ears were still ringing and stinging from the mortars. However, it was exciting to use weapons with such power and menace. I imagined lobbing those bombs into the German trenches, and seeing every Fritzy tossed into the air like a rag doll. I was a bit surprised by my aggression. It felt like the mortar was an extension of my arms, my fists. I grew a foot taller and forty pounds heavier.

We weren't too concerned about our last day in training at Aldershot. We should have been. I know that we all pictured, in our minds, the whole company fumbling with gas masks for most of the day, until we got it right. McKnight didn't tell us about "the shed".

The gas session started with the company gathering on the same hill rise that we assembled on yesterday. The team of McKnight and Carley were with us, again, to provide the finer points.

"Today, B Company, you will learn how to use your gas mask with your helmet while in the battlefield. It is extremely important to have the equipment tightly fitted to your face and helmet, with no leaks to the outside air. Mustard gas and Chlorine gas can be fatal. If they don't kill you, then you will wish that they had. Now let's set up a demonstration."

Sgt. Carley appeared carrying a gas mask and a helmet. He held the mask so that all of us could see it, and then he pointed out the various parts of the mask. Next he attached the mask with clips to the front of his helmet and pulled the contraption over his face. Sgt. McKnight made sure everything was secure, and he presented Carley to the audience as a combatant, ready for the onslaught of poison gas.

"We have brought enough masks along with us so that each of you will have a chance to practice. I warn you that it is not as easy as Sgt. Carley made it look. He is an expert. Isn't that right, Sgt. Carley?"

Carley replied, "Mfffft mumf mmmuff mmmufff."

"Yes, communication is not easy, with the mask on your face," McKnight said, as his audience hooted in laughter. "You will have to become proficient with hand signals when you are wearing these things. Sometimes, they fog up a bit, and your vision will be affected too. It is a sort of moral victory for the Krauts when they force us to wear these fucking things. They don't even have to release the gas."

Sgt. Carley doffed his mask, cleared his throat, and took over. "Follow me to the shed, B Company." He turned to his left and then proceeded at a brisk clip.

We fell in behind him, and began looking around and ahead for this "shed". The march took us behind a clump of trees where there was, indeed, a shed. It was a small structure that was constructed of wood planks and a normal tile roof. There were two doors, one at each end of the building, and two glass windows, one on each side. It looked like a small schoolhouse that could accommodate about twenty students. Near the front door, was a large table that was covered in gas masks. The last detail that I noticed was a large metal cylinder, with a valve on the top and hose that ran from the valve to the side of the shed, and then into the shed.

When we were settled in a circle around the front of the shed, Carley spoke up. "I need one volunteer to step forward and suit up." He immediately chose Elmer, who stood out because of his height. Carley grabbed Elmer by the shoulders and spun him around to face the battalion. Before Elmer could gather his wits, Sgt. Carley placed the mask in Elmer's hands and said, "Put the equipment on, just like I showed you."

Elmer fumbled around with the mask a bit, and then pulled it over his head so that his face was covered. He lifted his helmet, plopped it on the top of his head and then tried to fasten the clip to the front of the mask. Just as Sgt. McKnight said, it was a tricky maneuver. Elmer was having no luck, so Sgt. Carley leaned over and helped Elmer make the connection.

The instructions continued, "OK, Private, press on the front of the mask and make sure it is properly sealed to your face." Elmer pressed the mask with both hands, and made a slight adjustment to the alignment.

"Right, then! Let's proceed into the shed, and see if you have done the job good and proper. Once inside, we shall release the chlorine gas."

Elmer didn't budge. He turned his head toward Carley and stared (I think) intently at him. For a few seconds, they shared the stare. Then Sgt. Carley broke the silence, and by this time, you could hear a pin drop on the mud, in the midst of two hundred men.

"I'm sorry. Did I say chlorine gas? Ha, my mistake. We used up all our chlorine gas for demonstrations, yesterday. Fortunately, we are left with only tear gas. You are a lucky man, Private. You rookies need to pay close attention; there is nothing in war nastier than poison gas. When it was used near here, last year, on French troops, it left them gasping, puking and drooling. Then, the French soldiers began to drown in their own fluids. They begged their mates to shoot them to end the slow agonizing death."

Elmer continued his stare for a few more seconds, while he digested the information from the sergeant. Slowly, he moved to the front door. The front door was a double door, used to keep the shed sealed. Elmer gathered himself, and entered while the company returned to complete silence. The men that were at the sides of the shed could see him through the windows. They could see Elmer walk slowly to the centre of the shed, and turn around a few times while looking around the interior. A few minutes passed before Sgt. Carley signaled for Elmer to exit through the rear doors. He emerged to the sound of applause, and immediately pulled the mask off his face and dropped it to the ground. Everyone strained their eyes to see his expression.

There was utter silence. Elmer lifted his arms in a gesture of victory; there were no tears or snot running into his mouth, only a reddish outline around the perimeter of his face where the mask had sealed.

Carley gestured toward Elmer as if he was host of a Vaudeville show.

"Well done, Private. You succeeded; you had a proper seal to your face. It is time for everyone to give this a try. We will proceed with twenty soldiers at a time in the shed."

All the men got their equipment, and over the next hour or two, lined up to give it a try. Those who donned the equipment properly were able to stay in the shed for several minutes. The ones who erred, panicked very quickly, and bolted for the door and fresh air. Basins of water were placed nearby for these unlucky lads to immerse their stinging, snotty faces.

At the end of the demonstration, our company was joined by our CO, Lt.Thomson. He had a simple message for us.

"As you know, tomorrow you will leave for Fletre, and be billeted there. We have been attached to the Fourth Brigade at Vierstraat. We are to join them there, and then we will be moved into the frontlines with them. This will be your first taste of combat, your first look at Fritz. I am proud to lead you into the trenches, men. May God save the King, and may God look after us all."

We packed our gear the next day, and started our march toward Fletre, just before dusk. There was some rain to keep us miserably wet. Our greatcoats became very heavy when they got wet. This made me think of old Lenny, who must have been finding the going very tough. I couldn't see where he was, in the column, so I couldn't see if he was struggling or not. As we got closer to Fletre, we began to see shell holes and craters on the road. It looked as though Fritz was trying to mess up the road with his artillery, and made marching and wheeling equipment more difficult. I was beginning to realize that we were now in a land where nothing, absolutely nothing will be easy or convenient. We arrived at Fletre, just before dawn.

As we approached our billets, we were greeted by a young British Lieutenant. He gave us some great news. "When you have checked into your billets, 58th, please return to the farmhouse across the road."

We turned to see the farmhouse behind us. It was a grey plaster two-storey building that sported some shell damage to the roof.

"We have your mail delivery waiting for you in that house," the lieutenant announced with a big smile.

The battalion mates closest to him heard the great news. They immediately erupted in cheering and laughter. The men furthest down the column had no idea what the commotion was about. They instantly broke ranks and ran to find out what was happening.

I heard one soldier shout, "Is the war over? Did we win?"

You never saw men move so fast to their billets. Hell was breaking loose, as everyone rushed back to get their mail. It took some time to get distributed, and maybe an hour to get to the three Macs. Lordy, we got letters from Karen and Emma. The ladies co-wrote one letter to each of us. Elmer and I got letters from our mothers. Farquhar received a bagful for himself, the lucky "git"!

I couldn't help myself. "Farq, who the fuck sent you all that mail?"

Farq was beaming like a kid on Christmas morning. "Well, let's see. I got one from the sisters in London, one from Catherine and Peter in Toronto, one from Jesse in Aberdeen and one from … "

Farq stopped short with his mailing list, and gave us a queer look. "What?" He snorted.

"Come on, out with it, McLennan. Who is the last one from?"

Farq got very defensive, and started to move away from us. Before he could react, Elmer grabbed the letter out of Farq's hand.

"Nancy, Nancy Boseley!" Elmer shouted for all to hear.

Farq stood still, with a look of horror on his face. We had him. There was no getting out of this one. "Alright! Alright! Give me the letter and I will tell you all about it."

We went back to the billet shed to open our mail and give it a good read. We were so happy to hear from home. My mother sent some newspaper clippings, giving the names of local lads who had been killed or missing in action. Many of the names I knew from school or the streets.

The girls in London told us of some of their adventures. They had seen a Zeppelin pass over their neighbourhood. Some of their friends had signed up for the war. Finally we got back to Farq.

Elmer started the cross-examination. "So, what's the story, old chap? Are you in ... love?"

Farquhar gave him his reply. "You chaps are doololly," he said, in his serious voice, letting us know that this was no guff. "You know that I saw Nancy on more than one occasion in Niagara. I found her very pleasant to be with. She has a sense of humour, believe it or not."

We gave him a "get on with it" look.

"One day, she said something to me that I couldn't let go of, or get off my mind. It really bothered me. She told me that, despite all of the soldiers that she had 'spent time' with, not one had asked her to write to them or keep in touch. So I told her that I would be happy to write to her. She was delighted."

"Farquhar McLennan, you are so much more than a dumb football player," I told him.

I truly admit that I was proud of Farquhar for being such a gentleman. I was proud to be his long-serving friend, and there is no doubt that Elmer felt the same way. Farq was not a person who could be easily defined. His personality touched both ends of the spectrum. He was tough, yet he loved and cared for those who were weak or vulnerable. He was well-spoken and well-read, yet he could be as crude as anybody. He was a human contradiction. Above all, these traits made him a bloody interesting lad.

The battalion spent a few nights in Fletre. The weather cooperated and was cold, but clear. The next billet would be in the small hamlet of Locre, not much more than a dozen country houses. Each billet was inching us closer to the frontlines. The march from Fletre to Locre was about six miles, and from Locre to Vierstraat, was about three-and-a-half miles. The route marches that we conducted, back in Niagara, prepared us well for these Belgian manoeuvres. The weather was becoming more spring-like, giving us longer days and shorter nights. The temperatures were staying above freezing, but that just made the roads, farmlands and battlefields softer and muddier. Marching was slow and tedious. Some of the heavy equipment kept bogging down in the mud, and we would have to pull them out with ropes and lines. The mud clung to our boots and made them feel like they weighed ten pounds each.

We were supposed to link up with the Fourth Brigade at Vierstraat, and then we were to relieve the 52nd Battalion in the frontlines. The plan was to move us into the frontlines alongside experienced troops, so that we could get an introduction to trench warfare, with them as our instructors. It certainly eased my fears when I realized that we were not going to be battle tested alone and unaided. I couldn't forget our terrible beating at the hands of the 35th during the Great Trek. That was not a confidence-boosting experience, and made me very apprehensive about moving any closer to Fritz.

The distance between the Canadian and German trenches near Vierstraat was only about forty to fifty yards, almost eyeball to eyeball. In other places, the lines were much further apart. For the raw recruits, that distance, or lack of, seemed terrifying. The closest we had been to a German was our encounter with the submarine in the Atlantic.

"We will be able to talk to them, yell at them, and throw our garbage at them … whatever," Elmer observed when he heard about the close proximity.

Farquhar suggested, "Maybe some of them can speak English. Wouldn't that be interesting?"

It was a very unsettling thought, knowing that a group of men, less than a football pitch away from us, was waiting and plotting to kill us. How could we sleep at night? Maybe they will sneak over no man's land, and slit our throats while we slept? My stomach was knotted, and I knew that the other two lads felt the same. There was no turning back now. I am not a churchgoer, or a religious person, and neither are Farq and Elmer, but I was thinking about God now, and wondering how He could have let the world come to this state of disruption. How could He let us make all the terrible weapons of death and destruction, lay waste to such beautiful farmland and villages, and destroy a generation of good young men? Wasn't He a merciful God?

"May God have mercy on us. May God have mercy on us all."

Chapter 14

The End of Childhood

It was March 17th when we arrived at the front near Vierstraat. The weather remained clear and cold, making the ground a little easier to move around on. B and C Companies were chosen to go up front first. We had to wait until dark to make our move up through the communication trenches, accompanied by a guide. When we got to our positions in the front trench, the 52nd would take their leave and head back to a rest camp for some relief. The exchange of troops had to be completed in total darkness and in total silence. If Fritz detected us, he would let loose with a barrage.

Our Company gathered at our base in Vierstraat at sunset, and then proceeded into the communication trenches that would lead us to the frontline. I became separated from Farquhar and Elmer at this point. Somehow, they got behind me in the column. We followed the guides who knew the trenches, and would take us to our destination. We each carried about eighty pounds of supplies and some rations. The column moved in silence except for our footsteps and missteps. It was all too easy to stumble over some debris, and land with your face in the mud. I was so terrified that I couldn't remember what I had done in the previous twelve hours. My helmet felt so heavy and loose that I thought I would lose it in the trench.

After about half an hour, as we moved closer to The Front, my sense of smell was assaulted by the sickening stench of death. We had been warned about this. Many of the dead on both sides were left to moulder and rot in no man's land because it was simply impossible to bury them. There were occasions when the combatants called a truce to allow both sides to bury their dead; otherwise it was just too dangerous to send men out of the shelters to do the deed. Sometimes, exploding shells would release the dead from the wet bonds of soil to leave them exposed, once again, to the air, eyes staring blankly at the sky, mouths agape. What humiliation for the deceased!

The relief proceeded without a hitch at midnight. There was not much room to maneuver, when going into the trench. These were not the neat sandbag trenches that we had trained in at Niagara. There were roots and sticks protruding everywhere. The walls would crumble if you bumped them with your equipment. Communication wires ran down one side wall, sometimes catching and tangling our gear as we moved. The 52nd and the 58th had to pass each other in the communication trench, barely wide enough for one. How could you feel anything but confined? In such darkness, it was impossible to see much of the trench, so we had to feel our way around. The NCOs of the 52nd stayed with us to give direction, and set us up. Every communication was conveyed with hand gestures so Fritz wouldn't hear us. The NCOs literally grabbed a hold of us, and moved us to our trench positions. Fritz didn't react, so he was obviously unaware of us.

My mouth was dry and my heart was pounding. It seemed like I had forgotten every lesson I had learned in the last eight months. I had no idea where either Farquhar or Elmer was. My bladder felt suddenly full and I needed to piss like never before. I didn't know what to do, so I just let it go. I knew I was going to get wet here anyway.

Several men were selected for sentry duty, and the rest of us were instructed to climb into a dugout and try to get some sleep before sunrise. The dugouts were small caves dug into the parapet side of the trench, and were sometimes reinforced with pieces of wood or corrugated steel. They were placed a little higher than the bottom of the trench to keep the dugout floor dry. Two or three men could fit into some of the larger dugouts in order to sleep; however, most were one-man caves.

On the floor of the trench, on the parapet side, was a wooden plank firing step. The step was a foot higher than the floor of the trench so that soldiers could see over the parapet. Right on the bottom of the trench were the wood "duckboards" that were supposed to keep your feet out of the water. This had been home to hundreds of thousands of troops on both sides of the quarrel for almost two years. This had also been home to thousands of other troops who had somehow come into contact with the hot, sharp pieces of metal that both sides insisted on hurling at each other on a daily basis. They no longer dwelled in these dirty crevices with the rats and lice. They dwelled nearby, beneath the muddy sodden ground, with the worms, unable to draw another breath.

I found a dugout to share for the remainder of the night with two other privates. Our bunker was large, a bit larger than most, and the walls were lined with sandbags for reinforcement. Even the floor was covered with sandbags, which gave a measure of comfort when sleeping. I felt very fortunate to have this room, as some of the dugouts were much smaller and more open. We were able to arrange our groundsheets so that we had some temporary relief from the dampness of the soil beneath us. When we lay down on our sheets our feet protruded out into the trench. It would be a challenge to keep them warm and dry.

I knew one of the privates quite well, having met him at the tent city in Niagara. He had settled into a tent next door to me and my three tent mates. His name was Pte. David Waldron and he was well known among the troops because he kept an extensive diary. The brass hats would have been more than annoyed if they knew about his diary. The hobby was discouraged because of the possibility of it falling into the hands of the enemy. We made certain that none of the officers or NCOs knew of his journalistic activity. The other private, sharing the hole-in-the-wall with us, introduced himself as Pte. Jessop; Art Jessop. We had never met. Both men were young, about twenty, and as nervous as I was about being in this environment. We removed our helmets, and tried to make ourselves comfortable on the ground sheets. Without much talk, we laid our heads down on our kit bags, closed our eyes and hoped for some sleep. There were about six other men sharing this section of the trench, and though I didn't know them by name, I knew we would bond over the next few days. They also had dugouts to keep them relatively safe and dry.

Despite the piss in my pants and my soggy feet, I was able to fall asleep, mainly from exhaustion. My slumber was cut short when I was awakened by the sound of two rats trying to open my supply sack with their sharp teeth. I sat up and tried to kick them away from the dugout. They retreated a few feet down the trench, and then sat there to watch what I was going to do next. There was a standoff for a few minutes, followed by a wicked crack of wood against wood. A corporal from the 52nd, Corporal DeFoa, came to my rescue by slamming a piece of a tree branch down onto the head of one of the furry thieves. The rat released a death screech while his mate disappeared into the darkness. The corporal picked up the creature by the tail, and heaved it in the general direction of Fritz's trench.

"Tomorrow, Private, I will show you how we hunt these little buggers around here. Get some sleep."

"Thank you, Corporal."

As the sun began to rise, we were called to "stand to". The sentries had left their posts, and were moving into the dugouts for some sleep. We had to get our helmets back on, and head for the firing step to assume the ready position. Under no circumstances were we to expose our vulnerable heads above the parapet. There were steel firing ports called "loopholes" in place, hidden from the enemy by branches and debris, which pierced the integrity of the parapet. Through these holes, we could look across no man's land toward Fritz's lair.

I could hear a similar commotion taking place in the enemy trench, forty or fifty yards away. Orders were being given in the very distinctive but hushed German tongue. The fear inside me was stirred up again, and the stench in the air caused me to start retching. Thankfully, there was no food inside me to decorate the floor of the trench. I was feeling two opposing gut reactions; vomiting and starving. Within a few minutes I was able to compose myself and I looked around to see if I could locate Farquhar and Elmer. I couldn't see them in my trench, but I couldn't see very far down the length of the trench either. I felt mixed emotions, because while I missed Farq and Elmer, I was happy to have some new chums with me.

Our activities were shattered by sudden rifle fire from across the way. I lifted my rifle and moved to a loophole as quickly as I could. An NCO screamed, "Return fire!" I couldn't remember what to do next until the cracking rifle shots in my trench startled me, and jerked me from my paralyzing stupor. I thrust the Ross muzzle through the loophole and started to fire in the direction of the enemy. A cloud of smoke rose above the two trenches as the exchange of metal continued. I became aware of a new sound; one I had not heard before. It was the sound of German bullets whizzing over my head, or thudding into the parapet in front of me. Yet another sound was added to the volley of lead, as well; bullets began to clang against the steel plates of the firing ports. The exchange of ammunition lasted for about two hours, and then just shut down abruptly, and leaving the smoke to clear slowly away into the sky in silence.

After some minutes of inactivity and staring, I sat down on the firing step and contemplated what I had just experienced. I finally had a chance to look around me and take it all in. This was my first real look at the trench segment I had been assigned to, and slept in all night. The parapet was constructed with soil piled on top of sandbags. The parados (like a parapet) behind me was mainly sandbags. The duckboards beneath my feet were in decent condition (except for a red rat splat in one spot) and above the water. The trenches were dug with a traverse about every ten yards to prevent our men being enfiladed from the ends by the enemy. The traverses made it impossible to see more than five or six yards in either direction, presenting only muddy walls.

The ferocity of the exchange had left me stunned and exhausted. I never once saw who I was firing at. I never saw one Boche. I fired as many rounds as I could in the time we were engaged. My hands were shaking and my knees were knocking. It took some time for me to come down to earth and breathe normally.

"That was a hell of a baptism for you, Private." I looked up and saw that Corporal Defoa from the 52nd was talking to me.

"What was that all about? Did they want to give me a greeting?"

"Ha, that's what we call a 'mad minute' around here. Both sides do it on occasion. After 'stand to', we sometimes open fire across no man's land, in hopes of catching somebody being a little careless. You never know. Some Heinie might be eating his toast with his head sticking up a little too high. Bang! Goodbye, Heinie."

I thought immediately of Elmer and Farq. I had no idea where they were or if they were even still alive. We had never been apart like this since the beginning of Paradise Camp.

"Were there any casualties, Corporal?"

"None, Private. There almost never are, but we keep doing it. That's war!"

I felt relieved that my two chums were unharmed. "Thank you, Corporal."

The corporal moved on down through the trench and disappeared behind a traverse. There were about a dozen men from the 58th in the trench now, all checking their equipment and reliving their first brush with death in Flanders. No different than me. Scared to death and wishing they were anywhere but here.

Breakfast rations arrived from the kitchens a short time after the ceasefire. Everyone was starving, and I would have eaten that flattened rat if I knew where it was. They brought us bacon with fried potatoes, biscuits, jam and tea. The meal was served in closed metal containers, and it never felt so good to have some food in my belly. When I finished the meal, I decided to have a look around the trench, and see if I could find out where Farq and Elmer were.

I started out to my left, which was generally heading to the north. The duckboards made movement through the trench relatively easy. There was just enough width in the trench to get past the other soldiers as they engaged in their morning business. The trench was deep enough to keep me from becoming a target. As I passed each traverse, there was a new tableau of soldiers in front of me. I knew most of the men because they were from B Company. The NCOs from the 52nd were moving through the trench, giving instructions to our men. Despite our eight months of training, there was still so much to learn.

After passing a number of traverses, I came across Elmer sitting in a dugout. His part of the trench was a little deeper than mine, and, therefore, had provided a bit more living space. With his size, this was a little luck for him. I saw him first.

"Elmer," I shouted, "you jobby, you survived, dammit."

"Hey, Jonny! Wasn't that crazy?"

"I wasn't ready for that, Elmer. I couldn't react. It wasn't supposed to happen like that."

"Jon, I wasn't ready for it either. It started with no warning. No training will fix that."

"I hope you're right. I forgot how to do everything. Nothing came to me."

"We're not experienced yet, Jon. We're still green. Don't let it get you down. We just need some time in the front-line. The whole battalion feels the same as we do." Elmer's support was a welcome lift for me. I had rarely seen this side of him.

"I'll give it my best. You're right, Elmer. Tomorrow I'll be ready for it. Have you seen Farq?"

"Not a clue," Elmer answered, "but he can't be far. We're all B Company here."

"Did you get any sleep?" I asked.

"I couldn't sleep, Jon, I was too wound up and jittery. You?"

"I got some. Had a fight with a couple of rats in my dugout."

"I wanted to have a look over; I didn't see anything this morning. I want to see no man's land. I want to see Fritz. It is so frustrating to come this far and then not see him."

"You can't; you will get picked off if you try to look."

A sergeant, passing by us, stopped when he heard my request for a look. "You can have a look Private, but you will need a periscope. I know what it is like to be in the trench for the first time. Everyone is the same. All the new recruits need a peek at Fritz. You hear all these stories but you want to see him for yourself. Wait here and I will bring you a scope."

We had practiced with periscopes at Paradise and Bramshott. We waited only a few minutes for the sergeant to return with one. "Move down this way a bit and we will set it up," he said.

Within five minutes or so, we had the periscope set up, with the upper mirror hidden in some branches that were heaped on top of the parapet. The sergeant gestured for me to go first. My heart felt like it was going to pop right through my tunic when I looked into the scope. My hands were trembling. The quality of the image was hazy, but I finally got a view of no man's land. It was as flat as a billiard table but was cluttered with barbed-wire. I could see Fritz's parapet and it looked just like ours. There were puffs of smoke rising up into the air, which suggested that someone was having a smoke.

"Sergeant, why are there no shell craters out there?"

"We're too close," he said, clearing his throat, "too close together. The trenches, that is. When the trenches are this close, the artillery can't fire here because they might hit the wrong trench."

I thought I could see some soldiers lying motionless out there. I couldn't tell if they were theirs or ours. "Sergeant, are there dead soldiers out there?"

"Yes, Private."

He said no more, and I asked no more. "Elmer, you want to have a look?" Elmer took my place at the base of the periscope and took some time to survey no man's land. He took his time and moved the scope in both directions so that he could see as much as he could. Then he stepped back and looked at me.

After a few seconds, he spoke in a soft voice, "Not much to see ... kinda like looking in a mirror. Their trench and parapet looks just like ours."

"Their faces probably look just like ours, too," I added when I recalled Farquhar's comments about them being like us. "I guess only the uniforms and the language are different."

The morning passed without further incident. We spent our time tidying and repairing the trench. The water level in the bottom of the trench was low because it had been warm and clear for a few days. The weather seemed more like April than March, and that was good. The warm air also brought out plenty of rats, which were normally nocturnal. Some of us spent time trying to get rid of them using various techniques. We tried kicking them (too fast), and tricking them (too smart) but not shooting them as Elmer suggested. One of the men from the 52nd showed us a trick.

"It's easy. It's like fishing. Put a little piece of bread or biscuit on the end of your fixed bayonet. Hold it low to the ground near a traverse. Wait for Mr. Rat to come along to sniff at the bait. When his nose is right there … lean on the rifle butt. Voila! Skewered rat! Ha!"

Later in the day, Lt. Thomson came by to pass on some news to us. He told us to make sure the entire trench system was in top shape because Lt. Col. Genet was coming through for an inspection.

"Make sure your dugouts are in good order and the latrines are sanitary. Most important, make sure your weapons are clean and ready, and that your ammo is stored safely. Gas masks must be in good repair. He is coming through at 1400 hours."

Our supper rations came up just before nightfall. We were served bully beef, beans, biscuits and tea. I was very hungry by this time, so I certainly didn't complain, and neither did the other men in my section of the trench. We had expended a lot of energy fixing up our new home, and we were ready to try to get some sleep. This was our second night in the trench. Everybody was exhausted, and nobody had slept well the first night. Sleeping in a hole dug into the side of a dirt wall took some getting used to. Everything was cold and damp, with little chance of ever drying out. Ever. The putrid aroma in the air was as bad today as it was yesterday. We had to trust that our sentries would remain awake and alert through the night to warn us if Fritz was sneaking up to our trench for a surprise visit. I knew that those sentries were as exhausted as we were.

It was another cold night of broken and fitful sleep. I heard the rats again, but this time I didn't bother to get up and confront them. With my wool blanket and great-coat covering my damp aching body, I couldn't summon the strength to move.

My sleep came to an end with the words "stand to" being repeated outside of the dugout. Sunlight was beginning to paint the sky, calling us to duty. We dressed quickly and moved to our positions on the firing step. I was more in tune with my surroundings today, and felt ready to be effective if we engaged in another "mad minute". I moved to a steel loophole and peeked cautiously through the opening. I could see only a few degrees to the left and right. Straight across no man's-land was the German parapet, looking no different than yesterday. I wondered if there was a German soldier staring back at me from his loophole. It made me think, again, of Farquhar's comment about Fritz being no different than us. Did their officers have blue light brothels?

My eye caught a flash on top of the German parapet. A tiny fraction of a second later, I heard the distinctive sound of a rifle. I flinched and waited to hear the return fire from our side. There was only silence. I turned to look at my trench mates.

"What's going on?" I hollered to them.

"I don't know." Pte. Jessop answered.

Someone from the other side of the traverse screamed out, "Sniper, fucking sniper! We have a man hit by fire. We have a casualty! Medic, get a medic!"

My heart felt like it was going to explode. I tried my best to remain calm and professional. I still felt somewhat ashamed of my poor reactions to yesterday's firefight. When a sniper strikes, it usually means that someone has inadvertently exposed himself as a target. A soldier could be moving innocently in the trench, performing a normal routine, and get careless for one second. That is all it takes.

Within a few minutes, two medics hustled through the trench to get to the stricken man. They passed by my section and the traverse just south of us, and the next one over as well. Everyone remained at 'stand to', ready to fire if necessary. Everyone was thinking, "Who got hurt"?

For a long time, we remained still and tense, waiting for anything to happen. Finally, the medics came back through the trench, heading in the opposite direction.

Pte. Waldron spoke up. "How is he?"

"He's gone, Private. Bullet through the skull. Dead when we arrived."

"Do you know who he is?" I asked the medic.

"Didn't recognize him, Private. Lots of damage."

My breath left me, and I couldn't utter a word. I looked at my trench mates with the same lost expression that was on their faces. This was our first "killed in action". It seemed like there was something inside of me that that kept telling me that it wouldn't happen to us. Not the 58th. It only happens to other battalions or in the newspapers. Even through all of the fear and dread that I had felt about coming over here, I was not prepared for the actual event of death. It happened so close to me.

Pte. Jessop put his hand on my shoulder and gave me a gentle shake. "You alright, Private? You look really lost, upset."

"Uh, yeah, I'm OK, I guess. I wonder who it was."

"I'm sure we will get the information soon enough."

My concern was for Farquhar. I was certain that Farq wasn't as close as the next section. I would have been aware; I would have heard his voice or something. He would have ventured into my section yesterday. I couldn't stop thinking about him.

Eventually, the stretcher-bearers passed through our section to retrieve the fallen soldier. We couldn't leave our positions along the parapet, so we had to wait for them to come back through again, with the body of the dead soldier. As expected, a few minutes later they returned with the slain soldier. I was too afraid to look at him as he passed.

Pte. Waldron asked a stretcher-bearer, "Do you know him, Private?"

"I don't know him, but his chums gave me his name. Lance Corporal Clare, William Clare. God rest his soul."

I felt a combination of guilt and relief when I heard the name. Thank God it wasn't "Pte. Farquhar McLennan". I had known Corporal Clare since Paradise Camp. He was an Englishman who we admired for his leadership in field drills and practice. He was the first to come to our aid when we were struck by lightning at Queenston Heights. His voice was the first that my battered eardrums heard.

Breakfast rations finally arrived a bit later that morning, along with our first tot of rum. We didn't receive our rum yesterday because of the "mad minute". I hoped the rum would help us to digest our rations and ease the effect of the death of our corporal. It couldn't hurt.

The main event was supposed to be the arrival of Lt. Col. Genet this afternoon, but the anticipation was lost in our grief. My chief desire right now was to see and hear Farquhar and Elmer. Our time for the rest of the morning was taken up making sure the trench was in good shape. The excellent weather of the past few days had made the mission easy.

Col. Genet and Capt. McKeand arrived in our section of the trench a little past 1400 hours. We could hear him coming, actually, before he got to our section of the trench. He was coming into the trench from the north sector, and we could hear the conversation when he was next door to us.

"At ease, men," McKeand whispered, as he entered our section. It was still imperative to keep the enemy unaware of what was going on in our trench. "Lt. Col. Genet."

Genet made his entrance immediately behind McKeand. I couldn't help it, but the first thing I did was look at his boots. I remembered Farquhar saying, "He'll never get his boots dirty." Indeed, his boots were shiny and spotless.

Genet saluted and we returned the gesture. "Good day, men. I originally wanted only to look at your living quarters here, but sadly, we have lost a brave soldier of the 58th today. It hurts to lose a good man like Lance Corporal Clare, but we must not let that weaken us, or get us down. The Hun shall pay for this, and pay dearly. Let us not forget Corporal Clare."

As a group, we thanked the Colonel for his words.

Genet nodded to the men and then glanced at me. "Pte. McLaren. Good to see you. I saw Pte. McLean a few minutes ago. Where is McLennan? I haven't seen him."

I answered, "I think he is still further on down the trench, sir. Hopefully, you will see him shortly."

"You are probably correct, Private. Carry on. I still have some trench to see."

With that, Genet and McKeand disappeared around the next traverse. My group exhaled and relaxed.

"Well that was quick and easy. Now we can get on with the war," I said, as soon as the brass hats had cleared the trench.

"I guess if I played football, Genet would know my name too," Pte. Jessop said, with a hint of sarcasm in his voice.

The comment caught me a bit by surprise. It had never registered that Genet addressed me by name. Or that he had asked about Farquhar. "Art, I hope you are not offended by that. Football is Genet's baby, his passion. I can't help that."

"No offence, Jonny. We are all aware of that. Don't think about it anymore. He is just looking out for his prima donna football players."

The rest of the day passed without incident. I got stuck with sentry duty that night, which meant that I had to spend the entire night awake and alert on the firing step. I was equipped with a pistol that would fire a "Very" light into the sky if I suspected that Fritz was up to no good. A flare would shoot up into the sky and illuminate the battlefield until it returned to the ground. As the quiet hours passed, it was difficult to stay awake. The scratchy sound of rats, scurrying up and down the trench was a help in keeping me alert. A few times, I thought I heard a noise out in no man's land, resulting in me clutching my flare gun, and raising it in the night air in readiness. Every hair on my body stood up. It was so dark, I thought, if a Heinie crawled up to my parapet, I wouldn't see him until we were face to face, eyeball to eyeball.

When I wasn't fretting about a close encounter, I was thinking about those lifeless soldiers of whatever rank and nationality, who lay like piles of discarded clothes on the cold ground, their human form disappearing with each passing day. Why can't we go out there, and tend to them or reassure them that they are loved by someone and not forgotten, and give them a burial? We can't just walk away and leave them there.

With the emergence of the sun in the morning, my sentry duty came to an end. My first duty, before food and sleep, was to head to the latrine. I had to leave the frontline and take a communication trench back to the first support line. I made a right turn along the support trench, and followed my nose to the latrine. Those were the words used when I asked for directions.

The latrine was located in a short sap running off the trench. There was a board supported at each end that crossed the sap. Underneath the board was a shallow pit that contained four buckets. A soldier sat his ass on the board and hoped to hit a bucket. A person tried not to breathe much when in this area. This was far from Paradise.

As I entered the sap, I noticed a soldier already seated and going about his business. It was Farquhar.

"Shite, Farq! Fancy meeting you here on the cludgie!"

"Oh geez, you caught me! Pull up a chair, and make yourself comfortable."

"Let's not linger here. Let's finish our business, get the hell out of here and go talk."

We got out of that sap as quickly as possible, and found a spot to talk in the support trench. "I pulled sentry duty last night. What a nightmare," I said, as we sat down on some supply crates.

"Lucky you. I can do you one better. I was in the section where Corporal Clare was yesterday. He said he wanted a quick look over the parapet. I guess it wasn't quick enough. Sniper got him."

Both of us averted our eyes and looked down at the ground or whatever was down there. There was silence for a few seconds.

"Are you OK?" I asked.

"No, not really. I had just been talking to him. It happened so quickly. It is as if he's been snatched away from us. It doesn't seem real."

"Farq, just stay strong. We will get through this," I said, sensing that he was badly shaken.

"General Brock. Remember him? This is what he was warning us about. It can happen at any time and any place, but mostly when you're not ready. It was like a bolt of lightning. Bang, and he was gone."

We took some time to think again before anybody spoke.

"Did you see Genet?" I asked.

"Yes, he came through. He spoke to us, spoke to me. He looked pretty upset about the loss of Clare."

"I spoke to him, too. He asked about you. I told him that you were probably just around the corner. What did he say to you?"

"Just asked how I was doing, and was I ready to play some more footy soon? That type of thing. Then he left, on to the next section. Have you seen Elmer?"

"Yes, I saw him the other day in his section. He seemed settled. He was OK."

The conversation ended with Farq saying, "I don't think they will keep us here much longer. They want to bring us in slowly, give us a taste." We gave each other a pat on the back and headed back to our sections. I needed some food and some sleep, in that order.

I made my way back to my section, ate my breakfast, drank my rum and jumped into my dugout. Sleep came quickly and mercifully.

Sometime in the middle of my sleep - it was the middle of the day - my experience of life, as I knew it, was about to be permanently altered once again. I was shaken awake in my dugout by a distant rumble that shook the soil above down onto my face. I lifted my head and listened intently, thinking that I might have been dreaming. Then, I heard it again; this time I wasn't dreaming. The next sound, that shook the core of my body, was a mighty crash that was a little too close. I climbed out of the dugout to see what was happening, just in time to get pushed back in again. Pte. Waldron and Pte. Jessop were ducking into the dugout at the same time.

"What's going on?" I asked my rat-hole mates.

"German artillery! They're blasting our support trenches behind us. Stay here until it's over," Waldron told me. "Go back to sleep."

Jessop added, "Corporal Defoa said it will last all afternoon, until they smash all our trenches."

Then I asked, having to shout above the sound, "Are those the trenches that we rebuilt a few nights ago?"

"Yes, indeed. Those Goddamned trenches," Waldron shouted back.

"Shite! All that fucking back-breaking work for nothing! Shite! Shite! Shite!"

"Well, we have been using them," Jessop said, to console me somewhat.

The shelling did take up the whole afternoon, and finally ceased just before sunset. It was terrifying. It was deafening, and, by the time it had stopped my nerves were a bloody mess. I thought back to the fireworks at the CNE. I would never again be inspired by any damn fireworks display. I needed to recalibrate my sense of awe.

We received our rations after Fritz's temper tantrum finished. The evening remained quiet and the rats came back out, sensing that it was safe to do so. It was during this quiet period that I noticed another source of irritation – lice. I started noticing the bites and itch around my ankles. They must have been getting into my boots and under my puttees. We had been informed about the louse problem, and we knew what some of the remedies were. There was nothing I could do about it until we got out of the trenches and back to camp. What I would do for a hot bath right now!

Good news arrived at around 2200 hours when we were informed that A and D Companies would be coming up to relieve us. I was so happy that I started to cry. My emotions spilled out for all to see.

"Come on, McLaren, aren't you going to miss your dug-out-home?" Jessop teased.

I blathered back, "Get me out of here … now!" That's all I could say at the time. I had been here only a few days but I had seen enough. I thought about my father and I wondered how his first few days were in the Boer War. I don't think he heard anything like the punishing sounds of the artillery that I heard today. Times have changed and the weapons have gotten much bigger and even more terrifying, yet we have remained small and frail. We were destroying a generation of young men, but no one knew what the sacrifice was for. Everyone says "for King and Country" without thinking what that truly means. My country lay on the other side of the ocean, safe and separate from this quarrel. How did three young tire-makers from Toronto get pulled into this bloodbath?

Chapter 15

Getting Acquainted with Fritz

Just after midnight, we were relieved in the front line by A and D Companies. We were pulled back to some support trenches about one mile back from the front. German artillery could still easily reach us, so we always had to be alert for raining metal. Our withdrawal took place with no incidents and no casualties. The weather remained warm and fair. Everyone was happy to get away from the front line and have a chance to think and reflect. It was good that we were given a small dose to start with, and that we had experienced soldiers to guide us.

Our first day back in support passed quietly. The three Macs had an opportunity to reunite for most of the day. We met after breakfast and sat ourselves down in a dugout. It was a time to compare notes.

Elmer started off with his usual insightful question: "Jonny, how did you like those fucking big ugly trench rats?"

"Shite, yeah. But we did manage to get one with a big stick. They came by to visit every night."

Elmer continued, "Fuck, I guess we lost a man: Corp. Clare. I knew him from Niagara. He was alright ... it's fucking sad. Where the hell are our bloody snipers? Shite! We can't be careless here. Always ready, always on our toes."

Then Farquhar spoke. "Yeah, I was there when he got hit. He had just lifted his head to look over the parapet. It happened so fast, it took a few seconds to register. He was gone before we got to him. I felt so useless in that trench. I wanted to return fire, but how do you find a sniper? You need a spotter to find him. They always tell you, 'keep your head down'. His head wasn't up more than a few seconds."

"You have to be careful when you look through the loopholes, too," I added. "At this distance, they can hit you through the loopholes. All you can do is stare at the mud and crap in the trench."

We continued our conversation, but after a few minutes, the words dried up as the sound of a motorized vehicle began to get louder until it overtook our conversation. We looked up to see an aeroplane approaching our trenches from the East. It wasn't one of ours. It was a German scout plane looking for artillery targets. Its altitude was low: only a few hundred feet. We didn't welcome the visit but we did welcome the opportunity to use our rifles on a real target. Out came the Ross rifles and the chance for some revenge. We tried to judge the speed of the plane and lead with our aim before we opened fire.

The Heinie pilot pulled up as soon as he perceived the fire, and headed for a higher altitude. An anti-aircraft battery that was right behind our trenches began firing as well. The sound was painfully deafening. Realizing that it was "getting hot", the pilot did a circle to the west of us and departed.

Soon the droning of the radial engine faded away. We lowered our rifles and looked at each other. For the first time since I arrived in the trenches, I saw smiling faces. We had a feeling that we were no longer recipients of someone else's rage, but true soldiers, able to return fire and fend for ourselves. This was better than being at the firing range, even though we probably didn't hit the target. I felt like a combatant, and no longer a green beginner. God, it felt good!

A sergeant from the 52nd came by and informed us that we had now been spotted, and the pilot would report back to base in short order. We could expect some artillery soon. "Let's move back about half a mile to get clear of the shelling."

The company gathered up its equipment and proceeded down the communication trench to a new support trench. It didn't take Fritz very long to find the range of our original stopover and obliterate it with high explosive shells. All in a day's work. This is what life was like on the Western Front when there wasn't a big offensive raging. It was a chess game and we were the pawns.

After the excitement of the "Great Flanders Air Battle", we settled into our new home, and the three Macs got back to talking. I remembered something Farq had said a few days ago. I was curious to follow up.

"Farq, why the hell do you want to go back to school? You're a baker, you have apprenticeship papers."

"I wanted to be a baker before I came to Canada. Even when I arrived there, I still wanted to be a baker. But since I arrived and lived there and worked at Dunlop, I saw how new everything was; new roads, new buildings, new towns. I want to be new, too. I want to be a teacher."

"A teacher," I replied, a little bewildered. "Why a teacher? You never talked about that before."

"Well, I like to read and to write. I love to learn ... about all sorts of things. Nature, history, science, it all interests me. I think I could be good at it. I want to try."

"Farq, you would be a good teacher, and a good football player. I'm proud of you, laddy," I said.

Elmer added his opinion. "Shite, Fack, I'd hate to have you as a teacher. You're too fucking bossy."

"Well, I'd hate to have you as a student, Elmer. You're too fucking disrespectful."

The remainder of the day was quiet, once the shelling stopped. The rations were brought to us, and we used the time in the evening's good weather to relax and regroup. We bedded down for the night in our new dugouts.

The next morning began with a beautiful sunrise and warm air (for March). Breakfast, though, was interrupted by shelling. It seemed that Fritz was still looking for us, and shelled the areas behind the front lines for the rest of the day. We were informed that we might have to move again if the shelling started to come our way. In fact, a couple of times it looked like exploding destruction was moving in our direction, which caused the company to pack up and prepare to leave. Each time we got a reprieve, and we listened as the screaming metal monster crawled off in a different direction.

This led Farq to say, "Don't you feel like a tiny ant, and some big giant is trying to stomp on you?"

Elmer answered, "Bloody right, Fack. It's time to fucking fight back. We are always on the run."

The barrage lasted until the early evening. The continuous pounding of large caliber shells played on our nerves. Being confined to our dugouts, we felt the impact shock waves through the ground. The real terror was the sound of the incoming shells. We heard them whistling or whining as they approached our trench area. There were always a few seconds of absolute dread and helplessness as we waited for impact. One time, I became aware that I was clenching every muscle in my body in anticipation of my demise. Then, just like the passing of a summer thunder storm, it stopped.

When a sustained barrage ends, your brain is rattled. That is how we all felt. It was not easy getting any sleep that night. I swear that, long after the barrage, I could still feel the vibrations of the explosions as I lay on my groundsheet in the dugout.

The next morning arrived with a surprise - snow! Overnight, the weather had turned cold again, and coated the battlefield in white. It was a welcome change from the vast stretches of brown mud. The cold air, however, was not welcome.

Then, we got more good news. That night, after sunset, we were relieved by the 18th Canadian Battalion, and sent back to Locre. Fritz must have sensed the change because he launched another barrage to try to disrupt the relief. Two ORs were wounded by shrapnel.

Locre never looked so good. We billeted there for one night, then early the next morning, we marched to Camp F. Our two wounded men were sent to a hospital in France. The snow had finally stopped, but the weather remained cold and cloudy. When we arrived at Camp F, we were greeted by the Commander-in-Chief of the 3rd Division, General Mercer, and the Officer Commanding of the 9th Brigade, Brigadier General Hill. We performed a march past for the two big brass hats. By this time, we were exhausted and needed a rest.

The next day at Camp F was a fine respite. The camp was comprised of wooden huts that would be our sleeping quarters. We slept on the straw-covered floor, which provided some padding beneath us. We paraded to our first bath since we arrived in France from England. A few hundred yards from the camp was an abandoned brewery. The kegs were used as bath tubs, and the water was heated by the brewery boiler. These baths could handle about forty soldiers an hour; just what the doctor ordered. Everyone was itching (pun intended) to get rid of their lice. Also, we were able to launder our uniforms, where many of the lice were happily living. They made their homes in the seams of our clothes, and that is where they laid their eggs. We were shown how to run the seams over lit candles to remove the lice and destroy their eggs.

The baths and the laundry gave us a fresh, clean feeling. It was as if all the negative events of the past few days had been washed away. It was a great relief to be rid of the lice, which had left us with scabs and scratches. We spent one night billeted in Camp F, and then the next day, we marched to Camp D. The weather remained cold but clear. We stayed overnight in dugouts, and the next morning dawned cold with rain. Divine Service was cancelled due to the inclement weather, but in the afternoon, we participated in bombing and wiring classes.

The next day we paraded for baths again. We considered it an unimaginable luxury to bathe twice in the same week. Any thoughts that the Good Lord had abandoned us were now dissipated, or at least, suspended. It was absolutely amazing how something as simple as a bath could empower us. I could feel a sense among my mates that they actually wanted to get back to the front. Many of the men were eager to avenge the death of Corporal Clare. Other than the spotter plane, we hadn't laid eyes on Fritz. When one of our own was killed or wounded in action, it brought us to imagine Fritz as a dark, drooling ogre, which fed our rage.

After dinner was brought up to us, we were informed that we would march to the cinema. We didn't know what to expect. The cinema was a large hut; well not really a hut, but a building that could house the entire battalion, sitting on the floor. We were entertained that evening by a local band. The music took our minds off the war, if only briefly. They played different types of music for us, from hymns to songs from musical theatre.

The following day arrived cold and very windy. The dawn also ended our holiday at "Chateau Camp D". After breakfast, we were back on the march toward the mayhem. Marching above the communication trenches was made difficult by the cold north wind blowing directly into our faces. When we stepped down into the never-ending communication trench, we were sheltered from the biting wind, but we were greeted, once again, by the damp uneven trench floor and some deep puddles that made us wonder why we had even bothered to bathe. Our destination was the railway dugouts near Zielbeke. Along our route, we witnessed some of the artillery carnage for the first time. We were travelling in the daylight, and the communication trenches were not very deep. All of us had seen newspaper photos of the destruction, but they never really conveyed the true horror.

The flat terrain, mostly farmland, was pocked with craters and torn up unmercifully. Farmhouses and barns were reduced to rubble; sometimes there was nothing but a wall left standing, and a little evidence of a family's life scattered throughout. Along the roadways, we saw many lifeless horses with large bloated bodies, ripped and shattered by exploding shells. There were skeletons of vehicles: cars, trucks, carts and limbers, left to smoulder and remind everyone that this place was a bad dream; a nightmare. Christ! Advance at your peril!

Zielbeke was a small village that was situated further north than Vierstraat and closer to the Menin Road. This territory had been hotly contested for the past year and would be a sterner test for us than Vierstraat. There were a few bumps and rises in the landscape that both sides coveted. Any slight elevation gave an advantage to the side that occupied it. Being on top of a rise allowed the troops a superior view of the enemy's trench system.

We arrived at the railway dugouts in the dark at 2300 hrs. Our company, B Company, along with A Company, was dispatched to a spot called Maple Copse. This was a small sunken area that was forested, and was a few hundred yards behind the front line. The tall maple trees kept the trenches well hidden, but the Hun still liked to lob mortars into the area anyway. In some spots, the trees were only shattered trunks with broken branches, splayed out at grotesque angles. When looking at the wounded trees, one could almost hear them moaning in agony. Branches sticking up from the ground looked like the hands of dead men, frozen in time. I had lost contact with Farq and Elmer. They were assigned to a different "strong point".

Our mission at Maple Copse was to man several "strong points" for a period of a few days. Strong points were heavily armed locations, designed with a defensive purpose, and fortified with sand bags and tree limbs. Should the Hun break through the front lines, machine guns, bombs and rifles located in the strong points would slow their progress and protect our retreating troops. Some strong points in parts of the Western Front were built of reinforced concrete and presented a hell of a formidable challenge to the aggressor.

The next day, Capt. McKeand came through the trench at Maple Copse and paid us a short visit.

"At ease, men. Did you get any sleep last night?"

One of the ORs answered for us, "Yes sir. It was quiet last night."

"I'm just passing through. I am going up to the front line for a look-see. We will be in it sooner or later. Later, I hope."

Just as he turned to move up through the communication trench, he stopped and turned to look at me. "Private McLaren, you might be interested to know that those two Wonky fellows are getting trained back of the line as scouts. They said you might be interested, too."

"Not at this time, sir. I am happy being infantry."

McKeand gave a smile and turned again to leave. "Good Luck, Private. Stay safe."

Then he disappeared down the trench. I thought about those two little buggers volunteering me for scouting. Bollocks! Yer arse and parsley!

The remainder of the day was quiet, with no ammo being exchanged. Fritz must have needed a break as much as we did. The lull gave me an opportunity to write letters to the girls in London, and one to Catherine in Toronto. I envied them for being so far away from this miserable hole in the ground. I envied them their beds, their food, their warmth and their safety. I thought, again, of my relationship with God, or should I say, my lack of relationship. My parents were not church-people, and I was never inside a church, except for a few weddings and funerals. Was He punishing me for doubting Him, or not worshipping Him? Was He testing me as He tested His Son?

I decided to write a letter to my mum as well.

March 30, 1916

Dear Mother,

I received your last letter about 2 weeks ago. It takes about 2 weeks for your letters to get to me. I am always grateful to hear from you. I hope that you have been receiving my letters.

How is Dad doing? Is he keeping well?

The weather has been cold and windy, not very spring-like. We had some snow a few days ago. There is lots of rain and we are always standing in puddles. If you can, I would appreciate it if you could send me some socks. Lots of socks.

We spend a lot of time in our dugouts. These are like small caves that are dug into the side of our trenches. They provide protection from Fritz's shells but are not the most comfortable to sleep in. Everything stays damp here. We are hoping for some sun and warmer temperatures.

Farquhar and Elmer are doing well. We spend a lot of time together in the trenches. They told me to say hello to you and that they miss you.

We have not seen much of old Fritz. The battalion has not seen a lot of action yet. It is not as dangerous as most people think. We are all eager to have a go at Fritz, and show him what these crazy Canucks are all about.

The food that they serve us can't compare to home. We get lots of Bully Beef and biscuits, but I am pretty sick of them now. We are always hungry. It would be great if you could put together a food package for me with some cakes and muffins. If you can get me some Peak Freans cookies, that would be wonderful.

I should finish my letter now. I miss you and Dad. Keep well.

Your loving son, Jonathan

Pte. Jonathan McLaren

58th Battalion

The next day allotted us no time for letter writing or religious self-doubt. Fritz opened up with the heavy artillery on the Railway Dugouts, just after noon. We were safe in Maple Copse, but we stayed on alert all day until the shelling ceased. Unfortunately, five ORs were slightly wounded at the dugouts, but it could have been much worse.

A new day and a new month. It was now the month of April, and word came through for us to relieve the 113th Battalion in the front lines. A, C and D Companies were kept back in support, while B Company was sent to The Front. The relief was completed under the cover of darkness, as usual, at 2330 hours. There were no casualties. We got a quiet night's sleep and woke up in the morning to warm temperatures and clear skies.

We were in an area called the "left sector". This was a way of saying that we were at the left end, the northern section, of the trench system occupied by the Canadian 9th Brigade. Our position was a little south of the Menin Road and a little hamlet called Hooge. The trench here was in rough shape, and desperately needed some reconstruction. After breakfast and rum rations, we immediately got to work deepening the trench. The constant shelling a few days ago had left the trench somewhat filled-in. I met a new, very young, trench mate while I was shovelling. He had a nickname, "Tall Ted", earned by his gangly frame that reached six feet, five inches. He was all arms and legs. His full name was Pte. Ted Dance and he was very eager to deepen the trench. When he stood straight up the top of his head was clear of the top of the parapet, making him a sniper's dream. Until we lowered the floor and raised the parapet with the fill, he had to remain hunched over. The first order of operation was to remove the duckboards under our feet. Doing this left us standing in, and shovelling water, as well. Knowing we had to dig extra deep to accommodate him, I decided to give Ted some grief.

"Ted, you know this is entirely your fault. If you weren't so fucking tall we could be relaxing right now."

Ted just chuckled and said, "Yeah, I know. I'm sorry. I just can't help it."

"Look what has happened to my nice clean uniform," I said, gesturing to the wet mud slops covering my tunic and pants.

"Well, at least you look like you have been fighting a war."

I slammed my shovel into the wet ground and began taking another scoop. The tip of the shovel got caught on something. It appeared to be a piece of grey cloth. Part of somebody's uniform, I thought. I scraped around it a bit and revealed some more cloth and what looked like some white stone. Suddenly, my mouth went dry and my stomach began to churn. This was part of somebody's uniform and somebody was still in it. The white stone was a piece of bone. As I cleared away the soil more gently I could see the shape of a hand.

"Ted, come over here quick."

Ted arrived and stopped on the spot when he saw what I was looking at.

"Jon, that's a German uniform."

There was silence for a few seconds as we digested the scene.

I looked over at Ted and made a request. "We need an NCO and some sappers here ... oh, and stretcher bearers."

Ted disappeared down the trench. I felt very disturbed, but there was also sadness in my heart. This was somebody's son or father lying half-buried in front of me. He had rested here, lost to the world, known only unto God for months or more. I treated his remains with respect, and carefully began to brush the soil away from him. There, on his tunic, were the once-shiny brass buttons, and on his wrist was a watch, the time permanently set at 1651 hours. Perhaps a gift for his birthday. I backed away and sat down, folded my arms on my knees. The scene seemed unreal to me. I had never seen anything like this before, and I was unsure of what my eyes were registering. He almost looked like a filthy, discarded mannequin.

Ted arrived with the help that I had asked for. The remains were removed from the trench with the same respect that I had shown. He would be buried, whoever he was, somewhere behind the lines in a small military cemetery. If they could find a tag, he would be identified. Ted and I took some time to gather our senses and rest our rattled hearts.

One of the sappers walked over to us. "We see a lot of these around here. We are constantly burying last year's dead. At least this one will have a proper burial. There are thousands of them out in the fields, just waiting to be found."

By 1200 hours, the trench section was deep enough to accommodate Ted and keep him alive. We had to modify the firing step a little bit too. We lowered it about six inches so that he could use it. Our timing was impeccable; just as we were admiring our work, the Heinies started firing at us with machine guns and artillery. We "stood to" and waited to see if an attack was imminent. The barrage lasted all afternoon, and left my ears ringing and my brain vibrating. The damage was inflicted on the support trenches behind us, and they would have to be repaired again as soon as possible.

I looked over at Ted and said, "That must have been the welcoming committee. Thank God we mended the trench in time."

The day passed into night without further incident. Word got back to us that one man had been wounded by shrapnel. I drew sentry duty that night, and I benefited from some relatively warm weather. When darkness fell, I found a safe spot along the parapet to keep watch over no man's land. This was my second sentry stint and it was no easier than the first. Your ears became tuned in to every little sound in the blackness. The sky was slightly overcast, which resulted in little or no moonlight to help with the visibility. Every time a slight noise caught my attention, my mind started to construct a reason or source for the noise. I felt every fibre in my body tighten. If my imagination produced a picture of a large, heavily armed German assassin, I raised my Very light pistol in anticipation. If a second noise followed, I launched the flare. It arced into the air and produced a white light that lit no man's land until it faded away. Much to my relief, I wasn't the only sentry with an active imagination. Flares illuminated no man's land at irregular intervals all night long, casting ghostly, elongated shadows. The shadows danced and moved to the movement of the flare on its path up and down, causing me to perceive motion where there was none. As the night progressed, my nerves became frayed and my heart beat furiously. I became a prisoner of fear, which made the night seem endless. I scanned the eastern horizon again and again, for any hint of sunrise. When it finally arrived, it brought a guest.

The morning greeted us with fog rolling in from the east. When I first saw the fog, I thought that Fritz had released some gas. I alerted everyone in the area so that we could attach our gas masks before we were engulfed. As the fog moved over top of us, we stared at each other in anticipation. After a minute or two, there was evidence of the absence of poison gas. The evidence? Rats ran around our trench with little fear or discomfort.

Shortly after the gas scare, breakfast rations arrived and I headed for a dugout to get some sleep. Apparently, the day passed with only some sporadic sniper activity and the report of two wounded ORs. I was beginning to understand, more fully, how trench warfare unfolds. Each day brings its own challenges, and you never have any intuition as to what is about to unfold. The exception would be when we launch an offensive or a trench raid. If you weren't the giver, then you were the receiver. I felt fortunate that the exchanges had been limited and the casualties light.

The food that we received was bland at best. We always got canned bully beef, biscuits of some kind, a vegetable and tea. Occasionally, we got canned fruit or pudding. Sometimes, the bread we received was stale and if it was too stale, we used it for rat bait. We had certainly been spoiled by the fresh hot meals that were served to us in Niagara. At this point, my mind could barely retrieve those memories.

The view of the enemy opposite was always very limited, as I have explained. We were able to see the battlefield behind us, though, where the support and communication trenches were. The panorama was a wasteland of mud, boots, helmets, craters, large and small, smashed trees and the scars of the trenches that ran through the devastation.

There were no signs of life, except for the trenches. Not a bird sang, or flew about. No insects crawled along the ground or through the broken trees. There was only the detritus of war: empty shell casings, splintered duckboards, broken rifles, abandoned limbers and wagons, and, most graphically, assorted wooden crosses protruding through the muck. Under each of these crosses lay the remnants of lifeless soldiers, once, no different than me. They didn't even rest in peace. Their brittle bones were always in danger of being unearthed by exploding shells, shattered and scattered around the field with the rest of the litter.

We spent one more day in the front line. The enemy shelled our support trenches for most of the day, resulting in one more casualty. At the end of the day, we gathered our belongings and made our exit, relieved by the 43rd Battalion. We arrived back at brigade Camp E at 0200 hours. No casualties were reported during the relief. On my arrival at the camp, I felt that I was growing as a soldier; no longer a newborn infantryman. I was absorbing the sights, sounds and smells through the pores in my skin. Flanders was getting into my blood. That sense of dread that had hung around my neck like an anvil when we had first arrived was finally gone. I had to remind myself that I hadn't really seen anything yet. Someday I would witness terrible events that weren't meant for the eyes of any man, let alone a young man striving to find himself.

Chapter 16
War Games

The cold weather returned on our first day in Camp E. It felt wonderful to be able to sleep under a roof again, even if it wasn't a fancy hotel. I was finally able to reunite with Farquhar, Elmer, and even Lenny, whom we hadn't seen in awhile. I had an opportunity to tell my two friends about my encounter with Fritz in the trench.

Elmer asked, "Did that shake you up, Jon?"

"Aye, you bet your life it did. It shook me terribly, in a way I wasn't expecting."

"How was that? What happened?"

"He was so far beneath the ground, at the bottom of the trench. Buried by a shell or a shovel. Who knows? Lost and forgotten. He died for what?" It took some time for me to find the words. "Why did I find him? It felt like this was a message for me. A warning. That could be me someday, dug up from the ground to make room for another trench."

I could see inside Elmer's expression. He understood, exactly, what I was saying and my troubled thoughts, but he needed me to say more. I told him, "This war comes at you from every direction. It feels like you are prepared, then you find out you are not. They can teach you how to fire a rifle, but they can't teach you to deal with the consequences."

Then Elmer saw Lenny leaving a hut just a few steps away. "Lenny!" He shouted. Lenny turned his head when he heard his name.

"Hey, it's the three musketeers, and you're still alive! I thought Fritz would have got you by now."

"Where the fuck have you been?" Elmer asked.

"I've been working in the field kitchens, but not cooking. No, not me. They've got me filling the ration tins and carrying them up to the lines. Dangerous work, but somebody has to do it. If it weren't for me, you poor bastards would starve to death."

Elmer replied, "Thank you for keeping us filled with your fine food, Lenny."

It was no surprise that Lenny was not in the lines. It was just a matter of finding the right job for him. He was correct about the work being dangerous. We were told by one of the officers in the 52nd that sometimes the Hun knew what time rations were brought up to the front lines. They liked to lob trench mortars into the support lines to stop the rations from getting to the troops.

As we were speaking with Lenny, a shell spun over our heads, making an ungodly whining sound as it passed. It exploded about one hundred yards past our huts. Fritz was having some fun with his heavy, long range guns. We were supposed to know the gun by the sound of the shell and the explosion.

Farq guessed first. "Jesus, a 77 millimetre!"

Then, Elmer. "No sir; 5.9 inch, high explosive."

It was my turn. "Let's get the hell into the dugouts!"

We ran like rats to the nearest dugouts, and waited for what seemed like forever, until Fritz got bored which he eventually did. After an hour or so, the shelling stopped, and we emerged from the dugout, shaken, but unscathed. The rest of the day was quiet and uneventful.

After supper, each company was summoned, one at a time, to a nearby field for an address from Lt. Col. Genet. When it was our turn, the Colonel started his talk with words of congratulation for our first missions on the front line. He followed with a short eulogy for the men who we had lost. Then he informed us that we would be staying here for four more days, and would be participating in more field training, musketry, section training and company training. He finished with a special and very important announcement.

"B Company: I have some good news for you. While we are staying here at Camp E, we will be doing something other than regular training." He paused for a couple seconds to let all of us ponder the announcement. He was being a little theatrical. He had a very self-satisfied expression on his face as he nodded his head.

"I have arranged for a football match." Again, he paused and looked around at us. His audience reacted with a hearty cheer. The men behind us enthusiastically patted our backs and shoulders.

"On our last day here, we will play against the First Canadian Mounted Rifles. I hear they have a very good team, and they think they can beat us." Another dramatic pause while the satisfied smile remained on his face.

Raising his voice and sounding like a rector at Sunday sermon, he said, "Well, let's show them how wrong they are." Genet was truly excited.

Then he finished up, "Sergeant Shepherd would like to have a word. Thank you!"

Shepherd stood up, and strode to the centre of the battalion circle.

"Thank you, Lt. Col. Genet. I know that all of you would like to see our team in action again. We will start our practices tomorrow, and we could use some volunteers to work out with the team. We need about twenty of those who played on the company teams in Niagara. I would like to meet with you and the team when this meeting comes to an end. Thank you."

The address ended with the Battalion gathered together for the "Last Post", in honour of our dead, and we finished up with "God Save the King".

Afterwards, it was time to meet with Shepherd. He explained to us that our uniforms and equipment had been shipped to Europe with us. The men gave a loud cheer of pure joy. Like young children, we rushed to the crates to find our gear. We started practice early the next day, right after breakfast. We were relieved of our field duties.

The next day, we were greeted with rain, whipped at us by a vicious wind. Early spring weather can be unpredictable. The battalion went ahead with their field drills while the football team practiced as best we could in the poor conditions. The pitch was still muddy and slick. Shepherd made us practice slow drills to avoid injuries. All of us needed to polish our skills to get the rust off. It was liberating to be able to run and work unencumbered by our war gear. We were all fifty pounds lighter; what a joy! Once again, we could hear the sound of our feet propelling the new footballs through the air like mortar shells. We ran and played like colts in a pasture.

Game day arrived, windy and warm, perfectly suited to a football match. Camp E provided the home pitch for the game. What a pleasure it was to put our football uniforms on once again! I swear that when I held my uniform top to my nose, I could smell the sweet air of Niagara. The bright blue colour of our sweaters was such a contrast to everything my eyes had absorbed since crossing the Atlantic. We had seen nothing but grey, khaki, brown and then more grey. Here was a sweater that made me feel like I was under sunny blue skies in Niagara. When every player was fully uniformed in blue, we stopped what we were doing and stared at each other. It was a feast for the eyes! The whole team was confident, swaggering and in a different place than Flanders. It was if the war had suddenly stopped to watch the game.

There were no goal nets or field markers. We had to make do with branches for goalposts and boundaries marked by helmets placed on the ground. The pitch was still slippery but relatively flat, not a crater anywhere. The 58th stood along one sideline, and the CMR (Canadian Mounted Rifles) along the other. One other thing: having two battalions in close proximity was risky and we knew it. If Fritz caught wind of our game, he surely would lob some high explosives on us.

It became evident very soon, that the CMR was over-matched. We were a Division One team playing against a pickup team. By halftime, our boys were ahead two to nil. The Prosser brothers scored both the goals, but they were engineered by Farquhar's brilliant passing. He played a masterful, subtle game, preferring to stay back and pass up to his wingers, working his magic that way. It was such pure joy to watch him, after all the time that had passed since our last game. He was thrilling us and he knew it. I had to block but one shot on our goal through the entire half.

For the second half, Sgt. Shepherd used most of the substitutes and company players, who volunteered for practice. The two teams were now more evenly matched, and the game ended in a three to one victory for the 58th. As a prize for winning, the CMR presented us with a mangled German field gun. The battalions finished the day with a Belgium beer festival, supplied by locals and the 9th Brigade.

Genet met with the team after the festivities, and revealed that he was arranging more games for us, now that the weather was warming up. Then he dropped a bombshell. He was arranging a rematch with the 35th. We never saw that coming! I didn't even know that they were in the area. The team let loose a cheer for Genet. The meeting ended with a cask of rum and Belgian beef stew for the team. I had never seen Genet in such a good mood, and he spent the entire evening with us.

The next day was our last at Camp E. The weather had changed slightly, to warm and clear; a welcome gift for a soggy battalion. We had our church parade that afternoon in the "cinema", a large wood and corrugated steel hut, where the men could watch films. By 1800 hours, we were back in full military gear and headed back to the trenches. Rest time always passed too quickly.

I now fully understand what Genet had once told us about football being good for morale. As we were getting prepared to leave for the trench, the men talked of nothing but the football match. It was a sloppy, poorly played game, but we didn't care. It was a victory. The win over the CMR seemed to symbolically substitute, temporarily, for a win over Fritz. The men had more vigor in their steps when we headed into the communication trench that would take us to the front line.

The battalion arrived at the front line trench in darkness, and the relief was completed at 2335 hours. There was only one casualty to report; a soldier was hit by a stray bullet while still in the communication trench. There was always a danger due to stray bullets from either side of the line.

The soldier was not badly wounded. Sentries were set up and we bedded down for the night.

The following day proved to be eventful for two reasons. The first event was the disintegration of an unknown aeroplane in midair, not too far away from us. It just seemed to crumple up and fall to the ground. Everyone in my section of the trench stood and watched in disbelief. I think we all felt the same way, knowing that there was a helpless human in the cockpit and he was going to die right before our eyes. Such a helpless feeling! I heard no shots being fired at the plane. I never heard if it was one of ours.

The other significant event occurred later in the evening. The Germans opened up with a barrage of 5.9 high explosive shells on the trenches to the left of us. I had almost forgotten the ferocity and the volume of sound during a barrage. Again, I could feel the earth rumbling under my feet. Football was so serene by comparison.

The news came back to us the next morning, that there had been three killed and four wounded in the barrage. Our casualties were beginning to mount, and we hadn't yet really engaged the enemy in a battle. It was all just sparring, testing and looking for an opening.

The next few days passed with little activity, but the weather had changed back to cool and drizzly. Rain was a nightmare in trench life. Water ran down the walls of the trench bringing mud and debris with it. The walls began to erode and collapse in on us. Everything got wet and nothing ever dried out. We had to be careful to keep our Ross rifles clean and dry.

We were relieved from the front lines by the First Canadian Mounted Rifles (CMRs) at 0230 hours, and made it back to Camp B, through a cold drizzle at 0715 hours. Four men were slightly wounded by shrapnel during the relief. We slept in farm buildings again, sharing our beds with the animals. Good news greeted us after breakfast in the morning. Lt.Thomson, our company CO, announced that we would have baths now, and there would be another football game, this time against the 52nd Battalion in the afternoon. Oh happy day! The Good Lord was smiling down on us!

The excitement generated the next day over the football match was phenomenal. I saw Farq at the morning baths, and asked him how he was feeling.

"I'm good, Jonny. I feel much looser than I did before the first match. Trench life is pretty confining; you don't get to stretch your legs much. I'm going to find Elmer and have a run."

"Good idea. Do me a favour. When the two of you get back from your run, get some footballs and warm me up."

"Yep, absolutely!" Farq answered, as he headed off in search of Elmer.

Farq and Elmer, later returned with four footballs, and we spent time passing the balls around to each other, before finishing up with the two of them taking shots at me. I felt sufficiently stretched and confident for the game.

The afternoon game conditions were a little mixed. The air was warm, but it was breezy with scattered showers; not ideal for a match. Despite that, the game was another sellout, and the field was lined with two battalions of delirious fans. The pitch was slick and slippery, and that slowed the tempo of the game somewhat. There was a lot of sloppy play and missed passes in the first half. Farquhar played well, but the turf slowed him, and he didn't play with much open space. The half ended in a nil to nil tie.

The 52nd Battalion was a much better team than the CMRs. They played and defended well individually, and as a team. They would be a formidable challenge for us in the second half. While we were a superior team in pure skill, and our biggest fear was having that first goal scored against us. Then they would play a defensive style for the remainder of the game: a common football strategy.

The second half started with the 52nd pressing into our territory in a sustained attack. They were definitely playing for a quick first goal. In the first three minutes, I had to make three difficult stops. The last stop was on a corner kick header, and I just managed to get my hand on the ball when it was high over my head. Elmer retrieved the rebound and sent a beautiful long pass to Farq at midfield. Farq fielded the pass cleanly, and then sent a long drifting pass to "Tout" Leckie, who was steaming like a freight train down the right side of the field. It was a work of art. "Tout" took the pass and dribbled the ball into the area to the right of the goal. Farquhar followed up the middle and took a return pass. In a flash, the ball was past the goalkeeper. One side of the field erupted in a feverish frenzy. There was a khaki sea of waving arms. You would have thought that the war had just ended.

It was all downhill from there for the 52nd. Farquhar took over the game and owned the ball. Try as they might, the 52nd couldn't mount any comeback. The last goal was scored by Farquhar, near the end of the game. He dribbled through three defenders in front of their goal, and then slid a deft shot just inside the left goalpost. The game ended in a two to nil victory for the 58th, who let out a mighty victory cheer. The losers gifted us with a trophy made from a German shell casing. The casing was filled with beer and we drank it down in less time than it takes to load a trench mortar.

Genet approached to congratulate us.

"Nice game, men, though you had me worried there, in the first half. The rum is on me at the officers' mess."

The officers' mess in Camp B was a large dugout that was equipped with several wooden tables and several rum casks located in the safest spot at the back wall. It was large enough to accommodate the team and some officers, but we had to keep our heads down to avoid bumping the dirt roof. The room was reinforced with sandbags and timbers. The team celebrated, hoisting shots of rum and consuming salted crackers.

The morning arrived a bit too early for the football team. A lot of rum had been consumed the night before, in celebration of our victory. This was Sunday morning, and we were expected to be looking our best for Divine Service in the YMCA hut. Farq and I had a telling conversation as we were getting dressed.

"Jonny, I am feeling bloody uncomfortable with the treatment we get from Genet and his staff. He lets us use the officers' mess, and plies us with all the rum and food we can consume. Leckie is the only soldier who should be allowed in there. How does that go with the rest of the battalion?"

"I know what you mean, Farq. The men in my trench were a bit surprised that Genet knew my name when he came by for his inspection of our trench. It was a bit awkward when they made some comments. I don't know if it bothered them very much, though, because they never said anything again."

"Well, it's bothering me. I don't want any special treatment from Genet. The battalion and the ORs are a team, too. We can't be divided when we are in those bloody trenches. Our lives depend on our trench mates. There can never be any doubt in their minds that we will have their backs. The school boys get the special treatment. That is how it is."

I was a little confused. "Well, if you go back to school to become a teacher, won't you be a school boy then?" I asked.

"Jonny, you don't get it. I could never be a school boy. You are born a school boy. They live in a different world than we do. They are the upper crust, they live in big houses and run the world. Hell, you and I could never go there."

I understood that Farquhar was talking about privilege and wealth. I wanted to challenge him, maybe to open his mind a bit. In my mind, there are different classes of people, but that the wall that Farquhar saw can be climbed.

"Farquhar, I don't believe that. Don't you think that there are many who have started with very little and made something of themselves, and lived in those big houses?"

"I suppose there are always exceptions, Jonny. Perhaps, it'll be one of us."

We had a special visitor in the afternoon. Master Sgt. Billing of the Coldstream Guards, arrived to train our drill sergeants. He was an impressive man with a large bushy "handle bar" moustache. It was interesting to hear his booming voice as he worked with our sergeants, while we were busy with our own drills. There was a satisfaction in hearing the sergeants being lambasted for once, just as they do to us.

As it grew dark, three hundred and forty of our men were sent out for work detail in the support trenches. I never expected to spend more time with a shovel in my hand than a rifle. We were finding out that fighting Fritz involved much more than aiming and pulling a trigger. We were warned about this when we were back in Niagara, but I don't think anybody believed it. I spent another cold night digging out damaged trenches in near total darkness. I was very wary now, every time I planted the tip of my shovel into the soft mud. The memory of seeing a lifeless soldier at my feet was still vivid. I almost would rather have had my shovel strike a live shell.

The next three days were wiped out by cold, wet, windy weather. We were prevented from doing drills or providing work parties. We stayed in our billets and wrote letters, read letters and books or played cards. I wondered if the weather had brought a truce to the front line, too.

Our restful timeout was interrupted by a welcome announcement from Lt. Genet. It was an incredible moment when it happened. We were told that, when the weather cleared, there would be a football match against the 35th. The billets erupted in cheers. Every soldier leaped up on to his feet and danced around in a frenzy. I had seen nothing like it. It was mayhem. Inside of me, there were conflicting emotions. I was elated to see how much one football game meant to these men. It made me feel that I was contributing to their happiness and making this miserable war livable for them. Yet, I too, was bothered by the way the football team was getting some preferential treatment. I could feel what Farq was feeling and it unsettled me.

Indeed, the next day, April 20th, the 35th Battalion marched into our camp like the conquering Roman Army. Lt. Col. McCordick arrived in an automobile. When he got out of the vehicle, he handed a flagpole to his adjutant. The flag was unfurled to reveal the banner from Paradise Camp: "35th Battalion, Paradise Camp Football Champions, 1915". The men of the 58th were enraged. When they saw the banner unfurled, they booed and cursed at the 35th. The standard was suspended from two poles planted at midfield along one sideline. It was like waving a red flag at us.

"You're in for a beating today, ya wankers!"

"Better be ready for a beat'n, ya pansies!"

The football pitch was in terrible shape. It was soggy from all the rain we had received over the last few days, and it was still chewed up from our last game with the 52nd. Genet had ordered the construction of a viewing stand for the two

COs. As they did at Niagara, two chairs were placed on the riser, with a small table between them. He also arranged for some regulation goal nets to be set up on the field.

The two battalions stood along the sidelines, with the 58th on one side and the 35th on the other. The soldiers hollered insults at each other, in anticipation of the match. The two teams were bugled onto the field from opposite ends. Genet and McCordick made their entrance and strode up onto the riser and into their seats. A bottle of whisky was placed on the table between them. The crowd noise was so loud that we could barely hear ourselves talk.

Sgt. Shepherd signalled for the team to meet in front of our goal. We gathered around him closely so we could hear his words.

"Look at me, men! Look at me! Listen carefully. We want this game badly, but not half as bad as our CO. Our loss to these bastards stung us all. Now, the field is very sloppy, so don't get fancy out there. We have to make our passes up the field with fewer crossing passes. We want to take advantage of our speed, particularly Leckie. You Prosser lads, I want you to stay back a bit closer to midfield. We want to strike up the middle with McLennan and Leckie. OK, let's hear it!"

In unison the team yelled, "We are great, 58!"

The game started very tentatively because of the poor field conditions. It was very slippery underfoot, even in cleats. The ball changed hands frequently when players tried to dribble. It was becoming apparent that the only way to move the ball was with short, crisp passes. Farq was a master at this game. I felt that, at some point, the game would come to him.

We went through the first half without either team being able to register a shot on goal. Most of the play stayed stubbornly at midfield. At the sideline, during halftime, a large bowl of fresh oranges was brought out to us from the camp kitchen. I have no idea how Genet managed to get fresh oranges to Flanders for his team to enjoy. And enjoy, we did.

Sgt. Shepherd gathered us around for another briefing.

"So far, I like what I see out there. Watch out for their two wingers who are trying to sneak upfield for the long pass. McLean, watch up your side. Don't let him get by you. That winger has some speed. Farquhar, this is your time. Their midfielders are watching the Prossers on both sides. This will give you some room in the middle. Try to work the ball up to Leckie, and if they double team him, which I think they will, then you go for the opening. Has everybody got it?"

"Yes, sir!"

"Then let's go do it!"

The rain had picked up somewhat at halftime, leaving some puddles on the field. The conditions were such that whoever scored first would have a huge advantage. Being up by one goal would allow a team to concentrate on defensive positioning. The first few minutes of the second half would be critical. Both teams would be going hard for the first goal. From the opening kickoff, the 35th kicked the ball deep into our territory. Their left winger retrieved the ball in the corner and sent a beautiful crossing pass into the goal area. As if it had been rehearsed, their striker arrived at the ball in midair and headed it toward our goal. He hit the ball high toward the top right corner of the goal. I leapt with every ounce of strength in me, just to get a finger tip on the ball, and deflected it over the crossbar. The men on our side of the field were delirious and my teammates ran back to congratulate me.

Someone in the crowd yelled, "Atta boy, Jonny. You saved us, you bugger!"

Then good old Elmer reminded me of different times. "Makes up for your header at Niagara."

We survived the corner kick and took possession of the ball. The backs worked the ball up to midfield, giving Farq some open space. He took a pass, and immediately streaked straight up the field toward their goal. As the defenders drew toward him, "Tout" Leckie became wide open to his right. Farq chipped a floating pass over a defender's head and let Leckie run to it. Leckie took half a dozen long strides toward the goal and placed a perfect shot past their goalkeeper. It all happened so fast that, at first, everyone was stunned. It was a beautiful pass from Farq. The cheers erupted. The team hoisted Leckie in the air in triumph. But there were still thirty-nine minutes to play.

As expected, the 35th pressed us into our end of the field. We brought our wingers back and played a defensive formation. The puddles grew larger as the game progressed, and made passing and dribbling next to impossible. One of their midfielders became frustrated and enraged, and took it out on Farq with a vicious tackle. Farq sprawled on the wet ground in obvious pain. He seemed to be holding on to his left knee and grimacing in agony. Elmer took a run at the midfielder and knocked him backward a few steps. Both teams rushed to the scene and kept Elmer and his opponent apart. There was general milling about and finger pointing but peace was quickly restored. Neither player was given a red card, but they got a warning from the referee. The 58th crowd booed the call while the 35th cheered. Farq was able to get back up on his feet to test out his knee with a slow trot. He was able to move around on it well enough, and stayed in the game, though with a slight limp.

Now the 35th was getting more aggressive. Time and Nature were on our side, but it didn't stop them from having one more desperate go at leveling the score. They pulled all of their players forward and pressed us right back to our end of the field. Getting the ball near the goal was the problem. Everywhere they moved, they were met by a 58th defender. When we intercepted a pass, we would just take our time and kick it back to their end of the field. They would regroup and bring the ball back for another try. They pressed us deep, once again, and ended up with a corner kick when a shot glanced off Elmer. The corner kick was placed beautifully into the crowd of players in front of the goal. They missed the header but gained control of the ball in a great spot for a clear shot. The striker strode up to the ball and placed his shot off the crossbar. The ball ricocheted straight down in front of me, where I could dive on it. I dove at it, but it skittered away from me like a greased pig. I reached for it again, but I was too late. Farquhar beat me to it and instantly cleared it down to the other end of the field.

As soon as the 35th retrieved the ball to head back towards us, the referee blew his whistle. The game was over.

The men on our side of the field ran out onto the pitch. They hoisted Farquhar and "Tout" up on their shoulders. I looked over at the riser to see that the two COs were standing and shaking hands. I felt happy for Genet; I knew how much he wanted this game. I felt happy for Sgt. Shepherd because of the pressure he must have felt to win this game. He had prepared us well for this match, and he deserved as much credit as any of the players. I signalled to two players to help me hoist Shepherd up on our shoulders, and we carried him around the field while we were whooping and hollering.

As the celebration was winding down, McCordick presented Genet with the championship banner from Paradise Camp, and he invited our team to hold the banner high in the air. Then, Genet spoke.

"Thank you, 58th football, you have made me proud. And thank you, Sgt. Shepherd, for your hard work with this team. Thank you to the 35th for showing up today, in bad weather, and playing a hell of a game. And finally, to Lt. Col. McCordick for being a good sport in presenting us with the banner. I will give you a chance to win it back. Best two out of three!"

After the field cleared of soldiers, Capt.McKeand approached the two teams and told us to use the officers' showers, which, in fact, were ten suspended water buckets with holes in the bottom. He told us to get changed and meet up in the officers' mess for a post-game meal and celebration. Farq tapped me on the shoulder.

"I guess we are getting a pass on the work party tonight. I don't feel right about that."

"I know what you mean, Farq. Do you want to skip the celebration?" I asked.

"I sure do. Let's talk to Elmer."

"How is your knee?"

"It's sore, but it won't get me to Blighty."

We found Elmer and asked him if he was with us. "Absolutely, I want to be with the work party."

The three of us went to the showers at the officers' dugout, and as we undressed, we told the rest of the team that we were skipping the celebration. They looked at us in surprise. Then they looked at each other. Billy Prosser spoke up for the team.

"We are with you, Jonny. It's not right to let the rest of the battalion down."

One of the players from the 35th team heard what we were talking about.

"You guys are not going over to the mess for food and drinks? Why not?"

Elmer spoke up, “We are on work detail tonight. It’s not fair that we miss it while the others work.”

“I admire your loyalty, lads. Good for you and great game today; you were the better team this time. We’ll get you the next time.”

After the showers, the team went back to the huts to be with the rest of the battalion. When we arrived at the huts, the men were celebrating. Genet had issued rum rations for all. When Farq, Elmer and I returned to our hut, the soldiers there greeted us with puzzled looks.

“Farq, why aren’t you at the officers’ mess?” a private enquired.

“We decided to pass up the celebration and go on work detail instead. The whole team did, except Major Leckie. He had to go.”

There was a pause as the statement registered with the men.

“Well, we appreciate your gesture. Go celebrate; we might all be dead tomorrow.”

Farq quickly explained, “It’s not a gesture. This is where we want to be.”

The men in the hut surrounded us, cheered and patted us on the backs and shoulders. I felt released, inside of me, the warmth of solidarity, and the brotherhood of men. We would sacrifice our lives for each other in the blink of an eye, the click of a trigger.

Work detail that night was as unpleasant as ever. The daylong rain had turned the ground and the trenches into an endless bog. We had many trenches and roads to repair. Our boots would sometimes get sucked into the mud, and remain there as we lifted our feet to move. There were spots where men were up to their knees in mud. Lifting a shovelful of mud is a mighty feat. It requires so much effort that an average soldier is depleted in minutes. Making matters worse was the fact that we were attempting this rebuild in the dark. I would be embarrassed to see what our efforts looked like in the daylight.

The next day saw us depart Camp B for another location in Brigade reserve. There was no relief from the incessant rain. We arrived at our new camp, called the Belgian Chateau, just as it was getting dark. This camp was the least welcoming, least comfortable place that we had ever encountered. The Chateau was really only the remnants of what had been a chateau. It had been constantly shelled by long range artillery until there were only a few partial walls left standing in defiance. The Germans had their guns registered on this location, and so it was probable that we would be challenged during our stay.

Our sleeping quarters were large dugouts which were reinforced by hundreds of sandbags and corrugated steel plates. They were larger, deeper and more complex then the trench dugouts. The rain had made every inch of our living quarters damp and soggy. It seemed that every battalion that had passed here before us had used it as a garbage dump. There were broken pieces of military hardware lying scattered around the grounds. Not all of the garbage was military. Soldiers had simply left behind the remnants of their personal lives as well. Tin cans, empty packages, and cigarette cartons littered our path and had been absorbed in the mud. We were in a different world, not one of families and friends. This was a world where people came to die. When you know you are going to die, you can discard the frivolity of living.

It wasn't all bad. The following morning, Farquhar received a parcel from Catherine and Peter. He opened it in our presence, and we watched him as if it was Christmas morning.

"Don't expect me to share any of this with you two."

"Hey,Farq" Elmer answered, "I thought I saw our names on the box, too."

"Scunners! You wish!"

Farq reached into the box and removed some of the newsprint that had been put there for stuffing. We forgot the contents of the box for a moment as we each grabbed a piece of newspaper to read. For a few minutes, the three of us were home in Toronto.

Farq began to pull out the booty. First out were bars of soap.

Elmer couldn't resist. "She can smell you all the way across the ocean. Good choice!"

Next, Farq brought out a large tin of shortbread biscuits. He looked at us with a serious "hands off" look. Then he laughed.

"Go ahead, open it!"

We did. Six biscuits disappeared within seconds. Next out was a jar of strawberry jam, followed by a tightly wrapped rum cake. The last items in the box were a photograph of Catherine, Peter and William, accompanied by a short letter and a pencil drawing of a soldier by William. The letter had happy news of an expected little brother or sister for William.

Elmer stared at the photograph and said, "You are a lucky man, Farq, a lucky man."

When Farq finished reading the letter to himself he began to laugh.

I was curious so I asked him, "What's so funny, Farq?"

He lowered the letter and looked at me in a sheepish grin. "My sister says that I have to share the biscuits and such with my two mates or she will bash me in the head when I come home. Shite, how can she do that to me?"

Of course, Elmer and I made a move for the biscuit tin and opened it before Farq could react. Once we had the tin, there wasn't much Farq could do.

"I already shared with you two. Give them back!"

Music to my ears. We had been through a bit of nastiness in the last few weeks, and it was great to see that our sense of humour and brotherhood had survived. Listening to Farq and Elmer banter with each other brought back the warmth of our friendship and the warmth of last summer in Niagara. We had been through a lot together during the last month that had severely tested our level of maturity and our courage. What we didn't know was that we would be tested much more severely in the coming days.

Late in the afternoon, we again prepared to head out into the support trenches for work detail. The rain was still with us but the air was warmer and there was little to no wind. Our work party consisted of eight officers and four hundred and five ORs. Tomorrow was Easter Sunday, and we were looking forward to Divine Service, and maybe the day off. Our work party was given the job of carrying ammunition and supplies up toward the front line. It was a welcome change from digging in the mud in the dark.

Easter Sunday arrived with clear skies and warmer air. The usual rain clouds were replaced that morning by aeroplanes up above us. We saw some German scout planes giving us a look, and probably taking pictures. Then, their mission was interrupted by five of our own fighter planes that chased them away, to our cheering on the ground. It was an interesting diversion.

Just after noon, our normal, or what we thought of as normal, battle routine changed forever. It started with the whine and explosion of a single 5.9 inch, high explosive shell. The strike shook the ground nearby and sent out a shock wave that knocked people over. Large volumes of mud and dirt were launched into the air, only to return to the ground again and bury those who couldn't get away. Some men came to the aid of those who were buried. Others ran to the dugouts to seek shelter from the inevitable. Elmer, Farq and I made our way to the nearest dugout and retreated to the deepest part of the shelter. We were soon joined by several others.

The barrage began within a minute of that first shell. Our camp became a receptacle for a shower of high explosive fury. We could only sit helplessly in our dugout and hope that we wouldn't receive a direct hit. Every explosion sucked the air out of our lungs with the concussions. The earth became loosened around the sturdy walls of our dugout and trickled down on our heads. My ears simply couldn't absorb any more sound and I became deaf as a stone. Maybe that was a good thing because I could no longer hear the swelling whine of an approaching shell. As quickly as the bombardment started, it stopped. We sat and waited for it to start up again. Fritz liked to do that; he would wait until everyone came out of hiding, and then blast them again.

Eventually, we began to emerge from our dugouts. Looking around us, we could see how the terrain had been churned. Smoke still seeped out of the fissures in the ground. We began to look for injured or buried soldiers. We found one OR buried under the rubble. Someone spotted his foot sticking out of the rubble near the old chateau. By the time we dug him out, he was lifeless.

The shelling started again at 1900 hours, and we had to run for cover one more time. It was the same guns, 5.9 inch, with high explosive shells. The barrage lasted only until 1915 hours. It was a day that will be forever burned into my memory. I have never felt so hunted, so vulnerable. None of us had a thing to eat all day, yet no one was hungry.

We were all shaking and twitching, waiting for that next rude awakening.

When I looked over my shoulder, down to one end of my trench, I witnessed a heartbreaking sight. There were two soldiers who were suffering from "shell shock". One man sat on the ground with his back to a dugout. His elbows were on his raised knees and his hands covered his ears. He was weeping uncontrollably, his body convulsing. It was hard for me to look away, even though I wanted to. The other soldier stood still like a mannequin with a blank stare. He was silent and passive, like a lost little boy. There was nothing we could do for them except call in the medics to take them away from the front line for treatment. The chances are that they would be back to the action in a few weeks.

I thought of my father, and wondered if he suffered from shell shock. Sometimes I saw him stare off into nothingness, in mute agony. I felt myself a true victim, and one who could abide only lesser amounts of shock waves and flying debris than other men. Everyone has a limit; that is part of being human.

In war, a soldier can be destroyed in more ways than one. Would I rather die than suffer the indignity of shell shock? I had seen the silent dead, lying in no-man's-land, waiting for the worms to claim them. That image shook me, and left me feeling empty, lost, and numb. But seeing a man crying like a young child, unable to feel anything but horror, was beyond painful. Could anybody comprehend it? A dead man feels no terror. A doctor can't put a binding on horror. There is nothing a man can do until those demons tire of horrifying him, and leave. Perhaps we have pushed the game of war beyond the limits of man. Let it be a game for the gods.

Chapter 17

Into the Breach

We began the search for the dead and missing in the aftermath of the barrage. A couple of dugouts took direct hits. In one collapsed dugout, the body of Major Norman "Tout" Leckie was found, along with the body of Pte. Michael Johnson. In another dugout, three men were found alive, but severely injured. When the work crews had finished looking for casualties, their final toll was one officer and three ORs killed, and one officer and eight ORs wounded. The officer killed was our company second in command, Herbert Daw. We will miss him. Two men were victims of shell shock. A terrible day, a terrible Easter Sunday for the 58th.

"Tout" Leckie was a huge loss to the football team, as well as the battalion. He was a big man with blazing speed, and a great complement to Farquhar's skill and finesse. The two worked so well together. "Tout" was a natural athlete who could have excelled in any number of sports. Genet saw him play for the Toronto Argonauts in the Ontario Rugby Football Union, and before the war, Genet convinced Leckie to play association football for his team in Brantford. His loss to the team meant that a victory over the 35th in any rematch would be unlikely. He was popular and loved by the men of the battalion, and a genuine celebrity.

The Hun didn't forget about us. The next day, high explosive shells began raining on us after breakfast at 0900 hours. Fritz took a break in the early afternoon, and we held a funeral for Major Leckie. The Chaplain, Capt. Gordon, performed the military service, as our flag was lowered to half-mast. The solemn ceremony ended with two minutes of silence; a welcome relief from the constant roar of weapons. A lone piper stood on a slight hill nearby, and played the Scottish lament for a fallen soldier, "The Flowers of the Forest".

Farquhar recited two lines he knew from the lament, to Elmer and me:

The Flowers of the Forest, that foucht aye the foremost,
The pride o' our land are cauld in the clay.

That day, a battalion wept as one.

The lull in shelling made it seem like Fritz knew the battalion was in mourning, and deserving of respect. About one hour after we dispersed from the funeral, the barrage restarted. The men disappeared back into dugouts. The shells shook us, and crumbled dirt fell from the walls of our dugouts down onto us. If we were lucky, and far enough away from the detonation, only small parts of the walls trickled down onto our heads. Others were not so fortunate, and would have to be dug out of the rubble when the shelling stopped. We still hadn't time to repair the damaged dugouts from yesterday's barrage. Fritz kept up the onslaught until 1800 hours, then suddenly quit for the day. The first job was to find the buried men and dig them out. All were rescued unharmed. Our nightly work parties got to business, as usual, coming home with three more casualties, two of which were shell shock.

The next four days at the Belgian Chateau were characterized by intermittent shelling with the 5.9s and, one particular day, we were gassed with a type of tear gas that dissipated with the wind. Tear gas is not as deadly as the mustard or chlorine gas, and is more of a nuisance than a threat. The Hun went out of his way to make us put those miserable masks on our faces because it made life more difficult to endure.

The weather was growing warmer and more pleasant, making life a little more tolerable for us. We knew that we would be heading back to The Front at any time. Our battalion was sent to Zielbeke Bund, closer to The Front, for one day to serve in relief. We got in and out without casualties.

On April 29th, the 58th was sent to the right subsection of the left sector, in relief of the 43rd Battalion. We were back to being nose to nose with Fritz, less than a football pitch between us. We arrived in the trench at 0100 hours with one OR slightly wounded. We cleaned up the trench as much as possible and set up our dugouts with our few possessions. It was time for us to wait and prepare for battle.

On the following day, there was heavy shelling heard in the right sector. We were warned to have our gas masks at hand. We suffered no casualties, but there was considerable damage done to the trenches in that sector.

The first day of May is a German holiday welcoming spring: May Day. The brass hats warned us to expect some action from them. We were ordered to stand to, for the entire day. The morning was quiet, but at 1530 hours, Heinie began shelling two of our strong points with 77mm shrapnel. At 1830 hours he started with the trench mortars on our support trenches and dugouts. This continued until about 2030 hours, when suddenly we could see the Germans coming out of their trenches and heading straight for us. It was fucking real, and what we had prepared for in training. Goddamnit, I was ready to do some damage to Fritz! My hands were shaking a bit, but I was in control of them. I looked over the parapet and returned fire, as I had wanted to do since arriving in the trenches. We had trained so hard for this moment, and rehearsed, in our minds, the act of pulling the trigger and stopping the enemy in his tracks. The feeling of hitting the target on the range in Niagara, multiplied one thousand times.

We found that our signal lines had been cut by the trench mortars, so we had to rely on runners to get messages back to HQ. One of our men told me that Farquhar had been picked as a runner. My stomach knotted because runners had a large chance of being cut down by gunfire. They had to run the gauntlet in full view of the enemy.

With my heart pounding and my mouth totally dry, I set up to fire over the parapet. We had the advantage of the sun at our backs, making it easier to find our targets. The Germans were moving into the evening sun, and were hampered by the bright glare. I could hear our machine guns rattling, and our trench mortars firing into the face of the enemy. I made an effort to pick out one German soldier who was advancing, and fire my weapon at his chest. The distance to my target was, at most, thirty yards. I pulled the trigger and felt the recoil. I don't remember the sound; I was so focused on my aim. I saw a small puff of smoke on the lapel of his tunic and down he went. He didn't move, he just laid there, face down, his helmet flung to the side. I didn't have time to feel any emotions. That would have to wait. I needed another target. Our machine guns were taking a huge toll on them. The ground was littered with grey bodies. As I found my next target, he turned his back to me, and began to retreat to his own trench. A puff of smoke on the back of his tunic indicated another hit. I wasn't sure if it was my shot, but I was going to take credit anyway. The grey surge was stopped in front of us and was retreating, fading away. I fired one more time in their general direction in hopes of hitting someone. Then they were gone.

No man's land sat right in front of me, as I had always wanted to see it. If I had had a camera, I would have taken a photograph and sent it home for all to see. This, in my mind, was what I felt our loved ones would want to see: a battlefield littered with enemy dead and Jonny, safe and sound in his own trench with his gun barrel red hot. This is how I saw it before I signed up, before I saw Canadians dying in front of me.

There was a smoky veil rolling across the flat ground, and the smell of cordite in the air. The mud terrain was pockmarked with craters, and all the trees in the area had been splintered and smashed to the ground. Our trench mortars continued to pound their frontline and support trenches. Some of the Germans in the field were still alive, but badly wounded, moaning and twitching helplessly. The rest of the grey figures on the ground were still and lifeless. Then a feeling came over me that I had seen enough of no man's land and I didn't need to see anymore. My heart sank, and I asked myself, "Why don't I feel the euphoria of victory? I hit my targets and I brought the enemy down. What happened to that surge that I felt when I raised my rifle to shoot? Is this who I am? A few months ago, I would have cringed at the scene in front of me. Now I was searching for emotions, any emotions that I could take refuge in.

Sleep didn't come to me that night. It was a horrible struggle. I huddled inside a dugout and lay down, but I couldn't shake the nervous energy that surged through my body. Pictures of men running toward me, and falling, ran through my mind. I remembered an event that I witnessed when I was about twelve. I was walking to school one day when I saw a cat dash across the road and get run over by the large wheel of a cart. Its back must have been broken because it couldn't get back up to its feet. I heard its cries as it rolled and flailed on the ground until all the life had seeped out of its body. I could think of nothing else for the rest of the day. My mind ran that scene over and over again until finally, I was able to let it go. How long it took, I can't remember.

The other men in my trench were similarly affected. We talked about the ordeal for hours. I was not alone in trying to deal with the emotions of life and death. The war was showing us things that we weren't equipped to see or understand. Many of us were just starting out in life, and trying to establish ourselves in society. Now we looked around and saw what was happening to other young men with the same aspirations, but instead, we saw bits and pieces of them being picked up off the ground and placed into blankets. It was not supposed to be like that.

The Germans were nervous, as well. They sent up flare after flare all night long, in anticipation of a counterattack. I was sickened to hear the cries for help reaching out of the darkness of no man's land. It was impossible to not want to help them. Most heartbreaking, I heard the cry, "Mutter, Mutter!" I covered my ears so that I couldn't hear. It gave me some insight into what drove my father to seek silence inside of himself. As the daylight began creeping into the eastern sky, the sounds of lonely agony faded away. Fritz had removed some of his wounded during the night, leaving only those who were bereft of hope, and the dead.

It was a resounding but costly victory for the 58th, our worst loss of the war, so far. The horrible count was eight ORs dead and twelve missing. Fourteen ORs were wounded, and six suffered from shell shock. The German casualties had to be much higher.

The battalion remained in the front line trenches for four more days. There was intermittent shelling and several gas alerts during this time. The rain had returned just as the soil was beginning to drain and dry. We suffered more deaths and wounding than I cared to think about.

Before we left the front line trenches for relief, an opportunity came my way that I would have turned down just a month ago.

The Wonkys had been assigned, by general command, to a special training unit for trench raids. They weren't with us at the Belgian Chateau or Camp B, but at a separate camp with other scouts. They were taught the unique skills of cutting barbed wire, compass reading, bombing and night navigation. The brigade CO had given them plans to conduct a trench raid in our area of the front line. One of the Wonkys had requested Farq as a teammate. They thought that Elmer was too large for this kind of assignment. Stealth was the primary requirement. As for me, they thought I was too slow. Elmer and I were terribly disappointed about missing out. Farq volunteered when he was asked by Lt. Thomson. I would not have had the courage for this kind of duty if I hadn't performed so well during the Hun attack. I felt confident in my ability to act under duress, and most important, kill, if necessary. My new attitude had come to me as a bit of a surprise. I very badly wanted to go on the mission.

I made a visit to Lt. Thomson's dugout and begged to be included in the raid. My argument was that my lack of speed wouldn't be a problem. The men would be crawling on their bellies, for the most part. I told him of my excellent musketry scores at Niagara and Bramshott. I was lucky.

One man had backed out and left an opening. Thomson let me in.

The raid would need twenty-four men and two officers. These men would be divided into four teams. Each team had one bomber who carried a sack of Mills bombs. The other men carried a few bombs in their pockets, as well as knives or bayonets stuffed into their puttees.

Our objective was to crawl across no man's land immediately after the Wonkys had marked out a route for us to follow. We would approach Fritz trench in absolute silence, and kill or capture as many Hun as possible in the few minutes that we were there. The bombers would be first ones in, and would unleash their Mills bombs to kill men and clear the trench. Then, the other men would enter the trench with their rifles and travel in both directions, shooting to kill as they went. When completed, we had to get back home quickly and safely and bring back as many of our dead or wounded as we could manage.

Our mission was set for the early morning of May 3rd. The moon did not rise that night until 0500 hours, which gave us good cover of darkness. There was light rain falling. The Wonkys went out first, at midnight, and were given until 0100 hours to establish a route across no man's land. At the same time, our section of twenty-four men moved up to the front line trench. We had blackened our faces to make them invisible in the dark. I was in Squad B, and we were commanded by Sgt.White, a Limey from the east end of London. He was a wiry little guy that everyone liked; always had a joke and a smoke. Our job was to carry rifles, and stand along the German parapet in case German reinforcements came along while the other squads were down in their trench.

Sgt. White gave us a briefing. "Silence is the key to our success, men. We have to get right under their noses to make this work. I am carrying a whistle. When you hear the whistle, it is time to get out of the trench and back to our side. If anyone is spotted before we get there, you have to open fire and make a retreat. We will get covering fire from our trench. Good luck and good hunting."

Farquhar was in Squad A, and they were the ones who would toss their grenades into the trench and then jump in immediately after. Squads C and D were to do the same thing, but to the right of us. At 0030 hours, we crawled out on our bellies into the wet mud of no man's land. As I crawled, my hands sunk into the mud. I could feel the moisture soaking into my khaki uniform. My rifle had to remain clean and dry; a huge challenge in itself. It was a necessity that the men make no sound. Rain drops trailed down my helmet, and dribbled to the ground in front of my face. We waited in the light drizzle until we got a flash signal from the Wonkys. Ahead of us in no man's land at 0120 hours, we finally saw the flash of light from the Wonkys, and we crawled up to the spot where they waited for us. Wonky1 would guide Squads A and B, while Wonky2 would guide Squads D and C to our right. We had to trust in their ability to find the way. As we began our slow crawl toward the Hun's trench, the Heinies sent up flares every few seconds and then fired some shots in hopes of hitting something. Each time a flare went up, we flattened, then lay still until the light faded. Among our obstacles were the dead Germans who still littered the battlefield. The corpses were giving off a pungent, nauseating odour of decay that made silence a challenge. The natural instinct was to retch or cough when you got a noseful. In some places, we brushed up against the dead as we crawled, and swarms of blowflies would fill the air. When a flare went up, we blended in with the dead and they became our allies. I felt horror seeing their grimaced faces near to mine. Occasionally a breeze would move their tunic lapels, giving us a ghostly fright. I felt as if they were saying, "Leave us in peace."

Just a little before 0200 hours, we were close enough to Fritz's trench to hear them talking and their boots squishing in the mud as they moved about. One time, when a flare went up, I saw a sentry about twenty feet from me. I heard him clear his throat and adjust his rifle. Fortunately, he didn't see me or hear me. I tried my best to breathe easy and silently. I found that it was challenging to control my breathing. Crazy thoughts were going through my head. I thought of my mother and father. I thought about them back in Aberdeen, getting the news of my death. I had to remind myself to breathe slowly.

We launched our attack at 0200 hours. I saw Farq throw his first bomb into the trench, and I heard the other bombs going off to our right. When the Germans launched their flares, the sky lit up like it was the middle of the day. The sentry who was nearby saw me get to my feet and raise my rifle. He fired a shot at me and missed. I squeezed the trigger and watched him fall. Our men were down in the trench and I could hear the exchange of shots and the explosion of bombs. I could not see any reinforcements moving up to challenge us. I could only wait and listen to the "whomps" of the bombs and the screams of death coming from the trench. Minutes later, Sgt. White blew his whistle to end the raid. I reached down into the trench with my hand to help pull our men back up and out. One OR was badly wounded and covered in blood. It took several attempts to pull him up. I saw Farquhar running down the trench toward me, blood on his blackened face. But my heart felt pure relief in just seeing him.

"Farq, let's go. Get the fuck out now! Come on, man!"

I reached down and pulled him up; he was the last one out of the trench. We turned and ran as fast as we could back toward our home base. It was very dark and uneven in no man's land. I caught my foot on something and went flying head first into the mud. Fortunately, the 58th was covering us with fire from our trench, keeping Fritz down. Farq came back for me, pulled me up to my feet, and back to the safety of our trench.

Sgt. White gathered us together and ordered a roll call. We accomplished our mission with two men killed and three men wounded. Our dead were not recovered. The wounded were stretchered back to a medical clearing station. It was now 0250 hours. The remaining team members were taken back to a support trench, fed and given a very large slug of rum. My nerves were jangled. I didn't know what day it was or where I was. I asked for another shot of rum. Farquhar saw me sitting on the fire step and sat down beside me.

"Are you OK, Jonny?"

"No, I'll never do that again!" I said, and offered Farq a nip of my rum.

"Thanks. " Farq took a sip. "I can't stop my heart from pounding in my chest. Look at my hands."

Farquhar's hands were shaking. "Farq, you're bleeding. Your face."

"It's just a scrape. Some shrapnel. I still have my eyes."

The Wonkys were in the trench, saw us and came over. Wonky1 put his arm across Farq's shoulders and asked, "Are you hurt?"

"No, not me. You laddies did a great job out there. I'm proud of you."

Wonky1 answered, "We just got you dere. You did de rest."

Wonky2 held out a piece of cloth for us to see. "What's that?" I asked.

"It's dere colours. Prussian Guards," Wonky2 answered.

"Where the hell did you get that?" I asked in utter astonishment.

"I took it from de dead in no man's land. I cut it off de uniform."

The Prussian Guards were an elite outfit; the best the Germans had to offer. It was always important to know who you were up against in the opposite trench. This Prussian shoulder patch was good information for the brass hats. It told us, the 58th, something else: that the Hun would only use an elite unit against an enemy they respected and feared.

"One more thing," I asked Wonky2, "Where did you get those new black boots?"

Wonky2 gave me a wry smile and said, "De same Heinie!"

The Wonkys were living up to the promise that they had showed us in Niagara. They would have been wasted, just holding rifles in a trench. They had reached a very high level of competence as guides and scouts. I was proud of them for becoming a very important cog in our unit. Infantrymen like that are hard to replace. They had come so far from those two skinny waifs that showed up in Niagara just a few months ago.

It took some time after the raid for me to come to terms with my own role in the attack. I was beginning to appreciate my own competence and skill set. I still carried doubts and fears about killing a man standing so close to me. I feared the nightmares that would inevitably come about lying with the dead in the mud in no man's land. I was searching, once again ,for that emotional vocabulary that I still didn't have.

A medic came by and insisted that Farq get his wound cleaned up and dressed, as it could easily get infected. He went with the medic to the dressing station, located in a support trench. Tomorrow, we would have to debrief with Sgt. White and Lt. Thomas. We didn't know the results of our mission and we would find out at the debrief. The

Wonkys shook my hand and moved off up the trench. They seemed very calm and collected when you consider what they had been through.

The rain continued to come down on us, turning the trenches into streams. In some places, the duckboards were actually floating. We had to stay on the fire step to keep our feet dry. There was a gas alert early in the afternoon, but it was cancelled later towards sunset. At 2030 hours, we felt the ground shock of a mine explosion, to our left. At dark, Farquhar and I went back to the support trenches to try to get some sleep. It was there that we met Elmer.

"Shite, Farq. What happened to your head?"

"I took some shrapnel. It's not deep. No damage."

Elmer was happy to see us safe and sound, and was curious about what we had experienced. He asked us what we saw and if we got any kills. Farq answered first, "I know I killed a few when I tossed the bombs. The trench was pretty full when I got in. We may have arrived during a duty relief."

Then it was my turn. "A sentry was in front of me. He fired first and missed. I fired and got him. Shite, it happened so fast. I'm pretty sure he was dead."

Elmer's reaction was mixed. It seemed like he was sorry that he wasn't there, but he didn't get exuberant over the kills. He seemed a little tentative about the idea of taking a life, particularly at close quarters. I could empathize with him.

"Nice shooting, Jonny. I'm happy that he didn't get you first. You were pretty close to him, eh?"

"Aye, too bloody close!"

"You will get your chance soon enough," Farq said." You can count on it. That was only a warm up. We'll see some heavy action pretty soon."

Over the next three days, the weather was variable. Life was kept interesting by gas alerts, shelling and work parties. Our company CO, Lt. Thomson, was wounded by a rifle grenade that landed near him in the Gourock Rd. trench. The British troops who had been in these trenches before us gave them street names to identify them. Thomson was sent to the back of the lines for treatment. Right up to May 7th, our battalion suffered further losses of life and woundings; Capt. McNair and eight ORs were killed, fourteen men were wounded and six were victims of shell shock. That night, we were relieved by the 4th Canadian Mounted Rifles, and we arrived back in Camp D, our favourite camp, at 0600 hours. Camp D meant baths and a cinema.

The cold, wet, blustery weather returned and we spent the whole day resting and regrouping. That afternoon, the three Macs received a visit from Capt. McKeand.

"At ease, men. Pte. McLennan, how is your wound?"

Farquhar was surprised to be addressed directly. "My wound is nothing, really; a couple of scratches from bomb shrapnel. Just superficial, sir." Farquhar had a bandage wrapped around his head.

"Lt. Col. Genet sent me here to tell you that he wants to meet with you in his quarters at 1600 hours. All three of you. See you there."

With that, McKeand moved on to the other dugouts. We looked at each other, wondering what the meeting was for.

"Football," said Farq. "He wants to talk football, just like at Paradise Camp."

We arrived at Genet's quarters at 1600 hours, as ordered. McKeand was there, as promised, and ushered us into Genet's "office". The office was a very large dugout with sandbag reinforced walls, a desk, lights, telephone for communication, table and chairs, and a cot; luxurious by our standards.

Genet greeted us, "Come in gentlemen. I just want to talk a little football with you."

Farq gave us a knowing grin.

"I wanted to mention that we have arranged for the rubber match with the 35th on May 12. Pte. McLennan, because we no longer have "Tout" Leckie with us, Sgt. Shepherd wants to adjust your position. You need to talk to him about it tomorrow. We will arrange some practice time for the team. That will give us some advantage because the 35th will have no time to practice. McKordick is already complaining about it. How is your wound? ?Will it affect your game?"

"My wound is not really a wound, sir. My game won't be affected," Farq informed him.

"That happened in a trench raid, I understand," Genet said.

"Yes, sir. Shrapnel from my own bomb. We were in close quarters."

Genet had not paid any attention to Elmer and me. He seemed only concerned about Farquhar's health. Elmer looked over at me and winked. We knew that if Farquhar's injury was serious, the 58th would be sunk. That was Genet's nightmare. We couldn't lose Farq and "Tout" Leckie and still have any hope of beating the 35th.

Genet continued, "I don't want you three, or any other team members, volunteering for trench raids. Is that clear?"

"Yes, sir," we answered together. Something struck me as different from our first meeting with Genet, back at Paradise Camp. The three of us were not as diminished by the aura of power in Genet's presence as our Commanding Officer. The difference was that we now had ten months of training and constantly living in the shadow of death. We had leverage in Genet's desire to succeed in the sport of football as much as on the field of battle. There was some room for negotiation.

I decided to make a bid. "Col. Genet, I would like to add something, if I may."

"Go ahead, Private."

"The team, sir, your team, wants equal treatment with the rest of the men. No special treatment, sir."

"I'm not sure I know what you mean, Private."

Farquhar cut in, "Well sir, the use of officers' quarters and showers, and the food and drinks after games. The other men see that as a little excessive. Also, they see us getting time off from work parties to practice football."

"I see. I certainly don't see that as excessive treatment. I think it is earned on your part. What do they say to you?"

Farq answered, "They have said nothing. We can see it and feel it."

"And if we defeat the 35th, you want no celebration?"

Elmer took his turn. "Only if the whole battalion can join in, sir."

"I see." Genet paused for a few seconds to think. "Perhaps you are correct. If we are the victors in the rubber match, I will order food and drink for all. It will be great for morale. We have suffered some terrible losses in battle. Good, then. Is there anything else?"

"No sir."

Genet finished up, "Get some rest. I want you three ready for McKordick. And don't ever think that I take this command lightly. Every time that I receive a mortality or injury report from the adjutant, I feel the pain in my heart. All the men in this battalion are important to me, not just the team. You are dismissed."

We gave the salute and headed back toward our dugouts. Farquhar asked, "Do you think he will be good for his word?"

Thinking of our leverage, I answered, "I am pretty sure he will, Farq. He thinks this war is going to end soon, and he can get back to his civilian life, make money and play football. I believe that he does care for all the men, not just the team."

Elmer said what was on his mind. "I'm not so sure about that, Jonny. He is one of those chaps who flies through life without a scratch. He gets what he wants and he will do anything to get it."

"I agree with Elmer!" Farq said. "He is pulling the strings and we are on one end of them, the bottom end. That is how the world was, and how the world shall ever be."

Our next day brought two significant events. We had bath parade in the morning to get rid of all those little buggers that inhabited every nook and cranny on our tired bodies, and we were inspected by the acting Brigadier of the 9th Brigade, Lt. Col. Thompson. There was no shelling or aeroplanes to threaten us for a whole day.

May 12th arrived cloudy, but warm. We were interrupted by a gas alert at 0530 hours and had to don our gas helmets, which made eating breakfast a challenge. We had to pull the face mask up in order to get food into our mouths. More than a few men ended up with food and drink spilled on the front of their tunics and pants. Fortunately, the gas alert was cancelled at 1240 hours.

The 35th arrived at Camp D at 1300 hours. The big game was set to start at 1400 hours. McKordick, as usual, arrived in his big staff auto. The two teams headed into the officers' quarters to change into their football gear. When we came face to face with our opponents, we were shocked. Some of their best players were absent.

Our right forward, Bill Prosser, asked them, "Where are Flynn, McCain and Bonnell?"

Their team captain, John McMullan, answered, "Flynn was killed in action, McCain is missing and Bonnell lost a leg to a trench mortar. Where is Leckie?"

"Killed in action. Direct hit from a 5.9 inch h.e.," Prosser answered.

McMullan continued, "He was a good one. Your team will miss him terribly. When we lost our men, McKordick was devastated, as we all were devastated. They were three of our best. I think you will destroy us today. Some of us didn't even want to come. That's the way it goes. Nobody knows when it will be their turn. It happens in a flash of light and sound, like a lightning bolt from the sky, except it comes from the barrel of a Howitzer."

Farq spoke up, "Shite lads, we are so sorry for your losses. They were good men. Let's just play our game to honour our dead. And we will play for ourselves too. We could all be dead tomorrow."

"Farq, we will give our best if you give us yours," McMullan answered.

"Aye, we will." The two shook hands, and both teams raised a cheer in solidarity.

Both teams finished getting dressed and then headed out to the pitch. It was in much better condition than it was for the last game. The water had drained well and the field was firm. Speed was going to be a factor this day. The battalions had taken their positions on each side of the field, and the insults were being exchanged before the game had started. McKordick and Genet were in their seats with their shared refreshments. I couldn't see the usual blustery intensity in their gestures. The losses on both sides had dulled the rivalry between them.

Sgt. Shepherd spoke to us before the kickoff.

"I am aware of the losses their team has taken. Their coach told me that they were a bit demoralized and broken.

He assured me that they would give it their best. I told him that we would do the same. No pulled punches. Let's show our respect."

From the opening kick, it was evident that the 35th were the lesser team. The replacement players brought in to fill the shoes of the lost men were not of equal caliber. It took slightly less than five minutes for Farquhar to score. For most of the first half, the play remained in the 35th's end of the pitch. Only some spectacular saves by their goalkeeper kept the game close.

It was heartbreaking to see a team that was once our equal, or better, so diminished. We vowed to play at our best level, because if the circumstances were reversed, they would have done the same. It was the best way to honour the missing players.

Shepherd spoke to us at the half.

"I am proud of your game today. They are a great team and a great battalion. They don't want mercy, so keep your intensity at the highest level. Play your game as if it were your last. I know that those three chaps and "Tout" are watching you play."

The second half started with the 35th putting some pressure on our defensive backs. They worked the ball in close for two excellent scoring opportunities. Their centre striker laid a bullet shot along the ground that hit our left goalpost. The rebound shot right back out to their right forward, who tried to place a shot high into the top right corner. I managed to get enough of my hand on the ball to deflect it over the net. I think the fact that they failed to tie the game at that point took some of the wind out of their sails. From that point on, we took the game to them and forced them to play most of the game on their side of centre.

Farquhar was playing at centre forward, rather than centre midfield. He carried the ball less, but was in good scoring position many times. He scored his second goal at the 74th minute. It was a beauty. Art Prosser sent him a crossing pass and Farq headed it in. The 58th was up two to nil. We scored one more goal, just before full-time, to make the game three to nil. When the final whistle blew, there were no jubilant celebrations from the 58th. Both teams met at centre field and shook hands. The spectators flowed out onto the field to congratulate the two teams. In a demonstration of class and respect, Col. Genet fittingly returned the championship banner to the 35th team captain. Then he had four casks of rum brought onto the pitch and set up on tables.

The Colonel got up on one of the tables and addressed the two battalions.

"Soldiers of the 35th and 58th Battalions." He had to shout in order to be heard. Someone handed him a bullhorn. "Soldiers of the 35th and 58th. In honour of the men who have been lost to both battalions, I want to share a drink and a toast. Please form into company lines and we will distribute the rum to everyone. Congratulations to these two splendid teams and their coaches. Drink up!"

There was mayhem at first, but everyone organized into their companies and formed lines. We were happy that Genet had kept his promise. I looked for Elmer and Farq. I found them, surrounded by a mob of spectators at least five deep.

Elmer saw me first.

"Hey, Jonny, great game. Lovely save on that high shot. I thought he had you beat."

With that, several soldiers whacked me on the back to congratulate me. I worked my way through the crowd to be closer to Farq and Elmer.

I caught Farq's eye. "Good game, ya scunner. Loved that header."

"Thanks. Nice save on the high one, Jonny-boy. Where would we be without you, you old jobby?"

"I got lucky. Hey, Genet kept his word."

"I figured he would. We didn't give him much choice."

Elmer cut in, "Yeah, but I didn't expect him to serve both battalions."

"I'm happy he did. Nice touch for everyone," I added.

"Maybe I judged him too harshly," Farquhar said.

All of the 58th was aware it was a hollow victory. We were all deeply hurt when we lost friends and mates in the trenches. The rivalry between the 58th and the 35th was dead. We had common goals now, and we were no longer squabbling over trophies and banners at Paradise Camp. That seemed such a long time ago. The journey into Armageddon, the most uncivilized place on our planet, had changed us into something different. We were no longer the boys of football fields, church parades, pretty girls, and afternoon picnics. That was just a dream. War had taken us in a different direction, where we were capable of creating our own horrors, horrors for King and country. And in a war with no end in sight, things could only get worse.

Chapter 18
The Red Dragon

The day after the match with the 35th was quiet. We attended our morning church parade and then the "cinema", in the afternoon. At the cinema, we were treated to some movies about recruitment back home and also to some newsreels. It was a treat to be out of our dugouts because the weather was actually warm and pleasant. The time out of the trenches had been beneficial to the battalion, giving us a chance to heal our wounds and regain our strength. I had a chance to remove my boots and socks. This pair of socks had been plastered to my feet for weeks. I couldn't remove them in the normal manner; I had to shred them to get them off.

Orders came the next day, for us to leave this camp and march to Camp E in Brigade reserve. We were on two hours' notice, meaning if we were called to the front lines, we had to be ready in two hours to move out. Our time was taken up by physical, squad and company drills. Over the next two days, we were visited by enemy aircraft, but we managed to drive them away with ground fire from our Lewis machine guns and anti-aircraft guns. One of our planes plummeted down to earth, the result of engine failure. Sgt. Carley visited our company and D Company for rifle inspection. He was a perfectionist, and any little piece of fluff or dust found on a rifle resulted in a dramatic dressing down.

"Soldier, what is this crap that I am eyeballing right now? Did you eat your lunch while you cleaned your rifle? Is that a piece of bully beef that I am looking at?"

"N ... No, sir!"

"You have exactly ten seconds to get that mess cleaned up! Is that clear?"

"Yes, sir!"

"Let me see that weapon." Carley peers down the barrel and inspects the breech with one eye open and one eye closed. His eyebrows say more than most people can say with words. His targeted soldier is holding his breath.

"Catch!" He tosses the rifle back to its owner.

"Don't let me find you hiding your lunch in that piece, again! Am I clear, soldier?"

"Y ... Yes sir!"

When Carley finished, everyone took a deep breath. Our weapons were more valuable than any gems on planet Earth. Our lives and our mates' lives depended on them. No excuses were accepted for anything less than perfect.

We provided work parties of about 200 ORs each night. No casualties were reported, and we were not shelled during this time. The lull helped our hearing return to something near normal. It was a pleasure not having to shout at someone to be heard. Time was allotted to sterilize all of our water bottles and mess tins. It was not difficult to contract some kind of filthy disease in trench warfare. The rats contaminated much of our equipment with their excrement, as did the lice on our bodies. Men were constantly being treated for fevers of all sorts. Any effort to keep our utensils clean was essential.

One day, I got matched up with Privates Waldron and Jessop on a work party to the hamlet of Hooge, on the Menin Road. It would take us closer to the front lines. We were ordered to move some small arms ammunition up to the units there. The party consisted of two hundred ORs and eight officers. We started out just after dusk. It made me happy to be with those two soldiers again. It was a nice change from Farq and Elmer.

"Hey Jonny, we haven't seen you since the big football match. How are you keeping?" Waldron asked as we set out for Hooge.

"Hi, David. I am getting used to this place. How about you?"

"I'll never get used to this place; too many shells flying around here. Every kind: Jack Johnsons, coal boxes, whiz-bangs and h.e. sausages. Those fucking Johnsons are as big as a lorrie, and they can blow a hole the size of a village in a target or vaporize a whole platoon. What can I say? You gotta keep your head down or lose it."

Jessop spoke up, "I heard you went on a trench raid."

"That was the craziest thing I have ever done; nose to nose with Fritz. I am glad we got back in one piece. Not all of us made it back though. We lost two men."

The three of us compared our notes on close calls and shooting prowess as we carried our loads of ammunition through the communication trench towards Hooge. The route was in rough shape due to the constant pounding from German artillery. About one hour into our trip, we heard some gunfire in the east, followed very quickly by the shriek of approaching shells. We had been spotted.

The first shells went over our heads, and exploded about one hundred yards behind us. We dropped our loads and lay down flat in the wet trench, for cover. The next volley also went over us, but not quite as far. Fritz was trying to get his range. They must have had a spotter who could see us, and was directing the fire. The third volley was too close for comfort, and we had to abandon our mission. Our CO ordered us to turn back for Camp E. Waldron was in front of me and Jessop was behind. It was almost impossible to move quickly through the trench, but we had no choice, and we had to try.

The next barrage was, unfortunately, on target, and I could hear the eerie whine of an approaching shell. All I could do was brace myself for the force of an explosion. The impact was only yards behind us. The force of the blast blew me face first onto the ground, and covered me with heavy mud. Wet dirt filled my mouth and nostrils. I felt like I was drowning as I gasped for breath under the weight of the wet soil. I could feel the mass compressing me and my struggling lungs. Within a matter of seconds, I could hear someone above digging me out of my tomb. It was Waldron. Using his hands, he scooped the mud away from my face so that I could breathe. Someone else appeared on the scene with a shovel, and dug away the muck covering my limbs and body. The two men pulled me to my feet. My mouth was full of gritty clay and I tried to spit it all out, but with little success.

"Where's Jessop? He was right behind me," I sputtered.

We looked around and all we could see was mounds of mud and rising grey smoke. The darkness made it impossible to make out any details. As we groped around, we heard a muffled voice. It was close to us and under the debris. We listened for a bit, and heard it again. Waldron used his shovel to move some lumps of mud and prod around.

The shovel hit something solid and we began to dig feverishly. Within seconds, the mud covering Jessop's face was removed, allowing him to gulp deep breaths of air. The two of us grabbed his hands and feet and pulled him clear. He was conscious but disoriented.

Waldron said, "Art, it's me, David. You're safe, we have you."

Jessop was incapable of answering. We pulled him off the ground to his feet and supported him, me on the left and Waldron on the right. Because the trench was narrow, moving him back down to safety was a slippery, arduous trial. The big guns were still after us, and we needed to get out immediately. Another OR lit his torch to give some light in the trench. Several other soldiers joined us in carrying Jessop back to camp. We focused intently on every step and tried to ignore the shells that were exploding around us. I have no idea how long we took, but we eventually arrived safely back at camp with Jessop.

When we arrived, Waldron, Jessop and I were stretchered to a dressing station nearby. The battalion doctor, Capt. Cosbie, was called to look after us. His priority was Jessop, who was now more attentive and talking. The doctor took half an hour to look him over, and then declared him fit to return to duty. I was next, and it was obvious now that I didn't have any serious injuries. I told Cosbie what had happened back in the trench.

"Sir, a fucking large high explosive shell burst in the trench behind us. Obviously, it was far enough behind us that we didn't get vaporized. But we did get buried."

"I have seen a lot of this, Private. You wouldn't believe it. The only thing that saved you and Jessop was the mud. When the ground is soft, the shells penetrate deeply into it. You were hit by mud and debris instead of shrapnel. You are damn lucky men. I suspect that you two have concussions.

Take it easy for a few days on light duty. We will get you some clean uniforms."

Cosbie looked briefly at Waldron, and then told us to stay in the station until daylight. Word had got around camp about our adventure, and so we were greeted in the morning by a large contingent of our mates, who were happy to see us in one piece. Our mission was lost but we lived to tell about it. Now we needed some sleep and recovery time.

During that day, Waldron, Jessop and I were given kitchen duty instead of field drills. We were given the job of cleaning the empty food tins that were returned from the trenches. Our duties allowed us an opportunity to talk about our close brush with death. It instantly became clear that Jessop remembered none of it.

"I heard nothing and I was in total darkness. I only remember gasping for air and having my mouth full of mud. I don't remember anything about how I even got there."

I told them, "I am sure that I heard the shell coming. Pretty sure it was a 5.9 inch."

"Someone was looking after us out there," Waldron said.

"What do you mean?" I asked.

"Well, I mean that we should be dead. Maybe God was with us," Waldron answered.

"I don't know how I feel about that, David. Why did God put us out there in the first place? Or in this muddy hell-hole they call Flanders?"

Jessop stepped in, "I think God is with us here. We are doing His bidding. Fritz needs to be stopped from destroying all of Europe."

"This is a holy war?" I asked.

Jessop answered, "Yeah, I think so."

Our friend, Lenny, was nearby, and walked over to join the conversation. "I think if this was a holy war, God would end it Himself. He would send a plague or something."

I asked Jessop if he went to church back home. "Every week. Anglican. I was confirmed when I was twelve. Sang in the choir, at both the eleven o'clock service and at evensong."

Lenny said, "I'm R.C., but I never went to church. I only go to church parade here at camp."

I was still unsure of how God could take sides. "I don't think Heinie is evil, Art. How is he different than us?" I thought I was starting to sound like Farquhar. "They have mothers and fathers, sisters and brothers, just like us. They bleed the same crimson red that we do. I have taken lives here and I don't feel that God is guiding my bullets. If anything is true, He is sickened by this horror."

Before Jessop could answer, we were joined by another soldier from the field kitchen. He was a Lance Corporal, John Steckley, famous in the 58th for being the oldest recruit. Someone in Attestation, back at Niagara, had leaked that information to the men in the battalion; but not his age. We claimed that he was sixty years old, but he wouldn't agree.

"Not a day over forty!" he would reply.

When he came to Niagara, Steckley had a huge bushy black beard, speckled and streaked with grey. There was no hair on the top of his head, but it flowed out at the sides down to his collar. He looked like a big old lumberjack, but he cried when they cut his hair at Paradise Camp. To this day, he avoids haircuts, and still gets away with having the longest hair in the battalion. Not down to his collar, but bushing out from underneath his helmet.

"I heard you fellas talkin' about religion and such, here. Thought I might put in my two bits worth."

"Yeah, go ahead, John," somebody said.

"I think that we are heading for the Armageddon, the end of the world. It's in the last book of the Bible."

"Revelation," someone said.

"Yeah, that one. There is a story about the Red Dragon. My grandmother used to read the Bible to me every night, before bed. I always remembered the story of the Red Dragon. It starts out with the vision of a young woman who wears a crown of twelve stars. The moon is beneath her feet as she descends from the sky. She is pregnant and about to give birth. As the child is being born, another vision appears from the sky. It is a huge red dragon that has, I think, ten heads and seven horns. The dragon is on a mission to kill the newborn child, but just as it is about to strike, an army of angels appears to battle it. Eventually, the angels are able to defeat the dragon and save the child."

I thought for a second or two about Steckley's story. "Are you saying that the Hun is the Red Dragon, John?"

"I admit, that at first, that is what I thought. But then I remembered what my grandmother said about the story. She said that the Red Dragon represents a vision of the destruction of our children, our future. I think that the dragon is this damn never-ending war. When we are on the verge of destroying our future, God will send his angels to save us."

Jessop spoke up, "I know that story, too. I never thought of it that way, John. I never figured that this would be the last war, the end of times. That's too bloody scary!"

Lenny was next to speak. "Are you saying we are all, both Germans and Canadians, going to die?"

"That's about it!" Steckley proclaimed. "Then God will send His Son to take all of us to Heaven. That's the way my grandmother saw it. I think she's right."

I couldn't stay quiet. "Shite, John! That is so bleak. I can't go along with that. We might as well throw down our rifles and walk out into no man's land if we are all going to die anyway."

We all stood and looked at each other without saying a word. Everyone had a different way of looking at the morality of this war. Who is to say that Steckley was wrong? When you really thought about it, this war was absolutely insane. One man got assassinated in Serbia, two royal cousins couldn't get along and, all of a sudden, young men from all parts of this world were being blown to bits in the muddy fields of France, Belgium and Gallipoli. We fought over forty yards of bloodstained soil. This was not a war of God, or gods. I thought Farquhar was closer to the answer than anybody. This was a disagreement among the privileged, the noble class, and about using the young men of lesser pedigree to make the bloody sacrifice. It was the mothers of these young men who wore the crown with twelve stars, the crown of grief. The dragon was the colour of the blood that the men spilled onto the ground; this sacred ground. Enough said. We all, then, returned to our kitchen duties.

News got out that two of our NCOs, Sgt Major Drysdale and Sgt. Clayton, had been subjected to a court-martial, for drunkenness. The three Macs had a few pints with these guys back in Niagara. It seemed shameful for any man to be reprimanded for drunkenness in these conditions. We all should have been drunk. Both sides. What sober man could put up with this life? They were found guilty, detained for two days, and then did a week of latrine duty.

Our time at Camp D was topped off with bath parades by the company in the evening. It had been a while since our last bath, and it felt wonderful to get those fleas and lice off of our bodies. Shortly after our baths, we were informed that we would be relieving the 43rd Battalion in the frontline left sub-sector of the right sector that night. I was told to report to Lt. Thomson at 2200 hours.

I met up with Farquhar and Elmer at mess. They too, had been told to meet with Lt. Thomson.

Farq asked, "What do you think he wants?"

"God only knows!" I answered.

Elmer had the answer. "He wants to give us all clean uniforms, just like Jonny's."

Farquhar replied, "You know where they got his clean uniform, don't ya? From some poor dead chap."

"Well, he wouldn't be needing it, any more would he?" was all I could reply.

At 2200 hours, we reported to Lt. Thomson's dugout. The lieutenant had his left arm in a sling as a result of the rifle-grenade attack. Much to my surprise, the other members of the battalion football team were called to the meeting, too. Thomson addressed us.

"Gentlemen, I have been asked by Lt. Col. Genet to give you some news. We are reorganizing some of the platoons. You have been withdrawn from your platoons, and are now attached to Number Four Platoon, A Company. Your platoon will remain in the support trenches with the kitchen wagons. Any questions?"

None of us could say a word. We were stunned. I couldn't believe what was happening. The team was being sheltered from frontline duty. It was so obvious. Lenny was right all along. Genet was going to protect us, keep us out of action.

"Report to Sgt. Wilson of A Company immediately, for your orders. Good luck."

On our way back with the team to report, I could see that Farq was livid.

"Fucking cludgies! He's doing it! I'm out!"

"What do you mean, you're 'out'?" I asked.

"I won't play football. That's it! I won't play!"

We all stopped walking, and turned to face Farq. This was a chance for the team to talk it out before we reported to Sgt. Wilson.

"Farq, are you quitting on us?" Elmer asked.

"Wait, wait. Let's talk about this, eh?" Billy Prosser added. "If Farq quits ... I quit! I think all of us quit!"

All the other players made the vow, too. Billy was a senior member of Genet's team, back in Brantford. After "Tout" was killed, Billy became the captain of the team. His opinion carried weight with the men.

Billy continued, "We are all in this together. We're a team, and we've been through a lot of good and a lot of shit together. For now, I think we should report for kitchen duty and avoid being disciplined. Are we all in this?"

The players were in total agreement. Genet's hand-built team would cease to exist. The strings would be cut. We agreed to talk with Sgt. Shepherd about discipline because we were unsure of what, if any, repercussions there would be for refusing to play football. Farquhar summed it all up for the team.

"I have no objections to doing kitchen duty, it is not beneath me. Shite, I'm a baker. But I object to being taken out of the fucking line of fire with my mates in the 58th. This is not about me and it is not about football. It's about standing with the battalion as a team of one fucking thousand. I am willing to lay down my life for any man who fights beside me."

Billy shouted, "We are great, 58!", and the team picked it up, in repetition.

"We are great, 58!"

The players split up and went their separate ways to the dugouts to collect their gear and report to Sgt. Wilson of A Company. Wilson was a soft-spoken Scot with plenty of war experience. He had seen some action with the 1st

Division, the previous year in the Ypres Salient. He had taken some shrapnel in his left arm, and had been hospitalized in France. After his recovery, he was assigned to the 58th. He never regained full use of his left arm. We met up with him at his dugout, where he welcomed us to our new platoon. At midnight, Platoon 4, A Company made its way, with the help of a scout, to our home in the field kitchen enclosure. Lenny was already there to meet us.

"Jonny, what are you doing here? You loved it that much, eh?" he said, with a grin.

"Oh, I loved it. Couldn't you tell? These are my new chums, Number Four Platoon."

Lenny gave us the once-over and said, "And the whole football team too, eh?"

"Long story, Lenny. I'll fill you in later."

Lenny said to the platoon, "Welcome to the Sanctuary Wood Ritz; only the finest food and the finest service. My name is Pte. Long. Call me Lenny. I'll show you where your dugouts are, and you can stow your gear there."

The rest of the battalion was in The Front, in an area called Sanctuary Wood. Our outdoor kitchen was about half a mile behind them. Our job would be to prepare the food, put it into tins and deliver to the men in the front lines. This was not a job without danger. If Fritz could locate us, he would surely try to snuff out our stove fires. If he could figure out our supper time routine, he might try to disrupt it.

Our first day on the job was eventful. The air was warm at sunrise and the Germans started their day by shelling the nearby Cumberland dugouts with 5.9s high explosives. The dugouts were about half a mile behind us, in the kitchen. The shells passing overhead made us very nervous and hesitant to head up the communication trenches with the rations. If Genet wanted the team out of danger, then he didn't pick a very safe assignment for us. Anyway, the men needed to be fed, so we began our hike up the trenches to The Front with the food. Breakfast was served successfully, along with the usual panache, no food dropped on the ground or wrong turns in the trench system.

The shelling stopped around 1130 hours, and allowed us the opportunity to settle our nerves. The afternoon remained quiet, and we had a visit from Sgt. Shepherd, the team coach. Sgt. Wilson was with him, and we used our time to talk to them about our dilemma. Farquhar started the conversation with Shepherd.

"Sir, we, the team, would like to talk to you about a problem we have."

"Go ahead, Private. I'm all ears."

"Sir, we are fully aware that Col. Genet manipulated some of the platoons to put the team all together in one platoon and behind the lines. He did that to keep us out of the line of fire."

Shepherd responded, "Well, yes, the Colonel spoke to me about it. Based on today's fireworks, he could have picked a better location."

Sgt. Wilson joined in, "Do you men want to be moved further back?"

"No, no!" Farq answered. "Just the opposite. We want to be back in the front lines with our other platoon mates, in our original platoons. We want to fight Fritz, not cook pancakes."

"The 'old man' will have none of that. Forget it!" Shepherd said back.

Billy Prosser joined the conversation. "Sir, the team has decided to disband if Genet doesn't move us. We are all in this together."

Then Elmer spoke, "Sir, can we be charged with insubordination if we refuse to play football?"

Sgt. Wilson answered, "I don't think so. You could always claim that you were too injured to play."

Farquhar got back in, "The Colonel thinks this war will be over soon, and he will be back in Brantford with his business and his Division One team. *He won't have this Division One team if he doesn't listen to us.*"

"You are venturing into tricky waters here, Private, and I don't think you can win this. These are not normal times. Genet has life and death power here in the battlefield. He can court-martial you and put you in front of a firing squad and you will have no recourse. Maybe you should rethink this."

"We are all in this together, and we are determined. Can you speak to the Colonel on our behalf? Maybe set up a meeting with him?"

"Well, I can try that, if you want. I don't like your chances, but I will see him in a couple of days. Hold tight until then and we will see what happens."

The day finished with more shelling from Fritz, from 1930 to 2030 hours. Little damage was done to our trenches and dugouts. The night was quiet, and we managed to sleep well.

The next day dawned warm and dull, with Fritz waking us up at 0530 hours by shelling Vigo St. trench and trench 59, both at The Front, with 77 mm shells. Little damage resulted, but this time we retaliated with our field artillery heavies and trench mortar bombs. The reply caused Fritz to shut the fuck up. One for our side! Shite, I loved it when we hit them back harder than they hit us. It actually made life in the trenches worthwhile.

The following morning brought more shelling at 0500 hours; never a good way for us to start the day. They hit us again with 5.9s and 77s. We lost two more men to this barrage. Like the day before, we retaliated with our field artillery to close out the action. Several men were wounded and some suffered from shell shock. The next four days were a repeat of the same. Several tons of shells were traded, and several men paid the ultimate price for the madness.

While this was going on, the weather changed. The dry spell came to an end, and cool, wet weather moved in. Our clothes and gear had just dried out, only to get soaked right through to our bones again. We could never get warm when we were so wet. We shivered constantly, and only standing near the cooking stoves warmed us up.

On the last day of May, we were relieved by the First CMR (Canadian Mounted Rifles) Battalion, and we proceeded back to Camp C. Our relief was completed at 0230 hours, but we lost three ORs and seven were wounded on the journey. The rain had stopped and the air was warm, allowing us a chance to rest and get dry. We spent all of the first day of June resting and regrouping. We had been promised a bath day on the second of June, something we had been dreaming about for a while. The lice were eating us alive, and everyone was eager to bathe and de-louse their uniforms. Morale, though, remained very high.

Unfortunately, things don't always go as planned. June 2nd bloomed warm and bright, but shortly after breakfast, at around 1000 hours, we were ordered to 'stand to' and were put on one hour's notice to move out. Something was happening at the front lines. We could hear the rumble of heavy artillery and exploding mines, but we didn't yet know any details of the action.

At 1400 hours, we were put on one half-hour's notice. The sound of the artillery was still shaking the ground, and now we could see great volumes of smoke rising into the sky, obscuring the sun. At 1500 hours, we were ordered to 'stand to' and be ready to move at once. Nobody was thinking of bathing or de-lousing now. My heart was beating out of my chest and my palms were sweaty. Damn, it's the start of the Apocalypse and we were going to meet the Red Dragon and our Maker.

By 1600 hours, word had filtered back to us that Heinie had launched a major offensive in a line from Hooge in the north, down to Mount Sorrel in the south; a distance of about two miles. Their artillery had driven our men back from their trenches, a distance of up to five hundred yards. The First CMRs had been right in the centre of this attack at Observatory Ridge, and had suffered heavy casualties. We were fortunate to have been relieved one day before the attack occurred.

I had an opportunity to talk to Farquhar and Elmer.

"*Away an boil yer heed!* All hell has broken loose in our old trench. Fritz has gone insane and blown everything up. *Scunners!*" I yelled, in anger.

"Good thing we got our arses out of there when we did. Shite!" said Elmer.

Farquhar spoke. "It sounds like they blew a few mines under us. Looks like we might be called for stretcher duty. Fuck, I want at them!"

No sooner than Farquhar had spoken those words, orders came through for us to move to Camp F immediately. It was difficult to figure what the plans were for our battalion. We moved to Camp F as quickly as we could, and arrived at 1745 hours. As soon as we put our gear on the ground, we were ordered to the Belgian Chateau. When we arrived there, we took up positions in the trenches to the west of Kruistraat Rd. At 2130 hours, we were ordered to the Ypres Ramparts. We made our destination at 0230, and we were put under the orders of the 7th Canadian Infantry Brigade.

By this time, the big guns had gone silent. We had no idea how bad the situation was. The silence was more frightening than the fury of the guns. Word came back to us that

Fritz had taken our trenches in Sanctuary Wood, Hill 62, Observatory Ridge and Mount Sorrel. They had basically taken a big bite out of the Salient. We had lost two field guns in the battle, and the PPCLI (Princess Patricia's Canadian Light Infantry) and the First CMRs had been badly chewed up. We generally expected that there would be an attempt to recover the lost territory with a counter-attack as soon as possible.

As our platoon was getting into our dugouts for sleep, Capt. McKeand appeared out of nowhere.

"As you are, soldiers. Get the team together and come with me," he said, as he lit his torch.

We immediately left our dugouts and followed McKeand through the dark, and back into the ruins of Ypres. The streets were strewn with the crumbled remnants of buildings, and we had to be careful as we picked our way through. He led us to the bombed out shell of a hotel and we descended a short stairway into the darkened basement. There were bricks, glass and beams scattered over the floor. McKeand led us to a room at the back of the basement. He knocked on an old wooden door, and we heard a voice from inside the room. It was Genet.

"Come in."

McKeand pushed the heavy door open and a rectangle of light appeared on the floor in front of us. He stepped into the room, snapped his heels to attention and saluted.

"Sir! I have the team," he said.

"Bring them in, Captain."

There were fifteen of us to squeeze into the room. We stood to attention and saluted. It was not a large room, and we filled up all of the vacant space. Genet was seated behind an old table that had been set up as his desk, and was reading some papers in front of him. There was only one lamp in the room on a shelf behind him. It cast our long shadows on the wall behind us. Sgt. Shepherd was standing off to the side, behind the table. This is where Genet had set up his temporary headquarters.

Genet took his time, and then lifted his head and spoke from behind the table.

"Welcome men, to my humble office. You are probably wondering why I would call you here on such short notice. You know that the Hun has dealt the Canadian Corps a very bloody black eye. We have been pushed out of our trenches, and have suffered some heavy losses. We are currently preparing to retaliate, and get our trenches back. The fact is we have to move quickly. Sgt. Shepherd filled me in on the conversation you had with him the other day. He informed me that you would disband the team unless you were put back in the front line trenches. Is that correct?"

Billy Prosser answered, "Yes sir! We do not want to be segregated from our normal platoons."

"You want to fight? Is that correct?"

"Yes sir. That is what we signed up for," Billy replied.

"I admire your courage and conviction, but I have very little time to deal with these matters right now. You are aware of how much this team means to me and to the entire Battalion. I thought you would appreciate the chance to work in a safer environment. A battalion has to eat if it wants to win. There is no shame in kitchen and rations duty. We all can't be 'strikers', can we? Somebody has to keep the ball out of our net. I think I have a solution for the problem that will make us all happy. The 3rd Battalion has requested two platoons for attachment in the far right sector, down on the far side of Mount Sorrel. There is a frontline sub sector that needs to be manned for a few days while we plan our counter attack, and I can assign you and the third platoon to that area. The team will remain as part of the fourth platoon, A Company. I am sending Sgt. Shepherd to command your platoon. You will come under the command of the 3rd Division. Are there any questions?"

Elmer had one, "Will we see any action, Sir?"

"Probably not much, Private, but you never know. Any other questions?"

"Yes sir!" I answered. "When do we leave?"

"You have to leave immediately. Pick up your gear at the Ramparts, and two scouts will lead you down to the 3rd Division headquarters where you can report. Good luck and stay safe."

Just as we were about to leave, Farquhar spoke up.

"Sir, is the football team remaining in the fourth platoon for the duration of this engagement? Are we still segregated from our old platoons?"

"Yes, Private, that is what I said."

"And after this engagement, sir? What then?" Farq asked.

"We'll see, Private."

"I don't know if we can trust you, Colonel." Farquhar answered, causing his teammates to shift their feet nervously.

Genet glowered angrily at Farq, for a moment, before he spoke.

"I don't see that you have any choice, McLennan. This is exactly how the army works. I make the decisions and you have to trust that I am making the right ones. Yours it not to question my decisions - ever. That is how discipline breaks down in a battalion. You are to do what you are told, when you are told. We will let history decide about my decisions."

Farquhar wasn't finished.

"Will history remember how many games we won, Colonel, or how many goals we scored? Will history play the pipes at the graves for any of the ORs? Will history serenade their broken bodies to rest with a Scottish lament? Will we be remembered?"

The two men stared intently at each other and the room was absolutely silent. Genet would have crushed Farq, if the will was there, but Farq would have won if Genet had chosen that path. It was a classic battle of wills between two men from opposite castes. Farquhar always said that this was a game we could never win. Perhaps he was wrong.

Genet stood up from his desk.

"Private, we will handle this, one engagement at a time. I can make no guarantees after that. I can't read the future. Your determination to fight is admirable. You are dismissed."

As the team turned to shuffle out of the room, I was holding my breath. Please, Farquhar and Elmer, say no more. This was uneven ground. I didn't want this to end badly, in a confrontation and a court-martial. When we passed through the doorway, nothing more was said. The team headed back to the Ramparts, with a guide, to collect our belongings.

When we arrived at the Ramparts, we sat together as a team, to talk about the situation with Genet.

"Farq, you bastard: I admire your courage, but I thought Genet was going to rip you," Billy Prosser said. "I could never tell a Lt. Col. that I couldn't trust him. You've got some big fucking *bollocks,* Farq."

Elmer made an observation.

"The old man doesn't know where his fucking loyalties are. Is it football or is it the war? He saw what happened to the 35th, getting decimated. He's bloody well put himself in a corner."

Farquhar responded, "What the hell did I have to lose? We could play his game and hide behind his skirt until this war ends – if it ever ends. Then we would never have any self-respect. We could never look at ourselves in the mirror again. Every time we heard a lost comrade's name mentioned, we would feel the anguish of our cowardice. I love the game of football, like Genet does, but I have come to love the 58th far more. Look what we have been through together, in the last year. My hope is that we all survive the war and return to our homes and families as honoured soldiers."

I thought long and hard about Farq's words. There is going to be a bloody confrontation any day now. Both sides are going to sacrifice the best young men that their countries have raised from the cradle; the generation of the future. And for what? Two hundred, three hundred yards of desecrated soil? And, what of Farquhar and Genet: a battle within a battle? One will pay the price; or maybe both!

Chapter 19
The Universal Language

I thought the meeting with Genet went rather well. No one ended up in the brig, and that is all I wanted. It was difficult enough having a confrontation with Fritz without adding Genet to our list of enemies. I preferred calmer waters.

Our journey through the night, down to the right sector, beyond Mount Sorrel, was as gruelling and challenging as any we had been on. There were two platoons, totalling sixty-eight men threading through the communication trenches. Sgt. Shepherd was commanding Number Four platoon and Sgt. White had Number Three platoon. We had to keep switching trenches to make our way there, and we could not have done this without our guides. Some of the trenches were chewed up by shells and had disappeared into deep muddy craters. We had to be particularly wary of sump holes in the trenches. These were holes that were purposely dug into the trenches to drain off the rainwater. They could be seven or eight feet deep, but were usually covered with duckboards to keep soldiers from falling into them. When shells exploded nearby, the duckboards sometimes got moved off the holes. No one wanted that kind of surprise.

The sun was just coming up when we reached our destination. The area was much flatter than where we had just come from. Surprisingly, there were very few shell craters, and our guides led us right to the front lines. We found this very unusual because the enemy trench was only about one hundred yards away. We were in clear view of Fritz. I looked for Sgt. Shepherd to ask him what was going on.

"Sgt. Shepherd, what the hell is going on? We are conducting a relief in full view of the enemy."

"Don't worry, they won't shoot at us. This is a *live and let live* zone. Neither side will contest it. It has no military significance. We'll just guard our trenches and keep a vigilant eye on the enemy."

Farquhar was beyond belief. "What the fuck is this? Genet has done it to us again!"

Everyone stopped in their tracks and looked over the parapet at the Germans. There were at least a dozen heads peering back at us, and not even wearing helmets! What an unreal scene! We had just come from the bowels of Hell and now we were about to play 'good neighbour' with Heinie. Not one man in the two platoons could fathom the ridiculous situation they had just hiked into.

Farquhar continued questioning. "How long are we to stay here, Sergeant?"

"Genet said that he wants us to stay here until the counterattack is complete. Just a few days."

Elmer spoke up. "Are you all right with this, Sergeant? Don't you want to be at the front line?"

"Honestly, I am not all right with this. But orders are orders and I can't disobey them, even if I don't like them."

Elmer continued, "So we are all going to miss the counterattack? We just stay here and keep house?"

"That's about it, Private," Shepherd said.

As we were discussing our dilemma, the usual breakfast rations consisting of bacon, biscuits and tea arrived from the kitchen in the support trenches. The men stopped talking and sat down on the firing step to eat breakfast. Rum rations were served as well.

Elmer observed, "This is almost as good a service as at Paradise Camp."

Everyone was extremely hungry, so the protestations soon stopped and the trench grew quiet. It is difficult to talk with your mouth full. We were very tired and badly in need of sleep. After breakfast, the men sorted out the dugouts, and, one by one, made up their beds and began to fall asleep. Sgt. Shepherd took the first sentry duty while the men slept.

I shared my dugout with Elmer, while Farquhar was in a dugout with the Prosser brothers. Our predecessors in the trench had left it in very good shape. There was very little garbage or litter strewn about like there was in most trenches we had been in. Even the dugouts had been left clean and tidy. As much as we hated being away from the action, the men found their new accommodations surprisingly pleasant and welcoming.

Most of the men slept until mid-afternoon. At around 1400 hours, we could hear the artillery exchanges to the north of us. We didn't know if this was the beginning of the counterattack. We weren't getting any information from the 58th HQ. It was an uncomfortable feeling, being left out of the action. Our OC now was Lt. Col. William Allen of the 3rd Battalion. We were not getting any dispatches from them either. It felt like we were the poor little kids that never get invited to the party.

By 1500 hours, we were all awake and just milling about in the trench.

"What do you think is going on up there?" Elmer asked, to no one in particular.

Farq offered a guess. "It could be a counterattack. It has been going on for awhile. I can hear the heavies, so both sides are into it. I don't know what the hell we are supposed to do here."

"Maybe we could yell some Scottish insults at Fritz. I don't know any in German," Elmer said.

"Hey *boaby* mouth!" Elmer hollered, then chuckled.

Reluctantly and carefully, we stood up on the fire step and looked across no-man's land at Fritz. They were just going about their daily chores like it was a day at camp. We could see smoke rising from a fire of some kind, and plenty of smoke from the cigarettes that were being consumed. Occasionally, we would see a head bob up and then disappear.

"Mmmmmm! Maybe they are cooking some schnitzel over there," said Elmer. "Do you think they will share with us?"

"No harm in asking," Farq said. "Hey, Oy!" he shouted in the direction of the German trench.

One helmet-less head popped up, looked across at us and answered, "Hey, Canuck! *Willkommen neue soldaten.*" Then he gave a wave of his arm.

"What did he say?" Art Prosser asked.

"I heard Canuck and something else. Not sure what," I said. "At least they're not shooting at us."

"Are we supposed to trust these guys? They're Heinies!" said Art.

"Damned if know and damned if I'll try," I answered. "This is bizarre. I would never believe this if I didn't see it with my own eyes. How can we train to kill these guys for almost a year, and then be waving and yelling to them across no man's land, like they were our best chums?"

Sgt. Shepherd hiked into our section of the trench.

"What's happening here, soldiers?"

Fritz, across the way, just called out to us and gave us a wave," Farq answered.

"Listen, that is not unusual here. If those guys are stuck there for awhile, you'll probably get to know them. Happens all the time in this sector. There is a kind of trust that happens. You'll get used to it."

"I'll never trust those lads. They're fucking Heinies, and fuck, they'll blast us any chance they get," Elmer replied.

"They'll wait until we are trusting, then they'll gas us," Art added.

Just before he moved on, Shepherd said, "In a day or two, you will see that I'm right. Just wait." The sergeant moved past the traverse and into the next section of the trench.

"Better safe than sorry, my mom always said," I shared.

Farquhar joined in. "I see what is happening here. It all makes sense. If the piece of Belgium has a few ridges and bumps, it is worth thousands of lives; our fucking lives, and shite-tonnes of ordinance. However, if the piece of Belgium is flat and featureless, and has no strategic value, then save the ordinance for somewhere else. We are saving the schoolboys lots of money by not shooting anybody here."

There was silence as we contemplated the statement.

"Good point, mate. You have a good point there, Facker. It leaves me with an uneasy feeling. We think we are fighting for King and Country, maybe for the good of everyone, and then we find something like this... 'live and let live zone'. It bloody well makes you wonder," I said.

As we were finishing the day's work of setting up our dugouts and trenches for the night, Sgt. Shepherd came back through the dugout. He had some bad news.

"We received some terrible word from HQ this evening, men. During the German advance on our trenches, our division OC, Gen. Mercer and the 8th Brigade OC, Gen. Williams, were lost in action. They were doing reconnaissance in the front line when the heavy shelling started. Gen. Mercer was killed, while Gen. Williams was wounded and captured by the enemy. May General Mercer rest in peace."

We all repeated, "May he rest in peace."

"Sorry men, it is terrible news to burden you with. I must move on."

Everyone in our section was speechless. It took several minutes for us to come to terms with the news. Generals don't get killed in action very often. If the generals were doing reconnaissance, it means that they were preparing a plan for a strike against the German lines. Fritz beat us to the punch and we paid a heavy price for it.

Farquhar shook his head and said quietly, "Even the schoolboys pay the price here. It really is a place in Hell."

Later that evening, we drew sticks for sentry duty and Farquhar lost. I didn't think he would see any flares indicating trench raids through the night. For the rest of us, it would be a challenge to stay awake. The next few days were marked by the return of the rain, as well as general boredom. We still could hear the guns trading shells to the north of us, and none of us knew if the 58th was getting hit. It left us feeling helpless and, even worse, left out.

One cool rainy afternoon, while we were sitting in our dugouts, writing letters and reading, Elmer returned from the support trenches with a surprise.

"Hey, platoon!" he shouted, "Look what I found."

Everybody in our section of the trench stuck their heads out of the dugouts to see what trophy Elmer was in possession of. He was standing in the rain, soaking wet, and holding a football in one hand.

"Fuck, what?" Billy Prosser asked. "How the hell did you find a football in the trenches?"

"I looked into a dugout in one of the support trenches, and there it was."

"What are we gonna do with that? We can't play football here," I said.

"We can kick it up and down the bloody trench. What the fuck else is there to do?" Elmer replied.

Farq jumped out of his dugout and went down to the far end of the trench.

"Let's see you kick it down to me, Elmer."

Elmer placed the ball down on the duckboards beneath his feet and gave the ball a clean, light kick. The ball sailed, unhindered, down the length of the trench, about waist-high, and into Farq's hands.

"Ooo! Nice one!" Farquhar said, and made the return kick to Elmer.

The two of them repeated their efforts for a period of time, about fifteen minutes or so, and then Elmer got bored of it.

"Ok," he said, "who wants to take over?"

"Oh, what the hell," I said, "might as well give it a try."

Elmer and I exchanged places in the trench. I gave the ball a kick and Farq caught it.

"Hey, this is better than staring at those dirt walls," I said.

The two of us continued our little game for a while and then I said to Farq, "See if you can put one by me. Get it past and it's a goal."

Farq placed the ball at his feet, and then whistled a shot at me. It hit me flush on the beak. Whack!

"Oowwwwwwwww! Fuck! My Nose! It's bleeding! You fucking scunner!"

"Sorry, sorry, sorry Jon. I didn't mean to hit you." he said, trying to hold his laughter.

I went down on my knees and looked down at my hand. It was covered in blood. "Farq, bring me a dressing."

Farq went to his kit bag to get a bandage. Elmer and the Prosser brothers moved down the trench to tend to me. Somebody handed me a dressing that I held against my nose, which I pinched to stop the bleeding. I got back to my feet and tilted my head back, keeping pressure on my nose.

"At least you stayed conscious this time, Jon," Elmer quipped.

Farq was feeling bad about the accident. "Jonny, I didn't mean to kick it so hard. Is it broken?"

They always used to tease me about my nose, which was long and a little bent. I had big nostrils, people would say.

"Well, maybe you straightened it out for me." I gave it a wiggle and it seemed to be in one piece. "It's good, it's good. Give me a few minutes to stop the bleeding."

I sat back down on the fire step to recover and shake the cobwebs from my head. Then I heard Elmer ask the question, "Where's the ball?"

I opened my eyes to look around me. Farq, Elmer and the Prossers were looking around the trench and the dugouts for the ball.

"I don't think it's in the trench," Elmer said.

They jumped up on the fire step to look out into no-man's land.

"Oh shite!

Everyone stared at the ball. I jumped up to have a look. It was still rolling gently, helped along by the wind, toward Heinie's trench. "What the ... "

The ball eventually came to rest about ten yards from their parapet. By this time, several Heinie faces were peering at it, too.

"Farq, you kicked it. You go get it, "I said.

"Hey, you touched it last. I'm not going out there to get killed."

"Shite, Facker, they won't shoot you," I said.

Elmer cut in, "That's right, Farq. They won't. You'll be safe."

"Well, someone come with me then. Come with me, Elmer."

As we were arguing like kids in the schoolyard, a big tall Heinie jumped out of the trench and nonchalantly picked up the football. He stood and examined the ball as if he was looking for a name or something on it. Then he looked up at us, gave us a wave and then jumped back down into the trench with our ball.

"Well isn't that a bale of shite?" Elmer offered. "They stole our wee ball!"

Farquhar hollered at the foe, "Away an boil yer heed!"

Sgt. Shepherd hurried into our section to see what all the commotion was about.

"What the hell is all the noise and hollering about?"

Billy Prosser stood up and answered the Sarge.

"We ... uh ... we had a football in the trench and it flipped out into no-man's land. And...uh.. .this big Gerry filched it. Just like that." Bill snapped his fingers.

"McLaren, what's with all the blood?"

"I ... uh ... got hit in the nose. With the ball ... before it bounced out."

"You're like a fucking bunch of kids. Do I have to watch you all the time?"

"No, Sir!"

"Where did you get the fucking ball, to begin with?"

"That would be me. I found it, Sir. I found it down in the support trench. The last unit must have left it behind," Elmer said.

As this conversation was taking place in the trench, the big Fritz emerged from his trench, holding the ball in one hand and a white flag on a stick in the other.

When we spotted him, Shepherd yelled at the top of his lungs, "Hold your fire! Hold your fire!"

We could hear Sgt.White repeating the command in his section of the trench, just north of us. Everyone got on the fire step to have a look. Fritz walked slowly to the halfway point between the trenches, and then he stopped. He certainly showed no fear as he pushed the flag stick into the soft wet ground.

In perfect English, with no trace of an accent, he called to us. "Canucks! Do you want your ball back?"

Our side was stunned. We glanced at each other and then turned our stare back to the German.

"Sarge," I said, "what do we do?"

"Let me handle it. Stay put, but I want three of you at loopholes to cover me."

Sarge climbed up over the parapet and stood just in front of it. He stood there for a moment in anticipation of something ... anything. Then he spoke to the German.

"I am unarmed. Are you?"

The big German answered, "Yes, I am unarmed. Please approach."

I turned to the men in the trench with me.

"This goes against everything we have been taught. I can't believe what I am seeing. I don't trust them."

Sgt. Shepherd walked slowly toward the German and then stopped about a respectful ten feet in front of him. Shepherd saluted and the German returned it. They began a conversation that we couldn't hear at this distance. After a minute or two, they saluted again and Shepherd returned to our trench and Fritz returned to his.

Shepherd climbed back down into the trench. He shook his head a couple of times, and then he spoke.

"You are not going to believe this. They will return the football, but only after we play a game with them in no man's land. I heard the rumours about the Christmas Truce, but this goes beyond that. A football game in the middle of Flanders; in the middle of a war, yet. I ... I ... I'm losing my mind!"

Shepherd sat down on the fire step to contemplate.

Farq asked, "Who are they? Did he say?"

"No, he didn't, but I saw 119th on his shoulder patch. That is all I know. Oh, and he is Sergeant Kofler, their platoon CO."

I had an idea. "Why don't we play a game, then? It will be good for morale, just like the old man always says."

"Are you kidding me? We could get in all sorts of shite for doing that: fraternizing with the enemy for one; abandoning our weapons for two. Both would get us court-martialed."

Elmer stepped in.

"Why does anybody need to know? The brass hats are all too busy planning the counterattack, while we are all getting bored and unfocused here. This is just what we need. Isn't that right, Billy?"

Billy Prosser and Sgt. Shepherd had been long time friends in Brantford. They had been part of Genet's football squad for years. Billy had some sway with Shepherd. The sergeant had always thought very highly of Billy Prosser. He wasn't the most talented player on the team, but he was tenacious as a competitor. He worked harder at it than anyone on the team; the shortest player, but he could connect on headers above taller opponents. The coach loved that about him.

"I would love to play them, Sarge. What harm can it do? Nobody at HQ is paying any attention to us, and it is probably the same on the other side. This isn't no man's land; it's forgotten-man's land," Billy said.

Shepherd shook his head again and looked down at his feet.

"Let me go talk to Whitey in the other section. I'll be back in a few minutes."

The sergeant moved past the traverse into the next section to find Sgt. White.

"Wouldn't you feel a little strange, playing footy with the people who shoot at us, kill our friends and teammates, and poison us with gas?" Farq asked.

Elmer answered. "Well, you are the one who always said that they are no different than us. They have school boy issues too, don't they?"

"Yeah, Elmer, I can't argue with that. It still gives me the willies, though."

"We've been slotted into these trenches for quite a while now. It would be great to get out and run around for a bit. Stretch our legs. The field is a bit soggy, but at least, it's relatively flat. Could be fun."

Some minutes passed and Sgt. Shepherd appeared back in the section.

He told us of his conversation with Sgt. White.

"Whitey thinks the idea is boffo if we keep it short and sweet. No more than an hour. He says his men are up for it, too. Do we have any white flags?"

Farq deadpanned back, "We're Scots! There is no such thing."

"I have a white bandage, Sergeant," I said.

"Is it clean?" He asked.

"Of course!"

"Well take it out and tie it to a stick. I want to go back out and talk to Fritz."

I tied my bandage to a little branch that I had found and handed it to Shepherd. He took it and climbed back up over the parapet.

"Sergeant!" I said.

"What?"

"You look ridiculous!"

Shepherd gave me a scowl and said, "Shaddup!" He marched out to the middle of the field with the white bandage and waited for a response from the Germans. There was still a very light rain falling on the pitch.

Within seconds, Sgt. Kofler emerged from his trench and approached Shepherd in the middle of the field. The two talked for some time and we could actually hear sporadic laughter. Then they shook hands and returned to the trenches. Shepherd went to see Sgt. White first, before he came back to our section.

Shepherd arrived at our parapet and gave us the news.

"I told him we have a full-fledged Division One team here in the trench, and did he want to play against it? He said, 'Absolutely!' Then I said let's do it."

The men in Number Four Platoon let out a cheer. Off came the helmets, and they started to clamber over the parapet.

"Wait, wait!" Shepherd shouted. "We need to keep two sentries in the trench. Munn and Wright, stay in the trench until I relieve you. Bring two helmets for goalposts, and put them at the north end. Leave your weapons and harnesses in the trench. Let's go play!"

This was so surreal. My belly was churning and full of butterflies. What were we doing? These people are here to kill us, aren't they? Do they really only want to play football? The only Germans that I had been this close to were dead and rotting. These ones were warm and alive. Are they concealing weapons? I could clearly hear them chattering to each other in Heinie.

Both groups of soldiers ventured cautiously onto no-man's land. The suspicion was equal on both sides, and the picture it presented was an awkward one. No one knew how to comport themselves as they milled about the field, casting glances at the men opposite. It was like looking into a mirror, except the uniforms were grey instead of khaki. Most were young, like us. I had difficulty framing my emotions. It was an eerie feeling, looking at the enemy without guns or parapets in between us. Different emotions danced in my head, starting with fear, followed by mistrust, followed by anger enveloped in confusion. My stomach felt like it was puckering inside me.

Finally, the football that caused this self-conscious spectacle appeared from out of nowhere, bouncing and rolling between the troops. One brave German soldier broke ranks and ran to the ball. He kicked it back to one of his mates, who proceeded to step on the top of the ball, spin it backwards and then flip it up into the air. As the ball descended toward the ground, he kicked it swiftly across no-man's land to a Canuck. A smile came across the Canuck's face as he fielded the pass. He lined the ball up at his feet and sent a deft pass back to the German side. The men were beginning to speak a common language. The ball was traded back and forth for several minutes, and all the while, the gap between the two sides was shrinking and changing shape. Both sides could be heard laughing and shouting as the pace of the game picked up. Soon there was no German or Canadian side of the field. Both units were intermingled and enjoying the freedom from the trenches.

The impromptu game halted when Sgt. Kolfler whistled. He walked onto the field and retrieved the ball from one of his men.

"Let's get this game started. Form a line on each side of the field so we can shake hands." Kofler repeated the instructions in German.

Shepherd had the two platoons form a line in the field. The Heinies did the same and then approached us. The two lines began to pass so that we could shake hands with each Heinie. What do I say?

As the first Fritz approached me, I said, "Good Luck, Fritz."

"*Viel Gluck, mein freund!*" Fritz said, as we looked into each other's eyes. Then we shook hands with the firmest grip we each could muster. The greeting was repeated for each German in the line. When the formalities were done, we retreated back to the goal area at the north end of no-man's land. We gathered around the two sergeants and waited for their words. I was more nervous than our big game against the 35th. I could see that my teammates felt the same apprehension. Their puzzled faccs and lack of words were a giveaway.

Shepherd spoke to us in his familiar pre-game voice.

"I want the starting team line-up to take their positions on the field. The rest of you lugs, take to the east sideline. Everyone will get a chance to play. The team will start the game, and then I will start substituting players into the game so that everyone gets a chance. I want two of you to substitute Munn and Wright into the game, too. Is that clear? We want to play for a full ninety minutes. Or at least we will try. The field is a bit slick, so don't hurt yourselves out there. It is very easy to pull a groin muscle. Play fair and play clean."

With that speech done, Shepherd met up at midfield with Sgt. Kofler. They shook hands and then Kofler placed the ball, our ball, at centre midfield. He put two fingers in his mouth and let go with a shrill whistle. The game was on. The Heinie centre played the ball back to a midfielder. He measured up and blasted the ball down to our end where Elmer fielded it. He played the ball across the field to Chadwick, a midfielder. Chadwick placed a long pass up the right side to Art Prosser. It became a game of "keep away" as Prosser passed the ball back to Elmer. Elmer fielded the kick cleanly and began to move the ball up toward midfield. When a Fritzy approached him, he laid a lovely pass up to Billy Prosser, who fielded the ball at top speed. Billy dribbled into the left corner of Fritz's end. He spotted Farq streaking up through the centre and into scoring position. Billy led him with a beautiful pass and Farq manoeuvred the ball into the German goal. No one was keeping score, but we could see that the Germans immediately realized that they were overmatched. The 58th were able to control the ball for long periods during the first half. The Germans were clearly impressed by the seamless teamwork.

From that point of the game, our team backed off entirely. This wasn't about winning. This was about a release from the grinding daily routine of death and confinement in the trenches. We played this great game for the sheer joy of it, and it was beautiful. The men slipped and fell into the mud, but each one got up to his feet laughing. Passes were missed and chances were muffed, but no one cared. Canuck slapped Fritz on the back and Fritz returned the favour. There was no German accent detected in any laugh we heard. A laugh is a laugh in any language.

The two coaches began subbing in the other soldiers. Everyone had the opportunity to play and, at least for a short time, enjoy life as it used to be. I noticed that my apprehension was gone and forgotten soon after the first kick. I was in the game and in the moment. I stopped a shot from one of their strikers, and fell on the ball in the mud in front of the goal. Suddenly, I was pinned under a pile of laughing Heinies. All I could do was laugh and wait for them to get off of me. The weight got heavier when some Canucks jumped on the pile. It felt like my mud bath near Hooge a few days ago. Bring me a stretcher.

Part way through the game, after I had been substituted out, I heard the distinct sound of a radial aeroplane engine. I looked up and saw a plane passing over us at over one thousand feet. I couldn't tell if it was ours or theirs; not that it mattered. The players on the field stopped playing to look up. The pause was short-lived and the game resumed. We were having too much fun to care.

All too soon, the ninety-minute curfew arrived, and Sgt. Kofler whistled to end the game. Everyone had gotten the chance to play, even the NCOs. Every player was covered in mud but no one felt any discomfort. We had just accomplished more in ninety minutes than all of the generals in Europe had accomplished in two years. Why didn't they think of that? Let's play a football match to decide how much of France and Belgium we get. Then France and Belgium could play a match to see how much of England and Germany that they would get. Brilliant! Pure genius!

In a mirror image of the pregame ceremony, we lined up to bid our opponents goodbye. As we passed down the line, mud-covered faces grinned heartily.

"Thank you, Fritz, good game!" I said to each one.

"*Vielen dank, Canuck! Gutes spiel!*" I heard in return.

When I approached Sgt. Kofler to shake his hand, he spoke to me first. In English.

"Great game, goalie! We are not in your league."

"Holy shite! You speak perfect English!" He was easily taller than my trench digging mate, "Tall Ted" Dance. Blond hair and blond moustache. So German!

"Yes, I lived in Canada before the war. I was a police sergeant in Hamilton, Ontario."

"How the hell did you end up in a Heinie uniform?"

"Ha! Just before the war started, I came back to Germany, my homeland, for my father's funeral."

"I am sorry, Sergeant."

"Yes, it is OK. Thank you. Anyway, I was still at home when the war started. I got conscripted and here I am. What choice did I have? I do not want to shoot Canadians, or English for that matter. I have tried to stay away from the front line. I am sure you understand."

We shook hands and moved on. He was trying to stay out of The Front and I was trying to get into The Front. None of this made any sense at all. We had just spent the better part of an afternoon enjoying the company of our hated enemy. I could not fit this feeling into the compartment in my brain that is supposed to store and understand this kind of a situation.

Our two platoons took their time leaving the field. Nobody was in a rush to get back into their trench. The freedom of being above ground level was liberating. The freedom of not worrying about stray bullets was more than liberating. It was intoxicating.

Farquhar saw me and spoke to me first.

"That was a lot more fun than playing for Genet or Dunlop. Fritz enjoyed it as much as we did. They had a few good players over there, don't you think?"

"Yeah," I answered. "Don't let Genet see them. I enjoyed the game. It felt really strange, though. They are just like us: a bunch of blokes who just want to play football. The hell with all this killing."

Both groups took the opportunity to make some trades with the so-called enemy. Canucks swapped cigarettes for sausages, cookies for candies and buttons for pins. With each exchange, we shook hands and patted each other on the shoulder.

"Hey, did we get our ball back?" Farq asked.

I had forgotten about the ball. I spun around to look back at the pitch. I could see Shepherd and Kofler still at midfield and still talking. At that very moment, just before they parted, I saw Kofler pass the ball over to Shepherd. Then they shook hands and parted with a quick salute. Within five minutes, no man's land was devoid of soldiers. This day was astonishing. It changed the way I looked at the world. It changed the way I looked at the war and my enemy on the other side of no man's land. I began to realize that the next trial would be the next time I had to squeeze the trigger.

Chapter 20

The Battle of Sanctuary Wood

There was a sense of peace and harmony in our trench; an unbelievable tableau in the midst of terrible battles and loss of life. The men were all talking at once, eager to tell their chums about Fritz patting them on the back, Fritz complimenting a pass, Fritz trying to speak English. It sounded like a schoolyard at recess. Sgt. Shepherd was somewhat concerned about the scene in front of him. He realized, of course, that he was the CO of this outfit, and perhaps, he had ventured a little too far in allowing the game to happen. He had opened the proverbial floodgates, and now all he could do was wait for his men to calm down.

After some time, the unit grew tired of their stories and began to settle themselves. Shepherd seized the opportunity to address them.

"Fourth Platoon! Listen up! We had a grand old time today, playing footy with Fritz. However; and this is a big however, we must keep our big traps shut when we get back to the company. It didn't fucking happen! This free-for-all could get us all court-martialed. The brass hats don't want us fraternizing with the fucking enemy. So let's keep it to ourselves. Is that understood?"

"Aye, Sarge!" was the chorus.

The evening passed quietly, except for the soldiers of both sides occasionally trying to communicate with the men of the other side. Someone would holler a phrase in broken German and wait for a response, usually returned in broken English.

"Hey Rudy, haben sie mehr sausages?"

"*Nicht mehr*, Canutsky!"

This went on for a good portion of the night until both sides got too tired and finally fell asleep, like Boy Scouts at camp. The rain let up, but it remained unseasonably cool and the men got a good night's sleep.

The morning arrived as a repeat of the day before. There were plenty of clouds, the air was cool and there was a south-east wind. The south-east wind never brought pleasant weather, or pleasant anything else, for that matter. At least we didn't have to cope with the rain. The rations arrived on time, as usual, and along with them, a runner with a message from the 3rd Battalion. We were to be relieved later by two platoons from the 3rd. Our units were to travel back, that night, to reunite with B Company at the Belgian Chateau. Our time in Never-Never Land was over.

Our guides arrived at precisely 2300 hrs. We followed them back through the same convoluted trenches that brought us here. We arrived, exhausted, at the Chateau at 0430 hrs, and found some dugouts that were empty. Our uniforms were soaked through and our feet were cold, wet and sore. Out came the ground sheets and we collapsed onto them, totally spent.

On the morning of June 10, after rations were delivered, Lt.Thomson and Sgt. Shepherd arrived in the dugouts bearing important news for our platoon. They informed us of a company meeting at 0900 hours behind the Chateau. At the meeting, we would be briefed on our roles in the upcoming attack on the Germans in our old trenches. The attack would take place at 0130 hours on June 13.

"One more thing, platoon," Thomson said. "One of our observation planes flew over your section yesterday. It was taking photographs. The OC, First Division, saw those photographs. At first, he couldn't figure out what was happening in the pictures. Then, he figured it out. He was furious! You are getting off extremely easy, or maybe not! He ordered you back to the 58th Battalion in the front lines. Genet is a bit pissed off, to say the least. I don't know if this is the end of it. That is all."

Thomson left, but Shepherd remained behind. He looked at Farq, then at Elmer and finally, at me.

"Well, you got your wish. It could have been a court-martial, but the battalion has no time and no will for that now. They need us in the front line more than in a brig. I had to beg to keep my stripes."

Farquhar answered him with wry grin.

"We're sorry, Sergeant. We're happy that you kept those damn stripes of yours. You are damn ugly but we can't live without you."

Shepherd laughed and said, "Yeah, you could do worse."

Farq continued, "Sarge, some fucking awful, grim things have happened in this war, but what happened yesterday wasn't one of them. We may have been foolish, but it reminded us of who we are and where we are. I am glad that we did it."

"You know what, Private? So am I."

Later that evening, at the set time, B Company arrived at the location behind the Chateau. It was imperative that the Canadian Corps deliver a decisive blow to the Germans after the humiliation on June 2nd. The British had been very critical of us for losing the ground that they had fought for so valiantly. Our reputation was tarnished and needed to be avenged. The British thought that the colonial troops were inferior because they were mostly volunteers and not very professional. They had no idea how tough Canadians are. I couldn't wait to show them.

Lt. Col. Genet tried to address the company, but with the sound of large calibre ordinance still rumbling a few miles away, it was decided that he'd inform one platoon at a time. The officers had already been briefed and they knew the details. A large relief model of the battleground had been constructed, showing all the trenches and strong points. Each platoon and section was given specific instructions as to where and when they would attack, based on the relief model. We were given as much time as we needed to study the model and learn the layout of the trenches. The battle would be taking place at night, and that meant we would have to feel our way around.

Our company, B Company, was given its assignments: Platoon 1 would attack from the trenches known as Warrington Avenue and Gourock Road. Platoon 2 would attack up the Hill Street trench from Warrington trench. Platoon 3 would occupy Strong Point 15 and Platoon 4 would be lined up south of them down to Hill Street. I was assigned, along with Elmer, to Platoon 1.

Farquhar's bomber group, along with two sections of bombers from the 52nd Battalion, each soldier equipped with a sack of grenades, was to start bombing up Warrington Avenue. The attack would be launched at 0130 hours. The artillery barrage against the German lines had already begun that afternoon. The bombardments lasted about thirty minutes and then stopped. The tactic was to keep Fritz confused as to when the actual attack would begin. Our big guns had been augmented by the artillery units of the British, South African and Indian Corps. This was the largest concentration of firepower by the Allies so far in the war. No extra infantry units were available as backup, save one; the 2nd Dismounted Cavalry.

The 58th would be moved into battle position from Dormy House, to the west of The Front, and up into the trenches from Sanctuary Wood at the left (north), down to Maple Copse at the right (south). The 13th Battalion would be to the immediate right of us, from Maple Copse to Observatory Ridge. The 31st Battalion would be to the left of us, from Sanctuary Wood up to Zouave Wood. As a result, we were right in the middle of the tempest.

That night, June 11, we were ordered to relieve the 43rd Battalion in the front line at Dormy House. The relief was completed at 0330 hours, with seven ORs and one officer wounded during the transfer. It was still cool with a south-east wind. Armageddon was creeping nearer to us. All of us were hungry, but when the rations arrived, most of us found it difficult to eat anything. We just forced it down, knowing that we were going to need every ounce of energy to fight the Hun. A double ration of rum was served to calm our frayed nerves. We stationed at Dormy House, with A Company to the left and B Company to the right. C and D Companies were sent to Maple Copse in support and reserve.

After our morning rations, the artillery took over. The German positions were pounded with hot metal for ten straight hours. We watched, incredulous, as the large trees of Sanctuary Wood were blown into splinters. Massive tree trunks and root balls were thrown into the air, as if the hand of a giant had dug his fingers into the ground and angrily flipped everything in his grip. The smoke and dust obscured the sky and darkened the battlefield. We had to cover our ears to ease the agony of the concussions and sound.

I turned to Elmer and Farq and hollered, "How could anyone survive that?"

"There will be nothing left for us to attack," Farq answered.

"Let's hope so," Elmer added.

The barrage stopped at 1900 hours. It seemed like even the guns needed some time to recover and take a breath. A ghostly silence followed. We strained our eyes to see if we could detect any signs of life in the obliterated German lines. The smoke and dust drifted away slowly to the north, revealing a dead wasteland. All that was left of Sanctuary Wood were shattered tree limbs, scattered around at all angles, and forlorn black stumps. There were hundreds of craters still emitting ribbons of smoke into the air. The stillness was eerie and foreboding. We knew we would be moving through this piece of Hell very soon. We knew that we would witness the grotesquely posed broken bodies of young men who had made the terrible sacrifice. Where was the sanctuary of this place? Paradise Camp was paradise but this was no bloody sanctuary!

At precisely 2030 hours, the blanket shelling of the German trenches began again; it carried on for thirty minutes and then stopped. The artillery laid down a thick smoke screen which allowed our troops to move up to our starting points at 2100 hours. Then we had to wait patiently for almost four long hours, before we could go over the top.

The First Division was ready and waiting at Mount Sorrel and Observatory Ridge in the south, and the Third Division was lying in wait from Hill 62, through Sanctuary Wood and north to Hooge. In all, there were at least twenty-five thousand men ready to strike at Fritz's throat.

It was an interminable wait. The drizzle that fell earlier had now intensified to a steady rainfall. With each minute, it grew darker. It was almost impossible to see more than a few yards in front of the trench. Few of us spoke. What I hated most was the pathetic moans and gasps of the wounded Hun in the trenches and craters that lie ahead of us. We could see a body hanging from the limb of a raggedly severed tree branch close by. When we encountered the dead in the trench, we either had to step over them, or step on them. The broken tree branches and roots turned our advance into a deadly obstacle course. I couldn't think of any worse conditions in which to fight a battle.

Fritz would be shooting at us and lobbing mortars to stop our progress. It would be impossible for a normal human who has never experienced this hell to imagine the horror of it. I just wanted it to be over. We waited and waited as the time slowly passed. As the moment grew closer, we wished each other 'good luck'. We were all sharing the same thought: "Will we ever see one another again?"

At 0130 hours, June 13, the bombers began their move into the Heinie trenches. They lobbed their Mills bombs over the traverses into the laps of the unsuspecting Germans just ahead of us. I could hear the thump of each grenade as it exploded. The Heinies screamed and yelled as the deadly little bombs dropped on them.

"*Laufen weg!*" I was hearing a battle but not seeing it. My imagination had to create the picture for me. This was Farquhar's domain; the toughest job reserved for the toughest men. His section was heading up Warrington Ave., ahead of my infantry unit. I tried to picture what Farq and his men were seeing or feeling as they entered each smoking trench. The reality, no doubt, was more brutal.

At this point in the battle, the artillery on both sides was silent. We could hear the sounds of small arms fire, Mills Bombs exploding and men's voices barking out instructions in two different languages. We held our Ross Rifles ready, and waited for the command to enter the bloody commotion. Knowing that our mates were getting bloodied in advance of us, made the wait much more difficult. Occasionally, flares flew into the night sky giving us a surreal image of rising smoke, orange-white flashes rising out of the muddy ground and reflecting in the puddles. This is what Armageddon looks like for those who dare to see. The shrieking voices of the dying sounded like a banshees playing the accompaniment to this opera of horror.

Elmer was close by, with my platoon; close enough for me to see him. When the bombers had progressed far enough, we followed behind them. We dealt with the aftermath of their efforts. As we moved into sections of the trench that the bombers had cleared, we had to search the dugouts for survivors and kill them. There were, as I had foreseen, many dead and wounded to step over. With our bayonets, we had to make certain that they were all dead and unable to retaliate. With some hesitation at first, I thrust my bayonet into motionless German soldiers as I passed over them. This was sickening; it was much easier to pull a trigger. Some of them reacted with a pathetic tortured grunt and a flinch. Others reacted not at all. I was thankful that I couldn't see their faces. This is what nightmares are made of. Time stood still. Everything happened in an instant, looking like a frozen frame in a flickering picture show.

The planned attack was going well until Fritz found our range in Warrington Ave. with trench mortar bombs. They began landing just behind us, about twenty or thirty yards, but Fritz adjusted and moved them closer. At this point, we had to halt our progress up Warrington trench as the mortar shells started to find their mark. Shite, we needed to get the hell out of here, and find immediate shelter from the barrage. Our platoon turned back toward our starting point, about one hundred yards behind us. As we passed a sap that angled toward the enemy lines, I noticed two of our men trying to avoid the shells and moving out toward us. The second man was Farquhar. In a bright flash of fire, a mortar shell burst in the sap between the two men. The nearest soldier was blown off his feet in our direction. He landed face down near my spot in the trench, very badly wounded by the mortar strike. I looked up the sap toward Farquhar, but the view was obscured by smoke and dust. I couldn't see him. I screamed to my platoon mates that there were two men down in the corridor. I jumped over the first soldier to try to get to Farq. The mortar shells were still raining down on us. When I got to the spot where I thought he was, I looked down onto the floor of the sap. He wasn't there.

I heard a faint sound coming from further up the sap, and I moved in that direction. I lit my torch and, through the smoke and dust, I faintly saw Farquhar lying motionless. I manoeuvred close to try to talk to him, and knelt down beside him. His eyes were closed and his face was covered with blood. He coughed weakly and turned his head very slightly. Then he was still.

"Oh, Sweet Jesus! Farq! Farq! Can you hear me?" I begged, hoping for any kind of acknowledgement.

With the arrival of more mortar shells, it was almost impossible to hear if he made any sound. I carefully placed my left hand under his precious head and gently lifted. There was no response. There was no pulse at his neck. I became numb to everything. The inferno beyond the trench ceased to register. I knew, then, what I was looking at. The life had seeped out of his body and there was nothing I could do. I couldn't even weep. I gently placed his head back down on the ground and tried to burn the picture into my mind. I tried to memorize every detail of his broken body and bloodied uniform because I knew I would never see it again.

"Sweet Jesus, *Milis Losa*!"

Someone grabbed me by the back of my harness and pulled me to my feet and out of the sap.

"Let's get the fuck out, Private, before we get flattened!"

I was pulled back into the trench and pushed in the direction of our starting point. My mind was barely functioning well at this point, and all that I could see were sporadic flashes of the soldiers' faces that were hauling me back to safety. They kept me moving away from the action and back to a casualty clearing station in Maple Copse, where they sat me down on a wooden box. There, I sat and stared blankly while trying to process what I had just seen. I sat for a while with my thoughts. The sounds of the still raging battle were so far away in my mind as not to be heard.

"Where are you hit, Private?" A voice brought me to the present, and the light of the torch hit my face.

"Oh, I'm not hit."

"There's blood, Private."

"Uh...it's not mine. My mate's, Farquhar's."

"Come over to the tent, I want to examine you."

It was Captain Cosbie, our medical officer. Finally, a welcome sight for me. I was in turmoil and wondering if this was the way shell-shock felt. I looked down at my bloodied hands to see if they were trembling. The evidence was conclusive. I could not hold them still.

"Lie down on this table, will you, son?"

I moved to the table. The doctor's voice gave a measure of comfort, and that was exactly what I needed. My body wasn't pierced or broken, but my soul was tortured. I felt a panicky impatience. I needed help, and the desire to see my platoon mates overtook me. Their faces would comfort me. The pain would go.

I tried to sit up. Cosbie gently put his hands on my shoulders to keep me in place.

"Private, stay put. I need to look at you."

While I was lying on the table, Cosbie opened my uniform and checked me for wounds.

"I don't see any injuries, but you seem a little disoriented. I am going to give you a shot of rum and keep you here until you have fully recovered."

"Sir, I want to get back to my platoon. We were in Warrington Ave."

"You can't go back there. That area is too hot. We lost an entire bombing section there. Only one survivor."

"Where is my platoon?"

"I don't know, but they would have been pulled out and moved to a different trench."

"You don't understand, Captain, I need to go."

"You are under my orders here. Stay until daybreak and then you can go back to your unit. Here's your rum. Take it."

A nurse led me out of the tent, and then summoned another private to take me to a shelter. I was led to a dugout that housed three other soldiers. One of them was sobbing and talking to himself. The other two were staring straight into the unknown and shaking. I was with the shell-shocked. Maybe Cosbie thought I was shell-shocked, too. Maybe I *was* shell-shocked. Perhaps tomorrow, I would wake up and find out that everything that I had witnessed tonight was a shell-shocked dream.

I must have drifted off to sleep in the dugout. I have no memory of the wait for morning. When my eyes opened, there was light in the sky. My three dugout mates were no longer present, and I occupied the dugout alone. As I became aware of my reality, the memory of yesterday came storming back and hit me hard in the stomach. I didn't want to wake up. I didn't want to be here. I wished Elmer was here with me. Shite, I wished I was dead.

The artillery was still active, but more sporadic than last night. I could still hear small arms fire, as well. The battle was still alive.

Later in the day, Fritz picked up the pace with his shelling in Maple Copse, Sanctuary Wood and Zielbeke. Captain Cosbie came by the dugout to see me.

"How are you feeling, Private?"

"Not so good, Captain. I am hurting deep inside. Not physical though - you know what I mean."

"I absolutely know what you mean. We have all paid the price for being here. Every one of us has lost someone close to us."

"Have they found him? Have they brought Farquhar back?"

"No. No one has been sent out. There is still too much action in the area."

"I want to go get him, Captain. I have to."

"I am going to send you back to your platoon. You were in shock last night, but you seem to be better this morning. By the way, we have taken back all of the trenches that we lost a few weeks ago. Fritz took a brutal pounding, but we paid a terrible price for it, too."

Cosbie sent a scout to take me to my platoon. We found them hunkered down in our original support trenches near Warrington Ave. and Bydand Ave. The trenches were badly chewed up and in need of repair. There were many German dead scattered around the general area and in the trenches. They would all have to be removed and buried. We couldn't just leave them there, and they were all carrying weapons, which we could put to use. Many of our men preferred the German Mauser to the Ross rifles that we used. Some of the men never missed an opportunity to take souvenirs. My priority was to find Elmer. I didn't know if he was dead or alive. Finally, to my great relief, I found him, shovel in hand, repairing our trench floor.

"Mac! Elmer!" I called out when I spotted him.

He dropped his shovel, and ran to me. I wrapped my arms around him and hugged him. The hug lasted a few seconds and then I could sense that Elmer knew something was wrong by the desperation of my hug. Elmer pulled back and looked at me.

"Where's Farq?"

I couldn't summon an answer.

"Jon, where's Farq? Have you seen him?"

"I have."

Elmer was becoming alarmed. "Please Jon; tell me."

"He ... uh ... he died in my arms. Last night." Elmer covered his face with his hands. He held them there as he absorbed the words of Farq's death. He pulled his hands away, fixed his stare on them and spoke.

"What the fuck! What happened?"

"I saw him coming out of a sap. Just as he was getting close, a mortar shell hit him."

"Please God, no! Where is he?"

"Still there."

"Jon, we have to go get him."

"Elmer, the whole platoon was wiped out. We have to get them all."

"Let's go, Jon. Let's get some men and some stretchers and go find them."

"We have to get permission from Shepherd. I'll talk to him. You find some men."

Within a short time span, I found Shepherd nearby and asked for permission to retrieve the bodies.

"Absolutely, Private, get it going. You have to do it quickly because Fritz is going to start shelling us in retaliation at any time now. If he does, the mission has to be aborted. Do you understand? You have to abort! Do you know where to find them?"

"Yes, Sir. I was there when it happened. In Warrington Ave. I saw Farquhar get hit."

There was silence. Sgt. Shepherd just looked at me. Then I realized that he didn't know.

"I am sorry, Sarge. Farquhar was killed by a mortar bomb."

The grief was etched on Shepherd's face. A bond had formed between the two: Shepherd and Farquhar. There was the bond of football as well as mutual respect. Shepherd as coach and Farq as the dominant player. We could always see the joy on Shepherd's face when Farq pulled off another of his miracles. Pure joy and admiration.

Shepherd cleared his throat and said, "Get going. Bring them home."

Elmer had no problem getting recruits. When they heard that Farquhar had been killed in action, they all eagerly volunteered to go. They weren't aware, yet, that the whole bombing section had been wiped out. Elmer managed to get ten stretchers and twenty men.

We set out for the section of Warrington Ave. where the men lay. The distance was only a few hundred yards but we didn't know what we would run into on the way. Fritz may have moved a few men back into that area after we vacated. We sent three men in advance, armed with Mills Bombs, in case we met resistance. It was an eerie feeling, moving through the trenches that we had occupied in the dark, just last night. We could see things that we never realized were there. We passed a German machine gun emplacement that wasn't on our scale model or maps.

"Fucking schoolboys never told us about this one! Assholes!" Elmer said.

"Shhhhh! Quiet!" I said, "We don't want Fritz to hear us coming."

Then we arrived at the point where the sap intersected Warrington Ave. We moved quietly toward the edge of the sap, straining our ears for threatening sounds.

"We should find them up here," I said in a whisper.

We peeked around the corner to see if there were any Heinies lurking. It was clear.

"I want you three bombers to move up the sap in advance. Move up to the first block," I said, taking charge of the mission. There was no NCO to run the show.

We waited for the "all clear" from the bombers. When it came, we moved slowly into the sap. Even though it had been dark, I knew where we would find Farquhar. The thought of seeing him there made my stomach tighten up. It bothered me that he had been out here alone for the whole night and most of the day. Somebody, perhaps me, should have been here with him. It was like leaving a newborn child alone for the first time. And he was newborn, but not of this world.

I led the group into the sap. The rain was still falling and the bottom of the sap had a few inches of muddy water. It was quiet except for the sloshing of our feet and the rain spattering on our helmets. The group arrived at the spot where I expected to see Farquhar, but instead, there was nothing! We found a few of our helmets and packs in the mud, further down the sap, but no bodies. The bombers returned from the far end of the sap and relayed the message that they had found nothing. They also saw Canadian helmets and supplies but no men.

"If they were all killed here, something has happened to their bodies. The only explanation I have is that the Heinies have cleared them out and buried them," I said.

"Jon, are you sure this is the correct location?" Elmer asked.

"This is it, without any doubt," I answered, "It has to be!"

"We could go a little further up Warrington," Elmer suggested.

"No, this is the spot. We should turn back now."

As we turned to leave the sap, I noticed something that could not possibly have been seen in the darkness of the battle. Along the whole length and down sides of the sap, on the top of the parapet and parados, was a growth of small delicate ferns. Among the ferns, long stalks protruded, and at the end of each stalk, was a red poppy. With the chilly east wind, the poppies seemed to wave at us. The green and red was such a contrast to the grey-brown mud. Crystals of rain dripped slowly from the red petals and the green fern leaves. Even in the rain, the red poppies were vibrant and brought life to the scene. Vibrant like blood and vibrant like the Red Dragon. Perhaps Michael's angels had placed the delicate flowers there to take the place of the lost children and ease the suffering of their mothers.

"What are you looking at, Jon?" Elmer asked.

"The flowers, Elmer. On the parapet, the flowers of the forest."

"I never really noticed them before, but there they were, right in front of us. Everything else here is smashed except those flowers. How the hell does that happen?"

"I wish I knew. We should get out of here."

Nobody really wanted to leave. We thought we would be bringing Farquhar and the others home with us. I didn't feel right about leaving without them. A deep sadness came over me. I was feeling completely alone, as if I was beyond the reach of my family and my friends. They were on the other side of a wall and couldn't hear me or see me, but I could see them. It was obvious why I felt this way, but

I was aware that Farquhar must somehow, somewhere, be feeling it too; taken away from us, his friends, his team. He was lost to us, yet I was feeling his emotions on the other side of the 'wall'.

The group quickly made its way out of the sap and back to our base near Warrington Ave. On the way back, I stopped to check the remains of one German soldier in the trench. I wanted to see what regiment we had been up against. I rolled him onto his side to look at the shoulder patch.

"Elmer. Look at this," I said. Elmer moved to my side and looked at the patch.

"Holy Shite! The 119th! I hope this isn't one of the guys we met on the football pitch."

I looked at Elmer and said, "I guess we'll never know. There is not much left of his face. It looks like he took a chunk of shrapnel. Poor Heinie. Poor soul."

"I don't think I would have recognized him anyway. It seems like a century ago that we played the match."

The men back at base had been anticipating our arrival, and had sent for the chaplain. We explained that the sap had been cleared of all the dead. Thc chaplain wouldn't be needed.

Sgt. Shepherd was perplexed. "I don't know why they would do that, unless they had plans to move back in. But that's not going to happen. We have pushed them back to their old frontline trenches. I sincerely hope that our boys got a decent burial."

It didn't take Fritz much longer to start taking out his frustration on us. The massive shelling on our new positions started late in the afternoon and lasted until dark. Word came through to us that we were being relieved by the 60th that night. A, B and D Companies were sent to the Belgian Chateau while C Company was sent to Zielbeke Bund. Three ORs were wounded during the move. We spent one day at the Chateau, and then we were relieved by the 3rd Grenadier Guards and sent further back from The Front to the Dominion and Scottish Lines. The 58th was spent and in great need of a well-earned rest. There was not much fight left in us. Men can only be exposed to so much violence and fury before they become lame and ineffective. The fire inside each man slowly dims.

At this location, we were allowed baths and given new clothing and equipment. We were a battered and scarred battalion. Where once we marched proudly, with our chests sticking out, we were now bent over with pain and exhaustion. There were many small injuries to tend to. Soldiers had cuts and scrapes that came with being in the trenches and on the battlefield. Shrapnel flew in every direction and lodged itself in arms, legs, buttocks and faces; not enough to send us to casualty clearing stations. These wounds could be tended to with wipes and disinfectants. Our minds were wounded too. We had had our fill of blood, brain splatter, shattered arms and legs, and ravaged flesh. We just wanted to look at pictures of our mothers, our fathers, our wives and children.

A muster parade was set up so that we could take stock of how many and who had been lost in the Battle of Sanctuary Wood. We separated into platoon units to undertake a roll call. Sgt. Shepherd lined us up and began reading from his list. We could plainly see, with a look around, who was missing, even before the names were read out.

Each man who was present called "Aye, Sir!" to acknowledge the sergeant. He began his list ...

"Private Robert Boyd - 453254." Silence. We listened in hope. Silence. More names ...

"Private John Campbell - 451095." Silence. More names...

"Private Arthur Jessop - 451866." Again, there was silence. Art Jessop. My mind ran a news-reel memory of my dear friend. Our near-death experience in the mud. His smiling face. My emotions began to win the battle of wills.

"Private Farquhar McLennan - 451889." Silence. A lifetime of memories raced through my mind. I stared into nowhere as the tears ran down my face.

One soldier in line called out his name: "Farq!" We all knew his anguish, and silently said his name too. Two more names went unanswered in the roll call. How can you train or prepare for moments like this? Nothing will ever remove the heartache that we were all feeling. This day, this week will stay fresh in my memory forever. We shall remember!

The grim news when all was tallied was that twenty-six ORs were killed, seventy-four wounded, twenty-three lost to shell-shock and forty still missing and presumed to be dead. We lost several officers, as well. My friend, David Waldron was recommended for a military medal, earned by his bravery in carrying messages through heavy enemy fire, to and from headquarters during the battle.

The battalion had been hit hard, and needed new recruits to come in and replace the men who had been lost. It would take some time to integrate them into their units. One hundred and fifty-one other ranks were brought into the four companies.

The anniversary of the founding of the 58th Battalion was marked with dinners on June 23rd for the officers and on the 24th for the NCOs. Genet had started to put this tribe together exactly one year ago, in Brantford, and had now seen it through its first major battle. His pride would have been tempered by the sorrow of seeing so many men go down so soon.

During this time, a funeral was held for General Mercer, whose body had been found at Armagh Wood. Near the end of June, we had a visit and inspection from the Canadian Corps commander, Lt. Gen. Sir Julian Byng. The next day, the officers of the 58th had a visit from the new divisional commander, Maj. Gen. Louis Lipsett, who was the replacement for Gen. Mercer. The month came to an end with word that we would relieve the 42nd Battalion at Zielbeke Bund on the last day of June.

Before we took our leave of the Belgian Chateau, I talked to Elmer about writing some letters.

"Elmer," I said as we were packing our equipment, "We have some time today, we should send a letter home to Catherine."

"Yeah, I think we should. Let's write one together." Elmer's voice was softened by his sorrow. We put our packing aside and began to compose:

> Dear Catherine,
>
> I have no doubt that you have been officially informed of dear Farquhar's death. I am writing to you on behalf of our good friend, Elmer, and the rest of the men in Farquhar's No.4 Platoon, to express our sympathies in your bereavement. On June 13, Farquhar was working with his bombing section in a German sap in ██████. They were successful in driving the enemy out of their trench. The Germans began a heavy trench mortar barrage on the section that his unit was in. Unfortunately, the whole unit was lost in the shelling, save one. I had the opportunity to tend to Farquhar but it was too late to save him. He died, not alone, but heroically and with minimal suffering. We were unable to recover his body.
>
> His death was a huge blow to the company and to the 58th Battalion. They knew him as

> "Farq", but also took joy in calling him your favourite name: "Facker". He was also loved for his tremendous football exploits on the pitches here in ██████. We are an undefeated battalion in both football and war because of men like Farquhar. He was also loved because of his generosity and his humour.
>
> Catherine, he was as fine a soldier as he was a brother and an uncle. He was the best friend that Elmer and I could ever have, you know that. We vow that we will do everything that we can to recover his remains and give him a proper burial.
>
> We hope to be home soon to be at your side and do whatever we can to comfort you, your husband, Peter, and young William. One day, I will take it upon myself to tell William all about his wonderful uncle and what a fine soldier Farquhar was.
>
> Although I know that you and your family are heartbroken, there is consolation in knowing that he died valiantly in a noble cause. Your grief is shared by the whole battalion.
>
> Sincerely and with love,
>
> Jonathan and Elmer

"Beautiful, Jonny. That is a beautiful letter. Thank you."

"I want to write another one, Elmer."

"To whom?"

"To Nancy. Farq wrote to her often. She deserves to know what happened."

"Great thought, Jon. Can you put my name on it too? You're better at it than me."

"Absolutely!"

> Dear Nancy,
>
> We are writing to you, as Farquhar's best friends, to inform you that he has been killed in action. His platoon was engaged in a bombing action against the German line on June 13. A barrage of trench mortar bombs destroyed the whole platoon, but one man.
>
> Farquhar spoke very highly of his friendship with you. Your letters brought him much happiness and he always looked forward to receiving them. He had happy memories of the time the two of you spent together in Niagara-on-the-Lake.
>
> He was much loved by his trench mates in the 58th Battalion. He died in a valiant battle on behalf of his King and his country. Keep your proud memories of Farquhar and cherish them forever.
>
> Sincerely,
>
> Private Jonathan McLaren and Private Elmer McLean
>
> 58th Battalion, Central Ontario Regiment
>
> CEF

Chapter 21

Dark Clouds on the Horizon Again

September, 1939

June, 1916 was a month of baptism for the 58th. We had tasted glorious victory twice. The victory at Sanctuary Wood was historic for the new Dominion of Canada. It was the first large offensive, planned and executed by the Canadian Forces. The victories came at no small expense, for the Battles of Sanctuary Wood, Hill 62, and Mt. Sorrel, cost us eight thousand casualties between the 1st Division and the 3rd Division.

Ahead of the 58th Battalion laid the Battle of the Somme, Vimy Ridge, Hill 70, Lens, Passchendaele, Amiens, Arras and Cambrai. By the end of the war, on November 11, 1918, the Battalion had counted almost five hundred dead, over two thousand wounded, ninety shell shocked, fifty-five gassed, two hundred and sixty-four missing and thirty-nine sick. Those of us who attended training at Paradise Camp had very little chance of coming home unscathed.

Farquhar's remains were found in August, 1916, and exhumed. His body was reburied in Bedford House Cemetery south of Zillebeke. Most of those who were found could not be identified. In Flanders, their names are found on the Menin Gate, outside of Ieper (Ypres). Remaining in the soft ground of Flanders are the bodies of about sixty thousand Commonwealth soldiers; their names, too, are inscribed on the Menin Gate. The sacred ground of Flanders also holds the remains of similar numbers of German soldiers.

Oddly, Farquhar's body was found on the Canadian side of the front line. This would indicate that the Germans had never found his body or moved it. None of Farquhar's bombing mates were ever found. I had the opportunity to visit the grave site in Bedford House, two summers ago, and to pay my respects. I have never been so moved.

At Vimy, in April 1917, I took a bullet in my right thigh, shattering the bone and sending me back to Blighty for recovery, and ending my football career. I was sent to the Military Orthpaedic Hospital in London for surgery. The doctors and nurses took excellent care of me there. They were so good to me that I married one of the nurses immediately after the war, and took Barbara back to Toronto to raise a family. We had two children: a girl and a boy. I returned to Dunlop Tire for two years, and at the same time, earned my high school fourth form at night school. Then I attended normal school, and became an elementary school teacher in downtown Toronto. One of my duties at the school is to conduct the Remembrance Day Ceremony every November 11. The students and staff know that I am a veteran of the war and often asked me questions about it. I am fulfilling a dream that Farquhar and I shared, and he was my inspiration to become a teacher.

The fear that stalked me in war, the fear of becoming a broken man like my father, has never disappeared. There are times, since I returned from the war, that are coloured with melancholy and anxiety. I feel it more often in the dark, cold months of winter. The bouts usually last a week or two, and then I return to my normal self. I am always anxious that the bouts will be unending and I will spend the rest of my years on the edges of sanity. Barbara has been a wonderful help to me. She recognizes when I am not myself and gives me time and space to work things out. Her words sooth me and ease the anxiety, the pain.

The one chap that no one figured to get through the war unscathed, Elmer, did just that. Not even a scratch. Elmer also returned to Dunlop, and has established a fine career in sales there. He remains a bachelor and still enjoys chasing the ladies as ever. Who knows, maybe one day he will catch one?

The Wonkys, like Elmer, came home from the war showing minimal wear and tear. They both earned their stripes as lance corporals, and won Distinguished Conduct Medals. The veterans of the 58th had many stories to tell of the amazing Wonkys and their daring night-time trench raids. The Wonkys even managed to sneak into the German trenches one night and set their wooden latrine structures on fire! When the war came to an end, they returned to Toronto and purchased a pawn shop business on Church Street.

Lenny survived the war and returned to Owen Sound to be with his faithful friend, Sailor. He met a divorcee and married her. Lenny used his kitchen experience in the war to become a restaurateur. He called his restaurant "Paradise Palace".

Lt. Col. Harry Genet remained as commanding officer of the 58th until January 1918. During that time, he earned the Distinguished Service Order. He, too, survived the war and returned to Brantford and his career as an accountant. He rebuilt his football team but never achieved the success that he hoped for.

Peter and Catherine raised a family of seven on Epsom Avenue in Toronto. There were four girls and three boys. Unfortunately, Peter died when he contracted sepsis, after an injury on the job. The oldest, William, had to leave school at the age of sixteen and find work to feed the family. He had the last years of his childhood snatched away from him. He worked hard to look after his family, and I always stayed in touch with them and helped out when I could. Bill, what we call him now, married his sweetheart, Irma in 1937 (a wedding I attended). They had two boys in the first two years: William Jr. and James. Bill joined the Royal Canadian Naval Reserve to supplement his income as a furnace installer.

Twenty-one years had passed since the "Great War", as it was called, ended. The hallways of Europe became dark and dangerous, and it began to look like we would be at war with Germany again. The Red Dragon was voracious, and salivating with the thought of feasting on the next generation of young men.

In the first week of September, 1939, William received his call-up for duty in the Royal Canadian Navy. Great Britain, Australia and New Zealand declared war on Germany on September 3rd. Canada had not yet made the decision, but it was expected to come within days of the other three declaring.

I decided to visit Bill and Irma at their modest two-story row house on Salisbury Avenue, in the east end of Toronto, before he was called away to duty . It was close to the school where I taught. The house had a small lawn just in front of the veranda. The facade of the house, like the others on the street, was covered with red brick. Down the street and around the corner, was the Riverdale Zoo. It always delighted me when I visited Bill and Irma, because I could hear the largest animals roaring and howling at feeding time. It sounded more like the jungle than the city.

My hosts treated me to dinner, and the talk at the table turned, inevitably, to war. The newspapers had been very busy, covering the march of Hitler's troops into Poland. The citizens of Canada were strongly in favour of declaring war and sending our boys to Europe to fight again. Irma was worried that Bill would be going to war, and that she and the boys would never see him again. Her fears were not unfounded. I, more than anyone at that supper table, understood that!

After dinner and dessert, Bill invited me to sit on the veranda and have a smoke with him.

"It's a lovely warm evening," I said, as we rose from the table and headed out the front door. We sat down on the steps, lit our cigarettes, smoked and silently surveyed the streetscape for a few minutes. The sun was starting to descend in the west and we had to squint our eyes.

"I know I'll be on a train to Halifax, within a week, and to will report to HMCS Stadacona to get my assignment," Bill mentioned after he slowly exhaled a puff of smoke.

"Any idea what you'll be doing?"

"Probably escort duty. We will likely be escorting troop ships when everything is together. It will take some time to organize everything. I'm eager to get back on a warship and hunt German subs. That's what we trained for in the reserves. I hate to leave my family, though."

"I know exactly how you feel, Bill. I went to war, too, as you know. The big difference was that I was younger and didn't have children. That, having children, no doubt, makes it even harder to go away; hard for me to imagine."

"Yep, Uncle Jon (I insisted that he call me that), it'll be tough for me to leave them. Who knows when I will see them again? The boys will grow up without me. I never planned on that."

"At least you will be on a ship. I was on the ground - infantry. I took a bullet in my leg in 1917 at Vimy."

"Yeah, Mum told me about that. You were a hero."

"Ha, not me! But I was in the presence of heroes; all of them! All of the 58th!"

"Farquhar was your best friend, wasn't he?"

I took a deep puff on my cigarette, dropped it to the ground and paused.

"Yes, he was. He was a great chum, fun to be with. Hell of a football player."

I stepped on the butt and kicked it out to the street.

"Mum showed me some pictures of him and you and Elmer; your football team with your trophy."

"Bill, I promised your Mum when I wrote a letter to her just after his death, that I would tell you the war story of your Uncle Farquhar. I didn't get a chance to tell you when you were younger. Can I tell you now?"

"Why not? As you said, it is a perfect evening and I won't be here in a few days."

I pulled out a couple of smokes and offered one to Bill. He took one and we lit up again.

"Well, Bill, it starts with a train ride from Union Station to Niagara on July 12, 1915. Three best friends, Elmer McLean, Farquhar and me; the three Macs...

I've heard the lilting, at the yowe-milking,

Lassies a-lilting before dawn o' day;

But now they are moaning on ilka green loaning;

"The Flowers of the Forest are a' wede away".

Dool and wae for the order sent oor lads tae the Border!

The English for ance, by guile wan the day,

The Flooers o' the Forest, that fought aye the foremost,

The pride o' oor land lie cauld in the clay.

CONFIDENTIAL

ORIGINAL.

WAR DIARY

58TH CANADIAN INFANTRY BATTALION.

INTELLIGENCE SUMMARY

Army Form C. 2118.

Instructions regarding War Diaries and Intelligence Summaries are contained in F. S. Regs., Part II. and the Staff Manual respectively. Title Pages will be prepared in manuscript.

Page No. 2.

(Erase heading not required.)

For month of June 1916.

Place	Date	Hour	Summary of Events and Information	Remarks and references to Appendices
In the Field	7th		Rain S.E. wind Cool Enemy shelling continued in early morning. No movement of our men allowed during daylight and men suffered considerably while in cramped positions, Casualties 8 O.R. wounded, 3 O.R. killed 1 O.R. wounded (shell shock). Heavy shelling of village and Bund from 6-30 p.m. to 9 p.m. Supplied covering Parties for Pioneers, also working parties to clear battlefield and re-construct trenches. 1 platoon "B" Coy sent to village as re-inforcements. Rations at Transport Farm & Village "A" & "D" Coys. relieved "B" & "C" Coys.	
	8th		Rain S.E. wind Cool Usual early morning shelling - Casualties 3 O.R. killed 15 O.R. wounded 52nd Can. Battn. relieved forward Coys. but retained two platoons "A" Coy. in Rifle Pits. Fairly quiet all night. Rations as usual Transport Farm.	
	9th		Rain S.E. wind Cool Usual early morning shelling, Supplied working parties to clear up BUND Casualties 2 O.R. wounded. Supplied working, covering and clearing battlefield Parties. Rations as usual. Enemy obtained two direct hits on dug-outs at BUND.	
	10th		Rain S.E. wind Cool Usual early morning shelling Battalion resting in morning Casualties 5 O.R. wounded 3 O.R. wounded (shell-shock) Relieved by 43rd Can. Battn. and marched to BELGIAN CHATEAU rations to Belgian Chateau	
	11th		Cloudy S.E. wind Cool Relief completed 1-35 a.m. Casualties 1 O.R. killed 5 O.R. wounded 1 O.R. (Shell-shock) Ordered to relieve 43rd Can. Battn. in front line, quiet all night.	
	12th		Cloudy S.E. wind Cool Relief completed 3-30 a.m. H.Q. DORMY HOUSE "A" Coy. on left front & "B" Coy. right front, "C" & "D" Coys in support & reserve at MAPLE COPSE Casualties [illegible] Lt. W.E. Gusler wounded, 7 o.r. wounded. Rations as usual ZILLEBEKE VILLAGE	
	13th		Rain. S.E. wind. Cool. Ordered by Brigade to make a bombing attack up GOUROCK ROAD, HILL & VIGO Sts., BYDAND AVE. and DURHAM LANE with the object of retaking old Front Line. Heavy artillery support in early evening. 1.30 a.m. the attack was made, and was a complete success. The enemy retaliated with heavy and light artillery on our old Front Line and Communication Trenches and MAPLE COPSE. We captured 28 unwounded prisoners, and accounted for many of the enemy's casualties which were heavy. Casualties - Lieuts. G. Clapperton, E.C. Nicol killed; other ranks, not reported. Attached hereto is list of those recommended for recognition; the C.O's. report on operations to 9th Can. Inf. Brigade; and list of those mentioned in Battalion Orders. Rations as usual ZILLEBEKE VILLAGE.	

2449 Wt. W14957/M90 750,000 1/16 J.R.C. & A. Forms/C.2118/12.

Harry A. Genet. Lieut. Col.

Dedication

In loving memory of my great uncle, Farquhar McLennan and my father, William Law.

This story is dedicated to a generation of young men and women, on both sides of The Great War, who gave their lives, their health and their futures for a cause that I am yet to appreciate. Their stories captivated me and inspired me to write this book. Also, I dedicate this story to my son, Jonathan McLaren Law, who is currently, at the time of this writing, the same age as most of the young people who made this terrible journey in history. May it never happen again.

Acknowledgements

I give my hearty thanks to the dedicated people who assisted me in shaping this narrative: My two editors, Bill Prosser and Harry Posner; my loyal readers Glenn Carley, John Steckley, Bob Nicholson and Christine Jablonski; my feedback team in Bolton Writer's Ink; and finally my wife Beth, along with the members of my family and friends who provided the inspiration for some of the characters and incidents along the way. A special thank you to Karen Dallow and Jacob DeFoa, who assisted me in finding Farquhar's grave site in Bedford House Cemetery, Flanders, Belgium.

About the Author

The author was born in Toronto, Canada, in 1949. He attended the University of Toronto from 1968 to 1973, earning an Honours BA and a BEd.

A 40 year teaching career followed, highlighted by 34 years at Humber College in Toronto.

Richard co-authored a Statistics text book for first-year Business students.

Elementary Statistics
First Canadian Edition, Second Canadian Edition
ISBN 0-201-75209-3
Triola, Goodman and Law, 1999 and 2002
Addison, Wesley, Longman (now Pearson Education Canada Inc)
Toronto

Richard is now retired and living in Burlington Ontario with his wife, Beth.

References

1. *Second to None, The Fighting 58th Battalion of the CEF*
   Kevin R. Shakelton
   Dundern
2. *For King & Empire, The Canadians at Mount Sorrel*
   Norm Christie
   CEF Books
3. *Training For Armageddon, Niagara Camp in the Great War, 1914-1918*
   Richard D. Merrit
   Niagara Historical Society
4. The Library and Archives Canada
   First World War
   War Diaries of the 58th Battalion, CEF

91008566R00217

Made in the USA
San Bernardino, CA
16 October 2018